I0768954

leaf you hanging

KIRBY FALLS
BOOK 4

LANEY HATCHER

This book is a work of fiction. Any resemblance to actual persons, living or dead or undead, events, locales is entirely coincidental.

Copyright © 2025 by Laney Hatcher; All rights reserved.

No part of this book may be reproduced, scanned, photographed, or distributed in any printed or electronic form without explicit written permission from the author.

Any use of this publication to "train" generative artificial intelligence (AI) technologies to generate text is expressly prohibited.

Made in the United States of America

Developmental Edits: Nicole McCurdy, Emerald Edits
Editing: Ozor Edits
Proofreading: Judy's Proofreading
Cover Design: Blythe Russo

Print ISBN: 979-8-9910786-9-6

For the eldest daughters

content warning

This book features an ex-husband who cheated (off-page but with several references throughout), a main character with generalized anxiety disorder and fertility issues, and a cancer diagnosis and hospice (not a major character).

While the heart of *Leaf You Hanging* is still cozy, charming, and small-town delightful, there are heavier elements at play, which pack more of an emotional punch than the rest of the series. Bonnie and Jack have a huge piece of my heart. I hope you enjoy their HEA.

JACK

I wasn't *technically* on the schedule for the night.

I was trying this new thing called having work-life balance. Except, Magnolia Bar *was* my life, so I couldn't exactly say I was nailing this new outlook.

It was even more difficult to maintain my distance from the bar I owned because I lived upstairs, directly above my workplace. It was easy enough to pop my head in when I was coming or going instead of just taking a straight route through the building lobby.

Logically, I knew that Sasha, Luca, Kayla, Sebastian, and my part-timers could handle things. The bar was busy tonight. It was a September weekend in Kirby Falls, so, of course, the place was packed with tourists visiting our small mountain town.

Magnolia Bar specialized in cocktails, wine, and local craft beers from every brewery between Charlotte and Weaverville. The kitchen whipped up upscale appetizers, including a charcuterie board that had recently been featured on a famous travel blog.

The place was a well-run machine and a Kirby Falls staple for every leafer who visited our part of Western North Carolina in search of sweeping long-range views and photo-worthy autumn foliage.

But since I was an obsessive asshole, I couldn't resist the urge to give things a quick once-over before heading upstairs with my takeout from the Indian place down the block. Yet, when I stepped into the modern space with sophisticated décor, smooth jazz playing overhead, and low mood lighting, I did not expect to see over a dozen people crowded around the end of the bar yelling "Chug! Chug! Chug!" while a petite blond woman tipped her head back and polished off what looked like a pint of that new IPA from a brewery in Saluda.

Sasha, the no-nonsense twenty-eight-year-old bartender I'd hired right out of grad school, met my eyes and slowly lowered her pumping fist to her side. She ceased chanting and did her best to nudge Sorority Wannabe Barbie off the bar top.

My other female bartender, Kayla, caught a panicked elbow from Sasha and turned in time to see me making my way across the bar in quick, determined strides.

With wide eyes and a word from Kayla, Luca—the kitchen manager—rushed around the wide oak bar and helped the woman back onto a high-backed leather barstool as the crowd voiced their displeasure at the end of their fun.

Then someone passed Barbie another beer, and cheers resumed as she brought it to her lips.

I placed my plastic bag of to-go containers on the end of the bar and walked through the swinging half door to confront my staff.

Luca wisely scurried back to his kitchen domain while Sasha and Kayla attempted to look busy with customers on the other end of the bar. I turned to the small crowd gathered behind the little blond chuggernaut and gave them my best I'm-in-charge-and-you-should-fuck-right-off glare.

They got the message real quick. The group—mostly men, I noticed belatedly—dispersed, but the woman kept drinking, downing her second beer, since I'd walked in less than three minutes ago, like a frat party champ.

But she wasn't a college kid. As I took the time to really look, I realized she was familiar. And she was closer to my age—thirty-three—than any undergrad. Her short blond hair was styled in loose waves that reached just below her chin. She wore a dress that was fitted down to her waist. The spaghetti straps fell across pale shoulders and delicate collarbones. But I could see a red cardigan draped along the back of her stool to ward off the autumn chill.

Oblivious to my inspection, the woman finished the beer and thunked the glass onto the surface of the polished bar before saying "Whoopsie," and then moving the glass onto a coaster.

My brows rose involuntarily, and I finally turned away to corner Kayla, who was pulling a brown ale from the tap below the bar.

"What the hell is going on?"

Kayla winced. "Um, well. The thing is . . ." She trailed off as she leveled out the glass, focusing on not overfilling it.

If customers wanted to sit on bar tops and chug PBR like frat boys, then they could damn well walk two blocks east over to Mattie B's. That was the townie bar where locals shot pool and sang karaoke. The floors were sticky, the jukebox was too loud, and the owner had a baseball bat under the counter. And that was all well and good. If I were going to catch a basketball game, hell, that was where I went.

But those were not the vibes at Magnolia. We served a different clientele. We held ourselves to different standards. Sasha or Kayla should have broken up whatever the hell had been going on out here before it ever got far enough to organize and start chanting. Instead, they'd joined in, and I wanted to know why.

I took the brown ale from Kayla's hand and passed it to Sasha, who was attempting to slink by to get to the point-of-sale machine. "Deliver that," I said tersely.

Then I pinned Kayla with a don't-even-try-to-fuck-with-me glare and ordered, "Talk."

Kayla glanced over my shoulder quickly before taking a step toward me and lowering her voice. "She came in on a mission, okay? Her divorce is final, and we felt sorry for her."

I released a breath, something suspiciously pity-shaped lodged itself in my throat. But I ignored it. "You overserved her."

"Jack, I've known Bonnie all my life. She is literally the best person. She came and got me and Larry sophomore year when our ride ditched us at a concert down in Greenville. She filled my dad's freezer with casseroles for three months when my mom died. Bonnie takes care of everyone. She deserves to blow off some steam. She is allowed to celebrate her freedom from that asshole she married."

I swallowed.

That was why she looked familiar. She was Bonnie Clark—or Bonnie Whatever-Her-Married-Name-Was. The Clarks were leaders in Kirby Falls. They owned one of the biggest farms and agritourism stops in Western North Carolina. I played rec league softball on a team with Bonnie's cousin Will.

Shit.

This was messy. And the perfect example of why locals should stick to drinking at Mattie B's. It kept the drama contained. I didn't need this in my life. I wasn't even on the damn schedule.

I sighed long and loud.

Kayla grinned. "Bet you wish you'd kept on going to your apartment instead of checking up on us. Too bad you're paranoid and anal retentive."

She totally ignored my glare and patted me on the chest before returning to where thirsty customers waited.

"Sorry, boss," Sasha muttered when she breezed by. "And sorry about your dinner."

"My what?" I spun around to where I'd left my saag paneer and felt my jaw drop open.

Drunken Barbie Bonnie was going to town on a samosa from *my* take-out container. Flakes of fried dough littered the shiny bar top as she closed her eyes and moaned around a mouthful, "Ermahgerd, I loooove these."

I shook my head in disbelief.

Kayla was right. This was what I got for being a control freak. Work-life balance, my ass.

I approached the little dinner thief and plucked the appetizer out of her hand. "These are mine."

She squawked, a wrinkle forming between her brows. "I already bit off it. Can't I finish it?"

"No, you may not." I popped the lid back on the Styrofoam box. "When the cops catch someone in the middle of robbing a bank, Clyde, they don't just let them finish the job because they already started."

"It's Bonnie," she corrected. "The other half of the duo."

I shook my head. "No, Clyde fits you better. You're trouble."

Bonnie eyed me suspiciously, or maybe she was seeing double and trying to figure out which one of me to focus on. "You're not how I thought you'd be."

I tucked away the rest of my food—*Jesus, did she already eat all my pakora?*—then tied the bag closed.

Leaning forward, I placed my elbows on the bar and met her gaze. It was slightly more focused. "Oh, yeah? And how did you think I'd be?"

Her eyes were interesting—bright honey brown with a dark ring around the outside. Not something you saw every day. The frown she was trying her best to commit to looked strange on her face, like her muscles weren't used to the shape, flitting inadvertently toward a smile when she wasn't paying attention. Whatever lipstick she'd had on at the beginning of the night was long gone, and now her lips just looked soft and full and pink. She had a slight gap in her front teeth that was oddly endearing.

Then I remembered she'd swiped the dinner I'd been looking forward to and resumed scowling.

"I thought," she mused drunkenly, "you'd be less concerned with legalities."

I felt my brows climb high on my forehead, an uncomfortable weight settling in my stomach. At one time, I wouldn't have been concerned with something as minor as theft or even breaking and entering. But I'd left those days behind. I hadn't been a delinquent teenage asshole in a very long while.

But it did make me curious about what she meant by that and how the hell someone who was publicly intoxicated was staring down her nose at me from atop her high horse.

It just went to show you that small towns had long memories. Once you were labeled a loser, it didn't matter how many successful businesses you owned or operated; you couldn't shake the convenient brand in the end. Not that anyone, aside from my grandmother, really knew I owned Magnolia.

Bonnie didn't do the polite thing where you looked away once you'd dredged up someone's embarrassing past. She kept her gaze right on me. "You were two grades ahead of me. I had a free period in the afternoon to help with the yearbook, and Mrs. Crowder's window looked out over the practice field and the field house."

I nodded, knowing where this was going. It wasn't shame churning around in my gut, but it was close enough.

"You'd skip out of last period nearly every day," she said conversationally, no malice or judgment in her tone, a small smile tilting her lips. "I'd watch you get on your motorcycle and roar off down the street. A real lone wolf."

Then Bonnie cupped her small hands and held them above her ears and let loose a high-pitched howl that had every head turning in our direction.

I fought a laugh as I looked down at the wood-grain surface. But I brought my attention back to her when she said quietly, "You didn't know I existed. I was just a sophomore, and you were Mister Badass with your leather jacket."

"Still have that leather jacket," I said.

But she didn't seem to notice. "And your attitude. And your harem."

I frowned. "Okay, I don't think it was a harem." I heard Sasha make a choking sound to my left, but I ignored her.

"And you *still* don't know I exist," Bonnie said on a sigh. She placed her elbow on the bar and rested her chin in her hand. "We play softball against each other once a month."

Now that I'd placed her, I knew she played third base for the teachers' team, but I wasn't about to correct her. One time, she'd tagged me out on the ass and then followed me into the dugout, apologizing profusely, her face so red, I thought she might pass out.

But other than rec league sports, our paths didn't really cross—not in any meaningful way. She was right about that.

I didn't remember her from high school. Mostly because I'd been too angry and stupid to notice anyone like her. And now, well, why would I?

Bonnie Clark was a bright, shiny do-gooder. I didn't know what grade or subject she taught, but I was sure she excelled at it. She wanted to mold young minds and support future generations. I bet she came in early, stayed late, and bought classroom supplies with her own money.

In the Venn diagram of Kirby Falls, our circles didn't touch.

She was in the same category as all off-limits women. She was married, and I didn't fuck around with that.

I considered her for a long moment. "I know who you are. You're one of the Clarks. You're just not one of the farming ones."

She shook her head in a way that said she was very disappointed in her student. "And you're still a lone wolf."

Bonnie cupped her hands above her ears again and made to howl, but I pressed my finger against her lips, fighting a smile.

God, she was hammered.

"Can you call someone to pick you up?" I asked. "Where's your husband?" Then I winced, remembering what Kayla had said earlier.

Bonnie leaned away from my finger, gaze and voice going frosty. "I don't have one of those anymore."

I was not touching that with a fucking barge pole. "How about we call Will or your sister?"

"No, thank you," she replied primly as her blinks grew slower. "I'm here to celebrate. I am officially divorced, and I'm going home with someone. And some sexy long-haired pirate bartender isn't going to tell me what to do."

I blinked. *Sexy long-haired pirate bartender.* What the hell?

Then Bonnie's eyes closed and her head drooped fully into her hand. Her elbow slid along the smooth surface of the bar until she was slumped over, breathing deeply.

I shook my head. Passed-out Princess Barbie wasn't going anywhere.

"Kayla," I called, keeping my gaze on Bonnie to make sure she didn't fall off her stool, "can you get a hold of someone to come get her?"

My bartender answered, cocktail shaker in hand, "I already tried calling Larry, but she's out on a date. Mac is not answering. I don't have Will's number. And I'm not trying her parents. This will be embarrassing enough in the morning. Sasha and I are closing tonight. You should just take her home."

I stared at her incredulously. "Me?"

Kayla strained the alcohol into a glass, added a curl of lemon peel, and then delivered it to the woman in front of her before coming to my side. Speaking quietly, she informed me, "I heard she moved out of her grandparents' house over at the farm. So I don't actually know where she's staying. Danny kicked her out when he said he wanted a divorce."

I blew out a breath. Jesus, what a fucking prince.

Kayla and I watched as Bonnie's mouth dropped open, emitting a small snore.

I reached forward and shook her shoulder. "Hey, wake up."

Kayla whacked me on the arm and walked off.

Bonnie mumbled and attempted to straighten herself.

"Where do you live?" I asked.

Her eyes drifted closed again. "I can't tell you that," she slurred. "Stranger danger."

I placed my hands on my hips as frustration mounted. I just wanted this townie out of my bar.

Bonnie Clark was a fucking headache, right between the eyes.

I followed Kayla to the register, where she was ringing in an order for sriracha deviled eggs with candied bacon. "I'll finish your shift. Just take her home."

Her fingers moved across the touch screen deftly, but she didn't look away. "No, I need the tips."

"I'll pay you."

Kayla side-eyed me. "Just like a man. Trying to buy your way out of your problems." I rolled my eyes. "Besides, you have like ten minutes before she pukes all over the bar. Just take her upstairs, Jack. This isn't that hard."

"I don't even know her."

"You know her enough." Kayla's gaze moved over my shoulder and narrowed in obvious anger. "Or you could let that guy take her home."

Cursing, I spun around to find a very sloppy Bonnie giggling over some tech bro in head-to-toe Patagonia.

I approached with a scowl, but Romeo missed it completely.

"Hey, man. I want to buy the lady here a drink."

Straightening to my full height, I crossed my arms over my chest. "Seriously, *man*? Consent. Go look it up."

His bright white smile slowly slid into frowny confusion. "What?"

I indicated the woozy blond at his side. "She's barely upright. Get the fuck out of here."

Tech Bro opened his mouth to argue, but seemed to think better of it. He turned and went back to a table where four other similarly dressed tourists booed his apparent inability to close the deal with a semiconscious woman.

After some yapping from the guy I'd booted, his friends looked in my direction. And, apparently, they had enough sense to read the "fuck off" in my expression because a moment later, they got to their feet and left the bar.

If Bonnie minded that I'd scared off her one-night-stand potential, she didn't show it. Instead, she had a hand pressed to the base of her throat as she frowned down at the bar top. "I don't feel so great."

Fuck, I needed to get her gone.

I clapped twice to get her attention. That felt like something a teacher would respond to. "Listen up, buttercup. Since you won't tell me where you live, I'm taking you upstairs."

She was still pale, but she visibly perked up. "Ohhh, what's upstairs?"

"It's where I live."

"I can vouch for him," Kayla said, suddenly materializing at my side.

Bonnie's brows furrowed as she looked between the two of us. But then she released a long breath that I thought might knock her off her chair. "Okay, fine. But can I have the rest of that samosa?"

I rolled my eyes, but I went around the bar and gathered her sweater and purse. With her things and my bag of takeout in one hand, I led her back out into the lobby.

Despite stumbling twice, Bonnie refused to hold my arm as we walked slowly up to the second floor. She insisted she was fine. I tried really hard not to notice how short her dress was, and only accomplished it when I remembered that idiot downstairs trying to buy her a drink when she was barely awake. Asshole.

She kicked off her flats as soon as she walked in the door. Then she did a nosy lap of the living room, picking up and looking at everything. Admittedly, there wasn't much. I wasn't exactly a knickknack sort of guy.

I watched as she examined my books on the end tables, a wooden coaster set, several small paintings on the wall, my reading glasses, and the framed image of me and my grandmother—the only photograph in the apartment.

My lips twitched as she folded and replaced the blanket I'd left on the back of the couch before turning to face me.

"Where's your bathroom? I am about to be very sick."

The beginnings of my smile died abruptly.

I sighed. "First door on the left."

"Thank you." Bonnie nodded, then promptly bolted down the hall.

I placed her things on my kitchen table. The dinner I'd been looking forward to went directly into the refrigerator. Next, I set about filling a glass of water and getting out the over-the-counter painkillers. I made my way to the linen closet and grabbed a washcloth, wetting it in the kitchen sink.

Horrible sounds came from the bathroom, but we'd all been there a time or two. I was a thirty-three-year-old man, and I hadn't overindulged in quite a while, but I still remembered what it felt like to have your body reject all the alcohol you'd poured into it. It didn't take a genius to figure out why the Puking Princess had made some questionable choices tonight. There was a small part of me—very small, mind you—that could understand the desire to drink away the day your divorce became final.

The toilet flushed, and I lingered in the hallway a moment longer. I pushed the already cracked door open enough to see Bonnie sitting cross-legged on my bathroom rug, her head in her hands. Her dress was short, but the skirt was full. Thankfully, there was enough material fanned out to keep her covered.

A curtain of pale blond hair hid her face. She elicited a pitiful moan when I draped the cool cloth across the nape of her neck.

I sat down, facing her with my back to the cabinet below the sink. "Want some water?"

She actually growled, and I fought another smile. "Maybe in a few," I amended.

"Go ahead and laugh," she croaked, voice hoarse from the last five minutes of hurling. "I know you want to."

"I don't want to laugh," I said, but I was smiling.

I should have been annoyed, and I was—a little. This woman had caused a scene in my bar and eaten my appetizers. She was puking in my bathroom instead of at her own house, where she belonged. But she was clearly regretting her life choices. I could just tell she was normally a Goody Two-shoes and never did this sort of thing. Maybe she had needed to cut loose for the night.

Plus, there had been that whole thing downstairs where she'd brought up my past, reminding me that in the eyes of this town, I'd always be a teenage delinquent and general loser. That was the guy she remembered. Someone selfish and arrogant who ditched school. Someone careless who pulled pranks and didn't have friends. A lone wolf, she'd called me.

Maybe I liked the role reversal now. Here I was, the responsible one, while Little Miss Perfect was hunched over a toilet seat like a reckless coed.

"Everything is spinning," she slurred before slumping over onto my outstretched legs.

"What do you need?" I asked, meaning it, wanting to make her feel better. I didn't know where the urge came from. Maybe it was the desire to be different than the teenager she remembered. Not that she was likely to recall any of this in the morning anyway.

In response, she folded in on herself, curling into the fetal position with her head resting on my thigh. Lying on her side, she wrapped her arms around her legs.

Snagging a clean towel off the rack above my feet, I spread it over her bare shoulders. Then I brushed her messy hair behind one ear and moved the cool cloth from her neck to her forehead.

"That feels good," Bonnie mumbled, eyes shut tight against the spinning, as if she could stop the world from tilting out of control just by willing it so. And maybe she could. She seemed like one of those optimistic, determined people who were always ready with a guidance counselor quote and a can-do attitude.

I kept moving her hair out of the way, carding the strands back from her face so that the washcloth could soothe her forehead and along her temple.

It should have felt weird to take care of this virtual stranger. I'd never had much practice taking care of anyone. But as my fingers smoothed Bonnie's soft hair and she curled further into my side, I couldn't help but admit, it felt weirdly good to do something nice for someone else—especially someone who needed it.

"I hate myself," she whispered suddenly, out of the blue.

I frowned and opened my mouth to tell her that nearly everyone has overindulged at one time or another.

But then, eyes still pressed firmly closed, she confessed, "Because I'd take him back. If he asked. If he wanted me. Which he doesn't."

I had no idea what to say to that. I'd never been in a long-term relationship, much less married. I didn't know what it would feel like to be with someone like that . . . and then lose them. If she thought I'd judge her for the admission, she didn't need to worry.

But suddenly her chin wobbled, and I felt something twist inside my chest.

"I don't want to move on," she said roughly. "It feels too big. How could I throw away something I spent half my life building and just start over? I think—I think I'd rather be unhappy than be a failure. How fucked up is that?"

Not that fucked up, I thought. Pretty human, all things considered. And that was coming from a loser who never bothered to feel bad about throwing in the towel on a variety of things—school, sports, family. Everything but my current job. Magnolia Bar was the only thing I'd ever really accomplished.

But I stayed quiet, sensing she just needed someone to listen, not relate or commiserate.

Sometimes people simply needed to whisper the truth so it wouldn't be so loud in their own heads.

"He said he can't imagine fucking only one woman his entire life, but I think I might throw up if I tried to sleep with someone else." She swallowed hard, and her face crumpled, but she reined it in after a moment. "I'm pathetic," she slurred.

I didn't know what to say. Every thought in my head was how her ex-husband seemed like a piece of shit who she was lucky to be rid of. But that wasn't what she wanted to hear. Placating her by telling her she'd find someone else wasn't an option either.

So, I focused on the way her golden hair felt like silk between my fingers and told her something true, knowing she probably wouldn't remember it in the morning. "This, right now, is the kind of hurt that you think you'll never get over because you can't see the other side of it. You can't go around either. It's just too big. The only way forward is through. You'll get there, Clyde. It just takes time."

Her breath came out on a soft snore, and I smiled sadly down at the fucking disaster sprawled across my lap. She was passed out again.

My sage advice and moment of vulnerability hadn't even mattered.

I'd dredged up my memories like silt in a riverbed. Thoughts turned to my family and all those old hurts that I'd had to go through—just like I'd told Bonnie. I'd climbed them like a jagged mountain peak. With bloody knuckles and dirt beneath my nails.

But I'd made it, and I was better off for it in the long run.

I listened to the steady sounds of her breathing and knew instinctively that Bonnie would be too.

BONNIE

I was pretty sure there was a red-bellied woodpecker inside my head, going to town on whatever brain matter was left in there.

With a hand to my temple, I sat up shakily in a room I didn't recognize.

I supposed I should have been more alarmed, but I couldn't really envision the owner of this place being a serial killer, what with the glass of water and bottle of pain relievers sitting on the bedside table. And all the framed amateur watercolor landscape paintings on the walls. Also, the stack of library books on the dresser. I was on the waitlist for the second one from the top.

After I swallowed two pills from the previously unopened plastic bottle, my eyes snagged on a leather jacket hanging on the back of the bedroom door. Embarrassment had me groaning quietly as hazy memories flooded my system along with a pretty good idea of who that jacket belonged to.

Jack Ellis was every inch the small-town bad boy, except now he was in his early thirties. He was a few years older than me, but we'd gone to school together. Me, an overachieving goody-goody. Him, somehow both popular and a loner who hadn't known I existed. I'd seen him around town since high school, of course. We actually played in the same softball league. But Jack didn't know me, and all my knowledge of him was based on gossip and leftover teenage memories.

Currently, I was desperately trying to remember how I'd ended up in his bed.

A glance beneath the covers revealed the clothes I'd worn to the bar last night. My dress was rumpled, but my underwear was still present and accounted for.

I guess it wasn't so far-fetched that I'd ended up with Jack. He worked as a bartender at Magnolia. But when I tried to pull up the faces of the folks serving me drinks last night, only Kayla's and Sasha's came to mind.

The memory of a flavorful samosa rattled around for a moment before abandoning me.

I finished off the glass of water and figured it was time to face whatever hell I'd wrought.

This was what I got for trying to do something reckless and impulsive for once. A blinding hangover and humiliation so painful it rivaled my current headache.

I may not have behaved responsibly last night, what with trying to celebrate my divorce by finding some stranger to hook up with, but at least I'd taken myself to Magnolia rather than Mattie B's. The fancy *leafer* bar had really been the only option. If I'd gone to Mattie B's, I would have run into no less than five people I knew, probably at least one a member of my family. I was pretty sure the ground would have opened up and swallowed me whole if I'd encountered one of my students' families while trolling for a one-night stand.

But the longer I'd sat on that leather barstool at Magnolia, the harder it had been to convince myself that going home with someone was what I really wanted. That sticking it to a husband—*an ex-husband*, I mentally corrected—who didn't even want me, might not have been the best way forward. So I'd ordered a refill to loosen up. And then I'd gotten friendly, which was what always happened when I drank too much. Well, that and crying.

It didn't matter because I'd sailed right past tipsy, fun, and looking to get laid and straight into plastered territory.

God, I couldn't remember the last time I'd had so much alcohol. Maybe one of the very few college parties I'd attended during undergrad. When you'd married young and your husband was back in your hometown, you typically drove the hour and a half home every weekend to see him. College parties had been few and far between for bright-eyed, optimistic coed Bonnie.

Now I just felt worn down around the edges. Like a penny that had been in circulation too long, weathered, lackluster, and not worth picking up if you saw it on the street. Also, there was the hangover thing. My head pounded and my belly churned, and there was a very real possibility I was going to vomit in the near future.

A vague recollection of memories assaulted me. A clean bathroom with white subway tile, a fuzzy gray bathmat, and a pair of firm thighs under my cheek.

Maybe I'd already done plenty of vomiting.

Cupping my palm in front of my face, I breathed into it. My eyes watered, and I gagged a little. Yep, I had definitely spent a portion of last night puking.

That was confirmed when I opened the ajar bedroom door and spied the dim bathroom across the way.

Another memory came the longer I stared. A cool washcloth on the back of my neck and a deep, soothing voice in my ear.

I fought another mortified groan. Jack had been forced to take care of me. Last night, I had clearly been the worst sort of person: an inconvenience. I hated—*hated*—putting people out. That was why I always made sure I was on time, didn't ask for favors, obsessively washed my hands so I didn't get sick, and never let myself be a nuisance.

The only thing worse than being an inconvenience was being a politician or maybe a male podcaster.

With a deep breath, I peeked around the corner of the doorframe into the hallway. To the right was a closed door. And to the left was—*shoot*. I pulled my head back distressingly quickly, fighting nausea. If I was a turtle, I would have been back inside my shell.

Despite my effort to remain unseen, a deep voice called out a moment later, "Come on out, Clyde."

I frowned and then stepped into the hallway. "It's Clark, actually." Jensen, technically, but most people in town still thought of me as part of the Clark bunch.

Jack was right where I'd briefly spied him. In a comfy-looking chair, relaxed and sipping coffee in a masculine living room.

"Nah, it's your new nickname," he countered around a sip of caffeine. "We worked it out last night. Don't you remember?"

I swallowed awkwardly. "Afraid not."

The coffee smelled amazing. Perhaps my gaze was a little lusty on his mug because Jack tipped his head toward the kitchen. "There's half a pot left. Help yourself."

Help myself.

I'd been helping myself and everyone else for as long as I could remember.

When I stood there too long, contemplating my pathetic existence, Jack cleared his throat.

That got my feet moving. I hurried into the kitchen. The floor plan was open, and only a small island separated the two rooms. There wasn't room for a kitchen table, but all the appliances were top-of-the-line stainless steel numbers that I would have handed over my secret recipe for beef Stroganoff to own.

A clean striped mug was already sitting out on the dark granite countertop, next to sugar in a ramekin and a pint of half-and-half. My hand paused on the mug, wondering if Danny had ever gotten a mug out for me. Or topped off my glass or anticipated any of my needs. He sure as hell had never put them ahead of his own.

I shook off those bitter ex-wife thoughts and poured some coffee into the existential-crisis mug. Then I dumped in a healthy spoonful of sugar, followed by an even healthier splash of half-and-half. I stirred the sweet, creamy mixture with the sugar spoon and then washed it in the sink with the dish detergent and brush stored neatly in the nearby sink caddy. I placed the spoon in the drying rack before picking up my coffee and returning to the living room.

My instinct had been to leave immediately. Actually, my instincts were ill-prepared for this situation. In my wildest dreams, I could not have imagined a scenario where I got wasted in public and then went home with the town's motorcycle-riding bad boy, whom I may or may not have slept with but definitely vomited in front of.

If I considered it much longer, I was going to spiral. I would pour this cup of hot coffee over my head before I allowed myself to have a panic attack in front of Jack Ellis, though.

I engaged my lifelong civility and Southern manners and sat down on the leather couch so I could apologize for my behavior in his home and his place of business (I vaguely recalled people shouting "Chug!" while I obliged wholeheartedly). My behind sank comfortably onto the smooth surface. Was this where Jack had slept while I'd occupied his bed? Or had he been in there with me and woken up first?

When I managed to gather my nerve, I looked over to the man in the armchair. Jack was back to drinking his coffee and ignoring me. He was reading a thick hardcover book, and my gaze briefly snagged on the way his fingers turned a page.

Another memory, sharp as a thumbtack, hit me the longer I stared. A calloused touch. Fingers oh-so-gently brushing the hair away from my face and a low voice asking, *What do you need?*

I swallowed, startled by the remembered question. It was so . . . direct and . . . something else. Most people asked what you wanted or how they could help. *What do you need?* That put to mind care and comfort, priorities and unwavering focus.

But that was silly. Jack didn't even know me.

I forced my attention away from his long fingers resting on the page of his book. But then my gaze caught unexpectedly on the slim, round wire-framed reading glasses perched on his nose.

Looking away, I blinked several times while my brain misfired. Were bad boys farsighted?

I took another sip. The coffee was sweet—just the way I liked it—and it helped make my thoughts more coherent. For a moment, they'd simply been wheeze-filled internalizing . . . *glasses* and *jaw scruff* and *bare feet* and *hot motorcycle man* before fizzling out into the mental equivalent of drooling.

"Thank you," I blurted inelegantly. "For your help last night. I apologize for any inconvenience I may have caused and for the way I conducted myself at Magnolia. It was unbecoming."

It took some effort, but I turned to face Jack, who watched me with an amused expression. "That was a very, uh, formal apology for what went down."

My eyes widened, unsure of his meaning, before sudden panic flared and I burst out, "Did we have sex?"

His expression went stony. "Sorry, comatose isn't really my type. The snoring was mighty tempting, though."

Then his frosty gaze held mine while he took another sip from his mug.

I blinked as initial relief bled into abject mortification. Of course, Jack would be insulted. I'd basically accused him of taking advantage of a woman in a vulnerable position. I might not know him very well, but obviously that would be offensive.

"Right. I didn't mean to imply—" I cut myself off before I made it worse, and then concluded with a straightforward, "Sorry."

I didn't really know what I would have done if he'd said yes. Obviously, my anxious, over-prepared brain could definitely have a list thrown together by the time I finished this too-sweet coffee. Everything from scheduling a doctor's visit for an STI panel to selling my house and leaving Kirby Falls to ensure I'd never run into Jack Ellis again.

Either way, I'd always been good in a crisis. I would have figured it out. But, overall, I was very relieved I didn't have to. Despite my intentions last night, I wouldn't have wanted to spend the night with someone when I'd been so out of control.

I risked a glance at those circular wire frames and swallowed. And maybe I would have wanted to remember whatever hypothetical things happened in Jack Ellis's bed.

Just the brief thought had guilt and shame slithering down my spine, cold and clammy.

Despite removing my ring and being divorced for all of eighteen hours, and being separated for months before that, my brain still hadn't gotten the message that I was no longer a married woman. Or, more accurately, it just hadn't accepted it. I wasn't beholden to vows I'd made when I was eighteen years old. I didn't have a husband waiting for me somewhere. No more emergency contact. No one to share a home with.

Part of me thought I might hate Danny Jensen for the rest of my life, while the rest of me worried I was doomed to love him for the rest of his. I had a good heart, but I could hold a grudge better than anyone.

And wasn't *that* the problem?

When your husband got drunk at a bachelor party ten months ago and accidentally slept with a woman at the bar, you couldn't find it within yourself to forgive him. Even when he'd fessed up immediately and been genuinely remorseful.

Maybe forgiveness wasn't the problem. Perhaps it was more accurate to say I couldn't forget. Danny had apologized profusely. He'd said it never would have happened if he hadn't gotten so wasted.

As a result, I'd wondered who let themselves get so drunk that they'd cheat. The spiteful person who lived under a bridge in my heart poked her head up and answered, *Probably someone who'd already considered straying and had found a handy excuse.*

And here I sat. Hungover in an unfamiliar apartment after a night of drinking to excess. The irony was practically beating me over the head. But, in the end, I hadn't slept with Jack. Something inside me had held on to good sense and rational decision-making—probably that judgmental bridge troll. Or maybe I'd wanted to have sex with him and he'd turned me down. That thought was not only mortifying in my present state, but also so embarrassing that teenage Bonnie wanted to crawl into a hole and die.

"Well," I said, feeling phantom limbs tighten around my airways as my thoughts spiraled. "Thank you again for your help last night. I'll get out of your hair." His sweeping dark brown hair was probably long enough to pull back into a trendy little man-bun.

Jack nodded. "Your things are by the counter, on the barstool."

I smiled stiffly and rose. Sure enough, my red cardigan was folded neatly. Stacked on top was my purse and cell phone.

I washed my mug in the sink, feeling the weight of Jack's attention on me. When I turned, I caught him watching me curiously.

With my head down, I gathered my belongings and made for the front door.

"See you around, Clyde," Jack called, amusement evident in his voice.

Something about that made my stomach knot uncomfortably, like the too-cool boy from my youth was making fun of me. Or maybe it was the very real possibility that I shouldn't have downed all that sugary coffee.

Either way, I hastened my steps, repeating before I tugged the door closed behind me, "It's Clark, actually."

<hr>

By Monday afternoon, I felt a little less like death.

Who knew that hangovers at age thirty-one were slightly more debilitating?

It was nearing four o'clock and the end of my workday. I just had to finish lesson planning and prepping supplies for my fifth graders. They were starting their self-portraits tomorrow—the first major project of the school year for my big kids.

While I loved all my students, the kindergarten through fourth-grade classes could be messy and loud, and chaotic. Now in my tenth year as an elementary school art teacher, I'd explored a wide variety of media with my students. I enjoyed the mess and chaos, but I also liked focusing extra attention on my fifth-grade students, who could stay on task for longer periods of time and really apply themselves to bigger projects, like a self-portrait.

Tomorrow, we'd go over the basics, discuss proportions and how to start with a light underdrawing. Then I'd hand out the photographs I'd taken of each student in class today so they had some source imagery to work from.

I sifted through the wallet-sized images of chubby grinning cheeks and gap-toothed smiles. My students really were sweethearts. I loved my job, and I was grateful for all the time I got to spend encouraging my budding artists.

A pang worked its way through my chest, heavy and familiar. Danny and I had tried for years to get pregnant. It just hadn't been in the cards. And now, I didn't know what the future held for me. The old hurt took on a new, more desperate edge as I realized, once more, that my future looked very different than how I'd envisioned it.

"Hey, you almost ready?"

My attention snapped to the open doorway of my classroom. My teacher friend April Coolidge was grinning at me, waiting. We usually walked out together in the afternoons.

Despite the heavy turn my thoughts had taken, I couldn't resist the smile that tugged at my lips as I took in my friend. She had a new stain near her left shoulder, and half her bun had fallen out. April taught second grade, and by the end of the day, she typically looked like she'd survived a battle.

I cleared my throat and stood from behind my desk. "Yeah, I'm packing up now."

April approached and gave me a cautious once-over. "You holding up okay?"

I fought the urge to grind my molars and, instead, gathered my bag from my bottom desk drawer and snagged the loop of my water bottle. "Yep."

Of course, she was going to ask. April was a year younger than me, and we'd been teaching at Kirby Falls Elementary together for the last eight years. We went to lunch often and saved each other seats at staff meetings and in-service days. We were friends. She didn't know all the gory details of my divorce from Danny. No one did. Not my family, not my sister, not even my best friend, Candace.

But April knew enough. And last week I'd been married, and now I wasn't.

"I'm fine," I insisted when she continued to watch me suspiciously.

As I turned off the lights and we exited my classroom, I felt guilty for dodging her question. I knew she was only asking because she was concerned. I couldn't tell if the awkwardness I felt was really there—hovering in the air between us—or if I was just imagining it because I was so worried about keeping the peace all the time.

Finally, in an effort to smooth things over, I touched her shoulder near the orange smudge on her white blouse. "What's this from, Coolidge? Paint?"

April looked down where I'd indicated and then brought the fabric to her mouth for a quick lick.

"Oh my God! Don't do that," I scolded, but I was laughing too.

"Not paint," she replied, unbothered. "Cheeto dust from lunch."

I chuckled. "Your Cheetos, at least?"

She grinned and nodded, what was left of her chestnut-brown bun flopping with the movement. "Oh yeah."

We continued walking toward the front of the building, and as we drew closer to the school entrance, April murmured a familiar countdown. "And in three . . . two . . . one."

Sure enough, as we passed the window that looked into the main office, our principal, Mr. Brinkman, glanced up from a stack of papers he was straightening. The office manager was already gone, and he was the lone occupant this late in the afternoon.

And just like every other day, he gave us a smile and a wave through the window.

April and I returned his greeting, waving until he was out of sight. My friend's bony elbow found its way to my ribs in a teasing gesture.

"Don't start," I mumbled tightly. I couldn't deal with her insinuations today. Not when I was technically single for the first time since I was fourteen years old. She'd been claiming Mr. Brinkman had a crush on me for years.

Alex Brinkman was a good guy. He was the kind of administrator who supported his teachers and really listened to students and parents. Alex had been my principal at Kirby Falls Elementary for the last five years, and I valued and respected him and the work he'd done in our community. He'd been a transplant from Wilmington, looking for a smaller school and a slower pace. And, if April was to be believed, the tall, handsome educator was looking to settle down. But he'd never once made a move on me. I'd been married, after all. He was just . . . pleasant and attentive. Plus, he smiled a lot.

"Mmhmm," April hummed meaningfully.

"He's just being friendly," I argued, pushing open the front doors of the school and breathing in the fresh autumn air.

Thankfully, April let it go as we made our way to our vehicles.

"See you tomorrow, Jensen," she called out, like she did every day.

Only this time, she froze as realization set in. April's eyes widened as they met mine over the tops of our cars.

Being in a school setting, we tried not to use first names around the kids. So most teachers tended to call one another by their last names.

"It's fine," I said quickly. "It's still my name. I heard it fifty times from students all day long today. I'm okay."

Some of the panic left April's face, her brown eyes softening as she nodded. "You're right. I'm sorry. I'm being dumb."

"You're being a good friend. But I promise you I'm alright." I threw in a smile for good measure, one that even showed the slight gap between my two front teeth.

"Okay. Night, Bonnie."

"Good night," I offered, hurrying into the front seat and pulling out of the parking space before she could see the tears welling in the corners of my eyes.

When I stepped into my mudroom ten minutes later, all I could hear was . . . quiet. There was a ticking sound coming from the kitchen, the modern cuckoo clock I'd saved up for and bought myself three years ago. My eyes adjusted to the dimness of the interior, and I scanned the rooms I could see from where I stood.

I didn't know what I was waiting for. Everything was still and silent in the house I'd fought so hard for, the place I'd gone into debt for and just *had* to have. The one stable thing I'd thought I needed to get me through this transition.

When Danny had finally lost his patience with me and demanded a divorce, he'd asked me to leave. And I had. Not because I'd wanted to. Not because I'd stopped loving him. But because I'd been too shocked and ashamed to fight back.

I felt like a failure, adrift and unmoored. He'd cheated, but I'd been the one to cause our separation because I hadn't forgotten fast enough or been able to move on in a timely fashion.

So, I'd escaped. At first I went and stayed with Mac and my grandparents at their home over at the farm.

But when things started happening with our lawyers, I decided that I wanted the house. I made it a priority. Like if I could just hang on to this one symbol of my past life, I could cobble together a new one.

In the end, Danny had given up the house amicably, and I'd bought him out. Now I had a bright, shiny mortgage with my name on it. I hadn't wanted anything else from my husband, not part of his paycheck or retirement funds. Most people would think I was crazy to demand nothing.

But I didn't want anything from the man who no longer wanted me.

Now, though, I took in the living room that was too dark, thanks to the wood paneling I'd never liked, and the empty space where the television had been. The wall of faded rectangles, where framed photos once hung, now blank and barren because I'd shoved them under my bed in a moment of weakness.

It didn't really feel like home anymore. The walls and furniture held the heavy weight of regret and history, as if a battle had been waged here and there'd been no survivors.

I felt like a ghost, haunting these halls, lonely and adrift.

There were little pieces of me scattered all over this house. Hopes and dreams broken apart, collecting like dust in the corners. I was trying to decide if it was worth bothering to gather them all up again.

If I was being honest, it hadn't felt like home in quite some time. My relationship with Danny had been strained for nearly a year, ever since he'd cheated. I'd avoided my husband, needing space. And he'd given it to me. But when he'd tried to be affectionate or initiate any sort of intimacy, I'd frozen up, physically ill at the idea. I became so fixated on what I couldn't forget. The visceral pain and betrayal of Danny with another woman. Danny touching and being touched. My husband of thirteen years fucking some stranger in a hotel room two hundred miles away.

I slipped my shoes off without putting them away in the closet the way Danny had liked. Then I dropped my sweater and purse on the floor and left them there, too. No one was going to walk through that door and scold me for being a slob. Not anymore.

I hadn't realized how difficult it would be to untangle over a decade of marriage, logistically. So many bills to switch over. Cell phone lines and family plans to cancel. I'd needed to open a new savings account and update insurance policies, change points of contact and beneficiaries, and notifications for everything. All my recommendations on every streaming service were basically screwed up for life.

Plus, there was the fact that I'd known Danny since kindergarten. Our friends and families were tied together in a snarl that I didn't know how to pick apart. As a result, I'd ignored most everyone who wasn't related to me by blood. I had my school friends, but they'd always been just mine. Distancing myself from my husband's family had been harder.

Danny and I had started dating when we were kids. He'd been my first crush, first date, first everything. I had a grand total of one person I'd ever kissed in my whole life. Ironically, that wasn't something that had ever bothered me. I'd always thought it was romantic or something.

So the idea of dating—even someone as nice as Principal Brinkman—made my nausea from the weekend look like nothing.

What did you do when you lost the love of your life? Find a replacement? Try again?

I wasn't there yet and didn't know if I'd ever be.

I wasn't the only woman who'd ever been cheated on. Some couples managed to recover from heartbreak and infidelity. But it hadn't worked out that way for Danny and me.

With a sigh, I grabbed my pajamas off the guest-bedroom floor where I'd left them this morning and wondered where I'd be if I'd managed to just put my marriage first.

You are never going to let this go. You're never going to forgive me. Danny's accusatory tone was easy enough to pick out of my memories.

And so was my stilted reply. *I'm trying, Danny. I swear. But it's hard to— to forget, even worse to remember. I just need time.*

You've had time. Months and months. I made a mistake and I apologized. You won't even let me touch you, he'd spat. *I need to move on since you refuse to. You can't expect me to wait around on you forever. And maybe— maybe people aren't meant to only be with one person their whole lives. I think I want more. I want to see other people. I want a divorce.*

I blinked back into awareness, my East Tennessee State University hoodie clutched against my chest. With an angry swipe at my wet cheeks, I finished changing and went into the kitchen to grab a flavored seltzer water.

With snacks acquired, I got settled in bed with the remote control. It was late afternoon, but there was no sense in going through the effort to make dinner for only one.

I'd moved the television from the primary bedroom into the guest room as soon as I'd moved back into the house a few weeks ago. I couldn't sleep in the bed I'd shared with Danny. I just couldn't bring myself to do it.

I pulled up my favorite streaming service and selected the next episode of *Sons of Anarchy*. I'd seen this one plenty of times, but it was easy, and I already knew what was going to happen.

Before I got too involved in watching, I grabbed my phone and fired off a text letting my sister, MacKenzie, know that I wouldn't be at trivia tonight. Kayla would be there, and while I did want to talk to her about the other night at Magnolia so I could piece together what had happened, I wasn't willing to do that in front of my sister and my cousin Laramie, who made up the rest of our weekly brewery trivia team.

Mac: Everything okay?

Her reply was immediate, and I fought a wince. Mac had been worried about me since my separation from Danny. I supposed having a panic attack in front of your little sister would do that. But in my defense, that had been the night Danny had asked for a divorce, and I'd been upset and overwhelmed, seeking comfort from someone I knew I could rely on.

Nevertheless, the incident had made Mac hyperaware of me and my actions and moods and responses. I appreciated her vigilance and concern, but I was the older sibling. I should be looking out for her, not the other way around.

Mac checked in with me often and usually invited me to dinner with her and her boyfriend, Brady, at least once per week. And in order to put her at ease, I usually agreed. But she would undoubtedly question my absence at trivia tonight. I'd been so good about attending, even with everything going on, but I didn't have it in me tonight—still emotionally and physically worn out from the weekend. But I'd show up for softball later in the week to keep her from worrying too much.

I typed out my response, then hesitated. Should I use one exclamation mark or two? One, probably. That conveyed truthful enthusiasm rather than aggressive excitement.

Me: Yep!

Mac: How about dinner this week? Indian takeout?

My stomach clenched uncomfortably, knowing my baby sister felt like she needed to take care of me—to keep her spinster relation from wasting away or to keep me occupied so I didn't go crazy and have another panic attack.

Then I scolded myself. That wasn't fair. Mac had never once brought up my mental health or used it against me. I was internalizing all of this and apparently taking too long to respond because my phone vibrated with another text.

Mac: Garlic naan. Samosas. You know you want to.

A weird sense of déjà vu washed over me then. Samosas . . . why did that make me think of Jack Ellis? And why did I want one so badly? There was a hazy drunken memory there, but it was like smoke. I couldn't hang on to it before it dissipated.

I shook off my confusion and typed out, *Sounds good.*

We exchanged a few more texts before I told Mac I needed to go. The sound of a motorcycle revving on screen had me fighting another memory. This time, a different bad-boy biker.

I still couldn't believe I'd woken up in Jack's apartment. Churning awkwardness came roaring back. The horrifying cringiness of it all. I groaned aloud into the empty bedroom.

He'd seen me puke. He'd held my hair back and given me a washcloth. I'd been vulnerable and honest and horribly weak in front of a boy from high school. Someone I'd always been curious about and intimidated by in equal measure.

Of course, Jack was no longer that bad-attitude teenager skipping class and getting questioned by the sheriff. He was a grown man with subway tile and wire-framed reading glasses. He made coffee and perused historical fiction.

Obviously, he was different. People tended to grow up after high school. But Jack still made me uneasy and nervous. That familiar, uncomfortable awareness had stolen through me just the same. Of knowing how attractive and enigmatic he was. This loner with piercing hazel eyes and a huge chip on his shoulder. And how uncool and straightlaced I was by comparison.

I couldn't help but wonder, why had he helped me? Why had he taken me home and taken care of me? Listened to me ramble and given me shelter during the very apparent natural disaster that was my life.

Jack might be more grown up and responsible now, but some things were reminiscent of the past. He still had that slightly too-long hair, the strands artfully disheveled and curling around his ears. And he was still aloof and slightly disconnected from all things Kirby Falls. Despite living and working in our hometown, he didn't participate. Aside from rec league softball, he wasn't a joiner. Maybe that was a leftover from his rebellious adolescence.

As a fifteen-year-old Goody Two-shoes, I'd been kind of in awe of the troublemaking bad boy with a complete indifference toward authority. Jack had put me on edge back then. I'd wrung my hands and wondered what he might do next. It had been like watching a tightrope walker with my heart in my throat, certain the next step would have them careening toward disaster.

Teenage Bonnie had been a worrier too.

Now, though, my therapist called it generalized anxiety disorder. Apparently, it wasn't normal to worry so much, to spend your life planning for calamity—real or imagined.

My anxiety was basically doomscrolling my entire existence. Sometimes, at night, I couldn't sleep from overthinking. My brain didn't have an off switch, and I couldn't seem to locate the fuse box that would bring me peace. It was like replaying every mistake you'd ever made and even the ones you hadn't. It was the potential for it, what might have been, or what I could have said. Every interaction had countless possibilities, and since I was a thorough individual, I liked to imagine each and every one.

When your brain was working against you, there was no way to defend yourself. You were wrong, ill-prepared, underwhelming, and the villain in every scenario—and there were many.

My therapist, Nina, gave me exercises to combat my bombarding thoughts. And since my people-pleasing wasn't limited in any capacity, I tried to do everything my therapist told me. You know, so I could win therapy.

But the crappy thing about seeing a therapist was this: Sometimes I just wanted Nina to tell me what to do, explicitly and clearly. Not rationally help me sort through options while also giving no opinions of her own.

I tried to consider what Nina might tell me to do about this situation with Jack, but couldn't come up with anything.

Presently, I was warring with myself, fighting the urge to make and deliver some blueberry muffins as a thank-you gift, and also considering ducking down behind my steering wheel for the rest of my life should he pass by me on his bike.

My eyes strayed toward the screen, and the MC members gathered around talking in their riding leathers.

Mostly, I just wondered how long it would take to stop thinking about the way I'd embarrassed myself in front of my very own motorcycle-riding bad boy.

JACK

When I unlocked the door to Magnolia at 11:00 a.m. on Saturday morning, I did not expect to see a small child with a clipboard waiting for me.

Honestly, I'd been fully anticipating Bonnie Clark stopping by with an apology pie or thank-you cookies. She seemed like the type. And judging by how mortified she'd been sitting on my couch one week ago, part of me thought she might never be able to make eye contact with me again.

"Good morning, Mr. Ellis," the child chirped politely.

"Do you need some help?" I asked after doing a quick sweep of the lobby over her shoulder.

I hadn't spent a lot of time around children, so I wasn't sure the age of this one. With dark brown hair held back by sparkly clips, she could have been anywhere from six to fourteen.

The little girl smiled brightly. "My name is Jamie Santiago, and I have a business proposal for you."

I frowned and looked around again for the person responsible for this kid. "Are you lost? Do you need me to find your mother?"

She blinked her dark brown eyes at me, but her smile stayed firmly in place. "I have a phone. If I needed my mother, I'd just text her. Anyway, about my proposal. Can I have a few minutes of your time?"

This kid—Jamie—sounded like a politician or an annoying overachiever. "Should you be out on your own? Are you old enough for that?"

Jamie laughed like I was silly, and I noticed she was missing two teeth. "Mr. Ellis, I'm eight and a half."

Like that explained anything.

"My mom is waiting in the car," she added, tossing a thumb over her shoulder.

I peered out the glass doors of the lobby entrance, but it was too dim inside the parked cars to make out anyone's mother. "Let's just talk out here." Staying planted in the doorway, I eyed her warily.

"Okay!" She passed me her clipboard. "I'm the team manager and starting midfielder for the Brookline U9 girls' soccer club. We are in need of sponsorship for the upcoming season."

I stared, confused. Brookline was the name of an upper-middle-class subdivision between Kirby Falls and Miller Creek. I knew enough about sports to know that U9 meant that the players on the team were under nine years old or close to it, depending on the season's calendar year. Apparently, the team was made up of eight-year-old neighborhood girls. I still didn't know why their self-appointed leader was here, talking to me, though.

Jamie's smile widened. Make that three missing baby teeth.

"That's where you come in," she said helpfully. "We all voted, and your logo is the prettiest. We'd like to have it on our jerseys."

"My logo?"

She pointed to the window beside the front door of my business, where the Magnolia Bar logo had been overlaid in shiny gold foil. The cluster of magnolia blossoms hovered elegantly above the uppercase "MAGNO-LIA," which was underlined in decorative filigree with a smaller "BAR" beneath.

"You want Magnolia to sponsor your soccer team?" I was obviously struggling here.

"Yes," she replied, and I had the feeling that if she'd had a gold star on her, she would have stuck it to my forehead.

"You want a *bar* to sponsor your soccer team for children?" I sought to clarify. "Isn't there a rule against that or something?"

"No, Mr. Ellis. Any local Kirby Falls business can sponsor a soccer club. I'm told it's great advertising and creates goodwill in the community."

I blinked at the tiny politician.

"The details are all on the form I gave you," Jamie insisted, tapping the clipboard in my grasp for good measure.

I glanced down at the paper. There had to be twenty-five bullet points and three different places requiring initials and signatures. A Kirby Falls Parks and Recreation header was at the top of the form.

"A verbal agreement would be fantastic, but a completed form would be even better." She clicked a pen and held it out to me.

Was this kid seriously eight years old? She was frighteningly efficient. I was pretty sure I could hire her to do my taxes. She couldn't be worse than Scooter Bates, my current CPA, who seemed afraid of me.

This request felt like a lot of pressure. I didn't usually get involved in the community. Magnolia didn't sponsor booths at the festivals or holiday markets. Nor did we participate in anything beyond serving tourists year-round.

My attention returned to the little scammer, who was still smiling like a serial killer.

"Isn't there some other business you can ask?" I said.

Her enthusiasm wilted several degrees, and a tiny frown formed between her dark brows. "But you won the poll."

I scrutinized her expression, feeling an unwelcome tightness in my chest when her lower lip jutted out. "What would you need from me?"

Jamie brightened again. "A modest, tax-refundable monetary contribution for uniforms bearing the Magnolia Bar logo, and a few other housekeeping requirements. It's all there on the form."

I glanced at the approximately ten million words on the paper in my hand, wondering what child talked like that.

"Please, Mr. Ellis," her small, high voice said suddenly, finally sounding like a little kid.

Swallowing, I met her earnest, big-eyed gaze. Then I snatched the pen out of her hand and signed the form before she did something horrific like start crying. "Do you need the money now?" I asked.

Jamie accepted the clipboard and grinned up at me. "No, sir. You'll be contacted by the Parks and Rec Department. They accept check, cash, or money order." Then she handed me back a copy of the form I'd just signed. "That's for your records. Thank you, Mr. Ellis. The team will be thrilled."

And then Jamie Santiago hustled out of the lobby doors into the late-morning sunshine, her long hair bouncing the whole way. She climbed into a white SUV, and I stood staring after her like someone who'd been steamrolled by an eight-year-old.

***

The farmhouse I grew up in was about fifteen minutes from downtown Kirby Falls. It was on a quiet stretch of road and had one of those custom mailboxes that resembled the house itself. A two-story white traditional farmhouse with navy-blue shutters and a wraparound porch, complete with ceiling fans I'd installed a few years back and ferns hanging at intervals.

My grandmother was the only occupant since I'd moved out at eighteen. But she still kept an impressive garden in the backyard and a variety of birdhouses all over the property.

I parked my motorcycle in front of the detached two-car garage on a foggy Tuesday. The September morning was chilly as low-lying mist hid the rear of the property from view.

The doors to the outbuilding were closed, but I knew my grandmother was home. She preferred to park her giant sedan in the grass beside the front porch. The detached garage mostly contained my woodworking tools and equipment, but it had been a while since I'd built anything. The hobby had taken shape after my grandmother took a watercolor class nearly a decade ago.

She'd asked me if I could make a frame for her artwork, so I'd learned how to. It turned out I enjoyed woodworking beyond the simple projects I'd managed to finish back in my high school shop class. As I grew more skilled, I experimented with making shelves and birdhouses, planters and benches.

But I'd been too busy lately to start a new project. It was apple season in Western North Carolina, and the bar would be overwhelmed with tourists for the next two months, at least.

No matter how hectic my work schedule was, though, I tried to always make time for Lia Ellis. The woman had sacrificed a lot to raise me and put me through college. She'd put up with my moody, rebellious teenage ass, too.

We usually had breakfast together a few times a week. And last night, my grandmother had texted saying there would be eggs and apple butter this morning if I wanted it.

I came in through the back door without knocking. I could hear the radio playing in the kitchen and Lia humming along.

"It's me," I called, though I was sure she'd heard my motorcycle when I'd arrived. Plus, she'd had a sixth sense for when I was coming and going since middle school. Lia had been a master of catching me sneaking in and out, some innate skill possessed by all hard-assed, take-no-shit, independent women. Especially those who'd been on their own for the majority of their lives.

The night I'd vandalized the pastor's shed senior year, I'd found her waiting for me on the front porch, shrewd hazel eyes narrowed and knowledgeable.

Now, I cleared my throat and crossed the threshold into the kitchen to find Lia moving a rubber spatula efficiently around a skillet. The scrambled eggs looked fluffy and bright, and I knew she must have visited Laiken Scruggs's farm this week for a dozen.

"Mornin', Jack," she said, voice a little rough, like it always was.

"Good morning, Lia." I pressed a kiss to her cheek, placing the loaf of sourdough from the bakery at Grandpappy's onto the counter next to the butter dish.

"Ho ho, what's this?" she teased. "You braved the masses for fresh bread?"

"It was early enough that the masses were still asleep at their Airbnbs. Besides, your apple butter deserves good bread."

I glanced at the Orchard Bake Shop logo on the brown paper bag, my mind drifting to Bonnie Clark. It wasn't the first time I'd thought about the petite blond disaster since last weekend, and that in and of itself made me feel . . . off-balance.

I didn't need a reminder of why it was unwise to rely on people. Bonnie had been a wreck over her divorce and the husband who she insisted didn't want her anymore. I wasn't naïve enough to assume the demise of her marriage had been that simple.

But it was one more reason why relationships were messy. The more people you let into your life, the more power you gave away—almost always into the hands of individuals who would hurt you or disappoint you. If you let them.

I didn't need heartbroken Bonnie Clark to confirm any of that. I only had to look at the woman who raised me. The long gray hair and the weathered face. The stern frown lines that no longer went away.

Lia had lost her husband early in their marriage. And when she'd gained a grandson, she'd lost a daughter for her trouble. She knew just as well as I did that loss was a part of life. It was better to control what you could from the start.

My mother had been a wild child and town troublemaker, too. I guessed that apple didn't fall very far from the tree. As a young adult, she'd screwed around with married men, and, eventually, her luck had run out. She'd gotten pregnant with me at twenty-two and handed me off to Lia to raise. There'd been no birthday cards, no calls on Christmas. Nothing.

We never heard from my mother again.

If I'd never come along, Lia would still have her daughter. My mom wouldn't have run off and abandoned her life and her only family.

I didn't know who my father was. He'd never been in the picture, but it didn't matter. He was just another person who didn't want me. Another person who let me down.

My eyes strayed to Lia, who was dishing up scrambled eggs into a wide serving bowl.

I'd had stability and support thanks to her. Maybe we weren't overly affectionate or emotional, but we had each other's backs. Over the years, we'd shown up for one another when it mattered. She'd proven that family didn't always look like a mom and a dad and one point five siblings. We'd made our own way.

And, sure, I'd been a teenage fuckup, but Lia hadn't given up on me. That was what love really looked like.

Briefly, I thought of Bonnie again.

How could I throw away something I spent half my life building and just start over? she'd said with self-loathing and humiliation in her voice.

But I didn't think there was anything shameful about it. She'd wanted to fight for her marriage, not abandon it. While I didn't agree with the institution as a whole, I had to admire her determination and loyalty.

And if her stupid fucking husband was too selfish to see that, then he didn't deserve her.

"Slice your bread," Lia called over her shoulder, drawing me out of my pointless thoughts about a stranger.

I washed my hands and grabbed a cutting board from the cabinet. We worked quietly in tandem to get the simple meal on the table.

Once we were settled with full plates and steaming cups of coffee, Lia asked, "How's the bar?" Her question was accompanied by an accusing gleam in her eye over the rim of her mug.

My grandmother thought I worked too much. And while I'd tried the work-life-balance thing, I'd gotten sidetracked by Hurricane Bonnie this past week and hadn't managed to get back on course.

I'd stayed late every night and closed up for Sasha when she'd called in sick on Friday.

"Good," I said, once I'd finished chewing. It wasn't a lie. Magnolia was doing well financially. Plus, we had a stable work environment. I paid my employees a fair wage, and they stayed.

However, I knew that wasn't what Lia was asking.

She proved it a moment later by asking, "You got any plans this week? Seeing friends or going on a date?"

I shot her a look.

"What? Can't a grandmother be curious about her grandson's life?"

Sighing, I said, "We don't do that shit, Lia."

She scowled and focused on slathering apple butter across a thick slice of sourdough. "Well, maybe we should. You need to get out more. You need friends."

"I have you," I interjected.

"Friends your own age, Jack."

An uncomfortable knot formed in the center of my chest. I had people I was friendly with, people who I spoke to if I saw them around town. But I didn't make plans or go out with anyone. There were no group chats or text threads. Instead, I had invoices and payroll. Employees and paperwork.

I'd never been a joiner. No team sports or clubs back in high school. There'd been other boys who'd tagged along for my troublemaking, briefly entering my orbit, but they came and went. Same thing with girls back then. But when you did stupid, juvenile things and ended up questioned by the police or arrested, those types of friendships tended to dissolve real quick. I didn't blame them. I knew I hadn't been worth the risk or the effort.

I cleared my throat and tried to make my voice light. "You'd be lonely without me. It's not like you have friends either."

"I do, actually," Lia replied matter-of-factly. "I'm in a bird-watching group. I play trivia every Monday night. I knit down at Weaverly Place with my stitch and bitch group. I have a full and active social calendar. I'm thriving, Jack. You're just surviving."

Ouch.

I stared at my grandmother, suddenly feeling like I didn't know her at all.

She shook her head, frustrated and exasperated by me, which was nothing new. "You need a life that's not just managing that bar. Get a hobby. Go on a date. Hell, join a motorcycle club."

My pride was a touch wounded, not to mention the fact that I felt like a loser whose grandmother was more popular than he was. So I said the first defensive, contradictory thing I could think of. "I have a softball game on Thursday. I'm not just sitting at home, reading space operas and ironing my curtains." Although if I were in the market for honesty, I did fill my time with books most days. And I was currently reading a really good space opera.

"See"—she held up a hand—"now I'm worried you're actually ironing your curtains. Why would you even make that reference if it hadn't crossed your mind?" I opened my mouth to argue. I did not iron my fucking curtains. But Lia kept right on going. "Just put yourself out there, okay? That's all I'm saying. I won't be around forever, and you're young. You can't close yourself off and focus only on the bar. Or else you'll look around one day and it'll be all you have."

Thursday rolled around after another busy few days at work. Sasha was holding down the fort tonight with a couple of part-timers—Sebastian and Cody—so that Kayla and I could play softball with the rest of the Bar Hoppers.

The team was a mash-up of players from local watering holes. There were only two of us from Magnolia, and a few folks from Mattie B's, including the owner and star pitcher, Matilda Bartholomew. Firefly Cider employees made up the remainder of the team. Despite not being employed at one of the bars in town, Will Clark and his fiancée, Becca, joined in with us most weeks because they were friendly with the team captain, Jordan Rockford, who was also the owner of Firefly.

No one minded because Becca was a sweetheart, and everyone loved her. And Will had been a professional baseball player at one time. While he didn't pitch for the Bar Hoppers as he once had in the major leagues, he was still ridiculously athletic. There were no complaints about his participation.

This adult rec softball league was the only thing I really participated in. Maybe my grandmother was right about me needing a hobby. But I'd played Little League growing up, before I'd decided I'd rather be a teenager with a chip on his shoulder. Maybe that was why I'd done something so uncharacteristic and said yes when Jordan came by a few years back, saying they needed one more to start the Bar Hoppers team.

Maybe I'd wanted a chance to go back to a time before I'd been a small-town fuckup. Maybe I'd still felt like that surly teen and needed to make a change.

Either way, it was something I'd committed myself to, and it usually ended up being a pretty good time.

And with the accusatory voice of Lia still ringing in my head, I'd made the conscious decision to go out for drinks with my team after the game. They were good people, so they always invited me. This time, I wouldn't say no, like I always did. It still made me grumpy and uncomfortable to think about making small talk with my neighbors and teammates. People who already had a history together and who probably knew most of mine.

But I was going to do it, dammit. I didn't need my own grandmother feeling sorry for me.

I'd seen the opposing team listed on the schedule, but I wasn't convinced Bonnie would show up. Not until I got to the field and saw her warming up. Part of me thought she'd try to avoid me.

It had been a week and a half since she'd woken up in my bed, and from the way she'd thrown the ball well wide of her practice partner when she caught sight of me, she definitely hadn't forgotten.

I fought a grin and joined my team in the dugout.

For the most part, these weekly rec games were low stakes. Most people were in it to socialize and have a good time during our season, a few months of the year. The Teachers' Lounge was the least competitive team of the bunch, so tonight's game would probably be pretty casual, with lots of chatting between the benches and on the field. Weirdly, it was the over-fifty team formed from the pickleball club that you had to worry about. They were vicious, and usually a handful of arguments broke out over the course of the abbreviated seven innings of play.

When it was time to start, I slid my mask on and took my place behind home plate. Bonnie didn't make it up to bat until the fourth inning, but I gave her a smirk that had her promptly swinging at the first three pitches and striking out hard. Her body was tense beneath her sky-blue uniform tee as she trudged back to the dugout, bat in hand. I stared after her until Mattie got my attention from the mound.

In the bottom of the fourth, I hit a double to center field that went through Becca's legs. But I didn't make it any farther than second base as Rhonda Coates hit a pop fly to close out the inning. I got on base again in the sixth, but was tagged out by the high school principal, Jim Gentry, trying to steal second. Neither instance put me in range of Bonnie, who was a pretty solid third baseman.

She struck out again in the seventh, but she didn't say a word. No, *Hey, how are you?* Or *Thanks for holding my hair back.* Again with the silent treatment. To be honest, I hadn't seen that coming. I'd fully expected her to be awkward and appreciative—a repeat of that morning in my apartment.

But while she was doing her best to ignore me, I knew she was still aware. I caught her glancing my way a few times, her pale cheeks going a rosy pink before she managed to hide her face. I noticed the stiffness in her shoulders as a result, the way she held herself in check so tightly. It was clear I made her uncomfortable, and I wasn't sure why I found that so frustrating. Maybe she didn't want the reminder of the night she was trying to forget. Either way, I clearly needed to stop assuming I knew people after one brief encounter.

Things took a turn in the bottom of the seventh. The game was all tied up, and I'd just taken my place on first base after being walked by the pitcher. Will batted next and managed a double that just barely stayed in bounds and got me over to third, where Bonnie gave me a wide berth.

Jordan was up to bat, and the Teachers' Lounge pitcher and catcher were taking a moment to confer.

Some part of my antagonistic teenage self must have still been alive and kicking because I turned my attention to Bonnie and teased, "I'm not going to bite, Clyde."

Her pretty brown eyes snapped to mine in surprise, and she frowned. "I know that."

"Well, you're practically in the dugout trying to get away from me."

"I am not," she argued.

I tried to keep the amusement off my face at her combativeness, but didn't manage it. She huffed and crossed her arms over her chest, but her glove made the action cumbersome, so she gave up and let her arms fall back to her sides.

Suddenly, a voice called from behind her, "Bonnie, you okay?"

She startled, then immediately piped up with a huge fake smile, "Of course!"

I glanced briefly at the guy who stood on the steps to the dugout. Generic brown hair, mid-thirties, with his rec league tee shirt tucked into tan pants. He had administrator knight in shining armor written all over him. Someone was very aware that Bonnie Clark was no longer married.

She stepped closer to the bag, but she was still farther away than necessary. Then she hissed out of the side of her mouth, "You're getting me in trouble."

I nearly laughed. That . . . was a gross exaggeration for what had just happened. "Can't help it. That's what happens when I'm around principals in khaki pants."

Jordan must have made contact because Bonnie and I both startled at the sound of the bat cracking. But the ball went foul over the teachers' dugout.

"I might make a break for it," I teased some more. "Steal home if you're giving me so much leeway."

Bonnie took two tiny steps closer to me, and I grinned.

"Um, actually, I baked you some muffins. As a thank-you for"—her gaze dropped—"the other night. They're blueberry. I hope you like them."

I knew it. She was one of those people who sent thank-you notes and *followed up*, and probably majored in people-pleasing. Frowning, I didn't know why that bothered me so much. I liked it better when she was giving me shit for getting her in trouble.

I must have stayed quiet too long because Bonnie jumped in, her words rushing over one another. "I know muffins don't really make up for the"— she paused to swallow hard—"inconvenience."

"Inconvenience?" I repeated, dumbly.

She nodded, the bill of her baseball cap dipping down. "Yeah. Of having to wrangle some irresponsible drunk person. I still don't know how I ended up at your place, but I'm sure you had better things to do with your night. It was immature and inconsiderate of me. I hope I didn't get you in trouble with your boss."

With my boss. Christ. I nearly rolled my eyes.

But something about her self-assessment felt all wrong. Sure, I didn't know her very well, but I got the impression that irresponsible, immature, and inconsiderate were not adjectives anyone would use to describe Bonnie.

So I asked, "Do you do that sort of thing often, then? I've never seen you drinking at Magnolia before."

"No, of course not," she replied emphatically, as if the very idea were preposterous.

I put my hands on my hips and stared at her in confusion. "So what are you over-apologizing for? You already thanked me and said you were sorry—multiple times—Sunday morning. I know you meant it. I don't need you to prove it with blueberry fucking muffins."

"Right. Sorry, I shouldn't have—"

"Stop apologizing."

She frowned. "It's polite to acknowledge bad behavior."

I scoffed. "It was barely bad behavior." I'd done a hell of a lot worse in my day. Vandalism, breaking and entering. What was a little public drunkenness from the hometown sweetheart?

Bonnie's gaze narrowed further, and she gritted out, "I like baking, so it was no trouble."

"I don't want your self-flagellation muffins, okay?" I snapped, unwilling to let this go.

If she'd been wearing pearls, she would have clutched them. Bonnie opened her mouth to argue—I could tell—but right then Jordan Rockford ran up from the direction of second base.

"Uh, Jack," he panted out. "You want to maybe run to home plate? My RBI won't score itself."

It wasn't until then that I noticed the volume of the crowd cheering for the Bar Hoppers, the flurry of movement from the other team, scrambling deep in the outfield after the hit Jordan must have made that I hadn't registered.

Bonnie's wide, surprised brown eyes met mine for a split second before Jordan was pushing me off third base and toward home. I took off, crossing the plate just before the teachers' catcher snagged the ball and lunged toward me.

The umpire swept his arms out wide. "Safe!"

And then my team was on me, cheering and patting my batting helmet, offering high fives. When I managed to see over everyone crowding me, I couldn't find Bonnie anywhere.

Someone shouted out to both teams, "Drinks at Mattie B's!" and another cheer went up.

We eventually retreated to the dugout to put away our equipment, which the parks department provided. A few minutes later, leather jacket in place, I walked toward my bike. I caught myself looking around the parking lot to see if I could spot Bonnie. She was probably getting into a minivan or something equally fitting. But I didn't see her anywhere.

When I was twenty feet away, I noticed a bright spot of something on the seat of my motorcycle. As I got closer, I realized it was a turquoise Tupperware container, small enough to fit in my saddlebag.

There was a half sheet of notebook paper on top. A short message had been hastily scrawled in quick, messy script.

I read the note, an ironic smile twisting my lips as my fingers traced the torn edge. After a final glance around the busy parking lot, I still couldn't find the woman who'd been nothing but a distraction since she'd stumbled her way into my life.

Huffing a quiet laugh, I placed my catching glove and the Tupperware carefully into my saddlebag. Then I folded the note and slid it into my pocket.

I didn't know what it said about me that I couldn't accept her thank-you the way she'd intended. That I'd argued with her and goaded her into reacting, scribbling on a piece of paper she'd likely found in her car. Maybe now, the baked goods weren't just some people-pleasing gift to acknowledge something any decent human being would have done. It was quite possible they contained a little bit of spite that had me eagerly anticipating them with my morning coffee.

Finally, I revved my engine and took off toward Mattie B's, thinking about the single line of snarky text Bonnie must have written in a fit of annoyance. I smiled beneath my helmet.

Blueberry Muffins (dairy-, nut-, and self-flagellation-free).

BONNIE

A quiet knock sounded before I heard "Hey, Bonnie. You got a minute?"

I glanced up from my planner to see Alex Brinkman leaning in the open doorway of my classroom.

"Sure," I said, giving him a smile despite feeling the edges of it turning brittle and digging into my cheeks.

With hurried movements, I worked fruitlessly to slip errant papers back into my spiral notebook and to straighten the stack of mandala designs my fourth graders had placed on the end of my desk, all before Alex made his way across the room.

I wondered what my principal could want at almost four on a Friday afternoon. Surely he wasn't going to—

"So, our office manager was going through her checklist for the new school year, and she happened to notice that your background check was set to expire."

"Oh." I frowned, trying to mentally backtrack and remember how often that needed to be renewed.

"It's okay," Alex said quickly, stopping in front of my messy desk with a reassuring smile and his hands tucked casually into the pockets of his khaki pants. My attention snagged briefly on the tan fabric as I recalled Jack's teasing comment from last night about principals. And the smirk that went along with it.

"You're not the only one," Alex added helpfully, drawing my attention back to his face and away from his pants. *Good lord.* "You submitted the required contact hours and continuing education credits back in May. So it's just the background check left."

"Right," I said easily. But inside, I was shocked that I'd forgotten something like that. I was already reaching for my phone so I could pull up my more detailed online calendar. Surely I'd had a reminder to update my background check for the state. But as I scrolled backward and forward, I found nothing.

"I'm so sorry," I finally managed. "I can't believe I missed that."

Alex's smile was genuine. "It's really alright. You've had a lot on your plate."

I was mid-nod when my brain registered the implication from his statement. And by *a lot on my plate*, he meant my crumbling marriage and subsequent divorce.

My face must have reacted without my permission because Alex straightened and backtracked. "You know, with summer and everything. It's a busy time. I know my summers get away from me. All that freedom," he rambled.

"That must have been it," I agreed quietly.

"Well, I called around and they can take you at the sheriff's office this afternoon, if you can make it there before six. Just a couple of forms, a small fee, and fingerprints," he said cheerfully, like doing my job for me was no big deal.

Shame and guilt had my shoulders going tight. My principal felt so sorry for me that he'd taken time out of his day to handle this. "You didn't have to do that, Mr. Brinkman."

His affable smile slipped a little, and I felt like even more of a jerk. But it suddenly seemed important to keep this professional. The way I'd gone cold and clammy when I'd thought Alex might have been stopping by to ask me out solidified the fact that I was not ready for that. Not at all.

"It was no big deal," he insisted.

I nodded. "I'll be sure to hurry over to the sheriff's office and get this all taken care of. Sorry for the trouble."

Alex smiled, but his face was laced with sympathy. I'd seen the expression on enough people to know when I was being pitied. I'd heard it in their voices, too.

It was present in how carefully my mom watched me during family dinners—when she thought I wasn't paying attention. Or how Mac checked on me all the time. The way Magdaline down at Apollo's softened her voice when I called in a to-go order. Or how nosy Sheila Jessup said "How *are* you, honey?" every time she saw me at the grocery store.

"No trouble at all," Alex said. "Have a good weekend, Ms. Jensen."

"Thanks. You too."

He gave me another smile before turning and walking toward the door. I watched as April came barreling in and nearly collided with our principal. The second-grade teacher apologized, and my coworkers shared a laugh before Alex eventually made his way out.

April approached my desk, eyes wide and face flushed. She tucked a strand of brown hair behind one ear, and I noticed pen ink or dry-erase marker smeared down the side of her hand.

She exhaled roughly. "I didn't expect a traffic jam in your doorway."

"Yeah, me either." I started packing up my things. I could finish my upcoming lesson plans over the weekend. Plus, I needed to hurry over to the sheriff's office.

Ugh. I'd been looking forward to staying in panda mode for at least the next twenty-four hours. That was where I wore my most comfortable sweats, snacked liberally, and lazed around the house, not going anywhere or seeing anyone. Panda mode was sacred and necessary in order to recharge as a teacher. It was usually reserved for weekends, but not always.

Tonight, I'd planned on grabbing Mexican takeout for dinner and watching the 2005 version of *Pride and Prejudice*. Having a crappy week? There was a Darcy hand flex for that. Suffering from a hangover from hell and having thrown up in front of the coolest guy from your high school? Yeah, you'll need to watch Matthew Macfadyen walk through a foggy field at sunrise with visible chest hair and a long coat flapping.

Instead, I would be a little delayed in getting the weekend started. But that was okay. It was my own fault for dropping the ball at work.

"Sooo," April began with raised eyebrows. "What was Principal McCrush-On-You doing here?"

The look I gave her was one I reserved for smart-ass students who thought they were cute. "*Mr. Brinkman*," I emphasized, "stopped by to let me know that my background check will lapse soon and I need to go over to the sheriff's office tonight to get that taken care of."

"Wow, a personal visit." She grinned. "And all I got was an email from Mrs. Fowler in the front office."

I paused in stuffing my planner in my bag. "You need a background check, too?"

April nodded. "Yep. Five years fly by when you're trying to get a class full of seven-year-olds to stop eating their boogers."

"And do you have to go tonight to do your fingerprints and stuff?"

"No," she replied, still looking pleased. Then she tossed up some air quotes as she continued, "I am responsible for making my own arrangements to remedy the state of my licensure before October first."

I frowned. "Why would Alex . . . ?"

April had no problem jumping in when my voice trailed off in confusion. "Because he has the hots for you and will do anything to keep his favorite teacher happy."

"April, stop. He's just being nice." I resumed shoving my things into my bag, but a little part of me thought there might be some truth to her statement. I didn't want that, nor did I endorse that sort of favoritism. But I couldn't decide if it was worse than him going the extra mile for me because I was pathetic and distracted by my marriage falling apart.

"Bonnie. The man has a massive crush on you."

I couldn't look at her. I didn't want to think about that or hear about it either.

"It would be okay if you were interested," she said gently.

Despite the tenderness in her tone, my head jerked back as if she'd hit me.

"Or not," she amended quickly, eyes wide.

"I can't—I'm not—I'm not ready for something—" I shook my head as my breathing grew labored.

"Hey," April said softly, taking a step toward me, palms out in surrender. "It's okay. I shouldn't have suggested that. I'm sorry. There is no pressure at all."

I could feel my face flushing scarlet from my overreaction. My friend could tease me about Alex. That shouldn't have been a big deal. I just—I couldn't think about dating anyone, even in a hypothetical sort of way. It made every one of my muscles go tight. Made me feel like I was doing something wrong—cheating on a husband who didn't exist anymore. There was too much pressure, too much expectation.

I nodded woodenly and finished packing my bag.

"Do you care if we stop by my room on our way out? I need to grab Cocoa," April said. She was using her careful voice with me, like I might bump the edge of my desk and shatter into a million pieces. Although, to be fair, she had just witnessed my minor meltdown over the innocent suggestion of dating my boss.

"Of course. That's no problem."

Cocoa was April's classroom pet. The four-pound, black Holland Lop rabbit was a new addition to our school. As an animal lover, April had been begging for a classroom pet for several years. Earlier in the summer, she'd gotten the other second-grade teacher, Angie Morris, to finally agree to have a pet in her classroom too. With both grade-level teachers on board, Mr. Brinkman had signed off on April's request.

Cocoa was a sweet and sociable little thing. The students loved the rabbit and took turns feeding and caring for her. But on the weekends and over school breaks, April brought Cocoa home with her.

When we made it to the second-grade classroom, I gave the bunny a few scratches before April loaded her up in her carrier.

"Are things smoothing out next door?" I asked.

While Ms. Morris had agreed to host her own Holland Lop, she didn't exactly love having a classroom pet the same way April did.

My friend spared a glance at the darkened classroom across the hall and hesitated. "Not exactly."

"What happened?"

"Well," April began, "she's been leaving Oreo at school over the weekends. I guess her cat doesn't appreciate having another animal at home. And Morris has been asking students and their parents to take Oreo for school breaks."

I made an affronted sound. "Oreo stays all weekend by herself?"

April nodded tightly. "She has enough food and water and everything—I've checked—but you know how these little bunnies like to run and play."

"Yeah," I agreed.

Cocoa would do laps around the classroom if she'd been cooped up too long. She was so good with the kids and seemed to genuinely enjoy the attention they gave her.

My gaze strayed to Morris's classroom. I hated to think about the little black-and-white rabbit alone in there all weekend long.

While April hefted Cocoa and turned off the lights, I peeked in the room across the hall. Oreo's cage was in plain view on the opposite wall. It was pretty sparse compared to the double-decker bunny house April had for Cocoa. But the fluffy rabbit sat placidly in its pen. Poor thing.

"At least there's a night-light plugged in for her," I commented absently.

"Yeah, that's one of those air freshener ones. Morris says her room smells like a barnyard because of Oreo." My friend rolled her eyes.

Maybe I could talk to Morris, offer to help out with the rabbit.

I wasn't really killing it at taking care of myself right now, though. In fact, breakfast this morning had consisted of me eating shredded cheese over the sink. But it might be nice to have a part-time pet around the house. Someone to watch Mr. Darcy with.

Troubled, I stared at the rabbit a moment longer before catching up to April and Cocoa. Now wasn't exactly the time to push this. I needed to get over to the sheriff's office and get this background check done.

I needed to pull it together, in general. I was dropping balls and forgetting things, tarnishing my reputation at work, and feeding into the rumors and assumptions that I needed to be handled with care. Next, my boss would be questioning my competency. I didn't want Alex to keep making excuses for me and giving me a pass because he felt sorry for me.

Not to mention the irresponsible way I was behaving. Getting drunk at Magnolia, waking up in someone else's bed, arguing on the softball field.

It was humiliating to be the worst version of myself. I just didn't know how to find my way back to the person I'd been before my life fell apart.

Mary Beth Collins answered phones and dispatch for the sheriff's office. She was two years younger than me—in my sister Mac's grade—but she greeted me warmly and showed me where I could sit until the administrative assistant who'd be taking my paperwork and fingerprints was ready for me.

When I rounded the corner into the small waiting room, there was only one other person there, but he and his motorcycle helmet took up two chairs.

I was pretty proud of myself for not stopping in my tracks and walking right back out the front doors. Especially when Jack glanced up from the clipboard balanced on his muscular thigh. He had his little round reading glasses on again, and I didn't know why I found them nearly as attractive as the leather jacket stretched snug across his broad shoulders.

"Clyde," he greeted.

The urge to make myself smaller was nearly overwhelming. Some nervous creature living inside me was just waiting for the town bad boy to poke fun. It put me on edge, kept me bracing for a well-placed jab or a stinging tease at my expense. This man turned me into an uneasy sophomore again, forcing all my adolescent insecurities back to the surface.

But Jack just watched me, that same solemn, handsome face of his, endlessly patient despite my continued awkwardness.

"Hello," I finally managed and took the seat diagonal to him rather than the one to his immediate right.

I'd seen him less than twenty-four hours ago. If the somersaults in my stomach were any indication, I was still feeling weird about the blueberry muffin incident and our mini-argument at third base.

Leaving the Tupperware on his motorcycle with a snarky note hadn't been my finest moment, but he'd made me so irritated, practically calling me a martyr and pushing all my buttons.

I'd just wanted to do something nice. I'd only wanted to say thank you. What was so wrong with that?

I hoped he wouldn't bring the muffins up.

So naturally, the first words out of his mouth were "Those muffins were good. I had two for breakfast."

I swallowed. "That's . . . nice." I opened my mouth again to explain away my immature behavior the night before.

One dark eyebrow rose above the frame of his glasses. His expectant gaze practically dared me to apologize so he could call me on it.

I closed my mouth.

Jack grinned and then asked, "So, what are you in for?"

That startled a laugh out of me. "Just a background check for work. I'm a teacher," I added.

He nodded like he knew that, but I couldn't figure out why he would.

"Getting fingerprinted brings back memories," he said passively.

I searched his face for a side of bitterness with that comment, but Jack mostly just looked amused, his grin toned down to something quiet and nostalgic. Maybe. What did I know?

I couldn't help but notice he hadn't offered up a reason for his presence in the sheriff's office. What could he be getting a background check for? Starting a new job that required it? He'd been a bartender for a long time and seemed good at it. Admittedly, our interactions had been minimal, but he seemed to have the right combination of traits to tend bar successfully: aloof, personable, and hard to ruffle. I knew firsthand he could be a good listener. Then there was the whole contrast of a buttoned-up, fancy-dress-shirt-wearing employee with tattoos and longish hair. Upscale and rebellious at the same time. I bet the *leafers* loved him—the women at least.

"But," he went on when I'd zoned out, "you're a good girl, so you probably don't know anything about that."

"Yeah." I cleared my throat. "You've got me all figured out."

Jack watched me calmly for a moment before admitting, "No, I don't believe I do."

He was right, though. I didn't know why I felt disappointed about it.

I *was* a good girl. Always had been. Star student, responsible daughter and sister, reliable neighbor, model employee, and the furthest thing from a troublemaker you could get.

You couldn't say the same about Jack. He'd adopted the bad-boy reputation in middle school and then backed it up with vandalism and grand theft auto before graduation. I'd never heard more than rumors, but the gossip seemed to indicate he'd gotten lucky being tried as a juvenile and luckier still with a grandmother who refused to turn her back on him.

Jack had disappeared from Kirby Falls for a time, but I'd been in college and focused on other things. The whispers ranged from forced military enlistment to an electronic ankle bracelet and home confinement.

Then he'd popped up a few years later, bartending at Magnolia. His hair had been longer, and there'd been new tattoos peeking out from beneath the rolled-up sleeves of his white dress shirt. After that, he'd joined the softball league with the Bar Hoppers, and our very limited interactions began.

I made myself ignore Jack's teasing. I had my own clipboard to worry about. Soon, the only sounds aside from my rapid heartbeat were pens scratching across our paperwork. I filled in my name and address, and all the pertinent information. Before I realized it, I'd checked the box for *married* instead of *divorced*.

Cursing myself inwardly, I quickly scribbled out the mark and then circled the correct option.

My eyes darted toward Jack, but he was focused on his own paper . . . like a normal person. He hadn't noticed my mistake because why would he?

I was being ridiculous.

Angling my clipboard higher, I forced myself to slow down, to read every question thoroughly. No more scribbles and ink blots. No more slipups.

Eventually, a middle-aged woman I didn't recognize poked her head into the small, well-lit waiting room. "Bonnie Jensen?"

I stood quickly—too quickly. My pen went flying off the clipboard and onto the floor.

Jack leaned down and retrieved it for me, soft-looking black leather stretched taut across his back.

As he extended his arm and held out the pen to me, something rebellious whispered in my mind. Probably the same antagonistic voice that had me arguing with him about self-flagellation muffins on the third-base line.

Suddenly, my mouth was saying, "Am I allowed to thank you for that?"

Tiny lines crinkled near his eyes, fanning out to his temples as he grinned. His hazel eyes contrasted with the golden rim of his reading glasses. They looked nearly green in the fluorescent overhead lighting. "Sure. Knock yourself out."

I grasped the other end of the pen and said pointedly, "Thank you, Jack."

He didn't let go when I tugged. Instead, his smile widened. "You're welcome, Clyde."

We watched each other for a long moment, and those somersaults in my stomach resumed their floor routine.

Then an impatient voice called from the doorway, "Whenever you're ready, Ms. Jensen."

Whatever had come over me abruptly fled. I dropped my gaze, and Jack finally released the pen. Without looking back, I hustled after the sheriff's office employee, mumbling out an apology for making her wait.

When I finished up twenty minutes later and left the station, I made my way directly to my car and didn't let myself look for a shiny black motorcycle, or even the possibility of it.

five

JACK

Cursing, I hoisted the mesh bag of soccer balls out of the back of my truck. While my motorcycle was my preferred mode of transportation, I had the truck for bad weather, cold winter months, and hauling things for the restaurant or my grandmother.

I would have much rather been somewhere—anywhere—on my bike right about now, but apparently I had an *obligation to the community*. Or at least, that was what local busybody and Kirby Falls multiple committee chair and president of everyfuckingthing, Eloise Carter, had told me recently.

When the old crone had dropped by Magnolia last Friday morning, she'd informed me of my new position as head coach of the Brookline U9 girls' soccer club. Apparently, that seemingly innocent form on little Jamie Santiago's clipboard had been legally binding, and I definitely should have read through it.

I'd inadvertently agreed to coach the little schemer and her friends when I'd said Magnolia would sponsor the team and provide the funds for their jerseys this season.

No amount of arguing or cajoling had swayed Eloise Carter. That woman was a force. I'd thought I was stubborn. *Jesus.*

So I'd gotten the last-minute background check she'd arranged for me and bumped into Bonnie in the process, which had been an interesting encounter. Good to know she was still off-balance around me, and that my strange inclination to push her buttons hadn't gone anywhere either. During our squabble over the pen, there'd been a moment when a spark had ignited in her eyes, and her words took on a razor-sharp edge. I'd liked it—getting such a reaction out of her. And I thought she might have liked it, too.

But now I was outside of Kirby Falls Elementary School at 2:45 p.m. on Tuesday afternoon, as instructed, for our first team practice. The grass field was wide, and there was a goal at either end. It seemed too big for a bunch of eight-year-olds to traverse, especially playing in a seven-on-seven game.

Yes, I'd had to email the Parks and Rec Department coordinator for a list of rules for the fall league. I'd never watched a soccer game in my life, much less knew how to instruct players.

I heard the bell ring over the outdoor speaker as I was setting up orange cones. Last night, I'd attempted some online research to find soccer drills and activities for kids their age. But I was sort of hoping the girls would just know what to do, and I could, more or less, babysit for the once-a-week, hour-long after-school practice.

The first two children who joined me on the field were not on my roster. Two little boys gleefully tossed their backpacks to the ground and started dribbling near the opposite goal.

The taller of the two noticed me and jogged over with the shorter one following close on his heels.

"Is it alright if we use the other half of the field?" the boy with shaggy dark brown hair asked. He looked like he was around the same age as the kid who'd tricked me into this whole thing, but his mouth was a little too big for his face, like it'd had a growth spurt before the rest of him had caught up.

"Sure," I said. I didn't know what I was going to do with half of a field, much less the whole thing.

"I'm Jacob," the tall boy offered. His attention drifted to the tattoos on my forearms.

I casually pulled my sleeves down from where I'd shoved them earlier while loading the truck.

"I'm Charlie," the shorter one piped up.

I nodded. "I'm Jack. I'm coaching the Brookline girls' team," I added in case he was checking references or knew a way to get me out of this.

Jacob elbowed Charlie, and they shared a laugh. "Good luck."

I didn't know what that meant, but I wasn't about to start pumping kids for information. Even I, with my limited experience with children, knew that was not a good idea.

"I live in Brookline, too. Are you coaching the boys' team?" Jacob asked hopefully. "Because our coach last year wasn't very good and my dad left, so it's just my mom supporting my soccer career."

Jesus, kids were honest.

"Uh, no," I finally managed. "I'm only coaching the girls." They stared at me for a moment, so I added, "Sorry."

"Okay!" Jacob announced before running off. Charlie parroted his friend and immediately followed.

I sighed. That had only been one interaction with two kids, and I was already sweating. How was I going to survive the next hour with ten little girls?

I shoved the sleeves of my hoodie back up my arms before remembering Jacob's curious gaze and tugging them down again. Was I a bad influence? Would he want tattoos now?

I didn't have time to have an existential crisis over the art on my body because a pack—and I mean, a pack—of girls came running toward me.

My heart rate picked up, and I swallowed hard.

"Hi, Coach Jack!" the tiny traitor of my contractual obligation nightmares called when she got to the sideline.

"Hello, Santiago," I replied flatly. "You know, you failed to mention the coaching portion of your request when you approached me about sponsoring the team."

Her smile widened. I thought she'd lost another baby tooth since I'd seen her last week.

"It was all there on the form," she said, not even a whiff of apology in her tone. "It's always a good idea to review a legally binding contract in its entirety."

I shook my head, borderline amused. *This kid.*

The rest of the pack were sitting on the grass, changing into soccer cleats. Jamie went to join them. It was still pretty warm for late September, and the girls were wearing shorts and tee shirts with tall socks in a variety of colors.

I finished placing the cones at the corners of our practice space and found the team stretching in a circle, Jamie leading them in the center. Tentatively, I grabbed my clipboard with the attached roster and joined my players.

I didn't even have to say anything or call them to attention. Ten pairs of eyes focused on me, and I was pretty sure a bead of sweat found its way down my spine.

Clearing my throat, I said, "I'm Jack. I'll be coaching you this season." They continued to stare. Jamie gave me a thumbs-up and a grin. "Why don't you take turns introducing yourselves and let me know what position you play?"

I pointed to a girl with dark brown skin and a tight bun, indicating she should start things off. Clicking my pen, I prepared to make notes on my clipboard.

The kid stood with military precision. "I am Raeanne Holt. Do not call me Rae or Anne. It's Raeanne."

I blinked. "Okay, Raeanne. What position do you play?"

"Captain," she replied easily and then sat, returning her attention to tying her cleats.

Uh, okay.

Jamie piped up, "Raeanne is new to our grade. She has lots of experience from her old soccer team. I think she'll make a great captain."

My eyes flicked to Raeanne to see how she would respond to Jamie's brownnosing, but the little girl remained stoic and offered a single, solemn nod. Jamie beamed.

"Right, next," I called.

A tall, skinny girl with a long, dark ponytail climbed to her feet. "I'm Rosie. I play defense."

I made a note. "Would you like to tell us anything else about yourself?"

"No," she said flatly and then resumed her seat.

"Okaaay." I tilted my pen in the direction of the next kid.

She was easily the tallest person on the field, save for me, and looked a little formal with her tee shirt tucked into her shorts. "I'm Tori," she said quietly. "I play goalie."

I noted that she had gloves next to her spot on the grass, and I jotted that down on my paper.

Another child popped up and did a little twirl. "Hi, I'm Gia. I wanted to be a cheerleader, but my mom said I had to do this. My preferred position is sub."

I . . . didn't think that was a position, but whatever. "Thanks, Gia." I smiled tightly.

The next kid didn't even bother standing. She had a tie-dye tracksuit on. "I'm Judy Douglas, and I can only come to, like, one game this season. I only signed up because I heard the jerseys were going to be really pretty. I like singing and dancing and acting."

"Right." I fought a sigh and made another scribble on my roster.

Three more girls introduced themselves, and thankfully, they were here to actually play soccer.

Then two players stood up together, and I realized how similar they looked.

"I'm Callie," one blond child said.

"And I'm Michelle," a nearly identical one echoed.

"Our parents make us play for exercise," Michelle added. "But please don't make us. Callie has heart palpitations if she runs too fast."

I stared, alarmed. "What's too fast?"

"At all!" Michelle insisted. "If she runs at all."

"Shouldn't you have that looked at by a doctor?"

"Great," Michelle huffed. "Now you're making her feel bad."

And sure enough, Callie's lower lip trembled.

Oh, shit. I was already making one of them cry. "Uh, sorry, Callie," I said quickly. "We'll take things slow."

Michelle crossed her arms and narrowed her eyes at me.

"Really slow," I amended.

Both girls sat, and I breathed a sigh of relief.

Finally, Jamie Santiago stood cheerfully. "Hi, Coach. I'm Jamie, as you know. I play striker or midfield."

Just then, a ball rolled into our circle.

"I'm ready to be the best I can be," Jamie added enthusiastically.

Jacob, the boy from across the field, jogged over and picked up the ball resting by Jamie's feet. "That sounds like the title of your autobiography," he said, Charlie giggling wildly behind him. He shot her a triumphant look and then sprinted away.

The gathered girls laughed while Jamie glared in Jacob's direction. She grumbled something under her breath and then sat back down.

There was a long moment of silence before I realized that I was the adult in charge and should probably get this show on the road.

"I thought we could start with some passing drills." Google had told me this was a pretty common occurrence at soccer practice, for any age group. "Find a partner. There are balls in that bag over there. And get started."

They stared at me.

So I clapped twice. They hopped up and got moving. Relieved, I made a note on my paper to order a whistle.

"These are size three balls," No-Nonsense Rosie called from the sideline.

I frowned. "Is that wrong?"

She gave me a look that insinuated *Duh, you moron.* Then she said, "I mean, those are for babies, but I guess you tried."

Wow. Okay.

"It's okay!" Jamie assured me with a grin. "We all have our own balls."

And sure enough, they each retrieved balls from their backpacks, along with shin guards and water bottles.

While chatting, the girls passed the balls happily back and forth for fifteen minutes as I stood there like an idiot with my clipboard, making fake notes and having absolutely no idea what we should do next.

Thankfully, I didn't have to figure it out because something on the sidewalk outside the school grabbed the team's attention, and the girls took off waving and shouting.

Alarmed, I tossed my clipboard aside, unprepared for mutiny so early on. But the kids stopped running once they reached their target.

The girls swarmed an amused Bonnie Clark—or Ms. Jensen, as the children were calling her—clearly on her way home for the day.

She greeted each child by name and smiled sweetly at them while they chattered animatedly at her. Words floated back to me on the breeze, snippets of their high-pitched enthusiasm about the team and practice.

Bonnie glanced over their heads and spotted me, her expression going from politely interested to shocked in record time. She let the kids tug her over to the field.

Before I could announce something—I didn't know what—Raeanne said it was time for a scrimmage and split the girls into two teams. They whooped and bolted onto the field.

Bonnie came to stand beside me while I watched my well-oiled machine chug away without me. She was wearing a flowy skirt with swirls of autumn colors and a gauzy white button-up tucked into it. A wide brown belt accentuated her waist, and if I wasn't mistaken, she was trying very hard not to laugh.

"So this was what the background check was for." Oh, yeah, she was amused.

I side-eyed her.

"They're a good group of girls," she offered, still watching the mini-game in progress.

"Sure. Even the diabolical mastermind with butterfly clips."

Bonnie finally turned to look at me, her grin widening. She chuckled and quickly brought a hand up to cover her mouth. "I'm guessing there's a story behind this?"

I sighed. "Santiago over there came to Magnolia looking for a sponsor for the team's jerseys and failed to mention that I was signing my life away as their head coach. Then Eloise Carter came calling and strong-armed me into the background check last Friday."

Her brown eyes sparkled. "So you're not actually into soccer?"

I huffed a humorless laugh. "No. I have no idea what the fuck I'm doing. And there are no parents here. I can't believe they just left their kids with me."

Bonnie laughed again. "Yeah, if there's an adult in charge, the parents are for sure going to bail. If you want them to stay, you'll need to explicitly spell out that it's not a drop-off practice."

Great. Not only would I be expected to talk to these kids, but I had to *communicate* with their parents, too.

Suddenly, the girl in the tie-dye tracksuit ran off the field. She grabbed her bag from the sideline without saying anything and bolted toward the parking lot.

Bonnie and I watched as Judy Douglas hopped into an old Pontiac waiting at the curb. A woman in the driver's seat waved out her open window.

"That's her mom," Bonnie offered helpfully.

"Who just leaves in the middle of practice?"

Bonnie's gaze cut my way, and she said seriously, "I'm sure it didn't have anything to do with your coaching ability." Then she ruined it by smiling widely.

"Ha. Ha."

"You know," she began, "my sister is dating a former college soccer player. Do you know Brady Judd? I could see if he'd be interested in helping coach."

I knew of the Judds. They were recognizable in Kirby Falls the same way the Clarks were. Small-town apple royalty.

There was a prickly, prideful part of me that didn't want Bonnie's help— or anyone's. But then my eyes drifted to the field where the scrimmage had devolved into most of the players sitting on the ground while Jamie and Raeanne looked on in disappointment. Gia was definitely FaceTiming someone, and Callie and Michelle were tossing Goldfish crackers into each other's mouths. *Christ.*

I didn't know anything about soccer. I also didn't know what to do with these kids. And I sure as shit didn't know how to motivate them. Turning down an offer for help from someone who actually knew that there were different-sized soccer balls was probably a dumb move.

Clearing my throat, I finally replied, "Thanks. That would be really great."

We exchanged numbers, and I made sure Bonnie saw me enter her contact name as *Clyde*. I bit down on a grin as she rolled her eyes at me, but she promised to talk to Brady tonight when she had dinner with him and her sister.

The kids must have known we were nearing the end of practice because they stopped looking for four-leaf clovers long enough to come over and tell Ms. Jensen goodbye.

"You'll come to our first game, won't you?" Jamie asked her hopefully.

"Of course," Bonnie said easily. "I wouldn't miss it."

"Coach Jack, your hair is long," Gia said out of nowhere. "You could have a man-bun if you wanted."

I must have made a face because Bonnie snorted in amusement.

"Why would I want that?" I asked.

All the girls chimed in at once.

"Because it would be cool."

"One of the Premier League coaches wears a man-bun."

"That would be way better than the boys in our grade with their mullets."

"And their perms," Raeanne added in disgust.

"And their permed mullets," Gia concluded.

I didn't know why, but I felt embarrassed by their attention. And then I noticed Bonnie nodding along with the girls, and my ears went hot.

Raising my brow, I asked her, "You think I need a man-bun?"

She narrowed her eyes like she was trying to picture it. "I think you could pull it off."

The team echoed their support.

Thankfully, the girls stopped speculating about my appearance as a few parents approached from the parking lot. I checked my watch, and thank Christ, this torture was over.

I cleared my throat uncomfortably for the hundredth time this afternoon. "Alright, your parents are waiting. No game this week. I'll see you next Tuesday for practice."

Without warning, the girls crowded around me, and I thought for one horrifying moment that they might hug me.

"Hands in," Rosie ordered.

Ah, a huddle. Sportsmanship and whatnot.

Cautiously, I placed my hand on top of the little ones stacked in the middle of our sloppy circle.

"You too, Ms. Jensen," Jamie said.

Bonnie reached in, her small hand settling warm and soft over mine. Our gazes met and held.

"One, two, three. Brookline!" Rosie yelled.

And the team chorused, "U9!"

Bonnie grinned at me, and I found myself smiling softly back. I realized suddenly that everything about this day had been entirely unexpected . . . but I didn't hate it.

Bonnie

After a delicious, if slightly awkward, dinner of Brady's sun-dried tomato pasta, I found myself tossing and turning and unable to sleep.

My restlessness was pretty common. A few nights a week, I struggled with my anxiety at bedtime. Usually, I thought about what I had left on my to-do list, and then I ran through scenarios of what I might be forgetting. The recent incident with the background check hadn't helped. My mind just couldn't seem to quiet.

Once I realized I wasn't getting to sleep anytime soon, I ignored my therapist's advice and grabbed my phone from the bedside table and started scrolling. It was just after three in the morning, and I knew my school day was going to be rough.

At dinner tonight, my sister, Mac, had been careful with me, the way she'd been since the divorce. Well, since I'd shown up on her doorstep mid–

panic attack back in the summer. I knew my sister was worried about me, but no matter how normal and fine I acted, she wasn't convinced.

Brady had been present for the panic attack, too, but he was less obvious in his worry for me. He did things like ask me to dance at weddings and walk me to my car, carrying leftovers and foisting them upon me.

Mac was a little more obvious in her attention because she wasn't a naturally soft sort of person. My sister could be pretty abrasive and salty. But it was like the divorce had put her on high alert. She was always aware of me and my reactions, doing her best to cheer me up or make sure I wasn't lonely. Her spiteful anger at Danny had made her even more loyal and steadfast toward me.

I appreciated her. I really did. But it was exhausting trying to reassure her that I was okay all the time. I felt like I was managing her emotions as well as my own.

I'd talked to Brady at dinner about helping Jack coach soccer when Mac had been distracted. It wasn't that I expected him to keep it a secret from Mac; I just didn't want to have to explain how or why I was involved. It would only raise more questions and make my nosy sister that much more curious.

Brady usually gave Mac one cooking chore to handle at every dinner. Since she wasn't a natural in the kitchen, the task usually required all her attention. And when she'd been keeping the breadsticks from burning, I'd quietly brought up coaching with Brady. He'd readily agreed, and I'd promised to text him the details for the next practice.

With that settled, I figured I could text Jack later and put him out of his misery.

He'd been so out of sorts with the girls this afternoon. It was the only time I'd ever seen Jack Ellis as anything but calm, cool, and collected. He'd looked on the verge of panic the entire time.

Honestly, it had been kind of sweet, in an amusing sort of way. The bad boy facing down ten second graders and defending his lack of a man-bun.

I giggled a little into the darkness of the guest bedroom and started a new thread in my messaging app.

I'd forgotten to text him earlier, but I'd do it now, and he could see my message in the morning and breathe a sigh of relief knowing that help was incoming. Friendly, affable assistance who knew his way around a soccer ball and was great with kids. I was pretty sure Brady could charm anyone.

Unsure of my opener, I typed my message and reread it a dozen times, like I was fifteen years old and texting my crush. That wasn't too far off. Jack definitely gave me butterflies, but I was over thirty. It was silly to be this worried about impressing him. Or more accurately, making a fool of myself.

Me: Hi Jack. It's Bonnie. Just wanted to let you know that Brady agreed to help out with the team.

There. Simple and to the point.

So I wasn't sure why I was fretting over it.

I debated adding my last name, but, in the end, I didn't want to type *Jensen* despite it being accurate. And I figured I didn't need any sort of closing. No plucky *Have a good day!* or *Good luck this season!* We weren't friends. I was just some woman who'd slept in his bed once. There were probably plenty of those.

After a deep breath, I made myself hit send so I would stop obsessing over a single text message. *Good lord.* Then I navigated over to my favorite social media app.

But almost immediately, a response popped up, and I dropped my phone on my face.

Oh crap. Jack had texted back. At 3:14 a.m.

Jack: Thanks for setting that up. The next practice is the same time, same place, if he can make it.

With thumbs fumbling across the keyboard, I hurriedly typed, *I'm so sorry if I woke you. I thought you'd see my message in the morning.*

Jack: What did I tell you about apologizing to me?

Me: Waking you in the middle of the night with a random text notification is a perfectly acceptable reason to say you're sorry.

Jack: You didn't wake me. I'm up.

Oh. Well, that was good. I was glad I didn't mess up his night.

A nosy middle-aged Southern spirit must have possessed my body because I found myself asking suddenly, *So, why are you up?*

My eyes widened, and I tossed my phone face down on the comforter in horror. What had I just done? I'd delivered my message about Brady, and now I was trying to keep the conversation going.

I could imagine several scenarios in which Jack Ellis would be up late. Maybe he was just getting home. Maybe he was wide-awake for a very fitting reason. I imagined him leaving the Sterling House Bed-and-Breakfast after hooking up with a gorgeous *leafer* from the bar. Tossing on his leather jacket and riding off down the street after rocking some woman's world.

I rolled over and buried my face in my pillow, groaning. What the heck was wrong with me?

But then I peeked at my device and saw light coming from beneath the edge of the plastic case. So quickly I should have been embarrassed about it, but I snatched up my phone and looked at the screen.

Jack: A drunk tourist picked a fight tonight at Magnolia. The cops came, and it was a mess. I had to deal with the police report and give a statement.

I winced, thinking about how he'd had to handle another irresponsible inebriated person. Bartenders had it hard.

Me: I'm sorry. That sounds like a pain.

Jack: I can practically hear you comparing yourself to a drunk leafer. Stop it. And stop apologizing.

That was a general I'm sorry, I argued reflexively, annoyed that he'd read me so easily.

Jack: I noticed you ignored the other part.

Before I could defend myself, he replied . . .

Jack: What are you doing up so late? Pretty sure it's past bedtime for most good girls.

Maybe I always felt uncool around Jack because he liked to keep reminding me how I was a good girl and he was a bad boy. Believe me, I knew how different we were—how different we'd always been. Maybe he felt like he needed to draw attention to those old roles to keep space between us. Or, more likely, he could tell I had an embarrassing crush on him.

I didn't have a quippy response or a funny answer. I was tired, and that was probably why I went with the truth.

Me: I have trouble sleeping sometimes.

It was something I hadn't told anyone besides my therapist.

Dots appeared and then disappeared for a while, and I figured that would be it. But as I was putting my phone back on the bedside table, it lit up with another message.

Jack: When I was a kid, I couldn't always get to sleep. My grandmother taught me this trick. To think about something good. Make a list of three of my favorite things. Like three favorite breakfast foods, or three favorite TV shows, or whatever it might be. It worked better than counting sheep. Maybe you could try that.

I smiled wistfully down at my phone, thinking how good I was at making lists instead of sleeping. I couldn't imagine this would actually work.

But I still typed out, *French toast with butter and powdered sugar, ham and cheese omelet, and Apple Jacks cereal.*

Jack: Toast and apple butter, scrambled eggs, and blueberry lemon scones from Cubhouse Coffee Shop.

My grin widened, surprised he'd played along. Even more surprised when another message came through.

Jack: Okay, now TV shows.

Me: Sons of Anarchy, Brooklyn Nine-Nine, Pushing Daisies. You?

Jack: Don't laugh.

I absolutely did.

Me: Promise.

Jack: The Office and Naked & Afraid

Me: AND?

Jack: and Ice Road Truckers

Me: OMG

Jack: It was compelling, okay.

Me: No, I believe you.

Jack: I had to Google Pushing Daisies.

I huffed another quiet laugh and typed, *I'm still bitter about that one. It deserved more than one season.*

Me: Favorite bands?

And the dots to indicate Jack was typing appeared again, as if by late-night magic.

We kept going, and some of the tightness wrapped around me, the kind preventing me from sleeping earlier, loosened its hold. My favorites were innocuous rather than damning. Confessions in the dark that wouldn't have made sense in the light of day. These were lists I didn't mind making. They were nostalgic and warm, rather than brittle mistakes or obligations holding me hostage, keeping my mind from rest.

I smiled more into the night than I could remember smiling inside this house in a very long time. I learned about Jack's favorite music and foods, the books he reread regularly, and the authors that he auto-bought. The way he took his coffee—black at home or an oat milk latte at a coffee shop —and his favorite sports to watch—basketball, hockey, and baseball, in that order. I was surprised by his honesty and giddy with the feeling of learning about someone new for the first time in quite a while.

And just like a weirdo on the internet, it was easier to be honest behind a screen. I was able to forget how twisted up Jack made me feel when he was just three bouncing dots. The one-sided attraction that made me awkward and tongue-tied in person was muted in the artificial glow of my phone. The hazy memories of that night in his apartment weren't front and center at the moment.

At some point, Jack's three favorites idea must have worked because I woke up to an alarm going off, my phone still clutched in my hand.

After silencing the noise, I blinked groggily until my screen came into focus. And there, at 4:48 a.m., after I'd failed to reply to Jack's request for my three favorite GIFs, he'd typed his final message.

Jack: Good night, Clyde. Sleep tight.

BONNIE

By six thirty the following afternoon, I was dragging.

My late night—or early morning, however you wanted to look at it—had caught up with me, and no amount of coffee could help. But I couldn't bail on bowling league tonight. It had been my idea initially—before my divorce—to form a team with my family and friends.

I'd asked Larry to participate, but my cousin had said there was no way we were getting her to put her feet into shoes that were still warm and moist from someone else's body. Apparently, bowling was a hard no for her, even when I'd suggested she buy her own bowling shoes like I did.

Becca, our newest resident of Kirby Falls and my cousin Will's fiancée, had a knitting group on Wednesdays and couldn't join us. And Chloe, my good friend who worked at Grandpappy's, had other obligations keeping her busy.

So our team became the Orchard Sisters with just me and Mac, and then my best friend, Candace, and her older sister, Joan, both of whom were Brady's sisters and worked at the apple farm across the street from Grandpappy's. We met every two weeks for league night down at the Lucky Strike Lanes.

I wasn't a skilled bowler on the best of days, but tonight's performance was sure to be in the gutter, literally. I'd mostly wanted to start a team for the social aspect—something fun to do with my friends and family that wasn't just book club once a month.

Looking back, I could see that I'd been lonely in my marriage. And then that marriage had fallen apart. Now, ironically, socializing was one of the last things I wanted to do. Mostly due to the fact that Danny also participated in a bowling league with his coworkers and friends from down at the garage.

The Begley Auto Boys were currently at the opposite end of the alley, thanks to Jemma, who worked behind the counter and handled league night. She'd greeted me tonight and called Danny a "fuckface who deserved the shittiest lane in the place."

It had been nice of her. Better than being asked how I was doing every five minutes.

"How are you doing?" Mac asked suddenly, holding out a plastic container of nachos. The cheese was violently orange.

I shook my head at the offered snack and kept entering our names into the score-keeping software. "I'm good."

I didn't think my sister actually wanted to hear that I was slightly nauseous over my ex-husband's proximity. And even if she did, *I* didn't want the world to know I was this weak.

Everything was so complicated. How could you still miss someone who'd broken all your walls and then buried you in them? That beneath the bitterness and resentment I couldn't seem to scrub away, there was a layer of hurt and bewilderment that somehow my marriage had ended here, with me tense and clammy-handed at the other side of the bowling alley, faking happiness.

My sister's concerned stare was burning a hole in the side of my head, but I ignored her. Finally, she gave up and walked back to the table behind our lane, her dark ponytail swinging.

Once I had the computer all set up, I joined my teammates.

"I got you a corn dog," Candace said, nudging the paper tray in my direction.

We cheers'd, tapping our deep-fried dinners together before taking huge bites. Candace was smiling so hard, hers nearly fell out of her mouth.

Candace Judd and I hadn't been friends long, but we'd clicked right away. She'd returned to Kirby Falls two summers ago after a bad breakup and job loss.

As kids and adolescents, we'd only vaguely been in each other's orbits. At five years her senior, I hadn't been in any of Candace's classes or extracurriculars, but I'd always known who she was, if not the details of her life. She'd been the popular girl, the valedictorian and the homecoming queen, whip smart and goal oriented. Candace had been a prime example of a successful small-town girl making good in the big city.

But she hadn't been happy there. Luckily, upon her return, she'd found her place, incidentally, working at her family's orchard. She handled things behind the scenes with social media and marketing, as well as on outreach and education, planning group tours and local student field trips.

Judd's Orchard was across the street from Grandpappy's—my family's farm—and had a somewhat smaller, more niche operation when compared to Grandpappy's sprawling acreage and year-round attractions.

Candace worked with her parents, her boyfriend, Mark Mercer, her brother, Brady, and her sister, Joan.

Speaking of Joan, she was watching us happily devour our corn dogs with a look of disgust. "I don't know how you can eat that."

"Junk food is good for the soul, Joanie," Candace told her sister before wiping mustard from the corner of her mouth.

I laughed into my napkin at the horror on Joan's face.

She was a healthy person who had nailed that whole treat-your-body-like-a-temple thing. She ran nearly every morning—on purpose—and ate well. At thirty-five, she was in way better shape than the rest of us sitting at this table.

I reached into my bag and pulled out the granola I'd made for her, along with the high-protein yogurt cup I'd packed before leaving the house. "Here you go, Joan."

Her dark eyebrows drew together. "You didn't need to do that."

Smiling, I assured her, "I know. But the food here isn't really your speed, and I didn't want you to be miserable until you could get home. I know you don't like to eat too late at night. There's a whole big batch of that granola. I'll bring the rest by the orchard for you."

"You made it?"

"Yeah. It has flax and chia seeds, almonds, pumpkin seeds, and a little bit of vanilla and honey."

"Thank you, Bonnie," Joan said earnestly. She was a serious person by nature, not given over to silliness or flights of fancy. Basically, the last person on the planet who would willingly plan a bachelorette party or be caught line dancing. Even still, I could tell she was genuinely touched by my gesture.

I grinned. "You're welcome."

See, that was how a polite exchange went when you made something for someone and they accepted it graciously. Jack could stand to take some lessons.

Speaking of Jack, I'd scrolled back through our early-morning texts more times than I should probably admit. In the light of day, I wasn't any *more* embarrassed, but I definitely wasn't planning on texting him again. I'd done my duty and sent the required message about Brady helping. Every-thing else had been . . . extra. A pleasant surprise. A surreptitious mishap. A nocturnal emission. *No, wait.* That wasn't right.

"Are we going to talk about why Brady went out today and bought a printer and is currently at home fighting with said printer in order to print out sample soccer training agendas and a practice schedule for a bunch of eight-year-old girls?"

"What?" Candace asked. "Why would my brother be doing that?"

"I don't know," Mac replied, fluttering her lashes. "You want to tell the class, Bon?"

Brady must have told Mac about coaching. I'd expected it. Brady was a good guy like that.

Sighing, I muttered, "It's because I asked Brady if he'd be willing to help coach one of the parks and rec teams. Some of my second graders."

"Did Eloise guilt you into volunteering or something?" Candace wondered before taking another bite of corn dog.

"No, nothing like that."

My sister wiggled her eyebrows at me and made a face that very plainly said, *Are you going to tell them or do I get the pleasure?*

I wiped my mouth on my napkin and placed it back in my lap. "Actually, I told Jack I'd try to get him some help. He's the one who was guilted by Eloise Carter, and apparently he doesn't know anything about soccer. I stumbled on their practice yesterday after school, and I saw a way I could help."

"You saw a way you could help," Mac parroted. "Okay, Mother Teresa."

Joan snickered.

"Wait," Candace said. "Jack who?"

"Jack Ellis, a bartender over at Magnolia," Mac answered helpfully. "I guess the bar is sponsoring the team, and he's the poor sucker stuck on coaching duty."

I watched as Candace turned that over in her head before her eyes widened. "Doesn't he drive a motorcycle and wear a leather jacket?"

"He does," Joan answered absently as she stirred granola into her yogurt.

My friend grinned at me excitedly.

Candace and I had binged three seasons of *Sons of Anarchy* together last fall. She knew how I felt about motorcycling-riding bad boys. That they were essentially my attraction catnip.

And looking at Candace's still-pleased expression, the one bordering on maniacal glee, she'd obviously completely missed the part about how it was all a *fantasy*.

Normal people didn't want to roar off into the sunset with violent MC members just because they looked good in their riding leathers. It was one thing to watch a television show and lust after fictional characters. Motorcycle gang members weren't actually my type.

And neither was Jack Ellis.

I didn't know if I even had a type. The only man I'd ever been with was tall and slim with light brown hair and a mustache I hadn't been a fan of. Danny was a quiet guy who spent most of his time in garage coveralls. He was close with his family, and I didn't think there was an adventure-seeking bone in his body. We'd been alike in that regard.

I made eye contact with Candace and gave her a subtle headshake.

She must have gotten the message because she tamped down her wide grin and didn't say anything else about motorcycle men.

A loud cheer went up at the other end of the bowling alley, thankfully drawing everyone's attention away from the topic of Jack. But when I tracked the hooting and high-fiving to the four grown men in the final lane, my gaze inadvertently collided with my ex-husband's.

My stomach clenched uncomfortably, and I looked away.

I thought suddenly that I was glad Chloe wasn't here and forced to face the decisions of her past. But it might have been nice to share this table with someone else who knew what it was like to be divorced from one of the Begley Auto guys, instead of being surrounded by well-meaning friends and family who were getting ready to ask me again if I was holding up okay.

Chloe Rockford, my friend and the bakery assistant at Grandpappy's, had married Keaton Begley right out of high school. They'd divorced a year and a half ago. But Chloe probably wouldn't have cared about Keaton being in her proximity. I was sure she'd hardly notice him hollering less than fifty feet away and making a big deal out of a strike. Because Chloe was happily remarried now. She'd moved on. She probably didn't even think about being cheated on and manipulated. Chloe had a new life, and she was living it.

I wondered how long it would take me to pull myself back together.

"Are you okay?" Mac asked quietly. Again.

I'd known it was coming. Instead of sighing, I met my sister's concerned gaze and nodded, aiming for a reassuring smile and landing somewhere in the vicinity of a pathetic lip tremble.

Mac furrowed her brows, helpless in the face of my despair.

I hated feeling weak. Reminders of my life *before* were hard to shake. There had been good years in my marriage, and Danny had been my best friend for the majority of my life. I didn't know how to put all that behind me, to stop mourning the loss and just move forward. To keep myself from begging for it back.

Maybe if Danny had given me a little more time, I could have—

Abruptly, Mac stood, distracting me from my self-pity. She looked determined, and that never meant anything good.

"He should leave," she spat. "We were here first. How long had you been asking to start a team? Oh, and *now* he decides to up and do it, when he never bothered before."

"Mac, please," I begged, fearful that she might do something public and rash.

She ignored me, too focused on defending my honor to actually hear what I was saying. "I'm going over there."

Desperation had me lunging across the table and cuffing her wrist. With strength I didn't feel, I kept her from walking off to confront my ex.

"Stop it," I hissed, panic making my voice unsteady.

I didn't want a scene. I definitely didn't need my sister to draw attention to the drama that was my life. I couldn't stand the thought of Danny seeing me this way, thinking I was anything but *just fine*.

I didn't pull out my big-sister tone very often, but I couldn't abide this. "Sit down, MacKenzie Eloise." But as the sound reached my ears, I realized my voice had come out broken and choked, like a call that had lost signal, pieces and parts dissolving into nothing.

Fear raised my heart rate, and my breath was coming too fast.

Mac's eyes widened, and she lowered herself to her seat in a hurry. "Shit. I'm sorry. I'm sorry, Bonnie. I wasn't thinking. Just breathe."

I did. I took great gulps of air as my nose started to tingle, always the first sign I was about to lose control—lose the fight against my anxiety.

Dammit. I did not want to do this here. I closed my eyes and focused on breathing in the here and now, the way my therapist had taught me. I listened to the rush of air through my nose, accompanied by the soundtrack of pins crashing and people talking. With every inhale, I catalogued the scent of fried food and decades-old cigarette smoke embedded in the furniture. My hands pressed into the smooth surface of the table, over and over.

I didn't know how long it took, but eventually my breathing evened out and my eyes opened. Mac and Candace and Joan were watching me worriedly. I didn't want to explain or discuss the anxiety attack I'd avoided just now. And I definitely didn't want to spend the next hour bowling.

"I'm sorry, Bon," Mac whispered again.

I nodded because I knew my little sister meant well.

"I think I'm going to head out."

"That's not a good idea," Joan said at the same time Candace insisted, "No, Bonnie. You shouldn't be alone."

"I'll come with you," Mac pleaded, guilt making her forehead wrinkle.

Shaking my head, I gripped the table and got to my feet. I was mostly steady. I could walk out of here and drive home and be just as fine as I pretended to be.

"It's been a long day. I'll catch y'all later."

I didn't look around to see if the coffee shop team on the next lane had seen me spiral out of control. Warmth was coming back into my face, a telltale blush working its way up from my neck.

With controlled movements, I gathered my bag and made for the exit. I wasn't stopping to change out of my bowling shoes.

When I passed by the concession stand, I glanced up to see Danny standing there with Keaton. His gaze met mine, and I was pretty proud when my steps didn't falter.

His brows furrowed, and his lips formed my name, but I didn't wait around to find out what my ex-husband would have said or done. I looked away and kept right on walking.

I was careful on the drive home, hands clutching the steering wheel as I focused on the beams from my headlights. At home, I left my clothes on the floor and changed into pajamas.

When I was lying in bed, I closed my eyes and remembered the last time I felt calm and in control—texting Jack in the middle of the night. It was easier to focus on that than the spectacle I'd made of myself tonight. I should have been relieved that I'd avoided a panic attack. My therapist, Nina, would have been proud of me, and I would tell her about it during our next scheduled virtual session. But I couldn't seem to find the relief. The sudden onset of emotion had been so very public.

Rationally, I knew it was silly to feel embarrassed or vulnerable. I was close to Candace and Joan and Mac. They weren't judging me or thinking less of me. But it was easier to hide certain parts of myself. Better to avoid being an inconvenience to the people in my life.

There had been a few panic and anxiety attacks in the months since my separation from Danny. Centering myself tonight, remembering the techniques Nina had taught me, and finding calm in the middle of the storm had been a big step.

"Three favorites," I murmured into the quiet room. Then I started with pizza toppings and moved on to ice-cream flavors. Next, I recited my favorite summer Olympic sports, followed by winter. Weary and exhausted from the long day and emotional upheaval, I was asleep before I hit the downhill luge.

Friday afternoon rolled around with another knock on my classroom door.

"Hey, Bon."

But it wasn't my principal with news to deliver.

It was my ex-husband.

I stood awkwardly as Danny shuffled through the open doorway. "Hi," I said cautiously, wondering what this little visit was about and hating myself for hoping he missed me.

I could count on one hand how many times Danny had been in my classroom over the years.

"How you been?" he asked.

The spiteful part of me that I kept locked away wanted to get angry, to tell Danny to get to the point and get out of my life. But there were other parts too, ones that were just as difficult to ignore. The girl who remembered holding hands for the first time on the bus in eighth grade or swimming in the lake with sunburned shoulders and full hearts. Or the young woman who'd gotten married under the gazebo at the farm and watched her groom cry when he saw her walking down the aisle.

"Good," I replied stiffly, a compromise.

He shoved his hands awkwardly into the pockets of his coveralls, and I hated that I knew it was because he was nervous. "Figured you'd be here late."

It had been a point of contention in our marriage. But I liked finishing up all my weekly grading before heading home for the weekend. Danny had gotten frustrated if I made us late for dinner at his parents' house on Friday nights. But I hadn't made us late. I always did the majority of the cooking, so we didn't miss anything. He was just chronically impatient and didn't like to wait on me. Plus, he thought eating after six thirty was the end of the world.

"Yep, still here," I replied, refusing to let that old bitterness bleed through. I didn't have to justify my decisions to him or anyone else. Not anymore.

A few more steps put Danny in front of my desk. I was still standing, unsure what to do with myself.

Finally, he said, "Got some news about Mom. Her cancer is back. Not much they can do about it this time. She's home with hospice."

My heart sank. Diane Jensen was one of the kindest people I'd ever met. I'd known her since I was fourteen years old, and she'd been a second mother to me. The separation had been hard enough to manage without feeling like I'd lost half my family in the process. But I had.

Danny's parents and sisters had all gradually broken contact. I realized it had been over a month since I'd heard from any of them. Not even about this.

I loved Diane. I couldn't just turn that off.

"I wanted to come by and see if you might visit with her," Danny said as I sat heavily in my chair. "She's been asking about you, but didn't want to bother you. I know it would mean a lot."

"Of course," I replied immediately. I wanted to see her. I might not be her daughter-in-law anymore, but I could still support her in this. "I'll get in touch with your dad and figure out when she's up for some company." I swallowed roughly. "I'm so sorry, Danny. Thank you for telling me."

His smile was tight. "Yeah. I'm sorry too."

We watched each other for a long moment. My instinct was to give comfort, to hug him or ask if he wanted to talk about it or if there was anything else I could do to help. But I'd promised myself I wouldn't offer something that wasn't wanted. I'd stop reaching for lifelines that had cut themselves.

Danny took a step back. "Well, I'll let you get back to it. Thanks, Bon. I know it'll really lift her spirits to see you."

He left as suddenly as he'd arrived, work boots squeaking on the linoleum.

I didn't know how long I stared at the doorway, forcing myself to breathe in and out.

Danny had touched down like a tornado, uprooting and leaving destruction in his wake.

Eventually, I finished grading and packed up my belongings. April had been sick most of the week with a stomach bug, so she wouldn't be walking out with me. I'd packed up Cocoa on Wednesday and taken her over to April's house along with some crackers, applesauce, and drinks with electrolytes.

The hallways were quiet. I'd stayed later than usual, and the custodian would be through in a little while to lock up.

The news of Diane's health decline weighed heavily on me, slowing my steps. She'd been through so much already. A breast cancer diagnosis nearly a decade ago, followed by surgery and chemotherapy. I hated the thought of her battle ending this way.

My pace slowed outside of Angie Morris's classroom, the night-light catching my attention through the window in the door. Little Oreo was alone again for the weekend, from the looks of it. I stepped closer and watched the bunny hop to the other side of the cage.

It was probably my heightened emotional state that made me impulsive. That was really the only explanation I had for why I tried the knob on Morris's door and then quickly slipped inside when it opened.

I located Oreo's carrier and supplies in the storage closet.

And twenty minutes later, I found myself struggling to exit the side door next to the cafeteria with a giant cage in my arms. Once I'd loaded it into my car, I glanced around to make sure no one had seen me. Then I collapsed into the driver's seat and released a long breath.

"It's just for the weekend," I told the black-and-white rabbit in my passenger seat. "I'll bring you back early on Monday, and no one will ever know you were gone."

I could see Oreo's nose twitching agreeably behind the mesh side of her carrier, and it felt a little like having a partner in crime.

Grinning, I started my car. "See, this would be an excellent time to nickname someone Clyde. Not when they're puking in your bathroom." I looked at Oreo seriously. "Don't puke in my bathroom, okay?"

I got Oreo set up at home, keeping her mostly out of the bedrooms. I was scared I'd lose her under a bed or something. Plus, I thought it would be easier for her to get used to my house if she wasn't overwhelmed at first.

Not that she needed to get used to anything. This was a one-time thing.

Probably.

I watched as she hopped and sniffed.

Then I dragged a hand across my mouth, fighting hysteria. I'd stolen a rabbit from a second-grade classroom. Good lord, was *this* rock bottom?

Oreo and I watched three episodes of a 2000s sitcom on my laptop in the living room. She sat with me and let me stroke her ears, and she made me laugh when she started nibbling my socks.

It was nice to have some company, especially tonight when my thoughts were mournful and tinged with heartache.

That night, as I lay in bed, I wondered what it would have been like to get the news of Diane's prognosis if Danny and I were still married. I could have been a source of comfort for the Jensens. I would have made meals and stocked their fridge. Visited and called, taken Diane to her appointments.

I would have wrapped Danny in my love, and we could have faced the heartbreak of loss together. That was what you did with a partner. Except now, he didn't have anyone to lean on, to help carry the weight or bear the burden.

But neither did I. And I didn't even have the right to mourn Diane as my family anymore. That had been taken from me, too.

Shame had me roughly scrubbing the tears from my cheeks. I was being incredibly selfish.

So I was relieved by the distraction when my phone lit up on my night-stand just after midnight. And then I was shocked because right there on my screen was a text message from Jack Ellis.

Jack: You up?

Jack: Okay, I realize how that sounded. I meant, are you awake, having trouble sleeping?

I laughed, the tearstained skin tight around my eyes as it crinkled in sudden amusement. For one wistful moment, I thought about what it would be like to get a booty-call text from Jack.

I braced for panic, for the sinking sensation of betrayal, to feel like I was cheating on my husband. But it never came. All I felt was the lightness of possibility, the flip in my belly that was attraction and giddy disbelief. A warmth settling low in my middle.

My mind went to places covered in tattoos. The dark scruff on his jaw. Little round glasses perched on a masculine face. I tried to imagine him in this bed. Knocking quietly on my door and sliding under the covers. His face was a solemn, stoic mask. Calm and cool and unaffected. I wondered what it would take to get that mask to slip.

Then I shook off the daydream with a regretful laugh and started typing, begging myself not to make it weird.

Me: I'm up.

Favorite movie theater snacks, he texted immediately, like he'd been waiting all day to ask.

I smiled, allowing myself the little fantasy. What was one more in the secret quiet of my bedroom?

Me: Popcorn with an obscene amount of butter, Cookie Dough Bites, and a fountain Coke. I will not be entertaining any other offers or taking questions at this time.

A pause before the bouncing dots appeared. I let myself have another little daydream, one where I imagined that little pause meant he was laughing on the other end of our conversation. Jack did that sometimes—waited for a beat or two before he started typing. Just for tonight, I'd believe it was because Jack found me amusing. He was, of course, too cool to use an emoji to convey his delight over my obvious charm. Obviously. And a GIF? Unheard of.

But Jack, leaning against his headboard, glasses on and smiling down at the screen of his phone. That, I could believe.

At least for tonight.

Jack: Another acceptable answer could be . . . Dr Pepper and popcorn with butter and Reese's Pieces mixed in.

Me: I will consider it.

Another pause. I rolled onto my side, grinning.

Jack: Three favorite alcoholic beverages.

Me: Low blow, Ellis. I'm still abstaining.

The longest pause yet. Then, *How could I be so inconsiderate? Three favorite holidays?*

I considered the question for a moment.

Me: Halloween, Christmas Day . . .

Me: And my favorite is Christmas Eve.

Jack: There's a difference between Christmas Day and Christmas Eve celebrations?

Me: Christmas Day was smaller, but still good.

That had been my time with Danny and his family. Diane and I used to put together a delicious brunch for the Jensens. My memories were shadowed with sadness now for a variety of reasons.

Me: But Christmas Eve night is our big party out at the farm. And when I was a kid, it was a really big deal. I liked the food, of course, and being with my cousins and aunt and uncles, but there was just something magical about Christmas Eve. Cold, clear nights, twinkle lights, and so much possibility. I remember all the excitement we had about Santa coming. My dad and uncles took it seriously. They'd stomp around on the roof after we went to sleep. Then leave tracks in the yard for the sled and reindeer.

Me: It's just always seemed like there was so much hope. So, it's always been my favorite. Even as an adult, with the magic gone, the possibility is still there, you know. Like anything could happen on Christmas Eve.

I'd typed a lot, and Jack had gone suspiciously quiet. I wanted to kick myself for making a big deal about family and holidays. It had never been a secret that Jack's homelife was different than mine.

So, I attempted to change the subject and sent *Favorite ice cream?*

The three little dots appeared, and I breathed a sigh of relief.

Jack: Rocky road, cookie dough, and vanilla

Jack: How about office supplies? I know you have at least three favorites of those.

I smiled drowsily. Sleep was catching up to me, chasing me down against my will for once. But I was grateful Jack had reached out tonight. I didn't know what it meant, if anything. But it went beyond feeding my juvenile crush with more of his time and attention.

He didn't know—couldn't know—but he'd given me comfort when I'd needed it. A soft place to rest my head for just a moment, long enough to gather myself before anything else broke apart.

Me: I know you're teasing me, but I actually do have favorite office supplies. Let's do three favorite pets instead.

Jack: Can I answer dog for all three?

Me: I suppose, if you're breaking the rules.

Jack: Sort of my MO, but since I know you're such a stickler, I'll add cat and . . . turtle to the list. Why, what are yours?

After a slow blink, my eyes drifted to the cage in the corner of my bedroom. I could hear Oreo drinking from her water dispenser.

Me: I don't know. I've heard rabbits make great pets.

JACK

When I got to practice the following Tuesday, all I could think was thank God there was a professional here who knew what the hell he was doing.

Then I watched Brady Judd put his hands on his hips and say loudly and indignantly, "I can so do the floss." And he proceeded to enter a dance-off with four giggling little girls.

Sighing, I trudged across the field. At least I had a whistle this time.

One of the non-dancing children—Tori, the goalie—spotted me and ran over for a high five. She said "Hi, Coach Jack" in a way that had me smiling down at my shoes after she ran off.

Brady finally caught my approach. With the dance-off apparently over, he said, "Alright, ladies, form two lines at half field. I'll be right there."

The players scurried off, ponytails swishing.

"Hey, man." Brady held out a hand. "Nice to meet you."

I took in the very tall twentysomething man in front of me. His smile was affable, and he looked athletic, like he knew his way around a soccer field.

"You too," I replied, accepting his firm grip for a shake. "Thanks for helping me out." Then I broke one of my own rules with the locals and said, "You can drink free at Magnolia whenever you want."

He chuckled in response, or maybe he was always happy and amused. "I'll take you up on that."

"I'll pitch in," I offered, indicating the girls hopping around in the middle of the field. "Just tell me what to do."

For the next forty minutes, I mostly chased down balls while Brady instructed the girls through various drills. He maintained a good balance of silly and serious, which kept their attention and earned their undying devotion. At one point, Gia faked an injury so he'd have to carry her to the sideline. I'd caught her sneaky grin over his shoulder and stopped him from frantically calling an ambulance.

Callie and Michelle provided commentary and support from their seated positions. They'd pulled the same heart condition routine on Brady, and I felt less like an idiot for falling for it when he, too, told them to play at their own pace. The twins had abruptly taken a seat right there on the field.

The little practice crashers from last week, Jacob and Charlie, were back on the far side of the field, and I noticed them looking on with a fair amount of interest.

Brady and I stood on the sidelines while the girls scrimmaged to close out the practice.

Near the end, Jamie was guilty of a handball when she'd reacted reflexively to the ball coming straight at her face.

"Sorry! That was my fault. I'll do better next time!" she shouted to the rest of her team.

Jacob, who had drifted closer to watch, laughed and said, "Another excellent option for the title of your autobiography."

Jamie scowled in Jacob's direction while Charlie high-fived him.

"Let's go!" Rosie called impatiently and took the indirect kick. Play resumed, and the boys went back to their side of the field.

I leaned toward Brady and murmured, "Do we need to worry about that? Isn't it bullying or something?"

Eyes on the field, my co-coach shook his head. "Nah. Jacob has a crush on Jamie. That's why he's teasing her. Take it from me, torture generally means he doesn't have an outlet for the way he's feeling about her. Wait and see, he'll end up showing his hand." A thoughtful pause. "Or Jamie will sit on his back and rub his face in an anthill. We'll keep an eye on them, just in case. But I'm guessing it'll work out. Hopefully it won't take a decade."

Sounded like there was a story there, but it wasn't any of my business. Thankfully, parents started rolling up to the curb a moment later. Brady had the girls gather the cones and put the balls away before Rosie led another team huddle and Brookline U9 cheer.

"Our game is at ten on Saturday at Tanner Park. Be there fifteen minutes early," I reminded them before they could all disperse. "I'll have your jerseys with me."

Their squeals of excitement could probably be heard from space.

"You working tonight?" Brady asked after everyone had gone and we were walking toward the parking lot.

"Yeah, till closing."

"I'll come by for a drink," he said before slapping me on the back and hopping in a dark pickup truck.

"Uh, okay," I muttered belatedly as I watched Brady back out of the space.

Then I made my way to my own vehicle, wondering what had just happened. I mean, I knew I'd promised Brady free drinks at Magnolia. But I didn't realize he was going to take me up on it right away.

Was this how adults made friends? An extrovert just sort of elbowed their way into your life and didn't leave?

Apparently so because twenty minutes later, after I'd quickly changed for my shift, there sat Brady Judd at the polished bar top.

I rolled the sleeves of my white dress shirt up to my elbows before stepping behind the counter.

Brady was in the middle of laughing with Kayla about something, a glass of whipped pineapple gose already in his hand.

"There he is," Brady called jovially.

"Hey," I muttered, sort of awkwardly, but if Brady noticed, he didn't seem to mind.

Kayla wandered away to restock glasses, and I felt the need to wipe something down. It wasn't even five yet. The bar wouldn't be busy for another hour.

I wasn't sure how to do this. Small talk with strangers was like pulling teeth.

Luckily, Brady didn't need any icebreakers or conversation starters. He took another sip from his glass, then said casually, "I didn't know you and Bonnie were friends?"

"We're not," I said reflexively, the lie sticky on my tongue. So I amended, "Not . . . really."

Bonnie and I weren't friends, exactly. *Friendly*, maybe. But I had no other way to classify her. A woman I kept running into. A distraction. The first person I'd taken care of, maybe ever. Someone I liked teasing. Abruptly, my thoughts turned to Jacob, the eight-year-old smart-ass giving Jamie Santiago a hard time because he had a stupid crush. Then I remembered I was a fucking adult, and what was going on with Bonnie was not the same.

Yes, I was attracted to her. She was beautiful and smart and funny. But she was also kind and sincere, real in a way I couldn't explain. Anyone would think so. It didn't mean anything.

Brady's friendly, open expression didn't change at my weird hesitation. He didn't call me a liar or give me a disbelieving eyebrow raise. "So how'd she get involved with the team?"

"The girls dragged her into it. She was leaving school during the last practice, and she could tell I had no idea what I was doing. She mentioned you and offered to talk to you about the team. I'm pretty sure she felt sorry for me." I chuckled, finally giving in to the urge to grab a rag from beneath the counter.

That was all true. But it wasn't the whole story.

However, telling Brady about Bonnie's drunken night in my apartment felt like going a step too far. I had a feeling she didn't want anyone to know about that.

"Nah," he said with a shake of his head. "I doubt she took pity on you. That's not really Bonnie's style. I know how much she hates it when she thinks people feel sorry for her."

I thought about that, and another little piece of the Bonnie puzzle clicked firmly into place. She hated being an inconvenience, couldn't stand the idea that she'd been weak in front of me, and felt the need to earn people's forgiveness with baked goods.

I was suddenly glad Bonnie hadn't overheard Kayla admit that she and Sasha had overserved her at the bar because they'd felt bad about her divorce.

Bonnie was prideful. I bet she didn't accept help easily either. Knowing this gossipy small town, she probably hated all the worried stares and heartfelt hugs, the knowing looks, and the soft-spoken "So how are you *really* doing, honey?" comments.

"Bonnie just genuinely likes helping people," Brady added, drawing me out of my thoughts before I could rearrange any more puzzle pieces.

I believed that too.

But who helped her?

Briefly, I entertained the ridiculous thought that maybe I had a little.

She'd fallen asleep texting me the other night, after she'd admitted she had trouble sleeping sometimes.

I didn't know why I'd told her about that trick from Lia. It had been something warm and tender from my childhood. Lying on a twin-size bed while my grandmother had asked me my three favorite pizza toppings or video games or baseball players. Things that didn't hurt to think about for a boy with no mother or father. Who felt separate and disconnected from his peers.

Soft reminders and cloaked comfort.

Maybe I'd had the urge to help Bonnie, a person who could only accept that help in secret, in the middle of the night.

I also didn't know why I'd texted her a second time on Friday and again on Sunday. Instead of delving too deep into my motivations, it seemed safer to indulge the silliness and wait for answers to innocent questions like her three favorite types of candy (Reese's Eggs, Reese's Hearts, and Reese's Trees, like a complete lunatic) or her three favorite *Star Wars* movies (*The Empire Strikes Back, Return of the Jedi*, and *The Force Awakens*, all acceptable).

We'd continued playing our innocent little game. I'd asked about her favorites instead of why she covered her mouth when she laughed. Or why she'd been drinking alone the day her divorce was final. Anything that pointed to me being too aware or too curious about someone who was so far out of my league that she might as well have been actual royalty in our small town.

I didn't know what any of that meant.

But I knew I liked talking to her. She was funny when she wasn't so damn worried about saying the right thing.

I'd looked for Bonnie this afternoon during practice, wondered if she might stop by on her way out again, say hi to the kids. But I hadn't caught sight of her. Maybe I'd missed her, or maybe she hadn't left work until after practice wrapped up.

I wondered if she'd really come to the girls' game this weekend. Had that been one of those empty promises that adults made to kids sometimes? Ways to smooth over awkwardness or questions you didn't want to answer. I couldn't see Bonnie doing that, though. Something told me she lied only about herself and only to keep from hurting other people.

I didn't know what would happen the next time we saw one another. I wasn't sure what to expect after texting someone in the middle of the night. Falling asleep with them on the other end of the line.

Everything about us felt like a secret. And Brady had confirmed it earlier when he'd asked if she and I were friends. I'd kept the truth to myself, wrapped it up warm and safe, and tucked it away in my pocket. Something just for me.

Despite my initial awkwardness with Brady, things smoothed out over the next hour or so. Mostly because of him. He was just good with people, whether they were my employees he happened to know or a random stranger two seats down at the bar. He put people at ease, and that went for me, too.

I relaxed and we chatted in between customers, talked sports and Kirby Falls politics. He invited me to the business owners' association meeting tomorrow, assuring me the snacks would be excellent because he was making brownies. I'd laughed, not promising anything because I didn't really do small-town involvement.

"I don't know if you know this," he'd said, "but you're on their radar now, Coach. There will be no more hiding behind this here leafer bar."

Brady stayed for one more beer before he'd said he was meeting Mac for dinner down the street at Apollo's. He'd invited me to go if I could get away from the bar for a minute. Said Bonnie would be there too. He hadn't given me a sly look or paused to gauge my reaction to that bit of information, but maybe I'd been looking for it too hard—expecting him to assume something. Maybe to warn me off his future sister-in-law, with me being from the wrong side of the tracks.

Later that night, after I'd closed down the bar and locked up, I pulled my phone out of my pocket as I walked up the stairs to my apartment.

There was an email notification and one new text message.

I made myself read the email first. Like I was saving the text message, holding on to it, drawing it out. The last piece of candy from my Christmas stocking, wrapped in a bow, going soft and melty in my hand.

Then I sighed because Brady had been right. The email was from Eloise Carter, the current head of the Kirby Falls Business Owners' Association, with a reminder for tomorrow's meeting. I briefly entertained the idea of attending. I was supposed to have the night off, my first one in a while. And there would be brownies.

Standing on the top stair, I swallowed and then switched apps.

Clyde: Brady yapped about practice all through dinner. I'm guessing it went well with the girls today?

I checked the time. 12:43 a.m.

Me: Yeah. He was a big help, and the girls loved him.

She replied before I could unlock my front door.

Clyde: Good. I'm glad it worked out.

Smirking, I typed, *Should I say thank you again? What is the appropriate number of thank yous to fully express my gratitude?*

My smile widened when her response came through, fast and sharp like I knew it would.

Clyde: Well, if you were actually grateful, you'd follow up with a baked good.

Me: Oh yeah? Something like . . . blueberry muffins?

Clyde: No, that would be redundant. You can't gift back the same thing you were already gifted.

Laughing, I paused.

Me: Right. They would probably cancel each other out.

Clyde: Exactly. Then you'd have to start all over again.

I gave in and just lowered myself to the top step rather than take the time to get inside my apartment.

Me: What would you recommend?

Clyde: Well, my three favorite baked goods are Pop-Tarts, caramel cake, and pumpkin scones. Unfortunately, they all contain self-flagellation, and I know you're allergic.

I snorted. God, she was in a sassy mood.

Me: Oh, I'm sorry. Did you think I was aiming to thank YOU? No, these baked goods would be for Brady.

Her reply was a GIF of some celebrity giving the camera a glare and a slow blink.

I chuckled again.

Me: I feel like we need to address the Pop-Tart thing. Those are not baked goods.

Clyde: Um, I heat them in the toaster.

Clyde: Usually.

Clyde: Sometimes I just raw dog them and eat them right out of the package.

I laughed so hard that I nearly dropped my phone.

Clyde: I cannot believe I just said that.

Clyde: Please ignore me.

Clyde: Pretend I did not just use "raw dog" in polite conversation.

It took me a moment to compose myself.

Me: I'm sorry. I cannot. I screenshot it for posterity.

She replied with the same glaring GIF.

Clyde: Okay, what are your three favorite baked goods?

Her embarrassment and misery were palpable, even over text. She was typing fast over there to change the subject. And I'd let her. Mostly because I didn't want her to freak out and stop messaging me. I liked having her here, like this. Right at my fingertips. Even if I should be keeping my hands to myself.

With my grin far from fading, I responded, *Blueberry lemon scones, sour-dough bread . . .*

I let the answer hang there, knowing she'd fill the silence with her curiosity.

Clyde: And?

Me: And your blueberry muffins.

The Kirby Falls Business Association meeting was being held in the library's meeting room. It had a podium at the front and probably ten rows of chairs with a narrow central aisle.

I stood in the back near the refreshment table.

The library hadn't really been on my radar growing up, which was ironic considering how much I read now, as an adult. I didn't have fond, paperback-scented memories of story time or library programs. There hadn't been summer reading events to keep me busy in middle school. Instead, I'd found trouble more often than not.

I caught sight of several local business owners, sitting and chatting in their seats. Margaret Mahroney from the flower shop downtown. The lady who always wore a bright caftan and owned Paperback Writer, the bookstore and gift shop I frequented.

I spied the Clark bunch in the front row. Bonnie was sitting beside a woman who looked like an older version of herself. I knew her parents were involved in the day-to-day running of Grandpappy's and assumed the person next to her was her mother. Maggie Clark sat on the woman's other side. She was my sourdough supplier and we were well acquainted. Two empty seats remained at the end of their row, and I wondered briefly if they were for Brady Judd and his girlfriend.

I didn't have to wonder long because a moment later, Brady breezed through the door I was thinking about escaping through.

"Hey, Jack. You made it."

I thought he was going in for a handshake, but instead, he thrust a large Tupperware container into my hands.

He grinned. "Take a few before the vultures descend. They're delicious."

MacKenzie Clark gave me a brief smile over Brady's shoulder before saying, "Bring me one of those. I'm going to sit down." Then Brady jumped like he'd been pinched on the backside.

If he minded, he didn't show it. Instead, his ultrabright smile widened. "Yes, ma'am."

"You want to sit with us?" Brady asked me as he popped the top off the storage container. "I can grab a chair from the back."

"No, that's alright," I replied, accepting the swirled brownie he passed me in a napkin. "I might have to take off early."

"I hear you. These things can get boring."

Just then, a throat cleared from behind him.

We turned to see Eloise Carter dressed in one of her uptight skirt suits, holding a file folder, likely containing the contents of tonight's agenda.

Unbothered, Brady greeted the elderly woman like he hadn't just been saying how terrible her meetings were. "Well, hello there, Ms. Carter. Would you like a brownie? I made them myself."

She sniffed. "No, thank you. I have a boring meeting to get started."

Eloise clipped away on her heels.

Brady and I shared a look.

"Smooth," I offered.

Brady chuckled. "Ah, well. She's never liked me. I kicked a soccer ball into her award-winning roses when I was ten. She's been holding it against me ever since."

"That feels on brand."

"Well, I'd better get up there." His hands were full of brownies wrapped in napkins. "See you, Jack."

Eloise Carter was just tapping the microphone on the podium when Brady slid into his seat. I watched him pass out his baked goods, noting that Bonnie shook her head, declining the offer before facing forward.

I guess if it wasn't a Pop-Tart, she didn't want it.

The meeting passed slowly. It was basically a rundown of sponsorship, fundraising, and volunteer opportunities for the fourth quarter. The Orchard Festival was over, but there would be plenty of events for local business owners to participate in between now and the first of the year, the Holiday Jamboree encompassing a lot of that.

"And next month," Eloise said succinctly, "we have trick-or-treating on Main Street. Candy donations are needed."

The woman made sudden, meaningful eye contact with me in the back of the room. If she thought her steely glare was going to faze me, she was mistaken.

I ignored her. I was still in the middle of the last thing she'd strong-armed me into.

Luckily, Bonnie piped up from the front row. "I can do that. I'll make sure to get options for kids with dietary restrictions."

"Thank you, Bonnie," Eloise said, her tone superior.

I nearly rolled my eyes. Here Bonnie was, not even a business owner, getting guilted into participating. She just couldn't say no. The people-pleasing gene was too strong in her.

The meeting wrapped up shortly thereafter. Neighbors stood and mingled.

A small crowd flocked to the Clarks in the first row, Bonnie surrounded by her adoring fans. I didn't see any khaki-wearing principals, so at least there was that.

I loitered, unsure why I had the urge to stay. There was a moment when I considered going to say hi to Bonnie. You know, in person instead of texting her like a coward. But it was pretty crowded at the front of the meeting space. Plus, I had no idea what I'd even say. *How are you? Are you sleeping okay? Want to text later and learn more about each other in bite-sized increments?*

Or, *Hey, you probably know more about me than anyone on the planet, and how pathetic is that?*

A rush of people made for the refreshments, and I sidestepped them, not wanting to lose a limb.

I was ready to turn and walk out the door, but then Sheila Jessup—another local busybody and gossipmonger—shifted, revealing Bonnie. And the look on her face had me pausing. I straightened, scrutinizing.

Maybe I was imagining it, but something about Bonnie's body language was like a flower wilting, closing in on itself.

Before I'd given myself permission, I was making my way across the room, mumbling excuse mes and avoiding curious gazes. I kept my attention on Bonnie. I could see the discomfort on her face morphing slowly but surely to panic. It was like watching a trauma response in real time.

Someone stepped on my boot, and I ignored it, looking for Judd or Mac or someone. Why was no one stepping in to help Bonnie?

As I drew closer, I heard snippets of conversation from Sheila. "Well, we've been awfully concerned. We hoped you and Danny could work things out."

Another older woman I didn't recognize offered her two cents regarding Bonnie's marriage, but I'd heard enough.

"Hey, Bonnie," I interrupted from several feet away.

Her attention snapped to me, eyes wide and stricken.

The nosy women in the semicircle around Bonnie turned toward me, but I didn't pay them any mind.

I kept my gaze on her. "Can you help me with that thing we talked about the other day?"

The startled expression she wore abruptly shifted as she processed my words. "Oh, right. Of course. That thing."

Then I held out my hand and she clutched it like a lifeline. I threaded our fingers together and pulled her toward me, moving us in the direction of the exit as one.

When we reached the double doors leading to the dim interior of the library, I slowed and asked quietly, "What do you need?"

Her breaths were coming fast, and I could see the urgency behind her eyes. "Air," she begged.

In my reckless adolescence, I'd been impulsive, rarely questioning myself or the decisions I made. Now, as an adult and business owner, I was more circumspect and responsible.

But in that moment, with Bonnie's hand squeezing the life out of mine and her request still ringing in my ears, shaky and unsteady, I didn't need to think twice. All I wanted to give her was what she needed.

So I led her to the parking lot, slid her arms into my leather jacket, and zipped it all the way up. Then I popped my helmet on her head and opened the visor.

"Your helmet," she protested, voice muffled.

I shook my head. "I'll be fine. We won't go far.

"Put your feet here or here." I indicated where she should position herself and helped her climb on behind me.

She sat stiffly, trying to keep distance between us.

"You'll need to hold on," I called over my shoulder.

Slowly, carefully, her hands settled lightly on my sides before sliding around my waist, her arms hugging me from behind. It took a moment, but I felt a deep exhale leave her as all her tense muscles finally relaxed against me.

I released a breath I didn't realize I'd been holding, refusing to let myself think about how good she felt behind me.

With a gentle pat to the backs of her hands, I let her know we were ready.

Then we were off, the autumn air cold and welcome against my cheeks.

I was careful, driving slower than I would on my own. It was dark, and while I doubted I would get pulled over, I'd take the ticket for driving without a helmet. She needed it more than I did.

And I couldn't stand another minute in that room with Bonnie slowly unraveling.

If she needed air, I'd give her wings.

Bonnie's warm body pressed snuggly to mine. Tense thighs bracketing my own. Her fluttering heartbeat, a hummingbird's wing against my back.

"You okay?" I called over the rush of air as I turned on to the highway.

Her answering squeeze to my midsection had me nudging the throttle.

The overlook wasn't far, but there wasn't much to see in the dark. Thankfully, that meant there wouldn't be any tourists around.

I parked the bike near the grassy rest area where picnic tables were scattered along the edge of the overlook platform.

I felt Bonnie shift to stand and lent a hand to keep her steady as she climbed off the bike. Then I joined her.

She tugged at the helmet. I detached the chin strap and helped wiggle it the rest of the way off before placing it on the bike.

Her expression was a little wild. Bright and alert, she gazed at me in amazement. She wasn't panic-stricken anymore, so that was something.

"That was . . ." she breathed, voice thin. "I can't believe . . ." And then, as if noticing the thin long-sleeved shirt I wore, her eyes widened in alarm. "Your jacket. You're probably freezing. Here—"

Bonnie worked to bring the zipper down in order to presumably return my coat.

But I stepped forward and stilled her hand. "It's okay. Leave it on. It'll keep you warm. I'm fine." She made to protest, the selfless martyr reporting for duty, but I ignored her. "Let's go sit down."

After a moment, she followed me to a picnic table nearby.

I sat on the tabletop, my knees bent, boots resting on the bench seat as I faced the mountain view. Currently, it was just layers of indigo and midnight blue going dark and fuzzy in the distance beneath a sea of stars.

Bonnie settled beside me, bringing with her the sweet scent of honeysuckle. She was close enough that she was probably determined to warm me with her body heat if I was going to force her to keep the jacket.

I fought a grin as I stared out over the horizon.

The inclination fled as soon as she said, "Thank you. For that back there. Saving me."

I couldn't pinpoint why her gratitude irked me so much. But just like with the muffins and the drunken night at Magnolia, I found myself shrugging off her politeness and manners. I didn't want to be one more person on Bonnie's grand tour of appreciation.

Maybe I wanted an explanation instead.

"What happened?" I asked, but I made sure my voice was measured and even, hiding the irrational irritation simmering behind my sternum.

She was quiet long enough that I looked over at her. Bonnie was staring down at her hands, fiddling with her thumbnail.

"You don't have to do that shit with me," I said. "I'm not judging you or whatever it is that you're worried about. I'm the town fuckup, remember? Juvenile delinquent, troublemaker, hellion, all-around asshole."

She finally met my gaze. "Don't say that."

I gave her a sad smile. "The truth has never bothered me, Clyde."

After a moment, she confessed, the words rushing out like they were racing through a yellow light. "I get anxiety attacks sometimes. A couple of panic attacks. Everything just builds up and then . . ."

"What does it feel like?"

Bonnie stared at me, considering. "My thoughts start coming fast. All the what-ifs stack higher and higher until I feel like they might collapse on top of me. My brain speeds up, everything rapid-fire. Then my body joins in. My breathing goes too fast, and my heart rate skyrockets. And for whatever reason, my nose starts to tingle, like it's falling asleep or going numb. Then I start to cry until I can't catch my breath. Feels like something heavy is sitting on my chest while my heart pounds against it, trying to battle its way out. You caught me before the tears but after the nose tingles."

"I'm sorry I didn't step in sooner."

"Don't be," she said stiffly. "It's not your job to look after me."

Rationally, I knew that. But I still didn't like the way it sounded.

Bonnie and I were . . . I didn't know what we were.

But I knew I liked her, and I hated that she felt like looking after her would be a hassle. Hearing her talk about her struggles with anxiety gave me a new piece of the Bonnie puzzle. I could imagine how much she'd hate being out of control, having her own body fight against her.

"How did you know?" she asked quietly, interrupting the way I was taking this new piece and turning it round and round, trying to fit it into place. "I'd thought I was hiding it well from everyone."

"Not from me," I said before I could think better of it. So I quickly added, "Plus, I don't think Sheila Jessup or Vera Sterling would notice anything that didn't directly impact them. The busybodies."

Bonnie smiled.

"Is it always about your divorce? The anxiety?"

She sighed, the smile slipping away by degrees, and I hated myself for asking. "Yeah. Well, I've probably had anxiety my whole life. But the attacks didn't start until this year . . . and all the stuff with Danny."

Danny Jensen. The ex. The man she still loved and would take back if he asked her to.

It wasn't my business. Marriages were personal. But I couldn't help hating the guy who'd made Bonnie doubt herself so much. Who didn't even have to be in the same room to hurt her.

Love made people vulnerable, and here was the proof, sitting next to me, wearing my jacket, her hands still trembling.

"Why didn't your family notice or swoop in to get you away from those gossips tonight?" I wondered.

"I never let them see me that way. Mac is the only one who might have noticed, but she and Brady had already taken off. And my mom and aunt, well, I'm sure they didn't realize. They're not bad people," she rushed to assure me.

"I know." I bumped her shoulder with mine. "I didn't mean it that way."

"It's just easier if they think everything is fine."

My gaze lingered on the side of her face, and I could see from her expression that she really believed that. Like she might be too much trouble for the people who loved her most.

"You should let them know you, Clyde. They might surprise you."

But she was already shaking her head. "I already feel like I'm walking around with a neon sign over my head that says damaged goods. It would make things worse if they knew I was seeing a therapist. They would treat me even more carefully. And I couldn't take that. You are the only person —" She cut herself off abruptly.

"I'm the only person what?" I asked, suddenly desperate to know.

She sighed, but admitted, "You're not nice."

Oh. Well, maybe I *didn't* want to know.

Then she turned to look at me, expression serious. "You're not nice, but you're *good*."

A bitter laugh escaped me. "There's a difference?"

"Stop it," she said, placing a staying hand on my tense forearm. "Yes, there's a difference. You took care of me when I was drunk. You never bring it up or hold it over me. You snapped at me about the muffins and gave me shit at the sheriff's office."

I rubbed an uncomfortable hand along my scruffy jaw, feeling my cheeks heat. "I'm not sure that screams good."

"It does because it was what I needed. You kept me company when I couldn't sleep. You are the only person in this town who doesn't treat me like I'm . . . fucking broken."

I watched her, suddenly afraid I'd say the wrong thing. And then I'd no longer be the one she looked for in a crowd, the person whose hand she'd accept without question. I wanted her to keep looking at me like that, soft and fierce at the same time. Like I was the glue holding all her pieces together.

So I tucked away what I really wanted to say. That she was so much stronger than she realized. And that she was better off without that piece-of-shit ball and chain dragging her down.

Or something altogether more dangerous, that she was the only one who bothered to see that goodness in me. And it might only be for her.

Instead, I gave her the response she needed, not the one I wanted. "Was that the first time you said the f-word out loud?" I teased.

She laughed, her hand coming up immediately to cover her mouth.

"Just curious because you kind of stumbled over it," I added as she whacked me on the stomach with the back of her hand.

I kept her from pulling away, threading our fingers together again. Standing, I tugged her down off the picnic table.

"Shut up," she said, but she was still laughing.

"That's okay. We can practice. You can tell me to shut the fuck up or fuck off."

We were facing each other, separated by hardly any space at all. Her hand was clutched in mine, but I felt like she was the one holding me.

"I don't want you to fuck off," she whispered, smiling and taking a half step closer until her shoes grazed mine.

I found myself leaning in, knowing it was one more bad decision on a mile-long list of ones I'd already made.

Bonnie met me halfway as I slipped my hands around her waist and drew her close enough that I could count every single one of her dark eyelashes.

"Yeah, I don't want to fuck off either," I confessed roughly.

Before she could even push up onto her toes, I leaned down and brushed her lips with mine. Just a brief touch. A question awaiting an answer. I didn't want to rush her or misread any signals. I knew she was hurting and maybe not ready for more than a motorcycle ride and a half-assed rescue.

But as I hovered there beneath an ocean of stars, waiting and hoping as my nose grazed the length of hers, I felt a warm hand slide into the hair at my nape.

Then Bonnie tugged me back down and slotted her lips against mine.

BONNIE

I could feel my heart beating, wild and untamed, inside my chest. But for the first time in a long time, it was in giddy anticipation rather than panic or dread.

My fingers wound through soft strands of dark, windblown hair, and I parted my mouth in welcome.

Jack Ellis was only the second person I'd ever kissed, but when our lips touched, I wasn't thinking about that or Danny or how I'd never planned on having another first kiss again.

There was only Jack. The warmth of his body in the cool autumn night. The smell of leather and leaves and something dark and tempting. How his hands had snaked beneath the jacket I wore and brought me flush against him.

For once, I wasn't thinking, only feeling.

The scruff on his jaw was delicious torture. I brought one hand around to cup his rough cheek, reveling in the feel of him beneath my touch. Then I tilted my head to deepen the kiss, giving a small bite to Jack's lower lip.

His hands slipped beneath his jacket that I still wore, fisting in the back of my shirt, and his own tongue met mine in answer.

Jack was patient. He let me lead, encouraged me to explore. I had a motor-cycle-riding bad boy in the palm of my hand, and it made me feel power-ful. But more than that, I felt wanted.

Eventually, a warm touch made its way to my lower back, fingertips dancing across my skin, lighting me up. I arched reflexively, bringing my breasts into firmer contact with Jack's chest. I felt his low groan vibrate everywhere we touched. That, too, made some prideful part of me sit up and preen.

Thoughts did their best to intrude, ready and waiting on the sidelines. I could feel them pressing close, ready to shame me or remind me I'd made vows to someone else. The desperate snarl of *what if* and *maybe* held behind fragile glass.

Then one of Jack's hands dipped low, and those thoughts drifted away like dandelion seeds on the wind. That eager touch coasted toward my back-side, then abruptly retreated, as if it had suddenly remembered its manners.

I'd tried the whole polite thing with Jack, and it hadn't quite taken. I wasn't sorry for it now.

Without breaking our kiss, I released his jaw and reached around to urge that hand right back down to my ass. Jack allowed it, smoothing over the denim covering me before squeezing, drawing me further against him.

His erection—thick and hot—pressed into my belly, and that did some-thing to me, too. I felt a little wild and a lot pleased, knowing that Jack was hard for me, from a brief make-out session with a good girl under the stars.

Attraction was a funny thing. That I could want so many different parts of this man, and delight in discovering them all. The studious, sarcastic acad-emic in his little round glasses. The leather-wearing white knight who'd ridden to my rescue and given me exactly what I'd needed. The comforting presence in the middle of the night who might as well have been taking my wounded heart and tucking it in tight.

I was overwhelmed by the possibilities and eager for them at the same time. So much newness and desire was exhilarating. I wanted to feel his hand grip my thigh on the back of a motorcycle. I wanted to straddle him in his chair and make him forget all about whatever he'd been reading. I wanted to lie alone in my bed and listen to his deep voice grow rough on the other end of the line, telling me exactly what he'd like to do to me.

A fantasy come to life.

The one right here and now, leaning into my touch.

I traced Jack's jaw and smoothed my palm down the strong column of his throat. My fingers skated along the ridge of his collarbone over to the rounded tops of his firm shoulders. I realized I wanted to take the same path with my tongue. To touch and be touched. Slowly, deliberately, with an end goal in mind. One I could feel even now, building low in my belly.

The realization had me toning things down, gentling my kisses, steadying my shaky control. Jack matched my pace without complaint. His lips were featherlight against my chin, my eyelids, the corner of my mouth. His hands came back to rest on my waist before we pulled away to look at one another.

His satisfied smirk had me grinning, suddenly relieved he hadn't appeared alarmed or regretful.

Finally, he pressed one last kiss to my forehead and said, "I'll drive you back. Your family is probably worried about you."

I frowned. "Why?"

"You were dragged away in the middle of the night by a—what did you call me? Ah, yes. A long-haired pirate. Oh, and a lone wolf."

A memory of that night at Magnolia abruptly assaulted me. "Oh my God. I howled in the bar, didn't I?"

He nodded slowly, impressed. Then held up two fingers. "Twice."

I groaned, covering my eyes with my hands.

An amused chuckle met my ears. Then Jack's gentle touch peeled my fingers away. He was grinning. "It was cute," he insisted, linking our fingers together once more.

My embarrassment was overshadowed by the feel of my hand twined with his. The gesture was casual and innocent, but I felt anchored to Jack—connected to him in this moment. And that was something I desperately needed. He was so steady and sure, and when I was wrapped up in him, I felt like nothing could touch me, not even my own doubts and fears.

Jack helped me with the helmet, carefully clipping the chin strap in place. His gaze remained warm and affectionate, and that took the edge off of the rest of my awkwardness.

Then we both climbed on the motorcycle, and he drove me back to town.

There would be time to fret over everything that had happened tonight. Later.

It was impossible to lose myself to my worries when I was on the back of Jack's bike. The sound and the vibration of the engine. The way the wind tugged at my clothes and the ends of my hair. The feel of the man seated in front of me, how his body shifted and moved as we flew down the road. How warm and solid and competent he was.

Despite the cold, I loved the way riding made me feel—free and unrestrained. I'd always thought I'd be scared if I ever managed to make it onto a motorcycle. But I wasn't. Maybe that had something to do with the man sliding a reassuring hand along my calf at the first red light downtown.

I grinned inside the helmet and tried not to squeeze him too tight around the middle.

When he made it back to the library parking lot, my car was the only one there.

Jack didn't say anything as he helped me off the bike, and neither did I.

I fought my instinct to thank him. For the rescue in the library, or for the ride that cleared my head, or for the kiss that rocked my world. I was grateful for all of those moments, but I knew Jack well enough now to know I should keep my thanks to myself.

He watched me, helmet in hand, in that quiet, solemn way of his as I made my way to my car.

I pulled out first and tried not to look for his headlight in my rearview mirror.

When I got home, the house was quiet, as usual. But I could feel the smile I wore, the one I hadn't been able to wipe away since leaving the overlook.

I returned a few texts from my mother, who had been worried about me. Not because she'd seen me leave with Jack, but because she'd seen my car in the parking lot but hadn't been able to find me. I told her I was fine and apologized for scaring her.

As I washed my face and got ready for bed, I thought back through my conversation with Jack. No one had ever asked me what my anxiety felt like. Not even Mac, who'd seen me in the worst of it. My sister had been too shocked at the time, and maybe she'd been too scared to bring it up afterward. I wasn't exactly receptive or open to discussing my mental health or my divorce. Nothing real anyway. I kept my interactions with my family safe and easy.

Jack's words came back to me as I patted my face dry. *You should let them know you, Clyde. They might surprise you.*

It was something to think about. Yet, I'd been honest with Jack tonight, and he hadn't treated me like I was broken. He had another one of my secrets, I realized.

Danny had never taken my anxiety seriously. He used to tell me to just let things go, like it was simple enough to release them into the wind. I'd had trouble sleeping for years, even before the affair. Just too caught up in my own head to let my mind rest. Eventually, I'd learned to go and lie on the couch so my tossing and turning or the light from my phone wouldn't keep Danny up.

It was nice to have Jack listen to me tonight and not make assumptions or tell me how to fix myself.

Admittedly, I'd been worried about seeing him in person for the first time since we'd started up our late-night texting. I'd thought our next encounter might be stilted or awkward. I'd wondered if we'd talk about the things we now knew about each other. Or if he would pretend our messaging had never happened. Would those texts that brought me so much happiness and comfort lately be another secret between us, too?

Luckily, an almost–anxiety attack had taken the pressure off.

Part of me wanted to chastise myself, to wallow around in mortification knowing that Jack had seen me during such a weak moment. That I'd needed saving in the first place. But it hadn't changed the way he'd looked at me, hadn't scared him away yet.

When I slipped into bed in my coziest pajamas, I closed my eyes and remembered whispered words and starry skies; the breathless rush of wind; the blur of trees in a single headlight; a quietly murmured *What do you need?*; dark hair threaded through my fingers; soft lips against the corner of my mouth; and soulful eyes focused only on me.

I thought about my favorite parts of this night.

And I didn't stop at three.

Danny: Hey, I'm planning on going to see Mom tonight too. So I'll just pick you up.

I stared at the text and tried not to let my annoyance get the better of me.

I'd spoken with Eldridge—Danny's father—a few days ago and set up a time to come and visit Diane on Friday afternoon. I didn't realize I'd be sharing visitation with my ex.

Guilt followed swiftly on the heels of that thought. Diane only had so much time left. She should be spending as much of it as possible with her loved ones, Danny included. I was the interloper here.

Me: I'd prefer to drive myself.

Danny: It's no big deal. I'll see you at 4:30.

I sighed. He knew what time I liked to leave school. It would be tight getting home and changed before he picked me up, especially because it was the weekend and I was fully planning on stealing a rabbit again.

I'd just plan on leaving a few minutes early. I knew how impatient Danny could be, and I didn't want to put him in a bad mood before seeing his mother.

At 3:45, April texted to let me know Morris had left for the day. I gathered my things and hustled down the hallway with the pet carrier I'd bought. I was in and out and home by 4:06 p.m. with Oreo in tow.

She had a brand-new pen and bunny house in the primary bedroom. It seemed like a pretty good use of the space since I wasn't using it. Once she was settled with fresh food and water, I hurried to change clothes and grab the applesauce cake I'd made for Diane. It was her favorite, and Eldridge had mentioned she'd been reluctant to eat lately.

I managed to slip out the front door just as Danny was pulling into the driveway. The house was a mess, and I didn't want him in there, judging me and reminding me what a poor housekeeper I was.

The short car ride was fraught with awkwardness in between stretches of silence. How did you make small talk with someone you'd been married to for thirteen years?

My eyes caught on his hands gripping the steering wheel and the bare ring finger there. I made myself look out the window for the rest of the drive.

I was relieved when we arrived at the small brick ranch-style home that Danny had grown up in.

That relief was short-lived.

Eldridge took the cake from my hands and ushered me inside to the kitchen. It was dim and quiet, like the house was already in mourning.

Danny's parents were older than mine, in their late sixties. They'd started their family with two daughters and were almost forty by the time Danny came along.

It felt strange to be back. I'd attended so many holidays here and cooked countless dinners, been squeezed around an oval dining table with my extended family. But now I was caught somewhere between the past and the present, a stranger with a familiar face.

Eldridge didn't treat me like a stranger, though. He enveloped me in a huge hug. "Hey, Bonnie girl. We've missed you."

My eyes welled as I clutched the older man. He still smelled like Old Spice and JFG Coffee, a quiet, calm presence who'd always thought of me like a daughter.

"I've missed y'all too," I choked out.

I could hear Danny in the bedroom down the hall, speaking to his mother. There hadn't been any other cars in the driveway, so I knew Danny's sisters were giving us some space.

Eldridge pulled away with a sad smile. "I'm sorry, Bonnie. I don't know what's gotten into Danny." I knew he wanted to say more on the subject, but I shook my head a little, and he nodded. "I just appreciate you coming to see Diane before—well, I appreciate you coming."

"Of course," I replied, squeezing his hands in mine. The urge to apologize was right there on the tip of my tongue, to say I was sorry for staying away. But I knew that was a lie. I'd needed time and distance. While I hated what the Jensens were going through now, I knew my role in their lives had changed. Some things just couldn't stay the same.

I made my way to the bedroom, swallowing hard when I caught sight of Diane sitting up in bed. It was a shock to the system. It had been a few months since I'd seen Danny's mother, but in that time she'd clearly lost weight. The lines on her face were more pronounced, and she looked tired and worn down.

"There she is," Diane said, grinning at me. "Danny, give us some time to visit."

"Yes, ma'am," Danny murmured before rounding the bed.

As Danny moved by me toward the door, he suddenly leaned down and pressed a kiss to my temple. I stiffened in response, but didn't want to cause a scene in front of his mother. She was still smiling at me, blue eyes warm in a weathered face. Then she patted the spot next to her on the bed.

I shook off my unease and sat down near Diane's legs, facing her.

She clutched my hand in both of hers. "It is so good to see you, honey."

"You too," I managed.

Diane and I chatted for the next half an hour. It had always been easy between us, and apparently, that hadn't changed even though I wasn't her daughter-in-law anymore.

She didn't bring up Danny or anything related to the divorce. She talked about the two nurses who checked on her in the mornings and evenings and helped manage her pain. She told me about Danny's sisters and their families, updating me on their lives.

About twenty minutes into my visit, Eldridge came in with three plates of applesauce cake for us. Diane made a fuss over it and even managed to eat half of the giant slice her husband had cut for her.

They'd been married a long time, and while neither were particularly demonstrative in their affection, they'd always been steady. I could see their love clearly right now. In the way Eldridge looked quietly relieved while watching her eat. With each bite she managed, some of the tension loosened in his shoulders. That might not have been a flashy sort of love, but it was the kind that endured. Caring for someone when they needed it, in sickness and in health.

It was hard to take, all this feigned normalcy. I wanted to cry. I wanted to wrap my arms around Diane's thin shoulders and tell her I was so damn sorry. That none of this was fair.

Instead, I made sure my eyes stayed dry and my tone upbeat. I stayed until Diane's lids started to droop and her evening nurse arrived. I kissed her cheek and told her I loved her, promising to visit again soon.

Then Danny and I got out of the way and back in the car.

He made a few attempts at conversation, but I was too worn out by my own emotions to manage his. My heart hurt for Diane and the rest of the Jensens. Seeing her so weak had hit me hard. There was a difference between knowing someone was dying and then facing it head-on. I wanted to be out of this car and alone.

I thought I might have mumbled "Thanks for the ride," but truthfully, I couldn't remember. I got out of the car as soon as it pulled to a stop, eager for escape and solitude.

But Danny parked the car and turned it off, following me up the driveway to the front door.

"Thank you for coming tonight," he said, footsteps hurrying to catch up. "It meant a lot."

How many times had I heard his boots outside on this very pathway? It was a slap in the face to hear them now.

I stopped my frantic retreat and closed my eyes briefly before turning to face him. His mother was dying. I shouldn't be so selfish and callous. "Of course. It was no trouble. I hate that this is happening to her—to all of you."

Danny nodded, looking down at his shoes.

I reached for the door, hoping that was the end of it. I needed to get away. I couldn't do this with him. Not right now, when my grief was so fresh, my emotions out of control and vibrating beneath my skin.

"So, how have you been?" he said quickly.

And when I turned back to face him, he was closer, at the bottom of the narrow porch stairs.

I didn't get a chance to answer or sigh or scream or any of the other things I wanted to do because Danny placed a hand on the railing and said, "Because you look good, Bon. Have you lost weight? That stubborn ten pounds you were always trying to get rid of?"

Then he smiled, blue eyes crinkling at the corners.

And something in me cracked wide open.

"What?" I demanded, tone hard and incredulous.

I'd ignored the liberties he'd taken tonight. The kiss in front of his mother. The hand on my lower back, ushering me to and from the car. How he'd tried to take my hand on the drive home. But I couldn't just sit back and take it anymore. I couldn't keep the peace and my mouth shut at the same time. Danny was taking advantage of the situation, weaponizing my grief and his, too.

I could only do this if there were boundaries in place. Everything felt too tenuous, a delicate balance that kept me functioning as one half of a former whole.

He straightened, perhaps sensing imminent danger. "I just wanted to talk. Is that so bad?"

"What do you want me to say, Danny?"

Exasperated, he threw up his hands. "I don't know. Tell me about your day or your students. Whatever you want."

I stared at the man I thought I'd spend my life with, suddenly realizing how starved for attention I was by the end. A year ago—hell, six months ago—I would have done almost anything to have Danny show any sort of interest in my life. I would have lapped up any little crumb of affection. Taken what I could get and been grateful for it. Seen it as some sort of sign that things were turning around.

But now? Now, I was only angry.

"You don't get to ask about my day or my job," I gritted out bitterly. "That's something reserved for boring married couples. Isn't that right?"

"You don't have to get so—"

"You want to know how I am?" I interrupted and dropped down a step to glare at him face-to-face. "If I'm happy or some bullshit like that? Which is it? You hope I'm doing fine without you, or so broken I can hardly function? You want to hear that I can't use fabric softener anymore because I remember how it smelled on your skin? Or how I found one of your shirts misplaced with my things and slept in it for a week? Or how I'm living out of the guest room now because I can't bring myself to sleep in our bed? Is that what you want to hear?"

His mouth opened and closed, suddenly unsure in the face of such brutal, devastating honesty.

I'd never spoken to him this way. Our fights had always been mild, passive-aggressive spats that cleared themselves up after a few hours or days of silent treatment. Even when Danny had confessed his infidelity, we hadn't had a knockdown, drag-out fight. I'd mostly been too sad.

But that wasn't to say we didn't know how to hurt one another. You couldn't spend so much of your life with someone without knowing the sensitive spots, the places that bruise the easiest. After some conversations with my therapist, I could see now that Danny had withheld affection—something that had always been important to me.

In the months we'd been apart, I'd foolishly hoped for a moment like this. One where he cared enough to ask after me, to maybe miss me a little. But now that it was here, I saw it for what it was—manipulation. And for the first time since we'd separated, I didn't think I wanted my husband back.

Maybe I wasn't happy . . . yet. But I hadn't been happy before either. My fingertips had forgotten the feel of his skin long before he'd put his on someone else.

Plus, I'd been lonely and depressed. Too focused on keeping the peace when I should have been demanding more for myself. More love, more time, more attention. And a husband who was faithful.

The realization knocked the wind out of my sails. My shoulders curved inward as grief struck me anew.

Finally, I said, "Leave me alone, Danny. I came with you tonight because your mother is one of the best people I've ever known. Not because I want to be friends with you and hang out in the driveway and chat. You wanted this. Now let me move on."

Danny swallowed hard and held his hands up in surrender. Hands that would always be a little grease-stained from his work. Hands that had held me and loved me. And then lost me, too.

My ex-husband retreated. After a few steps backward, he cast one last pained look in my direction and then climbed into his car and left.

I stumbled into the house as tears forced themselves down my cheeks. Collapsing on my bed, I grieved the unfairness of life, the family I'd lost. And then I mourned the end of my marriage, the way I should have months ago.

JACK

"Okay, girls," Brady said to the intent little faces staring back at him. "Just play your game. Keep your shape out there and remember to make smart passes. Use the whole field and give each other room to move. I know it's tempting to race down every ball, but trust your teammates. They'll have your back."

The girls nodded.

It was a bright Saturday morning, the last weekend in September, and the Brookline U9 girls' team was up against the Vultures from Lake Archer. Jamie and Gia had already been complaining about their opponents, saying they cheated and liked to play rough, always swooping in and scoring in the final few minutes, so there wouldn't be a chance for a comeback.

Brady had been good at changing the direction of the conversation, painting a positive spin on teamwork, and settling the girls before their first game.

"Hands in," I said.

Nine little hands stacked on top of mine, and I resisted the urge to smile at their determined expressions combined with glittery hairspray and French braids. Jamie had been right. The Magnolia Bar logo made for a nice jersey. The kids looked ready to go.

After our cheer, I consulted my clipboard and the starting lineup Brady and I had worked on. Gia lingered in front of me, the pale blue bow on the back of her head taking up a lot of real estate.

"I just want to say," she informed me, "that the man-bun was clearly the right call."

"Yes!" came a chorus of tiny squeals.

"It looks great, Coach Jack." Jamie gave me a thumbs-up.

I fidgeted, pushing my glasses up my nose, uncomfortable with the attention.

Brady's eyes scanned my hair and the strands that had been gathered into a short bun just above my nape. "Man, I'm jealous. My hair grows out all flat. I could never pull that off."

I rolled my eyes and focused on calling out the lineup. When the seven starters had taken the field, I glanced over to the sideline where the parents and spectators were gathered.

My little practice crashers, Jacob and Charlie, were sitting beneath one of the trees lining the sidewalk. They seemed to be watching covertly, and I wondered at that.

Then, my eyes caught on Bonnie. She was dragging a cooler behind her and following her sister, who had two camp chairs slung over her shoulder.

Bonnie wore jeans and a light blue shirt that made it clear which team she supported.

Her gaze met mine, and her mouth dropped open a moment before she smiled widely.

That reaction—so honest and forthright—knocked me off-balance and kicked my heart into gear. She was so sweet, so earnest, and distractingly beautiful in the early-morning light.

I lifted my hand off my clipboard and gave her a small wave. About that time, Mac stopped to set up her chairs, but Bonnie didn't seem to notice. She kept right on staring at me and stumbled into her sister.

I looked down at my clipboard, fighting a smile, thinking all those ridiculous man-bun instructional videos on YouTube might not have been a waste of time after all.

Maybe I wanted her to think about me. Maybe I'd been hoping she'd show up for the game this morning. I liked that she'd kept her word to the girls. Something that could have easily been written off as casual, an agreement made in the moment and then quickly forgotten. But of course, she was here. Bonnie didn't fall flat on her promises. She wouldn't leave anyone hanging. That just wasn't her.

I was glad she was here because I'd wanted to see her, too. I'd thought about that kiss more than a few times in the last three days. The way she'd felt hugging me tight on the back of my bike. All her softness and sweetness and the way she'd trusted me with her secrets. But I knew I needed to be careful.

Bonnie was just coming off a messy divorce, one she hadn't wanted. It made sense that her feelings would be all over the place and still tied up with her ex. She was vulnerable and probably not ready for . . . anything involving me. Not that I really knew what that might be.

I didn't really date. I wasn't sure what I could offer someone like her, beyond a roll in the hay.

A quick rebound.

But something about the thought of that had me gripping the pen in my hand a little too tightly. And when I told myself to stop being an idiot, I looked up to see the game had started.

I made myself focus, forced my attention on what was happening on the field. Not the blond sitting opposite, cheering her heart out for my team.

Brady shouted encouragement and direction. The girls responded, playing well together. But Gia hadn't been exaggerating; the Vultures played to win. Two girls with black jerseys received warnings for slide tackling, a move that wasn't allowed at this age.

Partway through the first twenty-five-minute half, a girl from the opposing team viciously elbowed Jamie out of the way well before the ball got within striking distance. Jamie went flying, her small body barrel-rolling on the grass.

Brady and I both stepped onto the field as the whistle blew, stopping play for the foul.

But Jamie gamely hopped to her feet, and I breathed a sigh of relief. "I'm okay," she told Raeanne, who'd hurried over to check on her. She winced but gave Brady and me a thumbs-up.

Shouts came from the opposite sideline. Angry little-boy squawks of protest. "That should have been a red card!" Jacob shouted from behind the line of parents in their chairs. "Get in the game, ref!"

Brady whacked me on the shoulder, drawing my attention. "See. Told you." He jerked his chin in the direction of the kid who was losing his mind over Jamie getting steamrolled.

I shook my head, then said, "What's a red card?"

My co-coach gave me a disgusted look. "Go home and watch an MLS game. Or at least Ted Lasso. Educate yourself, Coach. Come on."

Play continued until the whistle blew for halftime. Then Brady talked to the girls while they drank water in a circle around him.

A few minutes into the second half, a girl ran onto the field from out of nowhere. She had wild brown hair and just started chasing the ball down.

"Who is that?" I said, mildly alarmed.

"I don't know," Brady replied.

Raeanne was telling the kid to leave, and the high schooler officiating the game apparently didn't get paid enough to care that we had a feral child on the field.

"That's Addie," Gia said from my elbow. "I guess she got back from vacation."

The name rang a bell. There'd been one kid who hadn't shown up to practice yet. I was pretty sure she was on my roster.

"You can't just run on the field," Callie said from her place on the ground next to her twin, when the girl—Addie—finally made it over to us.

"How did you even get a jersey?" I wondered aloud. I'd just handed them out this morning.

She stood before us unapologetically. "I grabbed it out of your bag. When can I play?"

Brady and I shared a look before he crouched down to chat with the pint-sized thief.

We eventually got Addie subbed in. She was pretty good once she had a position and knew which way the offense was moving. But it didn't make a difference in the final score. True to the girls' warning, the Vultures scored in the last two minutes of play. They beat us 3–2.

While the girls dragged their feet over to the sideline, their disappointment was short-lived. Brady went around the circle of tired bodies and found a compliment for each one of them. And then Bonnie showed up with her cooler, and no one on the Brookline team seemed to remember that they'd lost this morning.

Bonnie passed out orange slices and packs of Goldfish crackers along with a Gatorade for each kid. She took the time to chat with her students and their parents. She checked in on Jamie to make sure she was really okay after that hit. And I overheard Bonnie telling Tori how brave she was to play in goal. The shy girl preened under her teacher's praise.

Eventually, Bonnie made her way to me as the kids surrounded Brady and Mac, giving helpful play-by-plays and asking if they were married.

"Tough loss, Coach," Bonnie said around a small smile.

"This may come as a surprise, but I'm not actually very competitive. I'm just hoping to survive the season."

Bonnie laughed, and like clockwork, her hand came up to cover her mouth.

I wanted to tug her fingers away and lace her hand with mine. Press a kiss to those smiling lips.

"Thanks for coming," I said instead. "You didn't need to buy snacks for the whole team."

Her brown eyes drifted over to the girls, smiling softly. "I know. I wanted to do something special for their first game."

I wondered how many times Bonnie had gone out of her way to make someone else feel special. Was there someone who did that for her? Or did everyone in Bonnie's life take her for granted the way her husband had?

Silence settled between us, and I thought about asking her what she was doing tomorrow. If she wanted to take a drive with me. I knew the weather was supposed to be nice, and the thought of her on the back of my bike with her arms wrapped around me was a welcome one. I wouldn't mention the fact that I'd picked up another helmet for her.

But then I started second-guessing myself, wondering where I thought this thing with Bonnie was even going. *Rebound* whispered in my mind again, and I nearly flinched. I thought about that khaki-clad principal who'd stared at her longingly and would probably be a much better match. I wondered what I could possibly have to offer that might be good enough for someone like her.

"Well, I'm going to pack up and head home," Bonnie eventually said. I'd been too busy wrestling with my own cowardice to keep up with the conversation.

We shared a long look, and I knew she was giving me a chance, a moment to step up and say something—do something. Ask her out or whatever people did with women they couldn't stop thinking about. Women they'd recently kissed.

But I allowed time to stretch, unfurl itself and pull taut.

I cleared my throat. "Thanks again for coming."

The moment snapped like a rubber band.

Bonnie nodded to herself, giving a resigned little smile that said, *Well, at least you tried.*

And I almost reached out and grabbed her hand.

But instead, she tucked a strand of blond hair behind her ear and walked away.

Gritting my teeth, I watched until the team bounded up, surrounding me in a halo of light blue and friendship bracelets, asking for high fives before they left. Several of the girls' moms came up and introduced themselves.

I tried to casually peek around the women to see if I could find Bonnie. Maybe I could stop her, tell her I'd text her later. Or maybe—

Gia's mom boldly reached out and squeezed my bicep, drawing my attention to whatever she was saying. When I looked over her shoulder again, I found Bonnie at the edge of the sidewalk watching. When our eyes caught, she quickly looked away and hurried to the parking lot.

I sighed, leaning away from the woman's touch. I managed polite conversation with the rest of the parents, and I avoided flirty smiles and uninvited touches, hating that Bonnie had seen that.

And hating that I hadn't been brave enough to ask for what I really wanted.

The bar was busy that night, and I was on the schedule to close. The kitchen had already run out of buffalo chicken flatbread, so I knew it was going to be a rough one.

Around ten thirty, I was changing the keg for the raspberry chamomile hard seltzer when Kayla came up and asked me if I'd take the customer at the end of the bar.

"Does he need to go?" I asked, washing my hands behind the counter.

It wasn't unheard of for some of my female bartenders to ask for a hand. Sometimes men got too friendly or couldn't take a hint. But Kayla usually wasn't shy about telling someone to back off.

"No," she replied, jaw set. "I just don't want to serve him."

I followed her glare to a man at the end of the bar who looked vaguely familiar, like he'd been in a time or two, but I couldn't place him. He looked like he was in his mid-thirties. Thin mustache, receding hairline, bland expression. The pale blue button-up was baggy on his slim frame, but the blond he was chatting up didn't seem to mind.

"I got it," I told Kayla and then made my way down the length of the bar.

I didn't notice anything weird when I took their order. Then we got another rush of tourists, and I put the man and his date out of my mind, checking in occasionally to grab refills. At some point, the chair beside him emptied before the guy moved down to set his sights on a different blond.

After we announced last call, I started closing out tabs and running receipts for the stragglers to sign.

The name on the last card had me staring down at the blue plastic in my hand.

Daniel Jensen.

My gaze shot to the man. He had a different woman beside him now. Maybe the third or fourth one he'd chatted up tonight. His arm was on the back of her chair as he smiled and toyed with a strand of her honey-blond hair. It looked like he might be about to close the deal and be rewarded for his efforts.

My hand tightened around the credit card reflexively, and I scanned my memory from the last few months, recognizing that he'd been in more than a few times. Bartenders were good with recall. Repetition always helped, though. And this guy—Daniel Jensen—had been regular enough that my eyes narrowed now. I couldn't remember much more than that. Always coming in alone, but rarely leaving that way.

He was picking up women in my bar and had been for a while.

I thought about Bonnie, weeks ago, curled up on my bathroom floor, crying over this man. I racked my brain but couldn't recall if he'd been here on the prowl before that night.

Kayla walked up and started organizing her own stack of receipts.

"Is that him?" I confirmed quietly before clearing the roughness from my throat. "Bonnie's husband?"

Kayla didn't even bother glancing up. "Yeah, that's Danny, her ex."

"And you didn't want to serve him because . . . ?"

"Because he's a dick," she said without missing a beat.

Couldn't argue with that. Everything I knew about him, I didn't like either. And, honestly, I was fucking dumbfounded that *he'd* been married to *her*. Bonnie could do so much better.

It wasn't just the looks thing, because I knew Bonnie well enough to know that shit wouldn't matter to her. But this guy, over there spouting cheesy lines, and trying—and failing—not to glance too often at some stranger's chest, was the human equivalent of wilted lettuce. He was as uninteresting and bland as a mayonnaise sandwich.

Seriously, what the hell?

"How long were they together?" I found myself asking.

"Since high school," Kayla replied. "Freshman year."

"Jesus," I breathed.

This was the guy she was so broken up over. The one she didn't want to give up on, who she'd devoted half her life to.

She'd been so young. Probably hadn't known any better or to hold out for someone who would have earned her love instead of claiming it for himself. I bet he'd never put forth any real effort because he'd known all along he'd landed someone loyal and devoted.

I slapped the credit card on the bar top with a little more force than necessary.

Danny straightened abruptly, peeling his eyes off the woman's rack.

I wasn't sure what expression I wore, but it must have been hard enough to have Danny standing and scrambling for his card, urging the woman beside him to stand as well.

Then I turned and walked into the kitchen to keep from telling him to get out and never come back. Luckily, by the time I finished going over the side work and running the last of the glasses through the industrial washer, Danny and the blond were gone.

I shook my head, wondering if the douchebag even realized he was picking up women who looked like his wife.

No, not his wife. His *ex-wife*. Bonnie wasn't his anymore.

It was after three in the morning when I got back to my apartment. I didn't know if Bonnie was awake. In fact, I hoped she was resting well. I hated to think she was losing sleep over that asshole.

But I didn't want her to lose sleep over me either.

So I pulled up our text thread and started to type, knowing it was a terrible idea.

But I couldn't stand to think that she'd assumed I was flirting with those moms this morning. That I was someone who would kiss her one night and pretend it never happened the next. She was the only woman I was thinking about—couldn't fucking stop thinking about. And I didn't want her to wonder.

It wasn't that I owed Bonnie anything. We were . . . I didn't know what, beyond a starry night sky, a stolen ride, and a handful of possibility.

But I knew I didn't want to be just some guy she'd kissed once.

So, yeah. Maybe I didn't know exactly who I wanted to be to her, but I knew it was more than that.

BONNIE

I'd spent the last ten minutes lurking in my living room and glancing out the front window. Jack was due to arrive any moment, and I was telling myself to just be cool about this.

It was worth a try, but so far, no such luck.

When I'd woken up to a text message from Jack, I'd stared at it for a few minutes, not really believing it.

Jack: The weather should be nice tomorrow. I'm thinking about taking a ride on the parkway. Would you like to come with me?

The parkway was the Blue Ridge Parkway, a stretch of road that wound through the nearby mountains, complete with gorgeous views and scenic overlooks. You could ride all the way into Virginia if you really wanted to. Since it was very early October, the leaves hadn't hit their peak yet. So the route wouldn't be as busy as it could be.

Despite the invitation and the fizzy, anticipatory feelings it inspired, I hadn't replied right away. Yes, it would be nice to spend more time with Jack. I liked him. He made me feel unsteady, but in a good way. One that made me a little brave. But after the kiss, I didn't know what to think. Was he interested in pursuing something with me? I didn't know how to feel about that possibility.

I was barely divorced, and I knew what people would say if I started up *something* with Jack or anyone. Besides, I didn't know if I was ready for anything like that anyway. I'd told Jack that I liked him because he didn't treat me the way everyone else did—like I was broken. But the truth was, I felt a little broken. Like my old self was buried in quicksand, and every time I tried to dig her out, I lost another inch.

I still had a hard time believing Jack wanted anything to do with me. I was a thirty-one-year-old divorcée with anxiety. A boring art teacher who stole rabbits and went to bowling league. That felt like more trouble than Jack was used to. Or like the benefits didn't outweigh the effort. Or somewhere in between the two.

Either way, I was skeptical.

I'd seen all those women surrounding him after the soccer game. All the smiles and flirting. I could easily imagine the attention he received at Magnolia's every night, too.

So why would *he* want to take *me* out on his motorcycle?

I still didn't have an answer after a cup of coffee and two strawberry Pop-Tarts, but it seemed rude to wait so long to respond.

Me: Sure. That sounds like fun.

His reply came pretty quickly, telling me he'd pick me up at 11:00 a.m. and not to worry about the helmet. He had one for me.

I wondered at that a little, but I was attempting to be cool, so I didn't ask.

Instead, I was pacing in front of my window and gnawing a raw spot on the inside of my cheek.

Suddenly, it was 11:02, and Jack was pulling into my driveway. My heart rate kicked up several notches, and it was time for my antiperspirant to go to work.

Jack looked effortlessly cool and so handsome. His dark hair was a little disheveled from the helmet, but it suited him. Overly polished and put together would have clashed with his general vibe. He wore his leather jacket and dark boots with light-wash, well-worn jeans. The thought of pressing my body up to his for the next hour or so made heat rise in my cheeks.

I glanced down at my thick cardigan and jeans and felt another jolt of nerves in my midsection.

"It's not a date," I mumbled as I hurried to slide my ID and some cash into my pocket. "Be. Cool."

With a deep breath, I opened the door and stepped out into the fall air just as Jack reached the porch.

"Hey," I said. I could hear the tremble in my voice and hoped he didn't notice.

"Hey." He smiled. "You ready?"

"Yep. Yes. I'm ready."

His grin widened. "Okay, then."

I followed Jack to the bike, where he unstrapped a second helmet and passed it over to me. "I thought we could ride north to Thompson Ridge and stop for lunch at the Rhododendron Inn up that way. Sound good?"

My gaze drifted from the motorcycle back to Jack. "Yeah, that sounds great. I've always wanted to go there."

His hazel eyes searched my face before he said, "You okay? You seem more nervous now than when you rode with me the first time."

I let out a small, slightly hysterical laugh. Yeah, well, I happened to be in the middle of a public meltdown that first go-around, and now, well, I'd had plenty of time to freak out in advance. "I was a little distracted that night."

Jack raised a brow and took a step closer, bringing with him the scent of leather and a spike of awareness. "Oh, do you need me to distract you?"

The sound of my swallow was loud. I had no idea what to say or how to flirt with this man. I was so far off my game here that I didn't know how—

Jack laughed a little and plucked the helmet out of my hands before smoothing my hair back and wiggling it into place on my head. He raised the visor and met my gaze, his amusement settling into something fond and reassuring. "It's okay to be a little scared."

Then he held out his hand.

I took it just as easily as I had the first time, a sense of safety and comfort soothing the nervous energy inside me.

A moment later, I was settled behind him, wrapping my arms around his firm middle as he started the motorcycle and backed us carefully out of the driveway.

Then we were off, the sound of the rushing wind drowning out my busy mind. I took a deep breath of fresh mountain air, feeling my lungs expand and my heart pound out a steady rhythm against Jack's solid back.

There was more to see in the light of day. And it was gorgeous to behold. Mild weather, blue skies, and the sun shining brilliantly overhead. The leaves were just starting to change, golds and reds tipping the higher elevations as the mountains formed layer after endless layer in the distance.

I loved my home and couldn't imagine living anywhere else. There were times in the last few months when it had felt like a prison, too small and too confining for what I'd been going through. But out here, where I could catch my breath and see for miles, it was easier to remember why I loved it so much.

We rode for a time, and just when my body was getting a little sore from holding one position for so long, Jack signaled and turned onto a long paved drive that wound back up the mountainside. We passed beneath a canopy of trees and into a gravel parking lot.

We left the helmets with the bike and climbed the stairs to a small over-look on the front of the building. I'd always wanted to visit the Rhododen-dron Inn. It seemed silly now. Only forty-five minutes from my house, and I'd never made the time for it.

The inn boasted two levels of quaint, themed mountain-view rooms on the hillside just above the parkway. In May and June, the rhododendrons covering the valley below bloomed bright and bold, drawing tourists from all over. The inn also housed a restaurant that was open to the public.

It looked like we were early enough today to have our pick of seating on the covered porch. Jack and I got settled at a table near the railing as a server dropped off menus and glasses of water.

"It's so gorgeous here," I breathed, gaze focused on the view before us.

"Yeah," he replied. "It's a nice spot."

"I've never wanted to live anywhere else," I admitted, turning to face him. "I know some people probably think that's weird, but I just can't imagine moving away."

"Where did you go to college?" Jack wondered. "Did you stay local?"

"Not far. East Tennessee State."

"That's a pretty drive, too," he offered.

I smiled. "Yeah, it is. Did you always live in Kirby Falls?" Then I felt my stomach drop. I couldn't believe I'd asked that. It was intrusive and horribly nosy. "I'm sorry. Where are my manners? You don't have to answer that."

Jack chuckled. "You can ask me questions, Clyde. I don't bite." But his eyes sparkled with a hint of challenge, and I thought he might give me a little nibble if I asked nicely. "I've lived here most of my life. Took a few years and traveled, went to school."

I'd always been curious about what happened to Jack after his arrest.

"You can ask," he assured me, still grinning. "I'm sure whatever rumors you've heard are way worse than what actually went down."

I winced. "Military boarding school?"

He snorted. "Try community service and a GED. Reverend Price dropped the vandalism charges senior year. I got lucky with the judge on the breaking-and-entering stuff and everything that came after. The house arrest rumor wasn't too far off. But afterward, I traveled around a bit. Got my head on straight. Came back and took some online classes. Figured out what I wanted."

I listened to him explain the past, watching for agitation or disquiet as he ran through a laundry list of youthful misdeeds. But if he was nervous about revealing his history, I couldn't detect it. His gaze remained steady, fingers tapping the base of his water goblet absently.

Yet, there was something in the set of his shoulders that made me think he was bracing himself, waiting for me to pass judgment. If that was the case, he'd be waiting a long time.

"And what was it you wanted? What did you figure out?" I asked softly, curiosity to know this man beating out all my peacekeeping politeness.

"That I was wasting my life and hurting the only person who mattered. The only person who'd ever cared about me. I was tired of hurting Lia, my grandmother, and it took a while, but I finally grew up."

He'd mentioned his grandmother a few times now. From the way he spoke, it was easy to see he cared about her. No one ever talked about Jack's parents. As far as I knew, they'd never been in the picture. But that was more than I was willing to ask. No sense in dredging up painful memories when we could have a nice lunch instead.

Just then, a server came to take our drink order.

After she'd walked away, I said simply, "I don't think I've met your grandmother. What's she like?"

He took a sip of his water, and, distracted, I watched the long column of his throat work. "I don't imagine your paths cross very often. She does grandma things."

I smiled. "I love grandma things." Jack grinned and rolled his eyes good-naturedly. "Does she knit? Have a garden?" I leaned forward dramatically and whispered, "Does she can things from that garden?"

He laughed, and I felt like I'd won a prize at the deep rumble of his amusement.

"She would absolutely eat you alive," he said.

That had me throwing my head back. "What? Why?" I finally managed.

Jack shook his head a little, still amused. "You might have similar hobbies, but you're both so different. She's hard in a way I don't think you could ever be. We've never been good at being affectionate or open. Lia's been on her own so long. She's tough. Made herself that way. There wasn't a lot of room left over for softness."

"But she loves you." It was a statement, not a question.

"Yeah." He nodded. "Yeah, she does."

"And you think I'm a marshmallow," I accused, but sanded the edges down with a small smile. He wasn't wrong. I felt more vulnerable now than I ever had in my life. I wished I was tougher, like his Lia. But when you'd had the rug pulled out from under you, it was hard to regain your balance or to trust that the rest of the rugs in the house wouldn't upend you the next time you walked by.

That was what made Danny's infidelity and the end of our marriage so difficult. I'd been blindsided, completely caught off guard. As a result, I had a hard time trusting my instincts, and if you couldn't have faith in yourself, then courage was hard to come by.

"I didn't say that," Jack replied flatly. "I just said you were different. It wasn't a judgment. Lia's a gruff old woman who's set in her ways. You work with kids every day. You're patient and kind and generous with your time. And you have this big family that you've devoted yourself to. Lia only has me."

I glanced down at the tabletop. It was nice of Jack to leave out all my bad qualities.

"But," he added, as if reading my mind, "you're also stubborn. So maybe you do have something in common with my grandmother after all."

"I am not stubborn," I argued. I was totally stubborn.

His hazel eyes sparkled. "If you say so."

"I'm not," I insisted.

Jack grinned and opened his menu. His attention was focused on the list of food items when he said, "Stubborn isn't a bad thing, Clyde. It's easy to see that you're dedicated to your students, your family, and your friends. Stubborn just means that you don't give up on people. You hold on."

My stomach did a back handspring at his matter-of-fact words. The simplicity and certainty there. Jack was right, but my inclination to hold on wasn't necessarily a good thing. I'd stubbornly refused to give up on my marriage until it blew up in my face. I'd taken all my hurt and betrayal and held on to that, too. I used to think blind devotion was something to be proud of. Now I knew the truth. Something had better be worth your time and effort. It should be deserving of your love before you went all in.

"You're a glass-half-full person," Jack was saying. "An optimist. You trust and love freely, and you care about other people. You see the beauty in the world around you." He gestured to the mountain view I'd been mooning over since we got here.

"You make me sound like some dewy-eyed romantic."

He closed the menu and placed it beside his elbow. "You disagree?"

I didn't know why this felt like an admission. Like Jack had seen a little too much, peeling back the protective layer around my heart. Or maybe my reluctance was due to the fact that all those traits he'd mentioned made me his opposite—someone he saw as silly or naïve.

But the old Bonnie had been like the woman he'd described. And maybe I was still mad at her for being so clueless, but part of me wanted her back.

I was a person who read romance novels and listened to Taylor Swift. I loved *Pride and Prejudice* and *North and South*. I appreciated manners and wanted someone to bring me flowers for no reason at all. I secretly wished for a serendipitous meet-cute or a surprise birthday party. I hoped lightning might strike and that the love of my life would turn out to be someone who put me first and not the man I'd wasted half my life loving, the one who'd thrown me away for a bachelor party in Gatlinburg.

Instead of saying any of that, I huffed a quiet laugh and admitted, "No. You're right. I suppose I am a romantic."

"I guess I admire that about you," Jack said. "You've probably noticed I'm pretty cynical. I don't see the world the way you do. My family is small and complicated. I haven't known people with healthy marriages. My parents weren't married. Well, my dad was married, but not to my mom. And working in the bar, I see guys picking up a different woman every week. Occasionally, with a tan line on their ring finger."

I fought an internal wince at that, a reminder of my own marriage.

Jack cleared his throat and glanced away from me, a flash of *something*, there and gone in an instant. I didn't have time to wonder as he continued, "I guess what I'm saying is, relationships have always seemed like this alien thing where you have to check in with someone constantly, and you can't make your own decisions without consulting whoever's in charge. It's feeling jealous or possessive or any number of overbearing emotions. It's keeping the peace at the expense of your own. Or it's just a tool to announce to the world that you have ownership of someone else."

I wasn't sure how much to read into Jack's words. Part of me thought he was warning me away. Subtly telling me not to get any ideas about the two of us. But that optimistic, glass-half-full girl thought maybe we were just having a conversation, getting to know one another.

With most people in my life, I knew their backstory. All the history. I'd been part of the timeline from the beginning.

With Jack, everything was brand-new. I was learning as I went, and while the big picture was there—this cynical, aloof, cool guy with a chip on his shoulder—all the little details would need to be uncovered and brought into focus.

So, I went with my instincts and treated this like a conversation between two people who were trying to understand each other. And I decided to tell him the truth so he could know me better. Not act like some woman on a date worried about scaring a guy off with too much honesty up front.

I said with a shrug, "I can see that. But I was lucky enough to have good examples of loving, healthy relationships. My parents, grandparents, and great-grandparents were all happily married. And, honestly, I *liked* being married. I liked saying to the world that we were a team. We were in it together. No keeping score unless it was us against everyone else. Someone to have your back and give you high fives. A best friend and a roommate and a secret keeper, all in one. The person that you could share an eye roll with and a million inside jokes. Someone who is always on your side, no matter what. Even if that means telling a hard truth. Because all they want is the best for you. A teammate." I paused. "That's what I wanted anyway."

A dull ache opened up in my chest. I'd hoped for all those things, but my marriage had turned into something else. There had been loneliness and disappointment. Missed calls and unanswered texts. Walking on eggshells amid obligation. Danny went from being the person I knew best to a stranger sharing my bed.

Jack watched me carefully. He looked like he wanted to say something. Maybe to disagree with me.

But again, I went with honesty.

"Danny used to buy me these chips I loved," I started. "And he loved them, too. Nine times out of ten, I'd go to grab a snack, and the bag would be there, but when I opened it, there would only be crushed bits at the bottom. He'd joke that he hadn't eaten them all and made sure to leave me some."

Jack was frowning, and I gave him a sad little smile before continuing, "But what was left in the bag wouldn't have amounted to more than a single chip. I know it sounds silly or arbitrary or nitpicky, but that felt like a metaphor for our marriage, you know. I think what I really wanted was to know that he'd been thinking about me. That he couldn't stop thinking about me—my wants and needs. I wanted to hear it in his voice and see it in the way he couldn't stop looking at me. I wanted a love that pulled its weight. Not just me and my determination dragging it around like a reluctant dog on the end of a leash. I want the love I deserve. Something bright and loud and undeniable. Not the leftover crumbs in the bottom of an empty bag."

I watched Jack shift uncomfortably in his seat.

"I'm sorry," I apologized. "That was probably more than you wanted to know. No one wants to hear about someone's ex."

Jack leaned forward, placing his forearms on the table and meeting my gaze head-on. "Don't be sorry. I feel like I learned more about you than I could ever understand about him."

I smiled, thinking that was a really nice way to put it.

The server showed up then to take our order, and I used the moment to regroup.

I made sure that the rest of our lunchtime conversation was easy and light. We talked about the bar and my job, and the girls on Jack's soccer team.

I laughed a lot, and he did too. It balanced out the intensity of our earlier conversation, soothing the burn of brutal honesty and some definite over-sharing on my part.

I found myself easily distracted by his throat working as he swallowed. Awareness crashed through me in a steady wave when he rested an elbow on the arm of his chair and cradled his chin in one hand—thoughtful and attentive as he listened to me talk about my family. A single diverting fingertip tapped lightly across his lush bottom lip, and I had a difficult time organizing my thoughts beyond a steadily building attraction.

I was a watched pot, set to a slow simmer, conscious of Jack's body and the way it moved. It made me curious, how those patient, rugged hands of his might feel on my skin. I was curious about a lot of things that had my stomach flipping over itself.

By the time we finished up our meal, I was looking forward to the ride back. It was hard to be nervous when you'd already shown your hand as well as your skeletons. And while this hadn't felt like a date, it had felt like the start of something.

Or, rather, I hoped it might be.

The second half of the trip went by faster than the first. I lost myself in the purr of the engine, the passing scenery, and the feel of Jack's body nestled against mine. Before I realized it, we were back in Kirby Falls, passing the orchards and farms on Highway 64.

A sinking feeling settled in my belly the closer we got to my house. Maybe I wasn't too far off from a first-date cliché, trying to hold some-one's attention without seeming desperate because I worried that all of this —all of me—might have been too much for Jack.

I didn't even know what I wanted, but I knew I didn't want it to end.

Maybe that meant more rides on the parkway or kisses in the moonlight. Meaningful conversations and getting to know him. Or late-night texts and Jack asking me what I needed.

"You seemed pretty relaxed on the way back," Jack said, accepting the helmet from my outstretched hand as we stood in my driveway. "Who would have guessed? A good girl turned biker."

I frowned. He was always doing that, creating space, highlighting our differences, reminding me who I was.

I thought about arguing, admitting I was selfish and judgmental. Or telling him about the time I'd snuck over here to the house in the middle of the night after Danny had kicked me out so I could dig up the orange daylily bulbs my great-grandfather had given me. Sure, I'd ended up replanting them after I'd gotten the house back, but whatever. It had been the principle of the thing. I hadn't wanted Danny to end up with my plants, so I'd risked trespassing and getting caught to get what I wanted.

I wasn't some one-dimensional good girl. I didn't fit neatly in the box Jack had labeled for me.

Instead of rehashing more of my divorce drama, I settled on, "I'm not *just* a good girl, Jack."

His face softened, somewhere between reluctantly amused and unwittingly fond. "I know, Clyde. I know."

Then he stepped close, and I sucked in an unsteady breath. Jack raised his hands and smoothed down my messy helmet hair. As he brushed the loose waves back from my face, I watched him standing there, looking impossibly handsome, smiling gently, those hazel eyes focused only on me.

As I stared, I thought how I'd never really asked for what I wanted. I'd always just taken the leftovers, made do with the crumbs.

My hands shook at my sides as Jack's thumb tucked a strand of hair behind my ear, the feeling of his tender care making my stomach dip agreeably.

I was tired of settling, of saying I was fine, of rolling with the punches and accepting the disappointment as my due.

Jack's words came back to me. *It's okay to be a little scared*, I reminded myself.

My fingertips settled on his waist, and I pushed up onto my toes.

Jack's hands cupped my cheeks as he leaned down to meet me.

But just before our lips touched, I blurted out, "I think we should have sex."

Jack paused, his nose a hairsbreadth from grazing mine, and blinked.

He pulled back to look at me, and I closed my eyes as mortification set in.

Warm, rough hands drifted down my neck to my shoulders, where they squeezed gently. "What was that?"

I forced myself to open my eyes, grateful when Jack didn't appear to be laughing or disgusted. "I don't know how to do this," I confessed. "I don't know how to date. I haven't since I was a teenager. Not that you're even interested in that." I fought the urge to close my eyes again. Jack didn't seem like the monogamous type, and he'd already said he didn't really believe in marriage or relationships. Plus, I was a boring elementary school art teacher. It was almost laughable that this ridiculously hot, interesting man would want to date me.

"Anyway," I said quickly, "I just thought—I feel safe with you. I like you and I'm attracted to you. We're adults." I snapped my mouth shut, then quickly added, "You can say no. Obviously."

Jack watched me, that same careful, solemn expression in place. "This feels like you're trying to prove something to yourself. But lucky for you, I don't usually drive the moral high road. So my answer is sure."

I shook my head. "Don't do that. Don't say that about yourself because it's not true."

He had the decency to look a little sheepish.

"And I'm not out to prove anything," I insisted. "I'm not killing time or ripping off a Band-Aid or looking for—for spite sex. I like you, Jack. I want you. I don't plan on having expectations or being overbearing or demanding. And we're friends, right? You and me? We could be friends with benefits. Is that still a thing?"

His lips twitched, and he squeezed my shoulders again. "Yeah, I think that's still a thing."

After a long moment that had me squirming, Jack finally said, "I'm off tomorrow night. Would you like to come over?"

I bit my lip before replying, "Yes, I would."

He grinned. "Okay."

"Okay," I echoed, smiling back.

And then he leaned in to kiss me. This time, I didn't even think about stopping him.

JACK

In the last twenty-four hours, I'd thought a lot about what might happen with Bonnie.

She'd agreed to come over tonight with a very specific purpose in mind. Yet I wondered if she might get cold feet. If, when the time came, she'd fail to show or she'd chicken out before she got what she wanted.

I'd thought about the length of her relationship with Danny and how she'd probably only ever been with her husband. Admittedly, that hadn't been a deterrent. Maybe it was my arrogance or pride talking, but I wanted to make this good for her.

I'd considered the fact that despite her assurances, she might catch feelings or be interested in more than I could give. Or the very real possibility that she might be unable to handle something casual.

There were a lot of thoughts swirling around in my head, most of them giving me pause and raising red flags. So I didn't know what it said about me that I hadn't once considered calling this thing off.

Bonnie's directness had taken me off guard yesterday. People were rarely so inclined to ask for exactly what they wanted. There hadn't been any subtlety on her part, but she'd also skipped over any scheming or game playing, which was kind of refreshing.

Part of me thought that Bonnie and I had been on a collision course since that very first night, with her drunk on a barstool and me completely baffled by her sudden appearance in my life.

She was someone I was attracted to, yes. But I also liked her. I enjoyed spending time with her—talking, texting, getting under her skin. And I hadn't had that with a woman . . . ever.

But a little voice inside warned that the timing could have been better. Even if we'd made it here on our own, naturally, without a roadside proposition, I didn't know if it was the right choice.

She was fresh off a heartbreak, still flailing around in it. Someone like her wouldn't just fall out of love with someone. She'd admitted as much, sick and miserable on my bathroom rug. I was more than prepared for a post-sex freak-out or even tears.

I was selfish enough to know I wouldn't turn her away, though. I liked that she'd asked for what she wanted, and, even more, I liked knowing that what she wanted was me.

So when—if—Bonnie got here, I'd do my best to put her at ease and make sure a night in my bed was really what she wanted. And if it was, then I'd make it a night she wouldn't forget.

A knock sounded just after eight.

I ignored the bright rush of anticipation as I made my way to the door, opening it wide to see Bonnie standing on the other side.

"Hi," she said softly.

"Hi," I replied, taking her in.

Bonnie wore a dress the color of the leaves on the Japanese maple tree in my grandmother's front yard. The deep red complemented her blond hair and made her pale skin glow. The hem of her skirt hit mid-shin, and the fabric looked soft. Everything about her looked soft and sweet.

The good girl standing on my doorstep, wanting to be bad for the night.

"Come in," I finally said, pulling my attention away from where her fingers were twisting themselves into knots.

She hesitated a beat, and if I had to guess, I'd say it was nerves keeping the soles of her ballerina flats glued to the floor.

The television was already on, and Bonnie's attention snagged there.

She smiled and looked at me. "I love this show."

That's what I'd been counting on. She'd mentioned the 2000s sitcom in our previous texts, and I thought it might go a long way toward taking the edge off any nervousness she might be feeling.

"Make yourself comfortable," I called as I went to grab her drink from the fridge.

Bonnie's attention stayed on the screen as she made her way into the living room. A moment later, she laughed, the sound familiar and happy, like she'd heard that joke before but couldn't resist her reaction.

I returned and sat next to her on the couch, passing her a fountain soda in a glass from the bar downstairs.

"Oh," she said, accepting it. "Thank you."

Her gaze found the bowl of popcorn, glistening with butter, on the coffee table in front of her. Then the packages of Cookie Dough Bites stacked neatly beside it.

Wide brown eyes met mine as her face did something complicated. Confusion wrinkled her brow, and her pink lips parted while a wondering smile fought to break free. I could see it in her expression. She was pleased but trying not to get her hopes up. Like maybe it was a coincidence that I'd arranged her favorite snacks for an impromptu movie night, and she didn't want to be wrong in case that wasn't the case.

"I got us some snacks," I said simply.

Bonnie watched me for another moment before her tentative smile finally wiggled out from beneath her uncertainty. "Thanks, Jack."

"Well, you do have to share with me."

Her grin widened. "I'll think about it."

I laughed, placing my own soda down on the table.

I could feel Bonnie's gaze on the side of my face before she eventually turned forward, her small hand depositing her glass beside mine.

I'd never seen this television series before. Bonnie explained a few of the running jokes, and I found myself enjoying it. Mostly, I found myself watching her as she smiled and laughed at whatever was happening on screen.

After two episodes, I felt Bonnie relax into me as she tilted the popcorn bowl in my direction. I leaned in, too, content to have her warm weight against me, the skin of her arm soft and smooth next to mine.

I watched her eyes dance. And the next time a joke landed and her lips formed a bright smile, I snagged her hand in mine before she could cover her mouth.

Two more episodes went by, Bonnie's quiet laughter easing the tension from her body.

I didn't want her stuck in her own head or worried about what came next. I couldn't do anything about her own expectations, but I could damn well make sure she wasn't anxious over mine. She was in charge here. Whatever happened tonight would be because she wanted it to.

My worries hadn't gone anywhere. Those red flags were still waving. But Bonnie was here. She'd shown up, and sometimes that first step was the most important one to take.

Eventually, she put her snacks back on the table and curled into my side. With her fingers wrapped around mine, her head dipped to rest on my shoulder.

It was another half an episode before I realized her laughter had trailed off. When I looked down, I caught the dark fan of her eyelashes against the tops of her cheeks and the steady rise and fall of her chest. And I smiled at the sight of Bonnie fast asleep, comfortable and relaxed in my arms.

Bonnie

"Clyde," a voice whispered somewhere near my ear.

I shivered at the sound, like something out of a dream.

A touch traced from my inner wrist to the center of my palm before circling slowly and then repeating itself.

I blinked my bleary eyes into a dimly lit room. The only light was coming from the kitchen behind us. Glasses and the remnants of our popcorn and candy were still visible on the coffee table from my tilted view.

Realization dawned and mortification gripped me.

I sucked in a sharp breath as I straightened away from the man at my side. A man who looked quietly amused.

Jack pivoted to face me, his arm bent, elbow balanced on the back of the couch as he watched me. "Sorry, it was getting pretty late, and I wasn't sure what time you needed to be up for school tomorrow."

I prayed silently that it was dark enough that Jack wouldn't be able to make out the fierce blush I felt on my cheeks. I couldn't believe I'd fallen asleep. I'd practically invited myself over *for sex*—I mentally hissed—and then passed out on the man. And after Jack had been so patient and accommodating. He'd even watched one of my favorite shows with me and gotten my favorite snacks.

I could still feel the phantom touch of his thumb circling the back of my hand.

"Hey," he said softly.

My attention jerked to his, as I paddled upstream against my humiliation and embarrassment.

"I don't have work tomorrow," I said, finally answering him. "We're on fall break Monday and Tuesday."

He nodded. "Well, then, I feel bad for interrupting your sleep. I know how hard that is to come by."

I closed my eyes briefly before opening them. "I am so sorry."

"Why are you sorry? Considering how tense you were when you first got here, I thought it was a good thing that you'd relaxed enough to sleep with me." He grinned, and I knew he'd phrased it that way on purpose.

I huffed out a humorless laugh. Of all the times for sleep to find me.

But he was right. I'd been uncomfortable when I'd arrived tonight. Frankly, I'd been a nervous wreck most of the day. So many thoughts and feelings had plagued me, making me question my sanity, wondering what the hell I'd been thinking, asking Jack to be friends with benefits.

I'd been with one man my entire life. I wasn't adventurous or experienced. Part of me worried I wouldn't be what Jack expected—that I'd be a disappointment.

I'd picked up my phone a handful of times earlier today, intent on texting him and canceling tonight. But in the end, my stubbornness and manners won out. I didn't want to be someone who broke their promise, no matter how inconsequential.

So I'd pasted on a brave face, ignored the knots in my stomach, and knocked on Jack's door. And he'd distracted me and put my restless mind at ease. So much so that I'd relaxed into a dreamless sleep, my head on his shoulder.

When I managed to lift my gaze, I found Jack still watching me, the corners of his lips tipped up, his hazel eyes bright and focused. I liked his attention and being the center of it. I liked the way his knee rested casually against my hip. I liked that he'd made such an effort tonight—for me— likely knowing I'd be taking a leap outside my comfort zone.

I'd never call Jack gentle. He was too jaded and world-weary for that. But he was gentle with me.

There were times in your life when you needed tough love. When brutal honesty and straight shooting were the only things that might get through to the heart of you. But that wasn't what I needed right now. I needed someone to shake things up, to be a guiding hand and a soft place to land. I needed room to breathe. To experience the unfamiliar in a safe space.

I needed someone who saw me in a way I couldn't see myself.

My gaze traced the lines of Jack's face. The firm edge of his jaw, the dark slash of his eyebrows, and the gentle rise of his cheekbones. He was every roguish, bad-boy fantasy come to life. A modern-day pirate with long hair and a wicked gleam in his eye.

But he was also a reassuring touch and warm fingers laced through mine. Someone who remembered all my favorite things and then actually gave them to me. Awareness and observation and intention. I didn't know if there was anything sexier than that.

Jack had this way of *really* listening to me. I'd noticed it before, but anytime I spoke, he focused. Most people were content to carry on a conversation while watching television or listening to the radio, driving a car or scrolling on their phone. But not Jack.

He consistently stopped whatever he was doing and gave me the full weight of his gaze. He watched me, read my expression, and heard me. It was almost as if he wanted to zoom out and get the entire picture, the full portrait of me. Like what I had to say actually mattered. No matter how small or trivial the topic.

When we'd watched television earlier, I'd felt his gaze on my face while I'd talked. It was a small thing that felt very big in my heart.

I had a bad habit of being intimidated by Jack, by his magnetism and attitude, by my own expectations and memories as well. In the back of my mind, I still saw him as the lone wolf, the rebel teenager I'd watched from afar. To have his attention—the full brunt of it—focused on me was . . . dizzying. It made me feel powerful. Unsettled in the best possible way. Like a second pulse in my chest. Awareness, bright and intoxicating.

"You could stay, you know," Jack said casually. "If you wanted."

Before I lost my nerve, before I let my insecurities stop me in my tracks, I leaned forward, bracing one hand gently on Jack's spread thigh, and answered him with my mouth pressed to his. I gave in to my wants and desires, the giddy pull in my middle that spoke of attraction and need.

Jack's lips parted, and I breathed him in. Leather and warmth, whiskey and something wicked that had me tugging him down on top of me. As I lay back on the couch and Jack's weight settled against me, I lost myself in the feel of him. Deep, drugging kisses that stole my breath. A rough hand gently cupping my jaw. My tentative touch slipping beneath his shirt, exploring to find the smooth skin of his back. All his firm muscles welcomed by my softness. And a growing hardness against my core that had me squirming, even as my legs widened in an effort to get him closer.

There wasn't any room for doubts and insecurity. There was just Jack, and he was more than enough to hold my attention.

My knees were bent, and I jolted as a warm hand wrapped around my ankle. The touch unexpectedly electric. Jack's rough palm skated up my calf and along the outside of my thigh, slowly gathering the fabric of my skirt as it went.

I panted into the dimness as Jack's lips brushed my jaw and then my neck. Little sparks of anticipation flickered in my belly as my body came wide-awake.

I wound unsteady fingers through Jack's long hair, holding him to me as his tongue traced the column of my throat. He found the sensitive spot along my collarbone, and I arched my back into his touch.

Jack took the invitation and nuzzled his rough cheek against my breast, but it wasn't enough—wasn't intimate enough for the ache building inside of me.

"Here," I whispered. "Let me." Then I wiggled to create space for my hands.

The dress I wore had a long line of buttons all the way down the front. Jack pulled back to watch as I unfastened the top four down to my waist, exposing the lace bra I wore. His eyes dropped to the sheer, pale fabric, and something deep in my core clenched at the way he licked his bottom lip before biting down.

Jack's gaze came back to mine, pupils dark and wide. He regarded me with that same watchful, patient expression. I liked that he was pacing himself, taking his time, taking care—with me.

There'd been some premeditation involved tonight. I'd asked for this, arranged it essentially. But I appreciated that he wasn't rushing through it, trying to get it over with.

"Can I kiss you?" he asked solemnly.

My lips twitched in sudden amusement. "You've *been* kissing me."

Only then did he grin, something teasing and mischievous that had heat spiraling toward my center. "What I meant was, can I kiss you wherever I want?"

I swallowed audibly before replying, "Yes," the word more breath than sound.

The hand that had trailed so leisurely up my leg gave my hip a firm squeeze, and then Jack slowly slid himself down my body so that he could focus his attention on my lace-covered chest. The movement of his firm stomach against my core had me muffling a little moan.

Jack's gaze snapped to mine wickedly. "Good to know."

Then his other hand pushed aside the fabric of my dress, and his mouth descended, hot and wet, right over the center of my breast. The feel of the delicate fabric caught between his tongue and my sensitive skin had me fighting another moan.

Fingers snaked inside my open top, molding themselves to my rib cage, pushing my breast more fully into Jack's waiting mouth. I kept my hold on his hair, clutching and desperate, tangling the dark strands.

He felt so good on top of me. His weight pressed me into the smooth leather of the couch. Jack was warm and possessive, attentive and thorough. The way he always seemed to listen to my words was reflected back intimately in the way he paid attention to my body. I was his sole focus. From the sounds I made as he licked and sucked and nipped at my flesh as the pleasure built inside me.

My hips were searching, my body needing something—friction, heat, just . . . more. More of Jack. More of this.

Sensing my restlessness, the hand at my hip reached around, finding the edge of my underwear and sliding north to palm one globe of my ass.

At the same time, Jack abandoned my breast, but before I could protest, his mouth found mine once more. He shifted up, using his other hand to brace himself as his erection settled right where I wanted it—where I *needed* it.

I groaned into his kiss, the sound equal parts needy vibration and gasping breath. I exhaled brokenly through the exquisite sensation as his hips rolled, jeans rough and welcome against my underwear and the bare skin of my inner thighs. He was impossibly hard and thick, and I closed my eyes as we moved together in a sensual approximation of sex.

Jack's hand on my backside tugged in time to his rhythmic thrusts, and I was too far gone to feel embarrassed about my impending orgasm. Lost to the urgency and the need, and getting exactly what I'd asked for without bargaining away my peace.

I wrapped one leg around Jack's hip, the heel of my foot digging into his ass, urging him on.

Jack made a rough sound before cursing and bearing down hard against my core.

"Oh God," I exhaled. Our lips brushed with every thrust, breaths quick and jagged against one another.

My nails pressed into the skin of Jack's back as pleasure tightened through my limbs. I felt the band between us stretching and stretching and stretching until suddenly it snapped.

I fused my mouth with Jack's and moaned as my orgasm struck. Waves of warmth and desire unfurling, loosening my taut muscles to make way for pleasure, over and over again.

My movements slowed, and Jack followed my lead. But before embarrassment or awkwardness could intrude, he was standing and bringing me with him.

I wrapped my arms around his shoulders and my legs around his waist as Jack held me. His erection nestled against me in a way that had my sensitive skin tingling.

He marched us toward his bedroom, the room dark and cool.

Jack set me down gently near the foot of the bed, hands at my waist to steady me. "Is this okay?"

"Yes." I nodded eagerly, cupping him in his jeans.

His muffled grunt of approval had me squeezing and stroking the thick outline through the denim. His forehead dropped to rest on my shoulder as his fingers went to work on the remainder of my buttons. Once the dress was unfastened, he pushed it over my shoulders and hips, all the way to the floor.

I paused long enough to step out of the pool of fabric before eagerly lifting Jack's shirt and tugging it off. His jeans and underwear followed.

I could just make out the hazy shape of him in the darkness. There was only the light sneaking in from down the hallway from the kitchen.

Jack led me to the bed, my heart beating hard in my chest as I lay back. Despite the orgasm I'd had on the couch and the anticipation spiraling through me, I was nervous again, bracing for this next step, lost to my thoughts and fears.

I heard a drawer open and close, felt the bed dip beside me. Then I nearly yelped as Jack's fingers wrapped around my ankle once again.

"It's just me," he said quietly, voice deep and soft.

I almost laughed. *Just him*. Good lord. If he only knew what he did to me. Silly-schoolgirl-crush sorts of things. Blushing cheeks and butterflies in my stomach. Wanting and needing. Thinking he might be the only person who knew this version of me. There was nothing that could minimize that. Not even his whispered reassurance against the shell of my ear.

But the drag of his hand up my leg was grounding. It was the way he'd touched me earlier. I knew it. It was familiar. An unhurried caress, slow and steady, causing my nerve endings to come alive and my mind to settle. To just feel.

Jack guided me toward him. Rolling onto my side, I faced his dark outline in the night, and his talented fingers dipped behind my knee, making me suck in a breath.

Desire coiled neatly in my middle, settling warm and heavy as I reached out and did some exploring of my own.

Jack was all firm lines and soft skin. My hand smoothed over coarse chest hair before following the line of it over a lean midsection. His hips jerked reflexively as my fingers brushed the velvety tip of his cock where it strained between us. I wrapped my fist around his length and squeezed. The sound Jack made against my cheek was rough and desperate, and I wanted to taste it.

Smiling against his mouth, I barely had time to stroke once, twice, and a third time before Jack freed himself from my grasp. He urged me flat on my back and loomed over me on hands and knees, his big body caging me in as he placed hot, wet kisses between my breasts all the way down to the waistband of my lacy underwear.

Despite my earlier agreement that Jack could kiss me wherever he wanted, I wasn't ready for this. Maybe I was crazy, but it felt too intimate or too soon; I didn't know.

So I reached for him, cupping his stubble-covered cheeks and guiding him back up my body. "I want you up here with me."

He came willingly, bringing his lips to mine in a kiss that left me gasping. But before he could settle himself, he rolled across the mattress, pulling me on top of him.

"You're in charge here," he stated roughly. "You set the pace." His hands smoothed rhythmically up and down my thighs, unhurried and encouraging at the same time.

Some unexpected emotion ricocheted through me. A weird combination of gratitude and fascination. What would it be like to take what Jack offered? To give myself permission? To stop worrying about pleasing everyone else for a change?

I shifted to get comfortable as I straddled his hips. My knee came into contact with something on the bed. I reached over, feeling the smooth edge of a foil packet.

For once, I knew exactly what I wanted.

I ripped open the wrapper and used both hands to roll the condom into place. Jack's hands tightened on my legs briefly, but he didn't move to help. I rose slightly, sliding my underwear to the side as I positioned his cock at my entrance. Then I slowly sank down as pressure and heat threatened to overwhelm me.

"Fuck," Jack cursed, his fingers digging into my hips.

I waited a moment, getting used to the invasion, the size, the way my belly had hollowed at the feel of him. When I could manage a full breath, I rolled my hips experimentally.

Jack cursed again, the sound a vulgar hiss from a tightly clenched jaw.

I let myself smile into the darkness, and then I started to move, doing what he'd told me—taking charge, setting the pace.

A thumb found its way to my clit, using the slickness of my arousal to rub tiny circles right where I needed it. I jolted at the touch, an arrow notching in the bowstring of my desire. Goose bumps erupted on my skin like the AC was going full blast.

"Yes," I moaned, my movements speeding up, every tilt of my hips pushing me higher and higher.

Jack was moving now, too. His hips rising to meet my thrusts, a perfect counterpoint. His other hand remained steady on my hip, content to let me lead.

"I'm close," I whispered as my movements fell out of sync.

The thumb at the apex of my thighs stopped circling. The teasing touch bore down directly on my clit, giving me pressure and heat and *yes, there . . . right there . . . oh, God.*

Through the flash of pleasure, the blinding intensity of it, I felt Jack's thrusts speed up, his hips snapping inelegantly as he reached his own climax.

He jackknifed up, clutching me to him as he groaned into my neck. I held on just as tightly, feeling raw and untethered, like I needed something to keep me from floating away.

Jack panted against my neck, exhaling heavy and warm. As seconds passed and his breathing slowed, he placed a soft kiss along my jaw.

"I'll be right back," he said, words brushing the shell of my ear and making me shiver.

He was careful with me as we separated, helping me onto the center of the bed while being mindful of the condom.

Awkwardly, I adjusted my underwear and attempted to piece myself back together while Jack shuffled into the bathroom across the hall.

My mind felt like a switchboard, warning lights pinging into existence as thoughts entered the atmosphere. I'd done it. I'd had sex with someone—someone who was not my husband. *Because I didn't have a husband*, my brain quickly corrected before I could drift into that minefield.

I'd had sex.

And it had been amazing.

Now I was sitting alone as the air cooled my skin, wondering what came next. Would Jack want me to leave? Did friends with benefits cuddle? Was I allowed to stay over?

No, probably not. I should—I should leave before I made things weird.

Quickly, I hopped up from the bed, eyes searching the darkness for my dress on the floor. I'd just bent over and gathered it in my arms when the light clicked on across the hall. I froze like one of those cartoon prisoners during a jailbreak.

"What are you doing?" Jack asked. My eyes hadn't adjusted to the sudden brightness, so I couldn't confirm, but I was relatively sure I heard amusement in his voice.

Squinting and blinking, I straightened, using the fabric of my dress to cover my nearly naked front. "Um, well . . ."

Jack was leaning against the doorframe of his bedroom, arms crossed and silhouette backlit. I could make out the laughing tilt of his lips, the arch of one expectant eyebrow, practically saying, *This ought to be good.*

I could also see that he was completely nude. He had a full sleeve of tattoos on one arm that I was eager to explore in the light of day. But despite my best effort, my eyes dipped below his waist, confirming what

I'd only felt earlier. He was so beautiful. Lean and strong. Wide shoulders with narrow hips, and his penis was—

"Bonnie," he said, definitely entertained.

My eyes jumped to his face as a guilty flush worked its way up my neck.

"What are you doing?" he asked again, stepping into the room and within touching distance.

I closed my eyes briefly, trying to shake off the lust and the instinct to ogle and objectify. He was just so aggressively handsome.

"I don't know," I admitted with a humorless laugh. "Should I leave? Am I supposed to leave? I don't know how to do this."

Warm hands enveloped my upper arms as he stroked leisurely up and down. "You should only leave if you want to." His hazel eyes sparkled before he leaned in and placed a kiss on the corner of my mouth. "But I think"—another kiss beneath my jaw—"you should stay." Then he gave a gentle bite to my earlobe. "Because I'm just getting started."

It was morning before I wanted it to be, my limbs heavy with exhaustion and my mind well rested for once. As I blinked groggily, pale morning light brought the nearly unfamiliar room into focus and, along with it, a sudden awareness.

Clutching the covers to my naked chest, I sat up quickly as soreness registered in my muscles. The kind of ache that reminded me of multiple orgasms and the man very much not in bed beside me.

At least this time, I didn't have the hangover from hell.

I took in the room, noting things I hadn't on my previous visit. The basic white walls, the tidy, spartan space that hadn't really absorbed the personality of its owner. The framed paintings were a bit out of place. Jack didn't strike me as a watercolor landscape sort of guy. But I'd learned not to assume things about people and their hobbies. After participating in and teaching summer art courses over the years, I knew that talent could be found in the unlikeliest of places.

My eyes drifted to the foot of the bed, where a shaft of sunlight spread across the quilt, highlighting my dress and underthings neatly folded and waiting for me. I grinned, my hand rising on instinct to cover the gap in my teeth.

I figured I should probably get dressed and figure out how awkward this morning after was going to be. A few minutes later, I'd smoothed my wrinkled dress down my legs and finger combed my short hair into something resembling order.

With a peek around the doorframe, I found Jack in the same chair he'd occupied the first time I'd snuck out of his bedroom. There he sat with another book—this one a paperback—and a cup of coffee, reading glasses on and feet once again bare.

My stomach did a little back handspring and stuck the landing.

"Hi," he said, his lips looking like they were on their way to a smile. Like maybe he was comparing the last time we'd been in this situation, too.

"Hi," I returned, stepping fully into the hallway.

"Come have coffee with me," he invited.

My feet were already moving. "Okay."

"Your mug is on the counter."

Something about the casual words and the ease with which he'd delivered them had my mind stuttering to a stop. My toes nearly tripped me up as my steps faltered momentarily on my way into the kitchen.

My heart shouldn't be beating this hard over something so minor, so utterly insignificant. But it was.

Sitting there, right where he'd said, was the same striped mug I'd used the first time we'd had coffee together, weeks ago, after a painful night and Jack's unexpected kindness.

My hand trembled slightly as I reached for the handle of the mug—my mug, apparently.

I didn't even have a mug that I considered mine in my own home. I just used one from a four-pack I'd bought at the grocery store after I realized that Danny had taken the ones we'd accumulated over the years. The handmade mugs from Bramble Pottery that I'd loved. The ones we'd bought at Dollywood when we were dating that had our names on them. Any number of various vacation souvenirs. All gone.

But I had a mug at Jack's apartment. The existential-crisis mug struck again.

The sugar and half-and-half awaited me as well. Only this time, I knew that Jack drank his coffee black, so he'd set them out for my benefit.

I pulled myself together as I stirred and washed my spoon before making my way carefully to the couch, coffee in hand.

Jack looked up from his book as I sat. Then he slid his bookmark between the pages and placed the paperback on the low table in front of him. It was a popular sci-fi title that I made a mental note of for my TBR list.

I noticed that the snacks from last night had been cleaned up. The popcorn and candy and soda that he'd gotten with me in mind.

Maybe there was something to be said for pen pals or long-distance letter writing. It helped you get to know someone—from the minor and the mundane to the big, messy life events. The text imprinting thoughts and ideas in your mind with a certain clarity that speaking on the phone couldn't quite accomplish. Aside from a shared experience, it could be argued that exchanging written words was the best way to get to the heart of someone. A search refined. The essential pieces narrowed down again and again until the truth could be neatly and efficiently extracted.

Jack and I had been texting for a while now, and he . . . knew me better than almost anyone, at least the current version of me. The one who was a little messy and heartsick, adrift in a way I didn't quite know how to reconcile.

Maybe it was silly of me to reread our messages to one another, to comb through all his favorite things. But when I considered last night and the ease with which I'd settled in here, I didn't think it was silly at all.

"What do you have going on today?" Jack asked politely after I'd been quiet for too long, lost in thought.

"Not much. I'll probably drop by my classroom and prep some projects for the week. Then I have trivia tonight at Trailview." *I have a stolen rabbit to check on, too*, I didn't add.

He paused with his coffee halfway to his lips. "I think my grandmother is on a trivia team there."

"Oh. Which one?"

"I'm not sure," he said thoughtfully. "I just found out about it."

I briefly considered prying, but I knew that Jack was private as well as protective of his grandmother. What we'd done last night had been pretty intimate, but somehow I didn't think that sex automatically qualified me for personal details.

"Well, I'm sure her team routinely kicks our butt. Mac is usually so focused on beating Brady that she gets so distracted our team usually loses or gets kicked out because of their bickering."

He smiled and finally took a sip. "They play on opposing teams even though they're dating."

"Oh yeah." I shook my head, recalling their antics. "It's a whole thing. They're hypercompetitive nutballs. I think it reminds them of when they hated each other, but in a fun way. Or maybe they just like the trash talk. Either way. I'll be at Trailview later attempting to answer trivia questions until Mac gets us disqualified."

Jack laughed, lines deepening on his stubble-covered cheeks.

Silence descended as we drank our coffee. He didn't reach for his book again, and I felt the weight of all that attention focused on me.

I'd had sex with this person, and now I wasn't sure what to say as we sat next to one another in his living room.

Despite the awkwardness, I was grateful. He'd taken my request in stride, and, more than that, he'd taken care of me, made sure I'd enjoyed myself. I'd *more* than enjoyed myself.

"Hey," I said abruptly.

Perhaps he read my intent or knew me well enough to expect the words that were about to fly out of my mouth, because Jack's eyes narrowed and he interrupted, "Don't. Do not thank me for last night."

My mouth snapped shut audibly.

Gaze intent, Jack uncrossed his legs, placed his mug on the table, and leaned forward. He snagged my free hand and held on tight. "The same way I don't want your apologies, Clyde, I do not want your gratitude. You had fun, right? Last night?"

My cheeks burned. "Yes," I managed, voice a mortified choke.

"So did I. We're friends, like you said. Let's just keep having fun."

I nodded. It sounded simple when he said it like that.

He hadn't been lying last night. We'd been up for hours, exploring and tasting, getting comfortable with each other's skin. I'd asked for what I needed and accepted what he'd offered. No strings or expectations. Jack had made it his mission to wring every ounce of pleasure from me until I'd collapsed in a boneless heap sometime around three thirty.

He'd been intense and focused but also gentle and fun. We'd laughed over awkward positions, and he'd teased me over the scratch marks I'd left on his backside. I felt connected to him in a way I couldn't explain with words. That was the magic of intimacy. It turned you into different people, the kind who were unknowable to anyone outside your perfect bubble.

Honestly, I wasn't sure where we went from here, so I was glad he'd addressed it head-on. I'd like more nights like last night. More of Jack's unwavering attention, his rough stubble on my skin, his strength combined with tenderness, the rough sounds he'd made when I'd touched him, and the feel of him all around me.

But then my attention snagged on the wrinkles of my dress. I'd be leaving here in the same outfit I'd arrived in yesterday. I thought about how I'd parked my car two blocks away from Magnolia to save us both from the rumor mill. I wasn't ready for what everyone would say about me this soon after my divorce. Plus, I got the impression that Jack didn't really date, so I didn't want to cause trouble for him. He'd had to deal with enough gossip over the years.

"That sounds good. To keep having fun," I clarified. Then I added quickly, just to dispel any fears he may have, "And I'm fine keeping this just between you and me."

A beat passed, and I wondered if I'd misread the situation.

"Of course," he replied after a moment.

I frowned. I'd thought for a second there'd been something on his face. An emotion, there and gone before I could identify it.

Jack brought my hand to his lips, pressing a kiss to the inside of my wrist. Then his grin turned roguish, the devil peeking through bright hazel eyes and gold-rimmed glasses. "Can I interest you in a tour before you go?"

My brows furrowed in confusion. "A tour?"

"Yeah. You saw the bathroom last time—mostly the floor." He grinned. "But I don't think you got a good look at the shower."

Realization dawned. "Oh, well. I'd hate to think I missed something. Is this a guided tour?"

He nodded sagely before standing and pulling me with him. "Very intimate. Highly personalized. Just you and your tour guide."

Heat and anticipation became an insistent tug. A pleasant warmth shimmered across my skin, like a hot afternoon in the middle of summer. The lure of Jack in the shower was undeniably inviting. Wet hair, slick skin, and the promise I read in his eyes was more temptation than I could resist.

So I didn't bother trying.

I slid closer to him, bringing our bodies flush before saying without a whisper of uncertainty, "Lead the way."

BONNIE

There were times in my life when staying busy had kept me going.

After the separation, for example. I'd buried myself in work and end-of-the-year school activities. There'd also been the months—years—when Danny and I had been trying for a baby. I'd needed to keep myself occupied after all those negative pregnancy tests.

I was the sort of person who found it necessary to have reminders, reasons to put one foot in front of the other in order to maintain my sanity. Those came in the shape of volunteering or extracurriculars, helping my mom or my aunt, baking, donating my time and energy, participating in farm events, those sorts of things.

And right now, it was sort of nice to be so busy and occupied. I hadn't really had time to freak out about Jack or my relationship with him. In the last few weeks, there'd been little free time to question my sanity or my decision-making. I was, truthfully, still riding the high of sex with Jack and showering with Jack and coffee with Jack, and getting knowing looks from Jack.

I'd left his apartment the previous Monday after a thorough tour of the shower. One that had my front pressed to the cold tiles while Jack pushed into me from behind. I'd left with wet hair and a big smile on my face.

Tuesday afternoon, I'd visited Diane and Eldridge again. I'd brought my former mother-in-law her favorite fried chicken from Roosters in Asheville, hoping she'd be able to eat. We'd had a good visit, and I was grateful they hadn't mentioned my plans to Danny. I knew they hadn't because he'd been texting me, asking when I'd like to go back over to see his mom. Annoyed, I'd ignored the messages.

Wednesday brought bowling league play. I'd been able to enjoy my time with Mac and Candace and Joan while also sneaking in some texts to Jack.

Thursday night had Jack and I facing off on the softball field once again. Only this time, I'd had fun with the flirty looks and the knowing smirks. Afterward, I'd followed him to his apartment and stayed over. We'd gotten up early for coffee and Pop-Tarts before I'd needed to be at school Friday morning.

I'd spent Saturday with Jack. Another long ride and a sunny day on the back of his bike. We'd gone east this time, through Miller Creek and beyond, stopping at a brewery to have lunch and listen to a band play. I'd stayed over again, liking the excitement and anticipation of being in his space.

This week had been just as busy. But between school, trivia night, and dinner with Mac and Brady, I'd found time to text Jack throughout the day and following his shifts at Magnolia.

Currently, it was Friday evening, and I was looking forward to my monthly book club night. Becca typically hosted out at the homestead, but it was Chloe's birthday, so we'd decided to celebrate a little. I'd asked Kayla to reserve us an out-of-the-way booth at Magnolia, and arrived early so she could hide a cake for me in the walk-in refrigerator. The upscale tourist bar wasn't our usual hangout spot. In fact, I could count on one hand how many times I'd been there over the years. But I thought the change of scenery might be nice, though. And if I was being honest, I wanted to see Jack in his element.

The man in question watched Kayla disappear into the back with a decorated Japanese cheesecake in hand before moseying over my way.

"This is a surprise," he said casually as he wiped down the bar. His forearms flexed, the tattoos shifting on his skin as he moved. My mind got a little distracted remembering how those forearms had looked as he'd braced himself over me in bed.

Ignoring the heat flooding my cheeks, I smiled reassuringly. "Don't worry. I'm not here to drink my weight in beer and cause trouble."

Jack's eyes sparkled.

"We're having our book club meeting," I offered. "And celebrating Chloe's birthday." I frowned, considering, then lowered my voice. "I'm sorry. Should I have cleared that with you? I didn't mean to ambush you at work."

He gave me a flat, irritated look.

"Right," I backtracked. "I take back the apology."

Satisfied, he replied, "Of course, you don't need to clear things with me. You can come by whenever you want."

"You're sure?"

He stopped wiping and pinned me with another stare. "I'm sure, Clyde. You don't owe me anything."

My lips parted in confusion. I didn't like the sound of that. But before I could argue or object, I heard the rowdy voices of my friends arriving.

Jack's eyes shifted to the door behind me. "You ladies get settled. I'll come over in a minute and get you some drinks."

Then he walked farther down the bar, and I couldn't pinpoint why I felt so disappointed.

With a final glance his way, I wrangled my group and led them toward our booth.

Chloe, the birthday girl, was accompanied by my sister, Mac, and our cousin Laramie—known as Larry to nearly everyone. We'd grown up with Larry. She'd been a permanent fixture for sleepovers and family vacations, along with our other cousin, Will. Mac and Larry were both outspoken and a little wild. It was no surprise that they were best friends as well as cousins. All of us were close in age and had grown up on the farm. As adults, I was the lone exception, finding work outside the family business.

Chloe had been in the same grade as Will and was married to his best friend. She'd also started working at the farm a few years ago as a bakery assistant to my aunt Maggie. Chloe was a sweetheart, and we all loved her.

The small group was trailed by the rest of our book club attendees. Becca and Candace were chatting about something, bright smiles on both their faces. Candace's older sister, Joan, brought up the rear as she eyed her surroundings with suspicion. Probably wondering how many tourists she'd have to deal with as a result of our choice of locale.

"Hi, birthday girl," I said, welcoming Chloe with a big hug.

She grinned, blue eyes alight. "Thank you, Bonnie. This is so great. I appreciate you setting things up. Making my day special."

"Happy to," I replied, meaning it.

"Classy, Bon," Larry called, flashing a thumbs-up.

"Yeah," Mac added. "I'm a little worried we'll get kicked out of the fancy-schmancy leafer bar."

"Then you'll just have to be on your best behavior," Becca teased as she scooted into the center of the booth. "It should be pretty easy without Brady around."

That earned a few laughs.

Mac gave her a mischievous grin. "I make no promises."

"He'll probably be by later anyway," Candace stated as she joined Becca in the circular corner booth. "He's with Mark and Jordan and Will down at Mattie B's. They're our designated drivers. We are here to celebrate Chloe, possibly to excess."

Good for them, but I would not be overindulging. Not after the last time I'd embarrassed myself here.

The six of us got settled in the booth with our bags and various gifts for Chloe, chatting and carrying on several conversations between us.

"Okay, I want to know what y'all thought of the book," Larry announced, drawing our attention.

I wasn't surprised that she wanted to get right to our discussion. The book had been her pick. A why-choose hockey romance with three heroes and one very sexually satisfied heroine.

Becca, Candace, and Mac started talking at once while I laughed and Joan covered her face.

Larry had just very loudly said, "I thought I was going to die when they started going at it in the locker room after winning the championship. And with their skates still on. That's some athleticism right there," when Jack walked up to grab our drink order.

"Hi, Jack!" Becca called brightly.

Mac tried to smother her laughter but wasn't terribly successful. In fact, most of the women looked highly amused at the, frankly, fearful look on Jack's face.

His gaze found mine in an expression that clearly telegraphed *What the fuck?* before he mumbled out, "I'll give you ladies some more time."

Then he turned and bolted back behind the bar.

Giggles erupted, including mine as Larry looked around in confusion. "What? Was it something I said?"

"Yes, you heathen," Mac said, whacking Larry on the shoulder. "You scared him off. Bonnie, you're on the end. Will you go to the bar and order some drinks, please?"

"Yep, I can do that."

We decided on some champagne to toast Chloe.

Jack was busy when I arrived. So I slid onto a leather stool—my stool, if I remembered correctly—and waited.

He approached cautiously, and a laugh burst out of me.

"We're really ruining the vibe of this place, aren't we?" I finally managed through my giggles.

His gaze warmed as he watched me get a hold of my amusement. "Nah. You were actually very popular the last time you were here."

"I was?"

"Oh yeah," he said. "A whole fan club and everything. You don't remember them cheering for you?"

"What?" I sat up, alarmed. "No!"

Jack chuckled and then slung a towel over his shoulder. He leaned in close, those distracting forearms resting on the smooth bar top between us. "What *do* you remember from that night?"

My eyes searched the immediate area like I might find the answers—or my memories—floating around somewhere. But there were only liquor bottles lining the wall behind the bar and warm bulbs dangling from a modern light fixture above our heads.

"Not a whole lot, actually," I admitted, attention focused on the wood grain in front of me. "A Long Island iced tea when I got here. Chatting with some people at the bar."

I remembered not feeling well at one point. Then that vague craving for the Indian restaurant down the street. And then all the things I didn't want to admit. The flashes of memory from Jack's apartment. His quiet words. The brush of his fingers against my temple. My tears on his jeans.

"Hey," Jack said, tipping my chin up to look at him. "You don't have to beat yourself up about that. It's behind you, right?"

I nodded, forcing away all the tangled *what-ifs*. All the things that could have gone wrong that night. The way I'd been reckless with my safety.

"What can I get you and your troublemakers over there?" he asked, making me smile.

His finger was still under my chin, making it hard to concentrate for a completely different reason. "A round of champagne to celebrate the birthday girl, please."

"I'll bring it over. You go have fun." His thumb swiped my chin softly before he released me to my friends.

Drinks and discussion continued amid lots of laughter. Kayla brought out Chloe's cake and served it while we sang "Happy Birthday." The tourists at nearby tables joined in, and a few even sent drinks over for us as the celebration went on.

A while later, Candace checked her watch and did her best to call everyone to order. She let us know that for our next meeting we would be reading a very popular romance book that had recently been adapted into a movie. We were planning to have our monthly book club discussion and then go see the movie together in November.

Joan groaned. "I think I'll sit this one out."

"What? Why?" Becca asked.

"Yeah, it has that hot guy in it playing the lead," Mac said diplomatically. "What's his name?"

"Dorian Masters," Chloe supplied.

"Yesss," Candace said. "He *is* hot. Come on, Joanie. It'll be fun."

Her sister rolled her eyes. "I do not have time for some pretty-boy movie star who's just going to ruin one of the greatest romance heroes of all time."

Larry and Mac booed while Becca tried her best to cajole Joan into going.

Eventually, Candace drew our attention her way again. "Okay, two more announcements." Then she seemed to hesitate before a huge grin took over her face. We all quieted and waited expectantly. "Mark proposed! We're getting married in December at the orchard. We don't want to wait."

Our group erupted again with well-wishes and delight. Larry hooted when Candace showed us the ring, which she was wearing on a chain around her neck until it could be sized. Becca was teary with happiness. Joan had a soft expression on her face while she watched her sister. And I was so very glad for my friend.

Candace and Mark Mercer were going to be ridiculously happy together.

More champagne arrived, and we toasted the happy couple.

I didn't really hear Candace's second announcement because I got distracted. I watched as Chloe clinked her glass with everyone before placing the flute down on the table without taking a drink. I frowned as she gave Larry, who was seated beside her, a gentle nudge with her elbow. The other woman reached out, quick as a flash, and snagged the glass before downing the contents. She gave Chloe a subtle wink as she put the empty flute back in front of her. Chloe returned the gesture with a grateful smile.

I forced my gaze away before anyone realized. It wasn't my intention to make Chloe feel awkward or obligated to share if she wasn't ready. Maybe I was wrong. Maybe Chloe wasn't pregnant, but it was the first thing that came to mind after witnessing her behavior. I couldn't remember seeing her drink anything besides water tonight, come to think of it.

If my suspicions were true, she and Jordan would be amazing parents. And I was happy for my friend.

So I couldn't figure out why the knowledge settled like a stone in my chest. Excited chatter continued around the table, but I couldn't focus. It seemed that so much was changing. Our little group was evolving. Larry was dating someone seriously for the first time in her life. Mac and Brady were nearly inseparable. Now, Candace and Mercer were getting married. From the looks of things, a baby would be on the way soon for Jordan and Chloe.

And I'd changed too, hadn't I?

I was divorced and starting over.

For so long, I'd been the only one of my friends in a committed relationship. I'd assumed the role of married woman. Being the responsible one, arranging events, giving advice, and planning celebrations.

Now I was single again, and miles away from where I expected to be at this point in my life. So far away, in fact, that I felt like I was going backward instead of forward.

"I'm going to get some more drinks," I said, standing abruptly.

I didn't even wait for anyone to respond. I just walked to the bar, eager for an escape and overwhelmed by my conflicting emotions.

I jolted when a hand reached for my elbow.

"Sorry!" Candace said immediately. "You took off so fast. I wanted to ask if you'd like to be a bridesmaid, but . . ." She wavered, and I hated myself a little more for making my friend feel the need to hesitate, to ration her happiness because I was such a damn mess. "I was worried. I didn't want you to feel weird or obligated."

"Of course I'll be a bridesmaid," I gushed, so touched and honored that she wanted me by her side on her big day. "It's not weird, and I would never feel obligated. You and Mercer deserve to be happy, and I want to be there to celebrate with you," I told her honestly as I reached out and pulled her into a fierce hug. "You're going to be the most beautiful bride. I can already see it."

Candace leaned back, eyes shining with happiness. "Thanks, Bonnie. And thanks for saying yes."

Emotion threatened. I smiled, grateful that my friend had found someone so worthy of her love. Mercer was a good man. She was safe with him. Safe to build a life together, a marriage and a family. Something that would last.

She squeezed my arm gently before heading back the way she'd come.

I took a deep breath and faced the bar, telling myself to put one foot in front of the other.

I hated feeling like this. It was weak and pathetic to be . . . I didn't even want to think the word.

Jealous.

I was jealous of my friends—people I loved.

How could I be both happy for them and envious at the same time? It was proof that I was a terrible person. That I couldn't just celebrate with everyone else. That I'd felt compelled to get away.

Jack caught sight of me right away, and whatever he read on my face had him frowning.

"Hey," he said, rounding the bar and coming toward me. "What happened?"

I had no idea what to say. Shame kept my tongue glued to the roof of my mouth.

Jack's hazel eyes watched me worriedly. But I wasn't in danger of having an anxiety attack. This was a different sort of breakdown.

I felt weary, in my heart, down to my bones. And so damn disappointed in myself.

"Bonnie," he tried again, voice soft and coaxing. "What do you need?"

There it was again. That question. Need versus want. Jack's choice of words might not have made a difference to him, but it meant something to me.

"I just need a minute," I eventually got out.

He glanced briefly toward our table before focusing on me. Then he held out a hand.

I laced our fingers together and let him lead me toward the back of the bar, past high-top tables and a row of booths. We entered a hallway. A door on the left marked the men's room, while a doorway was open on the right.

Inside, there was a small foyer with dark wallpaper in black-and-gold geometric patterns. A door on the far side was for the women's restroom, while the door closest to us was labeled "Powder Room."

Jack tugged me toward the powder room and, once he'd noted it was empty, guided me inside and closed the door behind us. He removed a ring of keys from his pocket, locking the door from the inside.

It was quiet, the change in location enough to have my shoulders relaxing. There was a long counter beneath a mirror. Baskets of products occupied the space as well as a vase of flowers, boxes of tissues, and bottles of lotion. Two couches lined adjacent walls with a low footstool in between.

"What is this place?" I asked as I ran a hand across the soft upholstery of the couch.

Jack shifted uncomfortably, drawing my attention. "Initially, it was for Sasha. After she had the baby, she needed a place to pump while she was on shift."

"That was really thoughtful of management."

He pressed a hand along his jaw awkwardly, like the thought of talking about a woman breastfeeding made him itchy. I fought a smile.

"Yeah," he agreed, "afterward it became a powder room. The tourists seem to like it."

Now that I'd gotten a good look at the place, I thought Larry had mentioned it. She spent more time at Magnolia than the rest of us on account of Kayla being her best friend since childhood. She often visited her friend while she was bartending.

I eyed the couch thoughtfully. "It is really nice. I think Larry passed out in here once."

"What?"

"Nothing. Never mind," I chirped.

The change of scenery had definitely distracted me from the wild emotions surging through me. My conflicting feelings were still there, but they weren't in danger of spilling out all over the people I loved—people who would be hurt, if they saw the truth.

"Thanks for bringing me here," I said.

Jack sat on the ottoman and patted the couch before him in invitation. "Do you want to talk about it?"

I took a seat, and he wrapped a warm hand around my calf. The touch beneath the hem of my flowy skirt was grounding and welcome. But I didn't think I could admit my failings and discuss why I'd been so rattled moments ago.

"I think it was just too much," I admitted instead. "I felt overwhelmed. I don't know."

He nodded, accepting my vague explanation.

My eyes lingered on him, the glasses he wore, and the few dark strands that had come loose from his tiny stub of a ponytail at the nape of his neck. Combined with the slim-fitting white dress shirt and the sleeves rolled up to expose his forearms, the tattoos there, he looked positively sinful. The studious rogue. A wicked fantasy.

"You're staring," Jack accused, his lips twitching.

I resisted the urge to cover my face. "It's the glasses. They . . . do things to me."

"The glasses?" he asked incredulously.

I jolted as the hand beneath my skirt moved behind my knee. "Yes!"

"I didn't realize you were into reading glasses, Clyde. These eyes are from the 1900s, you know. I need them to see."

"You're hot, okay?" I managed through my laughter.

He snorted.

"And, now," I added, "I know what you look like *naked*." I whispered the final word.

Jack rolled his eyes, but he was smiling widely. "Is that going to be too distracting for you?" He gasped dramatically. "Were you picturing me naked while we were playing softball yesterday?"

I laughed, and he grabbed my hand before I could cover my mouth.

"You're out of control," he teased. "I'm more than just slutty little glasses and a man-bun."

My giggles had me bending forward, collapsing into Jack's arms. "You're ridiculous," I managed through my laughter, suddenly amazed that he could draw out this happiness when I'd been so lost and adrift moments ago, trapped in a minefield of my own making.

Eyes alight, Jack encouraged me forward, onto his lap. I came willingly, straddling his thighs and draping my arms across his firm shoulders.

"That's alright," he said, the hushed words ghosting across my lips. "You can objectify me."

"Oh, yeah?" I breathed as desire clenched low in my belly at our proximity and his teasing.

"Sure. It's only fair. I'm imagining you naked right now." He paired the admission with a firm squeeze to my backside.

He grinned as he leaned in, pressing his lips to mine. The kiss flared into existence, hot and incendiary in an instant.

I sucked on Jack's tongue, groaning as his busy fingers worked their way up my skirt. Rough palms smoothed the length of my thighs before he cupped my center over my underwear.

Despite being locked in our own little bubble, I was conscious of being in a public place. I knew I couldn't be too loud, and part of me worried about Jack.

After a firm bite to my bottom lip, he retreated. "What's wrong? You got all tense. Do you want me to stop?"

"No," I panted, breath embarrassingly short after what we'd done. "I just don't want you to get fired."

Jack's expression fought valiantly between confusion and amusement. "You—you don't want me to get fired?"

"I don't want to get you in trouble. You're supposed to be working."

He sighed, but his hazel eyes sparkled. Then, as he spoke, his thumb found my clit and started circling. "I can't get fired. I'm in charge tonight, okay. You don't have to worry about me."

I nodded quickly, distracted by his thumb but also trying to focus on his words. He couldn't get fired. That was good. I guessed he was managing Magnolia tonight or something. "Okay."

He grinned. "Now, can I get back to getting you off? You are really ruining the naughty thing we have going on here."

"Sure," I replied, fighting a moan. "Sorry. I just couldn't get into the moment if I thought you were going to get in trouble."

"I know. You're such a good girl."

My lips parted at his words, a flush blooming beneath my skin.

"We'll explore that later." And then he was kissing me deeply, at the same time he swept my underwear aside and plunged two fingers deep inside me.

His mouth muffled the sounds fighting to get free as my hips pumped in time with his thrusts. And still, his thumb worked against that tiny bundle of nerves, driving me mad.

"Yes," I gasped, breaking our kiss. I bowed my head and pressed my forehead to his shoulder as I moved on top of him, desperate and seeking.

The scruff on his jaw was rough against the sensitive skin of my neck and collarbone, but I loved the feel of it, making all my nerve endings come alive. So, so alive.

"That's it," Jack murmured, voice low and raw. "Take what you need. That's my good girl."

My inner muscles clamped down on his fingers while his thumb finally gave me the pressure I needed. I was coming, my mouth firm against his fancy white shirt to stifle the low moan I couldn't stop.

After a moment, I leaned back and met his gaze. Eagerness was quickly replacing the loose, satisfied feeling in my limbs. I wanted to return the favor. So I reached for his belt, but Jack shook his head.

"You should get back before your friends come looking for you."

"Oh, right." I nodded awkwardly, disappointed that our time was up.

I wiggled back to try to stand, but Jack stopped me with a possessive hand on my thigh. "You want to stay over tonight? You could come with me to the soccer game in the morning."

I pretended to consider. "Will there be Pop-Tarts?"

He paused to consider. "That could be arranged."

I didn't know how to say how thankful I was for the way he'd taken control tonight and saved me in my moment of weakness. How he'd provided respite in the midst of my turmoil. The way he always seemed to know just what I needed, and if he didn't, he just came right out and asked. Something that seemed so simple, but was rare all the same.

It didn't matter that I couldn't find the words. Jack didn't want my gratitude anyway.

So I cupped his cheeks and kissed him instead. Something soft. A sweet press that lingered, saying what I couldn't.

Minutes later, I'd straightened my skirt and cleaned up, leaving Jack in the powder room so we could stagger our return to the bar area.

My friends were still at the table, talking and laughing. It was Becca who noticed my approach first. She smiled brightly as I slid into the booth.

"Bonnie, you're glowing." Then her eyes slid over my shoulder before widening.

I turned my head and watched Jack slip behind the bar, his gaze meeting mine briefly.

When I faced forward again, Becca had a gleeful expression on her face, and my stomach dropped. I opened my mouth, unsure if I should say anything at all or if that would just draw more attention to myself.

Panic must have been plain on my face because Becca's delight dimmed.

Before I could figure out how to salvage this, Mac called out, "Yeah, Bonnie always gets red-faced on wine. I'm the same way. I think it's a curse from our mother."

"Probably," I offered weakly.

"Oh, I get that way with tequila," Becca said helpfully, still smiling gently my way. And knowing the friendly woman, it was more in support than anything else. I had a feeling that if anyone could keep my secret, it would be her. "But that doesn't stop me from enjoying a margarita when the mood strikes." Then she winked.

I fought my laughter.

"Amen," Larry said.

"We should get margaritas!" Candace added.

"Great idea," Mac said, putting her hand up for a high five.

And I thought it was a very good thing that all of their significant others would be here soon to drive their drunk behinds home.

My gaze slid toward Jack at the bar.

After all, I had plans of my own.

thirteen

JACK

The Brookline U9 girls won their soccer game yesterday. Afterward, Brady and I had taken the team out for pizza to celebrate.

Bonnie hadn't made it to Apollo's with the rest of us. She'd said goodbye after the game, telling me to spend some time with my team.

The cynical, suspicious part of me thought she just didn't want anyone to see us together or to draw any conclusions about our sudden proximity.

Truthfully, I hadn't been all that surprised when Bonnie had asked that our friends-with-benefits arrangement stay between us. I knew how damn nosy the town was. They had their own Facebook group for gossip, for Christ's sake.

But I also knew that Bonnie was a consummate people pleaser. She had a reputation to uphold. Small-town school teacher mourning the love of her life and all that.

Maybe there'd been some weird disappointment regarding the secrecy, on my part. It was small and spiteful of me to take offense. I didn't have a problem with casual. All of my relationships with women had been short-lived, with absolutely zero expectations.

This felt different, though. Like Bonnie was ashamed. Embarrassed to have her friends and family find out she was sleeping with someone so soon after her divorce—someone like me. For some reason, knowing that Bonnie was sneaking around, parking blocks away from my apartment and hiding herself, made me feel dishonest and complicit in her deception. It wasn't something I ever anticipated bothering me.

Sure, we were just friends with benefits. Maybe what stung most was knowing that the *friends* part of our relationship was just as much of a secret as the benefits.

I wondered if she'd be as adamant for secrecy if that buttoned-up, khaki-pants-wearing principal had finally made a move. Maybe that guy was just biding his time, waiting for her rebound phase to wear off. Who knew? I was making a lot of unfounded assumptions.

Danny had shown up at Magnolia again last night. He'd bought drinks for various women, just like the last time. And an hour before closing, he'd found someone to take home. Something about watching him so brazenly live his life while his ex-wife felt the need to hide herself away made me irrationally irritated. Probably because I was the secret she felt she had to keep.

Bonnie had been a good girl her whole life. I could see how sneaking around and playing the part of the rebel might feel good for her now. Taking the former bad boy and small-town fuckup for a spin probably held some spite-fueled appeal.

My mind drifted to the good girl in question. She usually got annoyed when I called her that, but she definitely hadn't minded the night before last in the powder room at Magnolia. Yeah, she'd been into the sneaking-around part too. Maybe there was a latent wild streak in her after all.

She'd been eager and responsive to my touch, a willing participant in the little game we were playing. So damn sexy on my lap. Skin slick, cheeks flushed, moans muffled, and eyes wide and pleading as she'd come with my hand under her skirt. There was something about the way she looked at me. The want—no, the *need*—in her expression. The trust she placed in me. The honesty in those pretty brown eyes. I'd be lying if I said I didn't like it.

I'd delivered the fun she'd been looking for and the distraction. Then I'd sent her back to her table with her family and friends none the wiser. Back to the people who had no idea who she really was because she never let them see when she was weak or hurting. Bonnie was well-versed in hiding the vulnerable parts of herself.

She was hiding me, too. Like a liability. Just as troublesome and inconvenient as her emotions.

I shouldn't care. It shouldn't bother me.

For the first time in my life, I was someone's dirty little secret, and the knowledge wasn't as easy to shrug off as I thought it'd be.

"Hey, you okay?" Bonnie asked from the edge of the hallway, presumably where she'd emerged after cleaning up in the bathroom. Concern pinched her features.

"Yeah," I replied. "I'm good."

Jolted back to the present, I finished drying my hands on a kitchen towel. I wasn't sure how long I'd been standing there, lost in thought. Judging by the water droplets surrounding my feet, long enough.

It was Sunday afternoon, and I'd invited Bonnie over. She'd barely made it through the front door a half an hour ago before I'd pushed her up against it, taking her mouth in a hot, possessive kiss.

I'd been startled by how much I wanted her, unable to wait to get her into bed. Fucking her right there in my entryway. Her legs wrapped around my waist as I set a punishing pace that only had her yanking impatiently on the hair at the nape of my neck.

It was a rush to have her like that. The way she tasted and how good she felt. The sounds she made. How she didn't hide what she liked or what she wanted. Her responsiveness and the way she looked at me, always with a sense of wonder and sweetness. Like she was just as awed as I was that it felt this good every single time we were together.

Now, I watched her smile as she crossed to me in the kitchen.

She cupped my jaw and rose on her toes to press a kiss to my lips. "That was quite the welcome."

There was that sweetness again. It wrapped itself around me and squeezed.

"Too much?" I asked.

Her smile widened, eyes sparkling. "No, I liked it."

I placed my hands on her hips, thinking that maybe I'd been making assumptions based on my own insecurities. It could be that I was reading too much into the secrecy thing. There was something to be said for privacy. Maybe that was all she really wanted.

There was one way to find out.

"Are you hungry?" I asked. "Want to go grab some dinner? We could walk to the Indian bistro down the street."

I scrutinized her expression, bracing against my will as I awaited her response.

Bonnie hesitated, and I felt my jaw clench. I could practically see the gears turning as she considered her reply. I imagined her running through the ramifications. The gossip and rumors. What her perfect family might say. The people who would judge her for dating so soon, when her asshole ex has been picking up women for months. I watched the fear tighten her shoulders. And I fucking hated how much I cared.

"Um, could we get takeout instead?" she finally answered, voice quiet.

Well, now I knew.

I swallowed, making sure my voice was nice and even. "Sure."

Then I asked what she wanted and set about placing the order online for delivery.

Disappointment shimmered beneath a rising tide of anger. Irritation I didn't have any business feeling made itself known. Bonnie had made her terms clear, and I'd agreed.

I didn't play games, and I didn't get involved enough to have ulterior motives. So I didn't know what the fuck was wrong with me or why her rejection was bothering me so much. It was like she'd failed a pop quiz I'd sprung on her at the beginning of class. I was being unfair. But I couldn't do anything about my complicated emotions at the moment.

Bonnie drifted around my living room while I typed on my phone. Her sweater was still by the front door where she'd dropped it. She was barefoot in one of her long, jewel-toned skirts and a white camisole.

Unbothered, she lingered over one of my grandmother's watercolors while I stewed ten feet away, like an idiot. I'd seen Bonnie eyeing the landscapes around the apartment before. I figured it was the art teacher in her.

"Are these yours?" She caught my gaze over her shoulder.

"No." My tone was terse, and I worked to soften it, to relax all my bristling edges. After clearing my throat, I explained, "They're Lia's. The signature is probably cut off by the frame." Bonnie was studying one of my grandmother's earliest paintings and one of the first frames I'd made as a result. The craftsmanship was a little shoddy. I should probably replace it.

Bonnie stood on her tiptoes, examining the border. "Oh, yeah. I see it now." Then her voice shifted, the word emerging slowly, like she was coming out of a dream. "Magnolia."

I breathed out a sigh, knowing what she'd seen—what she'd realized.

I stared at the phone in my hand as quiet footsteps padded over to me. Soft fingers traced the delicate lines of my tattoo. From the blossoms shaded on my forearm and biceps to the flat, wide leaves weaving themselves in the space between. Bonnie's touch followed along.

"Lia is short for Magnolia," she said. Not a question.

I looked up, meeting her soft gaze as her hand concluded its exploration, fingers twining casually through my own. "It is."

"It's yours—the bar. You own it and you named it for her." Another statement, but this time it was laced with confusion.

Shifting uncomfortably, I pulled my hand free and took a step back. "Yeah, it's mine."

Bonnie watched me, that familiar little vee forming between her brows. "But no one knows?"

"It's not really a secret. No one has ever bothered to ask," I clarified. "They'd rather make assumptions."

And Bonnie had been pretty distracted with an impending anxiety attack at the one and only business owners' association meeting I'd attended.

"Why don't you just tell people?" Bonnie asked, still confused.

I huffed a humorless laugh. It wasn't that simple. Everyone supposed I was an overworked bartender, or if they paid attention, the manager on shift. I just didn't correct them. Seeing Bonnie's obvious surprise a moment ago was probably the reason I didn't broadcast it. It confirmed the fact that people made assumptions about me. What did she want me to do? Take out a billboard out on Highway 64?

"Why does it matter?" I said. "It's none of their business. Besides, to them, I'm just Georgia Ellis's screw-up kid. As worthless and wild as she was. They'd rather talk about what a fuckup I was in high school or how I should have been in jail for being a hellion."

"That was a long time ago, Jack." Her voice was gentle, like she was talking to someone unreasonable, an unruly child.

My jaw clenched. I wasn't irrational; I just knew that small minds and small towns didn't change.

"All I'm saying is," Bonnie added, "you don't have to hide that you own Magnolia or—"

"I don't hide it," I argued. "Most people are quick to assume and even quicker to judge."

Also, how dare Bonnie, of all people, criticize me about this? She hid herself every damn day of her life. From her friends and her family and her coworkers. From everyone.

Not from you, a traitorous little voice reminded me.

"Right, but you care," she accused. "This isn't some part-time job for you. You built Magnolia from the ground up. You love it. You named it after someone important to you. You're not just—"

"Just what?" I snapped when she abruptly cut herself off. "Just a bartender? Is that what you were going to say? Is being *just* a bartender not good enough for you, apple princess?"

Bonnie swallowed. "No, I didn't mean—"

My harsh laughter interrupted whatever apology she had locked and loaded. I could feel myself losing control of this conversation. How it had transformed, taking the shape of something private and painful that I didn't want to talk about. "Right. That's why I'm your dirty little secret. Slumming it with the low-life bartender until you manage to crawl out from rock bottom." Her face paled, but I kept right on going, intent on turning this around. To push until she was gone. Determined to destroy whatever quiet, secret thing we were building behind closed doors. "Your perfect family would hate to see you brought so low as to associate with the likes of me."

She fell back on her wounded-bird routine, shoulders hunched and voice hushed. "You don't even know them."

"Yeah, and whose choice is that?" I asked bitterly. "You sneak around with me because, God forbid, anyone sees you as a living, breathing adult woman. Safer to stay on that pedestal, isn't it? All while your piece-of-shit ex picks up tourists in my bar every weekend."

If she was pale before, it was nothing compared to the sickly pallor of her skin now. Bonnie looked gut-shot, stark and cold, and utterly stunned. She blinked quickly, and two tears beat a hasty path down her cheeks before she could scrub them away.

I should have known, I thought. That she wasn't over him. She wouldn't look like I'd just sucker punched her if she was really done with Danny. And why should I care about that? She was pretty damn honest when she was drunk on my bathroom floor weeks ago, saying she'd take him back if he wanted her. I couldn't imagine much had changed in the month or so since.

Still, something sharp twisted in my chest at the sight of those tears—at her obvious misery.

Bonnie turned without saying a word, hurrying toward the door.

I took a step—to what? Stop her? I didn't know. I shook my head, mad at myself for taking my frustration out on her. Bonnie didn't ask for this. We'd only been fucking for a few weeks, for Christ's sake. What was wrong with me? I watched her struggle to grab her things by the front door and hated myself a little more.

She left quietly, without a backward glance, shutting the door softly behind her. Even in her obvious hurt and anger, she couldn't just let herself slam a fucking door. Picture-perfect till the bitter end.

Thirty seconds later, and I was standing where she'd been, my hand hovering over the doorknob, thinking I should go after her and tell her I was sorry. Give her an apology of my own. Likely the only one between us that had ever been warranted.

Just as my fingers shaped themselves around the cool metal, a knock sounded from the other side.

Relief came swiftly as I flung the door wide. If she was back, even to argue, that was a good thing.

But that hope died as I met the wide, startled gaze of a delivery person holding the bag of takeout.

"Sorry," the kid murmured uncertainly. "I was just going to leave it."

I took the food without a word, forcing myself not to slam the door in the guy's face. It wasn't his fault, after all.

Nope. The only person I had to blame was myself.

Can we talk?

I'd sent the text two hours after Bonnie had left. I'd shoved the takeout in the fridge and gone for a long drive on my motorcycle, no destination in mind.

It was now Monday afternoon, and I was getting ready for my shift at Magnolia, and there was still no response.

Maybe she'd make this easy and just let it go. In the grand scheme of things, a few weeks with someone wasn't a big deal.

So I wasn't sure why I felt like I'd ruined something important.

I'd let my own screwed-up headspace mess things up, and then I'd lashed out at Bonnie for asking perfectly reasonable questions about my business. She'd just inadvertently pressed on a tender spot, one that was already bruised from the mental backflips I'd been doing.

I'd made a lot of mistakes over the years. Backed myself into plenty of corners. And there was nothing worse than starting a fight with someone you cared about when the only person you were battling was yourself.

Work went by fast. It was nearly a week before Halloween, and the leaves had hit their peak in Western North Carolina. Tourists were in town by the droves, and Magnolia was packed as a result. I ended up staying late to help Sasha and Kayla close up.

The first thing I did when the door was locked and the lights were off was check my phone. Still nothing from Bonnie.

I sighed, rubbing my forehead. Then I checked the time. 12:38 a.m.

It was late, but I could go over to her house. I knew her well enough to know that she'd probably be awake.

Mind made up, I slid my phone in my pocket and took the stairs up to my apartment two at a time. I'd change clothes and drive over, see if we could talk things out. Even if she didn't want anything to do with me, I didn't want it to end like this. I cared about her, probably more than was wise, and I couldn't stand the thought of those being the final words between us. That the last thing I ever did where Bonnie was concerned was to make her cry.

I was halfway up the flight of stairs before I registered the figure sitting at the top. My steps slowed, and my heart picked up at the sight of her blond head bent over a book on her lap. Regret settled in my middle alongside stark relief. She'd come. Bonnie hadn't written me off just yet.

She wore black sweatpants and an ancient college sweatshirt, fuzzy clogs on her feet. Her hair was pulled into a tiny knot on the top of her head.

At my shuffling steps, Bonnie lifted her head and met my gaze. Without looking away, she tucked a bookmark between the pages of her book and set it behind her on the landing.

"Hey," she said.

"Hey," I echoed, feeling shamefaced and heartsick all over again.

"I was already in panda mode when I decided to come over, and I didn't want to change," she explained, like that made any sense.

I closed the distance between us and sat next to her on the top step. "What is panda mode?"

"It's when I wear my most comfortable clothing and let myself relax. Usually, there are snacks involved, and I don't answer the phone. Laziness personified. A personal recharge. Unfortunately, you get the basic factory settings at the moment. No makeup or hair products. Just me. Although halfway over, I realized I probably should have put on a bra. Alas."

"Alas," I agreed, fighting a smile. "I'm glad you came. You didn't need to sit here all night, though."

Bonnie smiled down at her lap. "Don't worry. Bookworms generally don't mind an extended wait. It's where we do some of our best work."

Silence descended like a blanket over us. Despite an entire day spent thinking about what I wanted to say to Bonnie, I wasn't sure where to start. Sometimes you just had to start talking and let your brain catch up with your heart.

After a shaky breath, I admitted, "I'm really fucking sorry, Bonnie. I shouldn't have lashed out at you yesterday about the bar. It was stupid and immature. I'm sorry I hurt you to protect myself. It wasn't fair, and I regret it. And you asked for secrecy, and I agreed to it. I shouldn't have tried to punish you for it."

Bonnie nodded when I finished speaking. "I'm sorry too. And before you tell me to stop apologizing, I just want to say something here." She turned a little so she could face me. "Jack, I'm not ashamed to be seen with you. I'm not embarrassed or anything like that. I'm sorry if I ever made you feel like secrecy was more important to me than you are. There is a part of me—and you were right about this—that cares too much about what other people think. I didn't want nosy neighbors gossiping about me behind my back."

"You don't owe me anyth—"

"I do," she interrupted. "I do owe you an explanation. In the beginning, I just wanted—I wanted something for myself. Every interaction with you felt electric, a little buzz beneath my skin. Even when you irritated me or made fun of my muffins." She smiled at the memory of us bickering on the third-base line like it was something fond, and that made me ache even more. "I liked it. And I wanted to be selfish for once in my life. I wanted something that was just for me. I know how this town can be—judgmental and meddlesome—and I didn't want to scare you off."

Bonnie looked away following the admission, so I reached for her hand and squeezed, desperate for her to keep talking, suddenly grateful I'd been so wrong in my assumptions.

"I like you, Jack," she confessed, attention on our fingers braided together. "And I wasn't ready to let go of that control. It made me feel powerful, or at least like I held *some* power in the situation. Mostly because I was waiting for you to realize that I'm not worth the effort. I thought if I kept things easy breezy, in a way you were used to—casual, no commitment— that you might want to stick around."

I frowned, baffled that she possibly believed that to be true. "Bonnie."

Her smile was self-deprecating, but she finally met my gaze. "It's just hard for me to understand why someone like you wants anything to do with someone like me—someone boring and safe and a little broken."

"You're not broken," I insisted.

"Dented, then," she corrected with a humorless laugh. "On the clearance rack at the very least."

Her honesty and vulnerability made me want to wrap her in my arms and tell her about the woman *I* saw when I looked at her. The one with patience and love and understanding for everyone but herself. But I knew Bonnie wasn't in a place to have one more person discount her feelings. Men weren't put on this earth to prove women wrong. But I thought people forgot that, using their volume to drown each other out, when really all they needed to do was listen.

"I don't think you see yourself very clearly, Clyde," I said gently. "And I know you don't see me accurately."

But she shook her head. "I just keep waiting for you to remember that you're the coolest guy in school and I'm the mousey sophomore watching you from the window."

"You wouldn't have wanted to know me back then," I told her. I was sure I'd looked better from a distance. If she'd been close enough to be on my radar, I probably would have hurt her. I'd been young and stupid, on a path toward destruction, bound and determined. I would have taken her with me. "And we're not those people anymore, either one of us."

"You're right," she replied softly. "I think I keep trying to get back to the Bonnie I used to be, and too much has changed."

"You should try being the Bonnie you are now," I said, squeezing her fingers. "I think she's pretty great."

Her cheeks went a little pink, but she didn't argue. "We can be as public as you want to be. I'm not trying to pressure you or—or make you my boyfriend or something. I'm fine with casual. But we can be done with hiding. If you want."

"Okay," I agreed. "I'd like that."

I'd never been with someone long enough to have an argument, much less reach a resolution to one. There was something to be said for honesty and communication. I was glad Bonnie hadn't just given up on me and moved on. Grateful that she'd given me the chance to apologize for my shitty behavior.

"And I like basic factory settings," I said earnestly. "We should panda mode together sometime."

She grinned over at me.

"Or does that break the rules?" I asked. "Do you need to be alone to recharge? Would that still fill your bucket?"

Bonnie pressed her lips together like she was trying not to laugh. Then she confessed, "I really want to make a joke about you *filling my bucket*."

I burst out laughing.

She smiled and assured me, "But we can do panda mode together whenever you want."

"Yeah?"

"Sure." She nodded. "Do you have gray sweatpants?"

"Is that required?"

Her brown eyes sparkled. "No, just encouraged."

"I know it's late and you have work in the morning, but do you want to come in? I haven't had dinner yet. Thought we could heat up a midnight snack. I have samosas."

"Those are my favorites."

I stood and pulled her with me.

Fighting my own laughter, I replied, "Yeah. I know."

BONNIE

"Bonnie, can you check the pantry for more corn syrup?"

"Sure thing," I called to my mom, already making my way across the kitchen.

My family was gathered at my uncle William and aunt Maggie's farmhouse for our annual Halloween celebration. It was Friday, and the holiday was tomorrow. There would be trick-or-treating on Main Street, where Grandpappy's had a booth along with many other local businesses. But today was for family.

This was one of my favorite get-togethers. Every year, we prepped popcorn balls for the trick-or-treaters and drank apple cider. There was also a slew of Halloween-themed appetizers that everyone contributed, potluck-style. The central kitchen island contained the spread, and we generally grazed like farm animals throughout the evening.

Brady, Becca, and I were helping my mom and aunt with the popcorn balls while Mac and Will nibbled on mummy-wrapped pigs in a blanket, ghost roast beef sammies with melted mozzarella cheese, and a variety of other tasty apps.

Larry emerged from the living room, where my dad and uncle were watching a football game. Her girlfriend followed a moment later.

My cousin had come out to the family a couple of months ago. She'd nervously announced that she was bisexual at a family dinner and followed that up with the news that she was dating a photographer from Greenville. We'd been pretty stunned but ultimately supportive. It had been a long time since Larry had brought anyone around, and we were excited to see her happy.

She and her girlfriend, Corie, made their way to the slow cooker in the corner of the kitchen and refilled their cups with spiced apple cider.

"I've never had a popcorn ball," Corie said as she observed the assembly-line process we had going on.

I was in charge of popping the popcorn in the old-fashioned stovetop pot with a hand crank. My mom and Maggie were making the syrup on the burner next to mine. Once the popcorn was popped, I passed it off to Becca, who drizzled each batch with the sweet marshmallow syrup and tossed it together in a huge mixing bowl. Then Brady got to work in his food-prep gloves to shape the coated popcorn into balls before it cooled and set.

The countertops were lined with wax paper and a little army of popcorn-ball treats. Once we finished, we'd wrap them individually and tie them off with some orange-and-black ribbon I'd picked up at the arts and crafts store.

"Well, go on and try one, sugar," Aunt Maggie told Corie.

"Maggie's recipe is the best," Larry offered, reaching for one of the cooled treats as Brady playfully batted her hands away.

I dropped off the new bottle of corn syrup with my mom before resuming my position at the stove.

"Oh wow," Corie mumbled through a mouthful of sticky Halloween treat. "That's so good. Sweet and salty. I love it."

"I'm so glad, Corie, honey." Maggie beamed. The quickest way to my aunt's heart was to compliment her cooking. "And we're so happy to have you join us tonight."

Corie smiled shyly and tucked a strand of dark hair behind one ear. "Well, Larry made it sound like so much fun. Definitely worth the drive. I just love it up here. The farm is beautiful. And so is your home. I appreciate you welcoming me."

Events with the rowdy Clark bunch could sometimes be a trial by fire, but Corie had held her own tonight amid the ruckus. And anyone could see that she made my cousin happy. Larry had always been confident and outgoing, but she seemed softer and more playful with Corie at her side.

I remembered what it was like to have someone to share a smile or a look with at these family get-togethers. To have someone to grab you a drink or to touch your back in a casual brush as they walked by. A partner to check in on you to make sure you were good. Danny hadn't been that for me in a long time. In the end, he was mostly looking for excuses to get out of family dinners, or he'd be glued to his phone and distracted the whole time. But in the early days, he'd been happy to be here. It had been several years ago, but at one time, we'd had fun being the duo responsible for wrapping up the popcorn balls.

I watched as Larry stole a bite from Corie's treat before smiling softly to myself. Then I went back to spinning the popcorn around and around.

We were on the last batch of kernels when Larry piped up out of nowhere, "So, Bonnie, a little birdie mentioned they saw you yesterday."

"Oh yeah?" I asked, my voice casual. I knew where this was going.

I peeked over my shoulder and saw everyone watching me expectantly as Larry feigned nonchalance and reached for a cracker. God, my family was predictable. They'd probably already discussed this in a group chat and made Larry their representative to bring it up. I nearly laughed.

"I didn't know you'd taken up motorcycle riding," Larry said.

I kept my attention on the popcorn popper. "Yeah, it's pretty recent."

"You taking lessons or something?"

I bit my lip to keep from smiling. My nosy family members had obviously heard about my afternoon ride with Jack yesterday.

Since we'd decided to date—hang out, whatever—out in the open, I hadn't made a big deal about his invitation to hit the road after school. Jack had the night off, and it had been one of the last mild days we'd likely have for some time.

And I'd be lying if I said I hadn't gotten a little thrill when Jack had taken the long way to the parkway—the one that took us straight through the center of town, where any number of people would have seen us. Helmets didn't hide much in a small town, especially when the residents were motivated by gossip and running their mouths.

I thought about Jack's hand casually wrapped around my calf at the last stoplight on Main Street and fought a blush as I poured the rest of the freshly popped popcorn into the bowl.

"No formal lessons," I finally replied. "But if I'm spending time with Jack Ellis, I figure I'll pick up some pointers in case I want to get my own bike someday."

It wasn't a lie, but I didn't really have any plans to switch out my reliable sedan for something with two wheels. I mostly liked riding with Jack, but I wouldn't turn my nose up if he wanted to teach me how to drive.

Becca was waiting to accept the large mixing bowl so she could finish up her own part of the popcorn-ball process. Her worried blue gaze landed heavily on mine, but I gave her a reassuring smile and a pat on the arm.

I turned to face Larry and the others. Their expressions ranged from delighted (Larry) to curious (Brady) to visibly concerned (Mac) to perpetually grumpy (Will). "Before you chickens get all worked up, I'm fine. Jack and I are seeing each other, but it's pretty casual." I was proud of myself for not stumbling over the claim. It was true, but laid-back wasn't really in my wheelhouse. Their approval would always mean something to me, and the apprehension was stamped clearly across their faces. But I was trying my best, and that's what counted. "We're adults, and you don't need to worry."

Maggie shared an uneasy glance with my mother, but they didn't comment, and for that, I was grateful.

"Jack seems nice," Becca said sweetly.

"Yeah," Brady agreed. "He doesn't know anything about soccer, but he's great with the girls."

"You could do worse," Larry offered magnanimously.

I rolled my eyes.

"It doesn't matter what we think," Mac said, drawing my attention and everyone else's. "Bonnie's a grown woman and she knows what's best for her."

Warmth flooded the tiny cracks in my heart. It meant a lot that my sister, who'd been hovering and overbearing at times since my separation, was supporting me in this.

Then she went and said, "Plus, it couldn't hurt for you to have a little fun for once. And that man looks like he's capable of providing it."

Larry cackled.

Sighing, I gave Mac a pointed glare that she ignored, grinning widely and blowing me a kiss.

Conversation resumed, my family loud and opinionated once more.

Without really meaning to, I watched these people who'd loved and supported me throughout my life, and wondered how Jack might fit in.

My eyes caught on Corie, the newcomer, who'd been warmly welcomed and seemed comfortable with her new surroundings.

Would Jack fare as well? Or would so much togetherness be too much for someone who'd never had an extended family? Would the well-meaning nosiness put his back up, or would he be comfortable after a time? I could picture him in the background, quiet and watchful. Maybe out on the deck helping my dad or uncles or Will man the grill. But I could also imagine him chipping in, letting my aunt or mother direct him in the kitchen, charming them all the while.

It didn't matter. We weren't—we weren't like that. Things were casual and straightforward. You didn't force your hookup to spend holidays with your family. That had a way of complicating matters.

So I put any daydreams or imaginings out of my mind and focused on wrapping up the popcorn balls.

"You okay?" Becca asked quietly from where she'd joined me, already snipping lengths of ribbon and stacking them neatly at my elbow.

"Of course," I said, swallowing awkwardly.

"Because you don't owe anyone an explanation about you and Jack. If you're happy, that's all that matters."

Becca was a rare bird. She was sweetness and light and had fit in seamlessly with the Clarks, despite having a completely different experience with her own family growing up. Maybe that was why. She'd fallen in love with my family right along with my cousin Will. That sort of love was something she'd been missing, and we'd been happy to provide it.

I appreciated her kindness and comfort. She would have likely kept my secret for as long as I wanted her to. And I was grateful for that, too.

"I know," I assured her. "But it was silly to hide things, and I was doing it for the wrong reasons. It doesn't really matter what this town thinks of me. If they're going to judge me for moving on, then they might as well just go ahead and get it over with. Their opinions aren't the ones that matter anyway."

Becca grinned. "Amen."

Everyone pitched in, and we finished up our Halloween prep pretty quickly. I spent the next hour chatting with my family and eating copious amounts of dips and desserts. I took some time to get to know Corie and learned about her freelance photography business.

It was a good night.

Made that much better after I climbed in my car and pulled out my phone.

Jack: Okay, hypothetically, if I decided to contact Eloise Carter and agree to hand out candy tomorrow on Main Street, would you be interested in joining me?

I smiled and started typing.

Me: Hypothetically, I would be amenable.

I'd planned to help out at the Grandpappy's tent, but they didn't really need me. It would be a low-key evening as long as they didn't run out of treats. Two people could easily handle the booth, and there would be way more than enough Clarks present and accounted for.

Jack: You sure you don't have plans?

Me: There's nowhere I'd rather be than in costume with you in front of Magnolia. Surrounded by candy. Don't forget that part.

Jack: Costumes?

I huffed an incredulous laugh.

Me: It's Halloween. Of course, costumes.

Jack: For the children.

Jack: Just the children.

Jack: Right?!

Jack: Clyde, come on.

I waited in my dark vehicle, grinning down at my phone like a maniac.

Jack: Well, what are you dressing up as?

Me: Princess Peach. It's a huge hit.

I did it every year.

Me: I'm sure we can think of a good costume for you.

Jack: How about a bartender?

Snorting, I replied, *Nice try. What about a chef? Oh, or a doctor. Scrubs would be super easy. Or a cowboy.*

Jack: I think I have an idea. Something you'll probably like.

Me: Oh yeah? Is it gray sweatpants?

Jack: No, you pervert. Calm down.

I giggled before finally starting my car and turning the heat on. It was chilly tonight, but I'd been distracted by Jack's messages.

Me: Well, are you going to tell me?

Jack: Nah. It'll be a surprise.

***

"You were not kidding about that Princess Peach costume."

I grinned at Jack as I waved goodbye to the little girls dressed as Snow White and sat back down beside him again. That was probably the tenth picture I'd gotten up and posed for.

"She's a fan favorite," I replied with a sly look in his direction.

I'd nearly tripped over my own feet when I'd found Jack at the Magnolia booth on Main Street. He'd dressed up alright, and just when I thought he couldn't get any sexier, a tall, brooding pirate awaited me.

He'd let the scruff on his cheeks grow in a little thicker this week. With a red bandana tied around his head and a fake earring in one ear, he definitely looked the part. The tight black pants didn't hurt either.

We'd been handing out candy for over an hour. The crowds would eventually thin out as it got closer to sunset, with the older kids heading back home to trick-or-treat in their own neighborhoods. But this event was great for the little ones. The whole street had been blocked off for the festivities. There were bounce houses and food trucks, and plenty of tables and businesses to visit.

It had been fun interacting with the community. I'd seen a ton of students —current and former.

Just then, several of the soccer girls came bounding up to the table. Jamie was dressed in all black as a dour Wednesday Addams. The effect was ruined when she smiled widely at us, black lipstick framing her white teeth. Tori and Rosie joined her. Rosie wore a Bride of Frankenstein costume. And Tori was painted gold all over—even her face—and I wasn't sure why.

"Hey, girls!" I greeted. "I love your costumes."

"I'm the World Cup," Tori said proudly.

"Of course you are." I smiled.

"Coach Jack, you make a really good pirate," Jamie offered.

"Word," Rosie added.

I pushed the bowl of candy forward. "Have at it."

But Jack reached over with a staying hand. "I, uh, actually have something for them."

I watched curiously as he produced a plastic bag from beneath the table and pulled out full-sized candy bars, passing them to the girls.

They squealed excitedly.

"Thank you!" the girls chorused.

"You're an amazing coach-slash-human," Jamie added with a grin.

Jack must have felt my amused gaze burning a hole in the side of his face because he cut me a sidelong glance. "What?"

"You are a secret softie," I said, absolutely charmed by this turn of events.

He wanted to play the role of a grumpy bar owner forced to participate in community service, but he liked these kids. And I was willing to bet he enjoyed coaching them, too.

"Ms. Jensen, will you take a picture of us with Coach Jack?" Jamie asked.

"Sure," I replied happily, accepting the little girl's cell phone.

The three hustled around the table as Jack stood. They got into position on either side, grinning widely and saying "Cheese!"

Jack's smile was somehow both gruff and unbearably fond, and I was infinitely delighted that there was photographic evidence.

Jamie and the others hurried off with a "Goodbye!" and a "Thank you!"

I couldn't resist my amused grin as we resumed our seats and handed over the candy bowl to the kids who'd been waiting.

When his gaze caught mine, Jack rolled his eyes. "It was just a picture. You've been taking them with kids all night."

"Yeah, but those other kids just wanted a photo with Princess Peach. Jamie and Tori and Rosie wanted a picture with you, their coach."

He looked uncomfortable with the knowledge. Like maybe he hadn't expected the girls to remember him off the field. Or he hadn't anticipated making an impact anywhere down the line.

"I was forced into the coaching thing, remember? I don't like getting involved."

I pressed my lips together.

Jack frowned. "What? Just say it."

"What about the end-of-season party you threw for the team at Magnolia this week after their final practice?" I challenged.

"It wasn't a party," he argued, but he looked away.

"And the certificates you gave each kid with their little trophies."

"I found a template online and just printed them out."

"Jamie showed me hers," I said, voice soft from the sweetness he was intent on hiding. "It's framed in her cubby at school. The Most Organized on the Team award. That doesn't sound like a template to me."

Jack sighed, and I had to work really hard to keep the smile off my face.

"Just admit it. You like them," I encouraged. "You liked coaching those kids. You liked being involved."

His eyes rolled heavenward, but he grunted out a barely audible, "Fine. Coaching wasn't as terrible as I thought it would be."

My smile burst free. "Look at you. Community leader." I waved a hand at our surroundings. "Active participant in our local economy."

"I think you mean, Eloise Carter's whipping boy."

I laughed at his deflection before disagreeing gently, "No. You could have passed on trick-or-treating."

He eyed me, looking a little cagy. "Yeah, but that seemed like the easiest way to get her off my back. Next thing I know, it'll be the holiday market or the Christmas parade or the Spring Fling or whatever small-town event she can think up next. Believe me, I do not want to be on Eloise Carter's email list."

"Why does that bother you so much, Jack? Why wouldn't you want to be involved?"

Despite being born here and living most of his life in Kirby Falls, Jack had been somewhat of an outsider. His solitude contributed to his reputation. One of a self-contained man who flew under the radar. Who didn't need anyone's approval or support, and lived the life he'd chosen. Almost like he'd decided to stay in his hometown in spite of the gossip and rumors.

He didn't answer. Darkness rolled over his expression like a storm rumbling in. He was irritated, likely upset that I was pushing so hard. But this was important. He was already a part of this community. The only person who saw him as an outsider was Jack himself.

"You're one of us," I told him seriously. "This town is as much yours as anyone else's. It's okay to want to be a part of that."

After a long moment, Jack nodded, his expression still a little unsure, or perhaps disbelieving. But the dark clouds of his temper had drifted into the distance, like a summer shower over the mountains, just barely hiding layers of the hillside behind a gauzy curtain of rain.

"It's okay to be a little scared," I said, using his own words from a few weeks ago.

I could tell he remembered. His face softened, the last hint of bad weather dispersing on the wind.

Then he raised a dark brow in my direction, enhancing his roguish appearance. "Well, don't expect me to turn Magnolia into the hometown watering hole. The last local who picked my bar over Mattie B's is still causing all kinds of trouble."

Then he winked and shot me a grin that had me going warm all over.

Eventually, the shuffling mass of parents and costumed children dwindled along with the candy in our bowl. I saw a few more students and said hi to plenty of neighbors. Jacob and Charlie had even stopped by our table.

Jacob had been dressed as a king, his costume complete with a cape, crown, and royal scepter. Charlie had taken a very creative approach and put together a Chef Mario Batali costume with the help of his dad. They were polite and spoke to me, but they were obviously there for Jack. I knew the boys still frequented the girls' practices, and they'd attended every Saturday game I'd been to as well. I wasn't surprised at all when Jack passed the boys full-sized Snickers bars, further earning their hero worship and undying devotion.

We managed to make it to Jack's building just as the streetlights turned on. Following Jack, I gathered my layers of skirts and took the stairs up to his apartment. I could tell he wanted to peek in downstairs at Magnolia, but he resisted.

He'd gotten better about that, letting those scheduled to close up actually do their jobs without stepping in or checking to make sure the kitchen wasn't overwhelmed. Magnolia was well staffed, but it was obvious that Jack had a hard time letting go where the bar was concerned.

But tonight, he'd been content to lead me right up to his apartment, his hand wrapped around mine.

My phone buzzed in the pocket of my dress as we stepped inside. I looked at the screen after I removed my shoes and felt my stomach drop. Another text from Danny. This time, asking if I had time to talk.

He'd been sending these messages every now and then, and I'd just been ignoring them, but too scared of an emergency with Diane to block him.

"Everything okay?" Jack asked, swiping the bandana off his head and raking his fingers through his hair.

"Yeah," I replied as I turned off my phone. "It wasn't important."

I didn't want to talk about my ex-husband. I didn't want to think about him either. Danny had occupied enough of my thoughts for a very long time.

Jack shrugged out of the white lace-up pirate shirt, and suddenly my attention was fixed wholly on him. He unclipped the gold hoop from his ear and placed it on the counter before stepping close.

Carefully, he removed the crown from my hair. Then he reached behind me and found the zipper of my dress.

"You know some people would be into the Princess Peach thing," I said with a grin. "I can leave it on, if you want."

His eyes stayed on mine even as I felt the fabric slide down my body, the air cool against my skin.

Jack ran the backs of his knuckles along my spine, making me shiver. Anticipation bloomed, and something heavy and warm settled below my belly button.

He shook his head slowly from side to side. "No costume, Clyde. I just—" He paused, throat working as he swallowed. "I just want you."

All my teasing and amusement abruptly fled as he leaned in and pressed a lingering kiss to my jaw.

No matter what happened with Jack, I knew I'd probably remember this moment for the rest of my life. When Jack laid me down on his bed and made slow, sweet love to me, it was with the knowledge that for the first time in my life, someone simply wanted me.

And maybe—just maybe—I was more than enough.

BONNIE

I shoved the last of the clean clothes in a laundry basket and wedged it inside the primary bedroom. I'd dragged my feet on sorting and folding for a few days, but since Jack was actively on his way over, it was too late to do anything about it now.

I needed more time in the evenings after work. But I'd been so busy lately with my weekly events—trivia, bowling, softball, and so forth—and spending nights with Jack, that I hadn't made cleaning up at home a priority. Actually, that was a lie. I'd never been a great housewife. The only thing I hated more than doing laundry was washing dishes. Plus, I was a bit of a pack rat. I liked knickknacks and collecting things. I didn't mind a little clutter. Danny and I had differed greatly in that regard.

With an impatient huff, I gathered up the rest of the items without a place from the living room and kitchen—unopened mail, art supplies for school, magazines, and shoes I tended to leave right beside the door—into another empty laundry basket. It joined the first in the bedroom mostly used for Oreo.

The rabbit watched me from where she sat placidly in the hallway. Likely wondering what the heck I was doing and why I was having a cleaning freak-out all of a sudden.

Well, Jack was coming inside my house for the first time. In the month and a half we'd been seeing each other, we'd always met up at his apartment. It didn't seem fair. I liked his place a lot, but I wanted him to know that I wasn't keeping him relegated to certain parts of my life.

Realizing I'd hurt him by keeping him a secret had been enough to push me outside my people-pleasing comfort zone. I didn't want Jack to think I was ashamed of our relationship at the expense of keeping the peace with a bunch of nosy neighbors. It wasn't anyone's business who I spent my time with—naked or not. I wasn't married anymore, and despite what the rumor mill churned out, there wasn't a timeline on getting your life back on track.

I blew a strand of hair out of my face and looked at Oreo. "Be nice to him, okay? I sort of like him."

That was maybe downplaying things. I did like Jack . . . a lot. In fact, I worried I was getting in a little too deep, especially since we were casual and undefined. I knew he wasn't seeing other people. We were together so much that it would have been nearly impossible. Since Halloween two weeks ago, I'd spent the night at his place more than at mine. I didn't mind the late nights waiting for him to finish up at Magnolia. The early mornings leaving for school didn't really bother me either. I just liked being with him. He made me feel accepted, safe in my own skin. Like, maybe, the current version of myself was worth knowing.

All those fizzy, nervous feelings he'd provoked at the beginning had changed at some point, shifted to something less anxious and more anticipatory. I wasn't waiting anymore for the bad boy to realize the good girl wasn't cool enough for him.

I liked his attention on me. It still made all my nerve endings sit up and take notice, but there wasn't a worrisome edge. Being with Jack was a little like being on a roller coaster. I could handle the wild turns and sudden drops, usually with a smile on my face and his hand clasped firmly in mine.

A knock came just as I was stacking the four paperbacks I was in the middle of reading into an orderly pile. I hurried to the front door, snagging the spare change I'd tossed on my end table and quickly shoving it into the pocket of my sweatpants.

"Hi," I said, a touch breathlessly as I swung the door open.

Jack's eyebrows popped up like I'd surprised him. "Hi."

I stared at him until he grinned and said, "Can I come in?"

"Oh, sure. Sorry. Welcome." Scolding myself for being weird, I moved out of the way so he could join me, you know, inside the house.

"Can I get you a drink?" I asked as he took in the open floor plan, eyes roaming over the living room, kitchen, and dining area.

"Yeah, thanks."

Glad to have some way to direct my nervous energy, I walked toward the refrigerator, rambling as I went. "It's a fixer-upper, I know. I had a lot of plans for this house that just sort of fell by the wayside over the years. Like getting rid of the wallpaper in the hallway and installing raised beds in the backyard." I opened the door and peered inside the fridge, moving things around to get to the beer I'd picked up on the way home. "And I know it's dark in here. I keep meaning to change up the window treatments. And the wood paneling doesn't help."

I nearly dropped the bottle in my hand when I closed the door to the refrigerator and found Jack waiting on the other side. "Oh my God!" I gasped.

He smoothly reached out and plucked the beer from my grasp before placing it on the counter next to us. Then he slid his arms around my waist and pulled me close. "Hey. You don't need to do that. It's your house. I already like it. It's comfortable and it smells like you."

I didn't have time to fret over what he meant by that before Jack's gaze slid past me to the hallway, where his attention stayed.

He drew in a short breath before saying, "Clyde, don't be alarmed, but there is a rodent in your house."

I turned to see Oreo sitting where I'd left her, nose twitching adorably.

A giggle escaped when I looked back at Jack, his expression somewhat alarmed. He was typically so hard to ruffle that I was enjoying this a little bit. "That's Oreo. She's a rabbit."

He glanced at me quickly, then zeroed in on Oreo, like he had to keep an eye on the dangerous animal threatening us. "You've never once said you had a pet rabbit."

"Well, technically, she's not mine."

Jack's eyes widened, and he shuffled us over a few steps until we were in front of the dishwasher. "It's coming over here."

I peeked over my shoulder, and sure enough, Oreo was hopping our way, curiosity getting the better of her.

"She's not going to hurt us." I laughed. "How are you afraid of a little bunny? She weighs three pounds."

"I'm not afraid," he claimed, tugging me faster around the end of the kitchen island. "I just wasn't expecting you to have a pet. Especially not one with such big teeth."

Shaking my head in amused disbelief, I reached down and plucked the rabbit off the floor. Jack straightened away from me and crossed his arms.

"See, she's friendly," I said.

He eyed the animal in my arms as I stroked her soft fur and smiled encouragingly.

"Are you pet-sitting or something?" he asked. "What do you mean she's not yours?"

Sighing, I said, "Oreo is a classroom pet."

"You have a class pet in your art room?"

"No. Not exactly," I admitted. "She's the pet in one of the second-grade classrooms, but the teacher doesn't like her very much. She leaves her at school on the weekends, and I just hate the thought of her being scared and alone. Rabbits are actually very social animals. Oreo loves the children."

Jack's brows furrowed in confusion. "So you what? Told the teacher you'd watch the rabbit on the weekends for her?"

I swallowed awkwardly and looked down at the sweet little baby in my arms. "Not . . . exactly."

A beat passed and then, "Bonnie, do you steal that rabbit every Friday and return it on Monday?"

I peeked at his incredulous expression. "Yes. But I'm going to talk to Morris—the second-grade teacher—about it. I really am."

Jack's attention dropped to Oreo before returning to my face. He still looked confused, but his gaze had warmed, amusement threatening as his lips twitched. "Wow, Clyde. I guess the nickname fits. You really are done living the good-girl life."

I smirked and took a step closer.

Jack jolted backward. "What are you doing?"

"Come on, Jack. Pet her. She's so sweet."

Another step followed by another retreat.

"Why can't you have a dog like a normal person?"

I shrugged. "She needed me. What was I supposed to do?"

He sighed but stopped running away. Tentatively, Jack reached out with a knuckle and stroked the top of Oreo's head.

The rabbit's nose twitched, but she stayed calm in my arms.

I resisted the urge to smile triumphantly. "She's soft, right?"

"I suppose," he half agreed.

"She has her own little bunny hut in the other bedroom, where she sleeps at night or stays when I'm out. Her food is in there, too. She's house-trained. She has a fuzzy blanket that she likes to hide under, and she hangs out with me while I'm watching TV. You'll barely notice her. And if she takes a chunk out of your leg or something, I'll put her up."

Jack shot me an unamused glare. I grinned.

"Pizza will be here soon," I said. Then I let my gaze slide down his denim-covered thighs. "Where are your sweatpants? I thought you were committed to doing panda mode tonight?" I teased.

"I am. I have a bag in my truck."

The November weather had taken a turn. It was currently cold and rainy, and was supposed to stay that way through tomorrow. Jack had left his motorcycle at home as a result.

When Jack returned, he had pizza boxes in his hands and a duffel slung over one shoulder. "Met the delivery guy in the driveway."

"Thanks," I said.

We gathered plates, napkins, and drinks, then took our haul to the living room, where our movie waited.

As soon as I hit play, I remembered the red pepper flakes I meant to grab. I knew Jack liked those on his pizza.

I set my plate on the coffee table and asked, "Would you like red pepper flakes? I have some."

"Sure," Jack said, but placed a staying hand on my thigh. "But I can get them. Just tell me where."

"Um, the pantry. About halfway down on the right. There's a little basket with spices."

He squeezed my leg and stood, making his way to the kitchen.

I watched him go, blinking away hazy memories and unwelcome thoughts. These moments were getting fewer and farther between, thankfully. Times when I made note of the differences between Danny and Jack. My life before and my life now. The stark contrast, black and white, night and day.

Danny had been all too happy to let me wait on him hand and foot. It shouldn't have been notable for someone to get their own red pepper flakes from the kitchen. But part of me still thought of Jack as a guest, and ignoring those habits and tendencies was hard. I wanted to fret over him and make sure he was comfortable, keep him content in ways big and small.

Attempting to banish the uninvited thoughts, I made myself reach for my pizza. I didn't want to think about the past. I didn't want to think about Danny, especially since he'd been relentless lately with the calls and texts. I'd visited his mother earlier in the week, so I knew his efforts weren't due to an emergency or anything. I'd been content to ignore my ex-husband. There wasn't anything I needed to say to him.

"What's this?" Jack called, drawing me out of my distracted fog.

I spun around to see over the back of the couch and realized he'd noticed the items in the bottom of the pantry. "Oh, those are my teacups."

"Do you collect them?"

I finished chewing, then replied, "Yeah. Well, sort of. They were my great-grandmother Geraldine's. She collected them. Had a big curio cabinet in the formal living room up at the homestead. She passed away before I was born, but I used to love looking at them as a little girl. My great-grandfather remembered that and gave them to me so I could start my own collection."

Jack was still over by the pantry, watching me, an expression on his face I couldn't quite place. "So why are they in here?"

Shame had me glancing away and clearing my throat. "Well, um, Danny hated them. Said they made me seem like an old woman. I didn't even drink tea. So I just stored them. It was easier that way."

I didn't want to see the look on Jack's face now, knowing it could range anywhere from pity to disappointment to disgust. I turned back around and faced the television and hit play on the remote.

Jack stayed quiet. Finally, after a moment, he took his seat, bottle of red pepper flakes in hand. Without a word, he placed an extra garlic knot on my plate. Those were my favorite.

I looked over and smiled, determined not to do something stupid like cry over a piece of bread or a shelf full of underappreciated porcelain. "Thanks."

"Anytime," he said, his hazel gaze steady.

After a few minutes of companionable silence while the movie played and we ate, Jack said, "You should put your teacups out somewhere. Maybe a shelf or a display cabinet. You could unpack them, if you wanted."

My throat was suddenly so tight, I wasn't sure if I could swallow. "Yeah, that's a good idea."

"And," he added quietly, "you don't have to hide all your stuff in the other bedroom, Bonnie."

I winced. "You saw?"

"Yeah, when I went to change into these gray sweatpants you're so obsessed with." His elbow nudged mine, and I snorted a laugh. "You said the bathroom was the door on the left."

With a resigned groan, I closed my eyes briefly. "Yeah, and there are two doors on the left."

"Yeah," Jack agreed, lips twitching.

"That's the primary bedroom," I confessed. "I can't—I don't sleep in there anymore. I prefer the guest room. But it works out great for Oreo. And I just didn't have the time today to straighten up the way I wanted to, before you came over. I know it looks like I'm a total slob."

A warm palm settled on my thigh and squeezed once more. "No, it doesn't. It looks like you panicked before I got here and gathered up all the evidence that you actually live in this house and tried to hide it. You're not guilty of anything, Bonnie. I'm not here to judge you or your laundry baskets. I'm actually pretty relieved that you're like the rest of us. Most people are a little messy. A little imperfect. I don't want you to be anyone but yourself with me, okay?"

I nodded as Jack's words chased away some of my embarrassment. Hope rose in its place, pushing through my middle like tender shoots through soil, roots delicate and fragile.

"I'll do my best," I agreed.

He smiled softly. "Okay, then."

His words were so easy and agreeable. Like my best might actually, truly, be enough.

I could feel myself relaxing. All my muscles unclenched as my body was drawn toward Jack, like a flower toward the sun. I wanted more of this. More comfort. More honesty. More of Jack.

He hadn't run away yet, I thought.

For now, these moments were enough.

I'd always been someone who'd held on a little too tight, clutching people and things with both fists for fear I'd lose them. I knew that whatever was happening with Jack was casual. I wasn't under any delusions about that. But seeing him here, in my space, offering acceptance and comfort, being exactly what I needed . . . I couldn't help but think I might never want to let go.

Jack

I wasn't sure what woke me, but I could tell from the moonlight filtering in through Bonnie's bedroom window that morning was still a ways off.

Intent on getting right back to sleep, I rolled over. But when I reached out to wrap an arm around Bonnie, I found cold sheets instead.

I blinked into the darkness before sitting up.

The clock on the bedside table said it was just after three.

I didn't hear water running in the bathroom or any sounds at all coming from the house.

So I slid out of bed to look for her.

I didn't have to go far. She was lying down on the sofa in the living room, her head propped on a throw pillow, blanket draped across her legs, and the light from her phone screen illuminating her face.

As I entered the room, my foot pressed down on a creaky floorboard, and Bonnie glanced up.

She immediately turned off her screen and sat up. "I'm sorry. I didn't mean to wake you."

"You didn't," I replied slowly, confused by her abrupt reaction. "Are you okay?"

"Yeah, I'm fine."

I couldn't see her very well in the dimness, but I could tell something was up.

I'd never gotten to this point before—with a woman or anyone, really. The place where you knew someone well enough to draw conclusions or make assumptions about their behavior. To be able to call them on their bullshit or ferret out the white lies they told everyone, including themselves.

Maybe Bonnie thought she was fine, but there was a reason she was out here on the couch instead of in bed with me, where she belonged. And I knew it. Maybe it was the tone of her voice or the quick way she'd apologized, like it was expected or she'd had plenty of experience doing it. She'd gotten pretty good at *not* saying she was sorry, especially since the muffin thing, but this apology had felt like a compulsion, completely out of her control.

Later, I'd think about what it meant to be in someone else's head. To have more than just surface knowledge to work from. But right now I wanted to figure out what was going on and how I could fix it.

So I said, "Scootch," and lay down on the couch next to her.

There wasn't a lot of room. Bonnie lay on her side, partially draped across my chest, her smooth, bare legs tangled with mine. She was wearing one of my shirts, but it smelled more like her than me at this point, and I liked that in a way I couldn't explain, even to myself.

After we finally got settled and no one was getting crushed or was in danger of rolling off the cushions, Bonnie huffed a quiet laugh. "You can go back to bed, you know. You don't have to be uncomfortable out here with me."

"I'm not uncomfortable," I lied. My neck was at a weird angle, and my legs did not fit, but I wasn't leaving her out here alone. "What made you get up? Was I snoring?"

"No, nothing like that." Her fingers drew lazy circles on my bare chest as she spoke. "I was having trouble sleeping. I thought I'd read on my phone until I could fall back to sleep, but I didn't want to wake you by moving around or with the light from my screen."

"I'm not a light sleeper," I reminded her, curious why she was so worried about waking me up.

I felt her nod, her soft hair brushing my cheek. "I know, but I'm used to—"

She cut herself off, and the resulting silence was suddenly very loud.

I considered her swift apology, the way she'd acted like I'd caught her doing something wrong. Not for the first time, I wondered what had happened in her marriage. If that asshole had hurt her, physically or otherwise. If he'd been selfish with more than just his love. I already knew he'd been critical of his wife. I worried that was why Bonnie constantly felt the need to be perfect all the time.

After six slow breaths that steadied my surging anger, I asked softly, "Did that use to bother your ex? When you had trouble sleeping?"

"Yeah," she finally replied, voice small. "I guess I just got used to leaving the bedroom and coming out here. It was easier to avoid the fight." My pulse thundered at her choice of words, a storm gathering. Then she added hastily, "Not *fight*. That's too strong for what it was. Mostly passive-aggressive stuff. But Danny didn't understand why I couldn't just sleep, you know. I'd get an exasperated sigh or an annoyed huff before he'd roll over. Sometimes he'd stomp out and go watch TV. It was better to just slip away to the couch and avoid that. I'd usually fall back to sleep at some point."

I thought about the guy who came into my bar—again this past Thursday night—to pick up women. The corny lines and the same ill-fitting blue button-up on a tall, reedy frame. The misplaced confidence. The ego. The smarmy smile below a too-thin mustache. The spineless piece of shit who'd thrown Bonnie away for what? Freedom? To fuck any woman who'd take him?

I wondered what had happened between them. Why couldn't Bonnie get over him? Why would she still take him back if she could? From everything she'd said and everything I'd heard, it didn't sound like there was much to miss.

It seemed a little like admitting defeat or showing my hand. Something that made me more vulnerable than I wanted. But I asked anyway. "Bonnie, what happened with your ex?"

Her throat moved against me as she swallowed hard. "He cheated."

I felt it like a punch, validation and anger swirling together and forcing me to take a steadying breath. I'd speculated, of course, but hearing her admit it was worse. I could only imagine how difficult that must have been—still was—for someone like Bonnie. A person so loyal and steadfast. Someone who I could never envision making that sort of mistake.

"It was a while ago," she explained quietly. "Last fall . . . at a bachelor party." Her laugh was bitter, all sharp edges and resentment. Nothing like the woman I'd come to know. "Cliché, right? He told me right away. Apologized and said it was an accident. That he'd been drunk, and it never would have happened if he'd been sober. We tried to move on and get past it. But I just . . . couldn't. I couldn't forget. I wasn't strong enough to let it go."

My thumb had been rubbing circles on her arm, just beneath the sleeve of the shirt she wore. But at her admission, I settled my palm against her shoulder and pulled her tighter into my chest. "I'm sorry that happened. It couldn't have been easy. But I don't think it had anything to do with you being weak, Clyde. Everyone has deal breakers. Their lines in the sand. No one would blame you for wanting a divorce because—"

"He asked for the divorce," she interrupted, and the rest of my words caught in my throat. "It was him. He got tired of waiting for me to get over it. I took too long. Danny said I was punishing him. But I just couldn't stand the thought of him touching me after what he'd done with someone else. So he decided enough was enough."

I worked to make my voice even. "I see."

Maybe Bonnie hadn't been able to move past her husband's infidelity, but clearly she was trying since she still wanted him. Her words came back to me, the misery in her voice, the tears she'd cried on my lap all those weeks ago. The whole reason she'd gotten drunk and emotional in the first place. *I don't want to move on. It feels too big. How could I throw away something I spent half my life building and just start over?*

She missed her life, and she'd been willing to fight for it. The divorce hadn't been her call.

Anger and jealousy twisted something ugly inside me. It made sense that Bonnie hadn't been able to just *get over* Danny's deception. Because when I thought about that asshole, his hands on her and the life they'd built together, all the years and the history, it made my jaw clench. I hated it. Couldn't fathom that she'd wasted so much time on him.

He wasn't worthy of her love or all the devotion Bonnie carried around with her.

Danny's not here, I reminded myself. Not anymore.

She had me. In her bed. In her home. In her life.

Our relationship had drifted like a boat on open water. I knew that we'd wandered past casual into something . . . more. Something unexpected and a little bit frightening. Because for the first time in my life, someone had the power to hurt me.

"Come back to bed," I urged. "We'll think of three things. And if that doesn't help you fall asleep, you can read all you want. It won't bother me. Just come lie down."

"Okay."

Bonnie let me lead her back to the bedroom, but before she could climb under the blankets, I stopped her. Reaching down, I lifted the hem of my tee shirt up and over her head.

"Three favorite places to be kissed?" I asked, my voice low in the darkness.

Her breath hitched, but I was already reaching for her hand and bringing it to my mouth when she replied, "The inside of my wrist."

I tasted the delicate skin there. Pressed my tongue against her as she ran her fingers through my hair.

Then I slid my hands over the smooth skin of her waist and leaned in to place a sucking kiss beside her collarbone. "Second favorite." It wasn't a question.

"Right there," she breathed, her pulse fluttering beneath my lips.

I was painfully hard inside my boxer briefs—the only clothes I wore. Bonnie's hand gripped the waistband as she pulled me closer.

"Last one?" I whispered against the shell of her ear.

She leaned back enough that I could see her face, barely visible in the moonlight, and tapped her lips with a finger.

I grinned and shook my head slowly. "That's not your favorite."

Then I guided her down onto the mattress, tugging her underwear off and lowering to my knees.

She widened her thighs, and I didn't waste time. I didn't wait for her to pull back or reassure me that I didn't have to, which was what she always did when I went down on her. Probably another reason I hated her fucking ex, and she should too.

I gave a long, slow lick through her center that had her crying out, the sound sweet and welcome to my ears.

I encouraged Bonnie to slide her legs over my shoulders. Then I tucked my hands beneath her ass and pulled her toward my waiting mouth. She was hot and slick, and the taste of her made me groan.

Using lips and tongue and single-minded determination, I feasted. Bonnie made these perfect little noises as her breathing grew heavy. Her fingers slid through my hair, and her hips took up an urgent rhythm around the pace I set.

I could feel myself leaking inside my boxers, desperate to be inside her, to feel her inner muscles clamping down on me. So I slid a finger inside her pussy and moaned as she squeezed me tight.

She was close; I could tell. Her body familiar. Her needs etched across my skin.

There was that understanding again. Knowledge and fluency in someone else that I'd never had before. I'd learned the things Bonnie liked and all the ways I could make her come undone. This sort of intimacy was different than anything I'd ever known. Being with someone you cared about was overwhelming but so, so good.

I didn't take that knowledge for granted now.

I added a second finger and thrust in time with every roll of her hips, intent on making this perfect for her. To drive away her doubts. To banish the ghosts of her past that lingered in every room of this house. To be what she needed over and over again.

Her fingers tightened on my scalp as I kept my tongue firm on her clit.

Then she panted out, "Wait. Wait. I don't want to come yet. I want you up here with me. Please."

I wasn't sure when it had happened, but I was beginning to think I'd give this woman whatever she asked for. A motorcycle ride by moonlight. A moment to hide herself away. A safe place to fall apart.

On shaky legs, I stood and reached for the packet from my wallet on the bedside table. I stepped out of my underwear and rolled the condom on before finding Bonnie's body with my own.

Her kiss was wild as I settled between her thighs and pushed home. She was hot and wet and perfect, and I knew this wasn't going to last long.

My hand wrapped around her thigh, encouraging her to spread wider as I tugged her leg up and over my hip. She made a desperate sound against my lips as my cock hit somewhere deep inside.

"Fuck," I cursed as her orgasm shook her small frame. The pressure and the warmth intensified until I was thrusting hard and fast, chasing my own release, desperate to be with her, to be close. Pleasure ripped from the base of my spine outward, everything going bright and loud for a split second before I was coming.

I pressed my face into Bonnie's neck, tasting the salt on her skin and the heat beneath my tongue. Her sweet honeysuckle scent filled my lungs, and I wished this feeling would never ever end. But I knew it couldn't last forever because nothing good ever did.

She was mostly asleep when I climbed back into bed after taking care of the condom. But her body still curved toward mine. I lifted my arm to make room, and she snuggled into my side, her small hand resting right over my heart.

"Stay," she murmured, voice slurred and drowsy.

I smiled. Where did she think I was going?

"For as long as you'll have me," I whispered in the dark, knowing she was already asleep.

JACK

It was another weekend at Bonnie's house. During the week, we spent the night at my place because it was easier. But we'd started staying at her house when we had more time together.

I'd closed the last three nights in a row at Magnolia. Kayla had practically shoved me out the door at nine, saying she and Sasha and Sebastian were perfectly capable of handling things on a Saturday night.

I knew they could. I really did. Yes, it was December and the tourists were in town for the Holiday Jamboree and other town festivities, but we had a good staff. I trusted them.

Honestly, I was grateful for the time off. I'd even been throwing around the idea of hiring a manager in the new year. Business was steady, and I could afford to bring in someone to take on more responsibility. But it was hard to contemplate loosening the reins on the only thing I'd ever accomplished in my life. Rationally, I knew Magnolia wouldn't fall apart without me. And if I did manage to hire someone to oversee the place in the evenings, that would free me up and make my schedule a little more convenient.

Throughout the week, Bonnie and I didn't get a lot of time together. Everything felt rushed and abbreviated. I was always in a hurry to close out, to lock up, to just . . . get to her. Worried she'd wear herself out waiting up for me most nights. I was just as desperate to get her clothes off as I was to get twenty minutes to talk to her about her day. I wanted to take her out and share a meal. I looked forward to her stealing my samosas over dinner.

Funny what a few months could change.

I'd given her a key to my place so that on the weeknights she came over—most of them—she could let herself in and relax. My schedule wasn't exactly set, and depending on how busy the bar got, I couldn't expect to leave at the same time every night.

Sometimes I woke her up on my couch, where she'd fallen asleep waiting for me. But it wasn't always about getting her naked. There were nights I just carried her to bed and wrapped myself around her, relieved to have her in my arms, knowing she was safe and sleeping soundly.

I should have been worried. Should have been scared shitless that in the last three months, this woman had somehow become the single most important part of my life. It wasn't just Magnolia anymore, or Lia. I didn't know if I was excelling at the work-life-balance thing yet, but there had definitely been progress.

It was Bonnie who occupied my thoughts. Soft skin and a sweet smile. Her body behind me on the back of my bike, arms tight around my middle. The way she breathed my name while I moved inside her, indulgent and demanding at the same time. The scent of honeysuckle finding me in my dreams.

My life wasn't just the bar anymore. I had something besides payroll and vendor shipments, employees and tourists filling seats at Magnolia.

There was Bonnie, but there were also emails from Eloise Carter in my inbox. Not to mention the little girls breathing down my neck about coaching soccer in the spring. I had a place in this town, with these people, in a way I'd never anticipated. And part of me knew that it had all changed because I'd let one person in.

"Are you really going to just stand there and ignore her?" Bonnie poked her head around the doorframe and stared pointedly at my feet, making sad puppy eyes. Well, actually, sad bunny eyes.

From my place on the couch, I glanced down at Oreo.

Truthfully, I'd gotten distracted while Bonnie had been in the bathroom, washing her face and brushing her teeth. I hadn't really noticed the rabbit sitting by my feet, desperate for my attention. But now that I wasn't thinking about all the ways my life had changed this fall, I could see more damage inflicted by the persistent little furball.

"This rabbit is obsessed with me," I called to Bonnie, who'd retreated down the hallway. "I have holes in my socks, Clyde. All of them."

I heard her laugh from the other room, the sound ricocheting through my chest and warming me through.

For whatever reason, the bunny was weirdly obsessed with me. She followed me around and nibbled on my socks when I wasn't giving her attention. I liked to tease Bonnie, but I'd honestly gotten used to the rabbit. I was more of a dog person, but Oreo wasn't so bad.

I picked her up and set her next to me on the couch, stroking her long, floppy ears.

A moment later, my phone buzzed in my pocket. I pulled it out and saw a text from my grandmother.

Lia: Breakfast is on in the morning. Eggs and grits. Bacon, if you're lucky.

Her typically brusque and abbreviated method of communicating was familiar, if not warm, and it made me smile. I usually saw Lia on weekday mornings, after Bonnie left for school. It had been a while since she invited me over for breakfast on a weekend.

My fingers continued to pet the rabbit's soft fur as my gaze strayed toward the hallway. Bonnie emerged in pajamas—another one of my tee shirts and some fuzzy pants that had snowflakes all over them—and gave me a sweet smile as she spied me with Oreo.

"Want some popcorn to go with the movie?" she asked, already standing on tiptoes to reach the stovetop popper she kept in the cabinet over the fridge.

"Sure," I agreed, a formality at this point.

My phone had gone dark, but I stared down at it for a long moment. Before I let myself think too hard, I pressed my thumbs to the screen and started typing.

Me: Could I bring someone? Would that be okay?

I watched the screen for nearly a minute as the smell of hot oil and the sound of popping corn drifted in from the kitchen. Then a surprisingly few letters appeared, considering how hard those dots had been working.

Lia: Yes

"Hey, Clyde," I called over my shoulder.

"Yeah," she replied over the rapid pop, pop, pop and the squeak of the hand crank.

"Would you want to come with me in the morning? Lia just texted and invited us over for breakfast."

The squeaking halted suddenly before resuming after a beat. "Sure," Bonnie said. "That sounds great."

I hadn't exactly told my grandmother I was seeing someone, but I'd noticed she'd laid off her spiel recently. Her typical, less-than-subtle nudges at me to get a life or a hobby or a girlfriend had been markedly absent. And her questions about Magnolia Bar hadn't contained the distinctive undertones of "you're going to die alone with a bar towel slung over your shoulder." I figured gossip about me and Bonnie had spread by now to her trivia team or knitting group or whoever the hell she spent her time with. In a town this size, it was inevitable.

I wasn't ready to examine too closely why I'd invited Bonnie along tomorrow. Things were feeling a little less casual now than when they'd started, but our relationship was still working. I wasn't looking for an arbitrary reason to end what we had going on. Maybe it was foolish, but I liked it, whatever it was—casual or not.

And maybe I wanted the two most important people in my life to meet. I could picture Bonnie's single-minded determination to charm my surly grandmother and, at the same time, Lia softening her own sharp edges because she knew that's what Bonnie needed.

The next morning, I awoke to a half-empty bed and the sound of a pan clanging somewhere in the house. The door to the bedroom was shut, but when I emerged into the hallway, I was greeted by the warm smell of cinnamon and vanilla.

A glance at my watch confirmed that it was way too early—not even six.

I blinked blearily as I walked into the kitchen. Bonnie was in my tee shirt and a purple floral apron. Fuzzy socks slouched around her narrow ankles. She was surrounded by mixing bowls and measuring cups as she transferred what looked like perfectly golden mini muffins from a pan to a cooling rack.

She caught sight of me and did a double take. "Shoot. Sorry. Did I wake you?"

"What are you doing?" I asked, my tone more confused than anything else. "I thought you wanted to come to Lia's with me."

"I do," she replied, then moved to set the muffin tin on a braided pot holder.

"I don't . . . understand."

Bonnie finally turned to face me, giving me her full attention. But I was tired and she was wearing an oven mitt and no pants, so my gaze drifted to where her thighs peeked out from beneath her apron.

"I wanted to make something to bring," she said, and my eyes reluctantly returned to her face.

I saw it then. The nervousness. The worry she'd hidden from me last night as we'd watched a movie before bed.

"And I wasn't sure what Lia would like or if she had any food allergies, so I made a few different things."

I took in the rest of the room and what I'd missed earlier—likely due to the no-pants thing. There wasn't just a single batch of muffins cooling. The kitchen table held a tray of what looked like sausage balls and a loaf of something with a shiny white glaze on top. There were more muffins—in two different varieties—occupying the island.

I frowned as my gaze drifted from one delicious-looking baked good to the next. "What time did you get up to do all this?"

"Oh, just a bit ago."

My brows went up, calling her on the fib. "It's just the three of us, Bonnie. You didn't need to go to so much trouble. Or any trouble. Lia is the one feeding us."

Her nose wrinkled in obvious confusion. "But I'm meeting someone new. And she's hosting. It's polite to bring something."

An alarm sounded quietly from Bonnie's phone, and she winced before silencing it and reaching for the door to the oven. "This is the last thing, I swear."

I sighed. It had been foolish of me to think the charm offensive would wait until we were standing in Lia's kitchen across town. Bonnie was so used to people-pleasing that she probably didn't even see what she was doing.

After she'd placed the final baking dish—some sort of cheesy hashbrown casserole—on the counter, I approached.

I turned Bonnie to face me, gently tugged off the oven mitts, and then pulled her into a tight hug. "You don't have to try so hard, Clyde. I don't think I've ever met anyone who doesn't like you. Lia is . . . she's gruff and opinionated. She's not soft, but she *is* an excellent judge of character."

I smoothed a hand up Bonnie's nape and cupped the back of her head before leaning back to meet her gaze. "You're going to get along just fine."

Obvious disbelief and self-doubt bloomed across her features. That little vee between her brows emerged—the one that I felt like a divot in my heart.

"I just want to make a good impression," she admitted.

A strand of blond hair had come loose from her little bun. With a soft smile, I tucked it behind her ear, letting my touch linger. "You know how to talk to anyone. I've seen it so many times. You're good with people because you care—because you have a good heart. It's not just you being friendly. You put people at ease. They want to know you, and so they let you know them."

Her lips parted, and she released a shaky breath.

"But in case of emergency," I offered, "just compliment her birdhouse collection and tell her she makes the best scrambled eggs you've ever tasted."

"She collects birdhouses?" Bonnie despaired. "Why didn't you tell me? I could have gotten her one from—"

I shook my head. "No."

"We probably have time before breakfast to stop by and—"

"No way. You already made enough food to feed an army. No presents. If you overdo it, she'll be able to tell. Just be yourself. That's more than enough."

Her fingers toyed idly with the waistband of my boxers, and I had to work hard to stay focused.

"Okay," she murmured grudgingly.

"Okay," I echoed. "Good."

She smiled, just a little. "Thanks, Jack."

I nodded. "Everything will be fine, I promise."

———

Bonnie

Everything *was* fine. Just like Jack had promised.

But just to make sure, I'd blurted out, "I love your birdhouses!" as soon as the door had opened.

Lia's shrewd gaze had slid from me to Jack and then back to me again before she'd ushered me inside—leaving Jack standing on the porch—and showed me even more of her collection.

The birdhouses lined the perimeter of the kitchen. They stood in all shapes and sizes at intervals above the scarred wooden cabinets.

It was a little surprising. This no-nonsense woman with her gray hair and stern features collecting something so delicate and charming. But maybe that was why I liked it so much. The habit had endeared her to me right away. Even if she hadn't been Jack's grandmother, I would have wanted to know the sharp-tongued widow who had a soft spot for birdhouses that looked like whimsical cottages and decorated her life with them.

Jack had reiterated that it wasn't necessary to contribute to the meal, but instead of arguing with me, he'd suggested that I bring the batch of blueberry muffins to share. Everything else had gone into the fridge or the freezer.

That was probably smart. I'd definitely overdone it. I could see that now. But when I'd woken up early, anxious over the prospect of meeting someone so important to Jack, I'd wanted to do everything I could to make our first interaction a good one.

I'd nearly burnt the popcorn last night when he'd invited me, surprise and hope freezing me in place. Obviously, I was curious how many women Jack had introduced to his grandmother, but I wasn't about to ask. It spoke of desperation and was, maybe, a little too honest. Not to mention, pretty telling about where my head was at.

But now our plates were scraped clean and we were sipping our second cups of coffee at the small round kitchen table while Lia asked me questions about teaching and my family and even Oreo.

Most of my nervousness had come to rest, settling into all the tiny cracks in my armor, but no longer overwhelming me. Jack was right. I did know how to talk to people. Maybe it was from spending over a decade as an educator. I'd been dealing with parents and administrators and peers for a long time. Plus, you never knew what ridiculous thing was going to come out of a kid's mouth. Teachers had to be quick on their feet and able to do a lot with a little. Even if Lia had been tight-lipped and grouchy, I probably could have coaxed some conversation out of her.

As it was, she was curious about me and obviously cared a lot about Jack. I could see it in her sharp glances and her quick tongue, the teasing between them that spoke of history. Even the indulgent way he called her Lia instead of grandma. Their relationship was unique. Maybe not overly affectionate, but it was still love. Something timeworn and tethering. Loyalty, plain and simple. And that was something I could understand.

Jack and Lia had survived hardship. They'd experienced loss together, and sometimes there was nothing more binding than that.

Their relationship was different than the ones between my family members, but no less impactful. The Clarks were a demonstrative bunch who gathered often and burrowed into each other's lives and business. But that wasn't the only way to show someone you cared about them.

Family filled any shape you put it in, like the air we breathed. It fit itself into the mold it was given. Through time and circumstance, loss and love. There was no perfect configuration or the right arrangement.

Jack and Lia had made a family out of what they had left, and bonds like those were often the strongest of all.

"You know Jack made that one," Lia said, drawing me out of my musings. She lifted one finger from the edge of her mug and pointed toward the top of the cabinet over the sink. "The one you were admiring just now."

My gaze focused on the birdhouse she'd indicated. It was a little bigger than the others, nearly grazing the textured popcorn ceiling. It looked like the perfect stereotypical family home that every child has probably drawn at one point or another. There was a door in the center with windows on either side. The dark roof, an inverted vee. But where the birdhouse's design was traditional and fairly basic, the details really shone.

The shutters on either side of the windows had been engraved, each line etched perfectly in a beautiful imitation of wood grain. There was a white picket fence that surrounded the house, obviously hand-painted with care and attention to detail.

"Jack made it?" I asked, eyes still soaking up every part of it.

"Yes, he built it," Lia replied.

Finally, I turned to him. "Are you a secret carpenter?"

Jack said no at the same time his grandmother said yes, causing me to laugh and Jack to roll his eyes affectionately.

"It's a hobby," he clarified and then took a sip of his coffee. "Nothing special. I'm out of practice anyway."

"Too busy with that bar," Lia murmured. Her comment had the smooth edges of an old argument. Something that had been sanded down with time and regularity.

Jack stiffened, and I could sense the conversation wandering into a hornet's nest.

That, too, was familiar. Conversations that repeated due to family members who wanted the best for one another, but maybe didn't quite know how to make that happen. So they just said it louder and more often.

Before the silence could stretch uncomfortably, I steered us to safer waters. "Okay, but back to the carpentry thing. What else have you made?" I asked Jack.

But it was Lia who answered, the note of pride in her tone obvious. "Oh, lots of things over the years. Shelves and cabinets. Mailboxes. Coffee tables. And the prettiest garden bench you've ever seen. I'll show it to you before you leave."

I was watching Jack as his grandmother spoke, so I witnessed the slow climb of pink into his cheeks. My heart—big and clumsy in the face of that blush—took a tumble over the sweetness.

Then something occurred to me. "The picture frames," I said softly and looked to Lia.

"That was how it started," she confirmed. "I took a painting class and asked Jack if he could make a frame for me. He'd had some experience from his woodshop class back in high school."

Her gaze drifted over my shoulder, like the memory was right there in the room with us. The firm line of her brow softened when she spoke next. "The first few frames weren't anything to write home about, but neither were my paintings. So we made a fine pair." Then she directed her attention back to Jack and smiled, her weathered cheeks creasing in new, unfamiliar lines. "But his craftsmanship improved."

"And so did her artwork," Jack added.

I grinned. "I've seen some. Of the paintings," I clarified. "In Jack's apartment. They're everywhere."

Two matching pairs of hazel eyes snapped to me.

"Is that so?" Lia asked.

Worry descended. Fear that I'd revealed a secret that wasn't mine.

At my panicked expression, Lia's gaze warmed, and she explained, "It's been a while since I've been over there. Jack usually visits me here."

"Oh," I said, then looked at Jack.

If he was upset, he didn't show it. Just calmly sipped his coffee while I fought the urge to backtrack or placate.

Instead, I stood and gathered the plates. "I'll help with the dishes, then you can show me that bench."

Lia rose as well. Nodding, she offered, "I'll wash and you dry. And then I'll show you my whole garden."

After breakfast and my tour of Lia's property, Jack drove me home.

Part of me thought he might want some space after sharing so much of himself with me, but to my surprise, he'd parked his truck in the driveway and turned to face me, asking, "How would you feel about learning to drive my bike? It's going to be chilly today, but the sun is shining. We could give it a try if you're interested."

"I'm interested," I replied, perhaps a little too eagerly, but I didn't care. I did want to learn. I loved riding with Jack, but it would feel good to do something myself for a change.

He nodded. "Want to go in and change into something warm? I can check on Oreo."

I ignored the way my stomach somersaulted and replied simply, "That sounds great."

And that was how we spent the afternoon. In the empty parking lot at the community college with Jack instructing me how to drive a motorcycle.

I could remember helping Danny install a ceiling fan in our bedroom years ago. As he'd strained to hold the motor and screw everything into place, he'd gotten so irritated at me, snapping out instructions before finally telling me just to leave if I couldn't be of any help.

But Jack was so patient, even when I got frustrated or needed another moment to practice with the clutch. He explained things simply and took the time to make sure I understood. Jack encouraged me to ask questions. Then he trusted me to be able to handle the bike on my own. He'd never once seemed nervous about me damaging his vehicle.

I hadn't expected it, but I could see now that Jack would make a good teacher.

And it was a nice feeling, realizing someone had more than a little faith in you.

seventeen

JACK

"Incoming asshole."

Kayla's words breezed by where I crouched, stocking limes in the refrigerator beneath the bar.

I stood up as Kayla continued directly into the kitchen through the swinging door.

Then out of sheer curiosity, I looked toward the front door of Magnolia.

Sure enough, there was an asshole incoming.

Danny Jensen wasn't wearing his customary blue button-up. He was in jeans and a white tee shirt. The tan work coat covered most of his thin frame.

If he'd ditched the one-night-stand uniform, I wondered what the hell he was doing here. Especially on an afternoon in the middle of the week. It was barely four o'clock and the bar was practically empty.

I didn't have to wait long to find out.

The man came right up to where I was standing and slipped onto the stool in front of me.

I wiped my hands with a towel to keep them busy. Too bad there wasn't anything to do the same for my mouth.

"What'll it be?" I practically spat.

Danny swallowed. "You're Jack, right? The guy dating my wife?"

I couldn't help it, I laughed. So that was how it was going to be.

"Listen, man," Danny went on, unburdened by forethought or self-preservation or anything as inconsequential as reality, "I don't want to fight."

Crossing my arms over my chest, I raised a challenging brow. "Oh, yeah? That's good to hear."

He straightened in his seat, perhaps realizing how a fight would likely go down between the two of us. Danny was about my height, but I probably had forty pounds on the guy. Plus, I was no stranger to schoolyard brawls, and I wouldn't feel bad about kicking his ass.

But I wasn't a fucking caveman, and Bonnie wasn't some shiny toy to squabble over like middle schoolers.

Danny changed tactics, offering up a good-ole-boy smile that did nothing to win me over. "I'm just looking out for you. Bonnie's not what you think she is."

"And what do I think she is?"

He shrugged. "What everyone thinks—that she's perfect. But she's not. She's a little boring, actually. Probably not like the kind of women you're used to—temporary and fun. And she's pretty tame in the sack."

Heat gathered in my chest, something bright and violent and reckless. A mistake waiting to happen. One with consequences like hospital beds and courtrooms. Maybe I was a caveman after all, because I wanted to beat the living shit out of this guy. But I refused to give him the satisfaction of getting a rise out of me.

I knew exactly what this pathetic attempt was. A desperate man who'd lost the best thing that had ever happened to him. And he was looking to score a hit without ever raising his fist.

Ignoring my fury, I kept my expression bored and glanced lazily at my watch for good measure.

Danny's dark blond brow creased in confusion.

Expectations were tricky like that. You couldn't bait someone with bullshit. There was nothing about this man I respected, so his opinions and his lies meant even less to me than he did.

Bonnie's ex shifted on his stool and decided to go in a different direction. "But if you're looking for something more permanent, you should know she isn't much of a housewife either. You can't tell it by looking at her, but she's kind of a slob. I don't know about you, but I like coming home to a clean house. Fresh sheets and the bed made every day."

I kept my gaze steady. "So make your own bed, Daniel." *And lie in it*, I thought spitefully.

When he realized he still wasn't getting anywhere with me, Danny leaned in and spoke low, frustration and anger finally spilling over into his features. "You're not good enough for her."

My bark of laughter made him jump. Placing my elbows on the bar top, I leaned in, too, as if I had a secret to tell. He shied away like a whipped dog, just like I knew he would.

"Well, which is it?" I asked. "Is she not worth the effort, or am I lucky to have her? Make up your mind."

"You never would have stood a chance with Bonnie if I hadn't—" Danny cut himself off abruptly.

I finished for him. "If you hadn't fucked up and thrown her away? Is that it?" My smile was mean, all sharp edges and bared teeth. But then my lips flattened, my expression going hard. "Don't come in here and act like you're doing me any favors, warning me away from her. The only thing we have in common is that neither one of us is good enough for her. But the difference is . . . I already know it, and you're just now figuring that shit out."

His nostrils flared.

"Find somewhere else to fuck around," I told him. "Stop putting on your cheap cologne and coming into my bar to pick up women who will never live up to the memory of the one you lost. Don't ever come back here again. Are we clear?"

Danny's gaze slipped over my shoulder, and I didn't have to look to know that Kayla was in the kitchen doorway, watching. I'd heard the door creak open a minute ago.

His pale complexion heated, and he glanced nervously around to the other customers who'd filtered in during our conversation.

He practically stumbled off the barstool and didn't spare me a backward glance as he made a beeline for the exit.

"Man, that had to feel good," Kayla murmured, coming to stand at my shoulder. "That guy is a fucking loser."

I made myself unclench my jaw, but I didn't answer her. I couldn't.

Yeah, Danny was a piece of shit. He'd cheated on someone who loved him and then put a timeline on her forgiveness. Even before all that, he'd taken her for granted. Taken advantage of her sweetness, her goodness. Her love. *Crumbs at the bottom of the bag.*

And, sure, it had felt good to throw his mistakes back in his face. But what about Bonnie? Some part of me worried that she'd be angry if she knew. Would she be glad that her ex clearly regretted his actions? That the prospect of her with another man had driven him to act?

Danny obviously wanted her back. He was a spineless coward, but coming here proved he was, at the very least, determined.

What did that mean for Bonnie and me?

That night in my apartment from months ago still haunted me. Her tears soaking into my blue jeans, and the heartbreaking confession barely whispered into existence. That she still wanted him—that she'd take him back, if he wanted her.

I had to prepare for the very real possibility that Danny was working a few angles and that one of them might pan out. Bonnie hadn't mentioned being in contact with her ex. As far as I knew, they hadn't spoken in a long time. But that didn't mean he wasn't still in her heart or the back of her mind.

How deep did her devotion go? Were the roots dormant beneath the surface, just waiting for a little attention to coax them back to life? Did they burrow down beneath whatever new, fragile thing we'd built together?

Kayla patted my shoulder before shuffling down the bar to greet our customers.

I needed to get back to work, but my mind was occupied—filled with what-ifs.

For all my talk of keeping things casual, I suddenly felt like the one in danger of getting my heart stomped on when Bonnie realized her old life might no longer be so far out of reach.

***

After Danny's little visit to Magnolia, I finished up some side work and then went home. I wasn't in the right headspace to deal with customers, and I knew my employees could handle closing up on a Wednesday night.

Bonnie had bowling league and was supposed to come over afterward, but she'd ended up going to Candace's house to work on wedding stuff.

I'd considered telling her about the encounter with Danny, but I hadn't decided one way or the other, and I didn't want to do it over the phone. But when she'd texted after midnight from Candace's and said she was too tired to drop by, I'd felt nothing but relief. So, I had my answer.

Why tell her about Danny's little visit and potentially pave her way back to that loser? She deserved better. She deserved someone who'd put her first for once. Not someone who couldn't appreciate her until he'd learned the hard way.

But what Bonnie did or didn't do wasn't actually my call. What she really deserved was to make her own decisions, even if that wasn't me.

Over coffee Thursday morning, I thought about all those teacups. Packed away and stored where no one could see them or appreciate them. I hated the thought of her burying parts of herself just to keep Danny happy. And how if she took him back, she'd keep right on hiding. Maybe she was still desperate enough to want her old life back, and her ex along with it.

And those teacups would stay in the box.

If there was going to be a countdown clock till the end of us, then I wanted to do this for her. I wanted her to have something that was hers. Only hers.

So I texted Bonnie, knowing she'd see the message during her planning period.

Me: I'm off tonight. Can I make you dinner at your place?

Her reply came through an hour later while I was grocery shopping at the Winn-Dixie.

Clyde: That sounds great. You know the garage door code. Make yourself at home.

I'd stood in the canned vegetable aisle and stared at her message so long that someone had to say excuse me to get me to shift over.

Make yourself at home.

Home had always been a foreign concept to me. Growing up, I'd been different than my peers. There'd been no mother or father or picture-perfect life. Lia had been the one showing up for teacher conferences and then, later, to the principal's office.

The farmhouse had always been the place I ran away from, sneaking out and getting into trouble in the middle of the night. Same for the town. Kirby Falls hadn't been a cage exactly, but near enough to one that I'd rebelled at every turn.

And then Magnolia had come along. The apartment above it, simple and comfortable enough, but mostly an afterthought. The smooth bar top and the leather-backed stools and the scent of lemon furniture polish were the only things that I'd felt like I'd earned.

But home . . . I didn't think I could point to a place or a time. My roots didn't begin and end with tradition or community. There was a very real possibility that home was a person. Blond hair, light brown eyes, and a big heart. And I was probably going to lose her, too.

I finished gathering the ingredients for lasagna and then made my way to Bonnie's house.

It was a meal I'd put together for myself a hundred times. Nothing special, but it was familiar, and I wanted Bonnie to have something to come home to for once.

I'd been here, in her space, enough to know where everything was. I found the mixing bowls, pans, and spices easily enough. Then I played a horrible game of what-if and imagined what the kitchen would look like with glass-front cabinet doors and a big bay window next to the dining table. It would let in more light and brighten things up the way Bonnie wanted.

Forcing my thoughts back to the task at hand, I finished layering ingredients in the casserole dish and then put everything into the preheated oven to bake. There were garlic knots from Apollo's waiting on the counter. I'd reheat those before Bonnie arrived.

With the food squared away, I gathered my other supplies and went to the pantry. As I counted out teacups and several matching saucers, I envisioned the overall shape and size of the cabinet I'd sketched out earlier. I'd toyed around with the idea of a wall-mounted shelf, but Bonnie had space between the entryway and the dining nook for a cabinet. I'd already talked to someone about the glass panes I'd need. I just wanted to measure the wall to get all the details right and ensure I was building it big enough to hold her collection—and to leave her some room to grow it, if that was what she wanted.

I'd tucked my notebook and measuring tape back into my truck well before Bonnie came through the door an hour later.

The lasagna was resting, and the house smelled like garlic and warm bread.

And I thought her unrestrained, radiant smile might break me in two.

She walked right into me, arms squeezing tight around my middle. "It smells amazing in here. Thank you for making dinner."

I nodded and pressed a kiss to her forehead. "How was your day?"

She beamed. "It was great. Even better now."

My throat was tight and I didn't know why. Maybe it was all the things I didn't think I could say in the time we had left, or the guilt over keeping my conversation with Danny a secret. Or it could have just been the way she was acting like another person making a meal for her was the best thing that had ever happened.

I felt sick knowing her excitement over something so small was because she'd gone without for so long. I'd bet my bar that Danny had never welcomed her home with a warm meal or a quiet, genuine interest about her day. Or if he had, it had been so long ago that Bonnie couldn't remember it over the other things he'd done.

The apathy, the disinterest, the betrayal, the way he'd given up when things had gotten hard.

As much as I didn't want to think about that jerk, maybe he'd be better if she took him back. Perhaps finally realizing what he'd lost had put things into perspective, and he'd treat Bonnie the way she deserved.

As we talked over dinner and Bonnie told me about her students, the upcoming winter break, and Candace's wedding plans, I tried to stay in the moment.

I tried to appreciate every single second with Bonnie.

But I could feel myself retreating, staying quiet and letting her carry the conversation. Shoring up my walls and guarding my heart against disappointment.

"You okay?" Bonnie finally asked while I was loading the dishwasher and she was wiping down the counters, a scene so strangely comfortable and domestic that I wondered what it would be like to do other things like it. To decorate a Christmas tree or go grocery shopping together. Suddenly, I wanted to put gas in her car or rake leaves in the front yard.

Was that love? Finding someone you desperately wanted to take care of? To do everyday, ordinary things with?

I cleared my throat. "Yeah. Just tired."

"Do you need to go back to the apartment or will you stay?"

For as long as you'll have me, I repeated in my head.

Out loud, I replied, "I'll stay."

I left off the sense of foreboding, the surety that I'd lose her, that it was only a matter of time.

Bonnie wouldn't understand. In her world, things were certain. Relationships were stable, and families were tight-knit. There were group chats and birthday parties, traditions and expectations. People stayed.

But for someone like me, I knew better. People left. It was what happened in life.

Part of me thought I should fight for her. That when Danny inevitably came to his senses, grew his fucking backbone and knocked on that door, that I should be the one to answer it. Show Bonnie that I could be the better man and then actually live up to that.

But that was putting my wants and wishes above her own. Bonnie had spent her entire life looking out for everyone else, slotting herself in second or third, or sometimes, not at all. She turned herself inside out and sideways for the people she loved, and I refused to be one more person using her up.

I wanted Bonnie to be happy and to have what she truly desired.

And if the life she'd spent decades building turned up on her doorstep tomorrow, I wouldn't stand in the way of that.

Sometimes loving someone meant making sure they had what they needed. And I did love Bonnie.

I just wasn't certain I was the person she needed most.

BONNIE

I was bowling the game of my life.

To be fair, I would probably still finish up with a score under 175, but that was fine by me. I was focused, picking up spares, and having a good time with my girls.

After a round of high fives following my strike during the eighth frame, I'd taken my seat with a grin still firmly fixed on my face.

Mac was up to bowl and away from our table when Candace asked, "So, Bonnie, how are things going with Jack?"

My smile wilted a little. Not for any real reason. Most of my concerns were imaginary. Or, maybe, *unfounded* was more accurate.

"Things are good," I heard myself saying. "We're casual, you know. Just seeing where things go. Having fun."

I could tell by the look on Joan's face that I hadn't been as smooth and composed as I'd hoped.

"Casual, right. And you're good with that?" Candace said. No judgment in her tone, just genuine curiosity.

"Good with what?" Mac asked as she slid into the seat next to me and snagged one of my fries.

I wasn't . . . nervous about answering. But I was reluctant. I could feel the words stalling out in my mouth.

For the last three months, Jack had been mine and mine alone. My friends and family had given me space and hadn't pushed after finding out I was dating the town loner and hot bartender from Magnolia. But I could tell they were curious.

Like right now. Candace's eyes were alight and her expression eager. I knew she wanted me to be happy. So did Joan and my sister, too. So I wasn't sure why this was so hard.

Maybe I was more worried about disappointing them if things started to fall apart. For months, I'd been kind of a mess. They'd been gentle with me—still were, if I was being honest. And I didn't want them to get their hopes up that Jack and I had some happily ever after looming on the horizon when that might not be where we were headed.

I still believed in happy endings and healthy relationships. My marriage to Danny hadn't broken that in me. But, truthfully, I didn't know what Jack wanted. Pressuring him to decide didn't feel like the best way to find out.

"Good with Jack," I replied, then grabbed a sip of soda. "Candace was asking how things were going. We're good. Having lots of fun."

Mac eyed me for a moment and then pilfered another fry. "Fun? Is that what we're calling it?"

"Ugh, MacKenzie." I whacked her on the shoulder.

But she shoved another fry in her mouth, unbothered. Grinning she said, "I'm just saying. A little *fun* never hurt anybody."

"And as long as you're on the same page," Candace added, "about expectations and whatnot, then you *should* enjoy yourself, Bon. Be casual. Have *fun*. Whatever. Ride that motorcycle—"

"Motorcycle"—Mac winked obnoxiously—"right. Ride that motorcycle to your heart's content."

Joan and Candace laughed at my ridiculous sister.

"Anything to add?" I asked Joan. Since everyone else was taking a turn.

Joan's dark brows rose in surprise. "No. Not at all. I'm the last person anyone should come to for relationship advice. And you don't need it anyway, Bonnie. You have good instincts. Always have. You just have to trust them."

I blinked, not expecting that sort of response from quiet, no-nonsense Joan Judd. It made the compliment that much sweeter coming from her.

"Thanks, Joanie," I managed.

She was right. There were little voices inside all of us. Ones that inserted themselves when the need arose. A nudge here. A prod there. But oftentimes, it was easier to ignore them. To stick with the known, if not comfortable. To plug along on the easy path rather than take the hard road and listen to those instincts.

I'd known that there had been problems in my marriage. I hadn't wanted to admit—to myself or anyone else—that things had changed with Danny. That maybe we'd grown apart long before he'd cheated. I'd felt under-valued in my marriage, ignored. More like a maid than a partner.

And now, my instincts were telling me something was off with Jack.

Things had been a little weird lately. After Jack had made lasagna for me last week, I'd noticed him pulling away a bit. No, that wasn't right. *Rationing* felt like a better way to describe it. Like maybe if he could keep everything between us nice and even, then it wouldn't get messy, or he'd have a better chance of staying in control.

My natural inclination was to assume I'd done something wrong. It was natural to place blame on myself because that was what I was used to doing, but I couldn't think of anything I'd done to inadvertently spook him. We spent a lot of time together. We did relationship things. Maybe initially, it *had* been all about fun and sex and exploring that part of myself. But I'd always felt safe with Jack. I didn't think I could have managed a one-night stand with a stranger.

The relationship part had come easy between us. I liked Jack and wanted to be with him, but I was trying to manage my expectations and not push for more than he was willing to give.

Obviously, I wanted to invite him to come with me to Candace's wedding in a few weeks. I'd love it if he—and Lia—spent Christmas with my family out on the farm. But I worried about going too far, demanding too much. I didn't want to sail across the imaginary line of casualness that we'd been dancing pretty close to for a while now.

I lacked experience to draw from, but I didn't think folks in casual relationships met each other's families or spent the night in each other's beds without sex being a determining factor. Were they supposed to share meals? Holidays? Where was the stop sign exactly?

They probably also didn't indulge their lover's weird pet bunny by holding it up to the window to show it the wild rabbits outside in the yard. When I'd caught Jack talking to Oreo in the living room the other day, I'd almost died from the cuteness. Nothing about that had felt casual to me.

But since he'd made me dinner last week, things had shifted. Jack was taking bits and pieces of himself and holding them hostage. Physically, I hadn't seen him much this week. He'd been working late at Magnolia. And this past weekend was the first one he hadn't spent at my house in quite some time. He'd mentioned he needed to be out at the farmhouse, helping Lia with some repairs.

I understood. Of course, I did. But I missed him.

Clearly, I'd gotten used to the rhythm we'd fallen into. The late nights together. His leather-and-whiskey scent on my sheets. How he always kissed my forehead when he saw me and really listened to me when I spoke.

We'd still been texting. So at least there was that.

"I'm going to run to the restroom," I told the table. "Y'all keep bowling. I'll be right back."

When I finished up and reemerged in the lobby, Danny was leaning against the counter waiting for me. It had been stupid of me to think I could ignore him for so long. But, frankly, I'd assumed he wouldn't put in the effort of seeking me out.

I hadn't even looked for him down at the other end of the bowling alley tonight. I hadn't noticed him or his team. He'd just been one more body in an ugly bowling shirt.

"You're a hard woman to get a hold of," he remarked.

"I can't think of a single thing we have to discuss, Danny."

He straightened to his full height and gave me a look like he couldn't believe what he was hearing. "So this is really how it's going to be from now on? You pretending I don't exist? We live in the same tiny-ass town, Bonnie. You can't just ignore me."

As if to prove my point, I moved to walk around him, but he sidestepped directly into my path.

I gave an exasperated huff. "What do you need to say so badly? You had me all to yourself for seventeen years. You couldn't find the time then?"

Danny rolled his eyes. "All to myself. Okay, sure. I shared you with the tourists and the townsfolk. With all the Clarks, the farm, the festivals, your students and their families. Maybe if you'd been more worried about keeping me happy instead of every other goddamn person in Kirby Falls, then we'd still be—" He broke off with a sigh. "I didn't come here to fight."

Scoffing, I crossed my arms over my chest, suddenly cold and growing more numb by the second. "Could have fooled me."

He lowered his voice and repeated, "I didn't come here to fight. I know you're dating that bartender and moving on. Sowing your wild oats or whatever."

I felt my mouth drop open at his dismissive words. *How dare he?*

Numbness quickly gave way to anger, white-hot and all-consuming. I took a step closer, replacing the careful distance I'd tried to maintain with blazing intention.

"You know what, Danny? You're right. I gave a lot of myself to this town and the people in it. But the only person who ever made me feel like it was a waste was you. I'm done apologizing for how I spend my time. What I do or don't do is no longer any of your concern."

I was close enough to see the embarrassed flush enter his pale cheeks. But I couldn't find any regret or remorse within myself. I was glad I'd said what I'd said. Danny needed to hear it. And he'd probably been stunned to hear me stand up for myself for once.

His eyes searched mine for a moment before he swallowed and said evenly, "I know that. I do. I just thought if we could talk for a minute. Slow things down and—"

"Bonnie, you're up," Joan interrupted, appearing like an avenging angel at my side. The look she aimed at Danny had him backing up a step, but her voice was eerily calm. "Time to go."

Danny's clear blue eyes turned pleading, but I ignored him and walked with Joan through the dim, hazy interior, back to our lane.

"You okay?" she murmured, just loud enough to be heard over the music.

"Yeah," I replied. And I meant it. For the first time, when confronted with my ex-husband, I didn't feel that familiar knot of dread twisting me up on the inside. There wasn't the painful pulse of my heartbeat in my throat, and I had enough air in my lungs. "Thank you, Joan."

"It was nothing. You had it under control," she said simply. Then, to my surprise, she walked past our table and out onto the approach area. She grabbed her bowling ball from the ball return and took her turn.

I looked to Candace and Mac as I resumed my seat, but they were deep in conversation, Candace showing my sister something wedding related on her phone.

Joan must have seen me, cornered by Danny in the lobby, and come to my aid. It wasn't actually my turn, and the others hadn't noticed me missing.

I watched as Joan took her second approach, knocking out pins nine and ten for a neat spare.

Candace and Mac whooped, offering up high fives as Joan returned to the table.

Before she could sit, I grabbed her in a quick, hard hug. She was tense, all hard, lean lines and toned muscles, but after a moment, she released a breath and patted me awkwardly on the back. "It was nothing," she repeated, for my ears alone.

"Not to me," I whispered back.

Then I released her and grinned. "Nice shot, Holy Roller."

She snorted a laugh.

"Yesss," Candace called. "A bowling nickname." She pointed to her sister. "I love it."

"No." Joan shot me a betrayed look. "No nicknames. Joanie is bad enough."

"Holy Roller! Holy Roller!" Candace chanted. Mac and I joined in.

Joan looked like she wanted to murder us, but there was a tiny tilt to the corner of her lips. "Okay. *Jesus*. Stop."

"Oh! She's already in the spirit," Mac clapped. "*The spirit*. See what I did there?"

We all laughed and continued our teasing.

Then it really was my turn to bowl.

And I didn't spare my ex-husband a single thought for the rest of the night.

Pun very much intended.

After another three days without seeing Jack, a sense of foreboding started to creep in. I found myself bracing, wondering if we needed to have a conversation. Would he officially break up with me, even though we weren't technically in a relationship? Or would he just fade away and out of my life?

Disappointment combined with something too sharp and unwise to name. I felt weak in the face of it, discouraged and heartsick over the possibility of what could have been.

But then Jack texted Sunday evening and asked to come over, and I was back to anticipating an awkward breakup.

Me: I'm running errands, but I'll be home in an hour. Meet you there?

Jack: Sounds good.

Jack: I've missed you.

I stared at my phone, confused all over again. Would you tell someone that before you ended things?

I did my best to push aside all my conflicting emotions as I finished up my grocery shopping for the week, but when the time came to start my car and leave the parking lot, I couldn't do it.

I sat there, dry-eyed, and stared into the darkness, wondering what I'd do if Jack and I were really over. With shaking hands, I scrolled back through our text conversations and found the early days. The late-night lists of our favorite things. The way he'd changed in my perception of him from intimidating bad boy to just Jack, this quiet, thoughtful guy who didn't feel like he belonged. But I knew without a shadow of a doubt that he fit with me.

You couldn't make someone stay or will a relationship out of apathy and indifference. I knew that firsthand. But if I could just figure out what had caused Jack to pull away so suddenly, maybe I could—

No.

I shook my head to dispel the urge to fix this by force. I couldn't do that. The situation with Jack wasn't a puzzle to solve. We needed to be adults and communicate, and that was all there was to it. I wasn't making the same mistake again.

With a deep breath, I started the car and shifted into drive.

I must have lingered in the parking lot of the Winn-Dixie for much longer than I meant to because when I got home, Jack was asleep on my couch with a rabbit on his chest.

I stood in the hallway from the garage, staring helplessly with five grocery bags weighing down each arm. A can of something must have shifted because a clang sounded, and Jack's hazel eyes blinked open. He took in the nose and whiskers six inches from his face before his gaze met mine. And then a sleepy smile emerged, one layered with aching relief and unguarded sweetness.

The bags thunked onto the floor.

Jack sat up, cradling Oreo carefully before depositing her on her fleece blanket that was folded neatly on the end of the couch.

Then he walked over and wrapped me in his arms. "I missed you, Clyde," he said as he pressed a kiss to my forehead. And I thought, *Oh*. There was no way I could have heard this sort of urgency in his text. The truth of his statement. Felt his scruff on my neck as he breathed me in and then sighed in relief.

"I missed you too," I whispered, a shaky exhalation.

But then my eyes caught on something over Jack's shoulder. Something that hadn't been there earlier today. It fit neatly between the windows leading from the entryway into the dining area. A gorgeous piece of furniture that I was quite sure I didn't own.

I released Jack and moved around him to get a better look. With every step, new beautiful details came into focus.

The back of the cabinet was flat and parallel with the wall, but the sides and front extended out at angles, like half a pentagon, with thin, delicate shelves along the inside. It was tall, nearly reaching the ceiling. The glass panes were clear and reflective between the honey-stained columns making up the cabinet. Beams shone down from discreetly embedded lights in the top interior.

"I wanted you to have something for yourself." Jack's voice came from behind me, close enough that I could feel his warmth at my back. "You shouldn't have to pack up the things you love and hide them away."

My fingers stroked a smooth line along the cabinet front to the delicate brass door pull shaped like a ring. The door swung open easily on smooth hinges, and I took in all the beautiful teacups shining like pearls on the shelves.

"You can rearrange them however you want. I just . . . couldn't stand the thought of them being shoved in the bottom of your pantry."

"You made this for me," I said, and it wasn't a question. I knew it in my heart. "That's where you've been for the last week and a half."

"Yes."

I closed the cabinet door gently before turning around and throwing my arms around him. "Thank you," I choked, unable to believe the gift he'd given me. Unsure how to accept something that I didn't even know I needed, something that could heal me in a way I'd never imagined.

It wasn't panic making it hard to breathe, but emotion—big, messy, inconvenient emotions. My arms squeezed him tighter as tears leaked down my cheeks.

Jack rubbed soothing circles across my back and shoulder blades, but it was no use. I was hiccupping, sobbing into his shirt.

How sad was it that a piece of furniture could instigate a total breakdown? But, truthfully, it was Jack, breaking down all the walls I'd put up to protect myself. From Danny's criticism and indifference, from people's opinion of me, from the failure of my marriage. The bricks laid carefully to prevent new hurt from ever getting in and the old hurt from ever getting out.

This supposed bad boy with a motorcycle and a bad attitude. I hadn't realized I'd needed to protect myself from his sweetness, his thoughtfulness.

Maybe I didn't have to. Maybe I could just accept it. Maybe—

"If I did something wrong or overstepped," he murmured suddenly, in between my broken cries. "If I touched a nerve—"

I pulled back quickly so I could see his face. "You didn't do anything wrong, Jack. I love the cabinet. Love that you made it for me. It's amazing and kind and thoughtful and perfect. And the sad truth is that I'm out of practice. I don't quite know how to handle someone doing something like that for me."

Face solemn, Jack cupped my cheeks and ran his thumbs beneath my eyes to wipe away the dampness clinging to my skin. "You deserve good things. You're worthy of someone making a fuss over you, wanting to take care of you, to see you happy."

I tried to smile but felt my eyes fill once more. I knew he was right. It was a topic I'd discussed with my therapist over and over again—feeling deserving of love. But it was one thing to talk about the hypothetical and another thing entirely when you had someone standing in front of you, actually doing the work.

Jack hugged me again, his strong forearms crossing over my lower back, and I let myself relax into the embrace.

And later that night, when we were in bed, I finally stopped lying to myself.

As Jack's hands and lips dragged over my skin, when there was only heat between us, I stopped trying to hold it all in. I acknowledged the truth— the one that had been swirling around inside me for a while now.

I was in love with Jack.

I worried that he could hear it in the wild beat of my heart. See it in my tender gaze. Feel it with every reverent press of my lips.

For all the ways I'd been trying to protect my heart, I couldn't do it by lying to myself anymore.

nineteen

BONNIE

Danny's mother died two weeks before Christmas.

The visitation was scheduled for this evening at Wheeler Funeral Home downtown, and the funeral would be tomorrow at the cemetery out near Miller Creek. All the preparations had been made ahead of time by Diane herself.

Her health had declined pretty rapidly in the last month. She'd been sleeping more and more during my visits, and I knew from Eldridge that Diane had been in quite a bit of pain.

Death was never easy, but sometimes it was a mercy.

That knowledge didn't stop me from grieving her—crying over her loss and wishing things could have been different.

I arrived in the parlor of the funeral home alone. Jack was working, but I hadn't mentioned the death of my former mother-in-law to him. I wasn't sure why. Maybe because I'd never managed to explain my visits to a dying woman over the last few months. It felt messy. Like I was still clinging to my past life in favor of my new one. But I'd loved Diane. She wasn't just Danny's mom. She'd been a big part of my life, too. I couldn't just stop loving her, like flipping a switch, especially when she hadn't done anything wrong.

I didn't owe Danny anything, and I wasn't attending the funeral for him. I was doing it for a woman who'd been like a second mother to me. And the grieving husband she was leaving behind.

Part of me worried about how Jack would interpret my dedication to my former in-laws, how he might read into my presence here tonight. Like it had been one more thing on a long list that I was unable to say no to.

I knew how Jack felt about the way I tried to keep the peace and make other people happy. I figured he'd look at me with knowing disappointment. However, it was wrong of me to project those reactions onto him. I wasn't married to Danny anymore—the person who'd actually made passive-aggressive jibes about my time and energy outside the home. I shouldn't be punishing Jack for mistakes my ex-husband had made.

I'd talk to Jack tonight and tell him about Diane. I'd explain myself because it was the right thing to do, not because I needed to justify my decisions.

The sickly sweet scent of flowers was nearly overwhelming, as was the crowd of people gathered to pay their respects at the small funeral home.

Diane had been a teacher in the community. Her influence was one of the reasons I'd become an educator. There were sure to be lots of her former students and coworkers from over the years, not to mention longtime neighbors and friends. Her passing would hit a lot of people hard.

I said hello to a few folks I recognized as I moved through the space. A television was looping a slideshow of photographs, and I stopped to watch. My already heavy heart squeezed with every grainy image that went by.

There she and Eldridge were in sepia tones, sitting in the back of an old Ford truck. They looked like teenagers. Then another snapshot from their wedding day, big smiles on both their faces. I watched as the little family welcomed their daughters and finally Danny. Then it was a myriad of memories from birthdays and holidays set to music, many with my own face staring back at me.

There was one photo I'd never seen before, though. It was taken in Diane's kitchen. She and I were in the middle of canning strawberry jam.

We weren't even looking at the camera, just quietly working side by side. Familiarity born of time and tradition. I could hear her voice telling me the secret was to add a teaspoon of butter to the jam while it cooked, right at the end.

I pulled a tissue out of my purse and wiped my eyes before finding my way into the main room, where the visitation was being held.

The receiving line was long, and I settled in to wait as friends and acquaintances occasionally came by to give me a hug or a kind word.

Eventually, I made it to Jackie and Meredith, Danny's sisters. Meredith's husband, Ollie, was with her, and I hugged them all and passed along my condolences.

Danny pulled me into an embrace before I'd even released his eldest sister.

I stiffened but said quietly, "I'm so sorry about your mom. She was one of my favorite people in the world."

He didn't reply, but I felt him swallow several times against my shoulder in an attempt to get his emotions under control.

With quick, efficient movements, I pulled away, unsure how to navigate this weird place with the family that had once been mine. Danny's eyes were red-rimmed and devastated.

But I moved over to Eldridge and offered what kind words I could. I felt his body shaking against mine, silent sobs wracking his thin frame.

It was difficult to take a step back, to leave these people with their grief, a sadness that I shared too.

I didn't realize Danny had reached for my hand until he tried to reel me back into his side.

"You should be up here with us," he said brokenly. "You're family. You were hers just as much as the rest of us."

My eyes widened, and I looked helplessly to Danny's father and siblings. Someone to step in and tell him that wouldn't be appropriate. But I thought they were all too grief-stricken to manage.

I shook my head, noting the folks gathered around the room starting to take notice and stare. Gently, but firmly, I said, "No, Danny. That wouldn't be right." Then I met the gazes of his family members and said one last time, "I'm so very sorry for your loss."

Finally, I tugged my fingers free from Danny's desperate hold and made my way to the exit.

The winter air stung my damp cheeks, and I pulled my black peacoat tighter around my body to ward off the sudden chill.

I wasn't aware of footsteps behind me until I was nearly to my car. Turning, I found Danny jogging across the parking lot.

"Danny," I sighed as he came to a stop in front of me, puffs of air leaving his mouth as he caught his breath.

"Just—I'm sorry, Bonnie. I'm sorry. I made a mistake. You and me. We belong together. Since we were kids. I promised my mother I'd fix this." His face crumpled for a brief moment before he composed himself. "Before she died, I told her I'd get you back. Put things right."

I closed my eyes, feeling fresh tears escape down my cheeks.

"You can't really want to throw it all away, Bon," he added.

My body was trembling. From the cold, from my anger, from bone-deep weariness . . . I didn't know. This wasn't the time or the place, but I couldn't let this go on.

So I kept my voice even and said, "No, Danny. I didn't want to throw it all away, but you did that for us. And you don't get to take it back now. I'm sorry about your momma. I really am. But stay out of my life."

<hr>

JACK

Bonnie was asleep on my sofa when I let myself in just after two in the morning. We'd been busier than normal, and I'd had to help Sebastian and Sasha close.

I knew something was wrong before I'd even taken off my shoes.

She was still wearing her winter coat, her body curved in on itself like she needed protecting. The blanket lay unused over the back of the sofa, despite being within reach. Bonnie's face was tense, even in sleep, and her mascara had run at some point, flecks of it around her eyes and temples.

Frowning, I sat down near her feet and wrapped my hand gently around her ankle. I kept my voice low so I didn't startle her and said, "Bonnie."

She blinked in groggy awareness before focusing on me. Then her face crumpled, and she reached for me.

I scooped her into my arms, drawing her tight against me even as my heart hammered in my chest.

This was it. She was here to break things off. Danny had probably gone to see her, made his play to win her back, and now she'd come to end things. Bonnie was a kind, empathetic person. Of course, she'd be upset at the thought of hurting me. That was the only explanation I had for why she was so out of sorts on a random Tuesday night.

Despite the warmth of her slight frame against me, I went cold at the realization. My throat was so tight that I worried I wouldn't be able to speak. That was probably a good thing. It would keep me from begging her to change her mind when the time came.

But then Bonnie choked out brokenly, "Danny's mom died," and all those what-ifs dissolved in the face of her unexpected announcement.

Her fingers tightened on the back of my shirt, so I ran my hand down her spine in a soothing gesture. "I'm so sorry," I managed.

Bonnie had been with her ex since they were kids. She'd probably been in his family's life just as long. This was obviously a difficult loss for her. Likely made all the more complicated due to her divorce.

"What do you need?" I asked softly.

She pulled back abruptly at my words, her face creased with worry and damp with sorrow. "I need to tell you something. Diane—Danny's mom— she had cancer. She'd been in remission for years, but it came back, and she was at home with hospice. A while ago, Danny came to see me at work to ask me to visit her. So I did. I went to see her every week—without Danny there. I brought some of her favorite dishes to try to get her to eat. But we all knew the end was coming."

I absorbed this and tried not to feel the weight of deception. Bonnie was grieving, and this wasn't really the time to question her motives. But I still asked, "Why didn't you tell me?"

"I don't know," she replied, looking down at her lap where she clutched one of my hands like she needed to keep me from pulling away. "I guess I thought you'd be disappointed in me. Or think I was being too nice or stretching myself too thin. But Diane was like a mother to me, Jack. I've known her since I was fourteen years old. I love—loved her a lot. Danny's father, too."

"I'm not your keeper, Bonnie."

"I know. And it's not fair, the way I assumed that. I guess I got really good at predicting the sticky spots in my marriage—the things that would push buttons or cause a fight—and did whatever I could to avoid them and keep the peace. It was wrong of me to apply that to my relationship with you. You've never once tried to manage my time or tell me what to do."

I nodded, ignoring the ache that caused in my middle, the comparison to her ex. But I understood. I knew there wasn't a deceptive bone in her body. The omission had been intentional but not malicious. And I wasn't the type of person who needed to know where she was at all times anyway. I'd never understood couples like that. Why would you bother being in a relationship if you couldn't trust someone?

It hurt that she hadn't leaned on me, though. Knowing she'd been visiting a dying woman and bearing that burden alone made me wish she'd been comfortable enough to tell me.

The situation with Danny's mother hadn't affected me directly. Not really.

The guilt I'd been dealing with since Danny's last visit to the bar reared its ugly head. That conversation had Bonnie stamped all over it, and I'd kept it from her, to protect myself, to extend my time with her.

"Danny came to see me at the bar," I blurted in a fit of guilt.

Bonnie's pain gave way to confusion. It was my turn to clutch her hand like a lifeline.

"He tried to warn me away from you," I admitted. "Talked a bunch of shit, but ultimately I think he realized that he"—I took a steadying breath—"he wants you back, Bonnie. He knows he fucked up, and it took knowing you were with someone else to get him to make a move. I know I should have told you, but I just . . . couldn't."

I'd been selfish. Withholding that information had allowed me to keep her a little longer. Realizing she had the knowledge now, and the fear of what she'd do with it, had all my muscles going taut. It was like awaiting the executioner's blade. It was only a matter of time.

"It's okay, Jack. Knowing wouldn't have changed anything. Danny—he's been texting and calling, trying to get in touch with me. I've been ignoring him," she rushed to add, and something in me went cold. "But tonight, he chased me out to the parking lot and told me he'd made a mistake. That he promised his mother before she died that he'd fix things between the two of us. That he wants me back."

I slid my hand out of hers. "I see."

Maybe Danny wasn't as much of a coward as I'd assumed, if he'd been trying to pin her down for a while now. And of course, he was using his mother's dying wish to his advantage. I shouldn't be surprised. Cornering Bonnie when she was emotional and vulnerable.

I shook my head. "So that's it, I guess."

"What?" Bonnie asked, baffled.

"You get your life back," I clarified.

"Are you serious right now? Why would I—how could I ever want that back?"

"The reasons you said. You didn't want to start over and throw away the years you'd spent building a life, a family, a marriage." The words came easily, like a pledge repeated over and over again. A reminder of why she and I were always going to be temporary.

"The really *unhealthy* marriage, where I was miserable and with someone who I'd grown apart from?" Bonnie's eyes were bright and incredulous. "I don't want Danny. I want you, Jack. How can you not see that?"

"But you said—"

"Months ago!" she exploded. "When I was drunk and vulnerable on the day my divorce was final. Are you holding me to that? After everything that's happened with us? Opinions change. Feelings change. Time passes. I couldn't possibly want him because I want you! I love you!"

For a moment, I let her declaration wash over me. The aching truth that this woman loved me back. That she could care about me that way. Like I might just be worth it.

I sucked in a breath and forced the knowledge away. It didn't matter, I told myself as I took another deliberate inhale.

Chest heaving, I stared at her, knowing she wasn't lying but still unable to accept it. It was too much pressure for someone like me. Being the undeserving asshole she wanted to give up everything for. Her past and her potential future, with the person she'd already invested so much time and love in. In the grand scheme of things, how could three months of whatever we had compare to a lifetime of what was in her heart?

She had connections and memories that I could never compete with. Hell, she had a whole other family who relied on her. One that still held her devotion and commitment. She was too good and kind to let her breakup with Danny impact her relationship with the Jensens.

I couldn't give her anything like that. There was just me, and I . . . I wasn't enough. I wasn't worth all that unwavering devotion that Bonnie seemed to wield so effortlessly. People didn't stick around for me for a reason. I wasn't enough. Bonnie just didn't know it yet.

So I restacked my walls—the ones that had kept me protected for years— neatly into place and hardened my resolve. "Don't do that."

"Do what?" she asked.

"Don't act like this is more than what it is. We've been casual."

Bonnie laughed, the sound watery and disbelieving. "We're together all the time. You've made sure you've been what I needed, every step of the way. You took me to meet your grandmother. You snuggle on the couch with my damn rabbit, Jack. And I'm in your bed every night."

"That's just sex," I argued, ignoring the softball lodged in my throat.

Bonnie's face paled, making the smeared makeup and red around her eyes more pronounced. The hurt and shock were plain enough to see, and I hated myself a little more.

But I kept going, trying to make her understand. Even if I couldn't tell her I loved her, couldn't confirm what she knew to be true, I would never hold her back. And that's all loving me would do.

"You were just killing time, Bonnie. You've known all along that this wasn't—wasn't going to work. I'm not . . . whatever you're looking for. I'm not husband material. I'm not Danny."

"It turns out," she replied quietly, "he wasn't really husband material either."

She wasn't getting it, so I said, "You keep holding on to this idea of me that you had back in high school. Some teenage fantasy. But here's the truth: If we had known each other back then, you would have tried to fix me. You would have wanted to tutor me or help me with extra credit or try to convince me to stop skipping school. But more than likely, I would have used you. I would have talked you into doing my work for me. I would have taken advantage of your kindness and your heart, and I would have ruined you. Dragged you down with me. You would have hoped to change me. And maybe you still do, if you're sitting here telling me you love me. That urge to fix me—to turn me into someone respectable, someone good enough for you—won't go away. And I refuse to be one more broken thing in your life that requires your attention."

I'd taken the wind out of her, but at least she didn't look like she wanted to argue anymore, and I was grateful for that. Because I didn't know how much longer I could sit here and wear her down. Parts of me were wearing away, too.

"I thought I had enough confidence or self-esteem or whatever to not even think about your ex," I confessed, giving her something true. "But I can't stand the thought of you comparing me to him. I don't want to be anyone's sloppy seconds or silver medal."

Bonnie huffed a humorless laugh that had me stiffening. "There is no comparison, Jack. I'm not lining up the two of you side by side and finding you lacking. I couldn't even if I wanted to. For me to compare you to him, I'd have to still want some part of him or miss him or see Danny as someone *worth* comparison. And I don't." She smiled then, and it was heartbreaking. "There's only you and me, and the happiest I've been in my whole life."

"You're lying to yourself," I insisted. "And you'll eventually regret it." *Regret me*, I added silently. "You lie to yourself and everyone around you to keep the peace. You act like it's your job to make everyone else happy. Do you even know what you really want, deep down?"

Bonnie frowned but didn't speak.

I gritted my teeth and forced out, "That's why I don't want you to handle me. To manage me and play peacemaker. I'd rather you get mad, get angry, or throw something. Show a damn emotion for once—one that's true, not something carefully calculated and stamped for approval and public consumption. The perfect version you trot out for your family— even your sister. You're never going to be happy being yourself if you're so worried about what other people think."

"And that's what this is? Something true?" she said, pointing in my direction. "Pretending you don't care about me. Pushing me away so you don't have to deal with something real. Because you don't get involved, right? You're not invested enough in anything to get hurt. Not this town, not your bar, not your soccer team, and not me. You're just easygoing Jack. You and your motorcycle and a big fucking chip on your shoulder. Well, fine. Have it your way."

I sat there as she scrambled off the couch and went to the front door.

Bonnie slipped her shoes on and grabbed her purse before whirling around, face pinched and angry. "You know, I'm sorry if you felt pressured by me. If I made you feel like I wanted more than you were willing to give. But I never thought—"

"Jesus Christ, stop apologizing," I snapped. "I'm letting you down easy, and you're fucking apologizing to me."

"Oh, is that what this is?" With a disappointed shake of her head, she reached for the doorknob. "Got it. Message received."

This time, the door rattled in the frame when it slammed behind her.

How painfully ironic that I'd baited her into standing up for herself, and she'd actually done it for once. I didn't know whether to be proud or miserable.

It didn't take long to figure it out. The longer I sat there, the heavier I felt. The weight of all the things I'd said tonight pressing down on me, burying me, drowning me in deep water.

I'd gotten what I wanted. Too bad it didn't make accepting it any easier.

BONNIE

Mac started talking before she'd cleared the front door.

"I got the last bottle of holiday custard. And the pizza and garlic knots will be here in twenty. I also ordered a Greek salad to split just so we could say we ate a vegetable at some point."

My sister's arms were loaded down with shopping bags, but when I moved to help her, she waved me off.

She dropped her supplies on my kitchen counter, and a pint of butter pecan ice cream went rolling onto the floor along with a box of Cookie Dough Bites and a bag of honey mustard pretzels.

With wide eyes, I stared at the mess of comfort calories. "Wow, you really went all out."

"Well," she said, swooping down to pick up the snacks that had tried to escape, "I figured if we were eating our feelings, then we should have some depth in the lineup."

Following my last conversation with Jack, I'd pushed through and made it to the weekend. I knew I couldn't let myself crumble, or school would be unmanageable. But today had been the last day before holiday break for both students and faculty, and now, I could let myself fall apart.

I'd texted my sister and told her Jack and I had broken up. She'd said she'd be over in an hour.

I really did love my sister.

But for a long time, I hadn't let her love me back. Not the real me anyway. Jack had tossed around a lot of bullshit on Tuesday night, but he hadn't been wrong about that.

I used to think I was the truest version of myself when I was alone, hiding myself away, tucking my fears and worries somewhere secret where no one could find them. But I think I was most myself when I was with Jack. I'd let him in. He'd seen the messy, imperfect parts of me and hadn't shied away.

It was time I let other people know the truth, too.

"Are we watching *Pride and Prejudice* or *North and South*?" Mac asked as she shoved another pint of ice cream into my freezer.

I took a deep breath and said, "I thought, maybe, we could just talk."

My sister's movements halted for a long moment before she replied casually, "Yeah. Uh, sure. We can do that."

I smiled at the surprise in her tone as well as the terrible attempt to hide it.

"Let's sit in the living room," I called. "Bring the pretzels."

Once we were settled on the couch, I turned to face Mac and told her the truth, for the first time in a very long time. "I haven't been a very good sister to you."

"Bonnie," she scolded, and I loved her even more for looking so affronted on my behalf.

Instead of arguing, I explained, "I've hidden a lot of things about myself and kept even more from you. Not just you, but Mom and Dad and Larry and everyone. I only wanted you to see the good stuff, like the shiny social media version of myself. I never even told you what happened with my marriage."

"I didn't ask," Mac said quietly.

With a sad smile, I told her, "Because you didn't feel like you could. I was so fragile and messed up at the time. And you didn't want me to unravel even more."

My sister's dark brows were furrowed, but she didn't dispute it.

It seemed silly now, after all this time, that I'd kept so many things from Mac and the rest of my family. I could have leaned on them. I could have told them the truth about Danny and the end of my marriage. It had taken some time, but I'd learned that I didn't have to do life alone. And the people who loved me the most had earned the chance to be there for me. Instead, I'd punished them and discounted them, taking their loyalty for granted.

"I want to be more honest," I said. "I want to be the sister you deserve. Let you see the messy side of me. The parts that are tired and anti-social and a little bit cynical. And I'm sick of keeping things from you just so you can keep this favorable opinion of me. I'm not perfect. I cry. I have anxiety. I see a therapist. I stole a rabbit."

Mac blinked.

I continued, "What I'm trying to say is, I want you to know me. I want us to have a good relationship—a real relationship. I love you, MacKenzie."

"I love you too, Bon." She reached over and drew me into a tight hug. "Even if you stole a rabbit, apparently."

I snorted into her shoulder.

For the next half an hour, I told my sister the truth. I told her about my marriage. How unhappy and lonely I'd been as Danny and I steadily grew apart. I admitted how stressful it had been trying for a baby for so long, while Danny refused to see a doctor or contemplate fertility evaluations and treatment. I told her about Danny cheating and how everything came undone over the course of ten months, ending with him asking for the divorce in a fit of frustrated impatience.

I only paused to grab the pizza and tip the delivery driver before resuming once more.

Mac listened and didn't interject her opinion or interrupt to call Danny a piece of shit, which I appreciated and knew must have been difficult for her.

I wrapped things up with how Jack and I had met. How I'd gone to Magnolia on the night of my divorce looking for trouble, but instead . . . I'd found him. Then I told her about falling in love with him slowly over the last few months. His surprising sweetness, his constant care, the cabinet. And then how he'd broken things off three days ago.

"I'm sorry I've been so closed off," I said, finally. "I thought if you only saw the very best version of me, you wouldn't worry."

"And I was smothering you," Mac replied matter-of-factly.

"No," I argued.

She wiped her hand on a napkin and placed her empty plate on the coffee table. "No, I was. Always texting, making sure you were coming to trivia, or inviting you to dinner with me and Brady. I definitely overdid it after you and Danny separated. But, Bon, I was so worried. Seeing you have a panic attack . . . I had no idea what to do. I couldn't even remember the last time I'd seen you cry. I think I was in shock or something. And it scared me enough that I never wanted it to happen ever again. So I thought if I checked on you enough, spent enough time with you, that I could keep you busy and distracted. That I could prevent it."

"And I do appreciate that, Mac. I know you care about me. That's never been a doubt in my mind. I'm going to do better. Be more honest. If I'm having a crappy day, I won't just gloss over it and say I'm fine."

"You could get mad at me, too. We could fight," she added helpfully. "Sisters do that. Tell me to fuck off if I'm being too much or suffocating you. Or if you need me to help you get through this thing with Jack, I can be here with pizza and ice cream whenever you want."

I smiled, grateful for my loyal, badass sister. But I didn't know what was going to happen with Jack, and I'd spent too much of my life doing things the hard way to try to fix this on my own.

"What happened, Bonnie? Did he hurt you?"

I sighed, but admitted, "Yes, but not how you mean. He found out Danny wanted to fix things between us and just assumed that he and I were done. Like I could just toss Jack aside and go running back to my married life. Like the last three months never happened." I frowned as I considered. "I think he was trying to be noble or something."

Jack had hurt me, but he'd hurt himself too. Walking away had been one of the hardest things I'd ever done, but I'd needed to protect myself.

There was a part of me that thought Jack would realize I wasn't going back to Danny. That with some time and perspective, he'd see the truth. My old life wasn't packed up in a box somewhere just waiting for me to dig it out and open it up.

I was changed. Things were different now. I didn't need to cling to the past because my present had been pretty damn good.

"Wow. He's an idiot," Mac decided.

I smiled, my tender heart agreeing and protesting at the same time.

"But you don't want Danny back, right?"

Incredulous, I stared at Mac.

"I'm just making sure!" She held up her hands. "You were devastated, Bonnie. People go back to their undeserving exes all the time."

I blinked. Maybe Jack's assumption hadn't been so unfounded if my sister thought I'd consider taking Danny back, too.

I wasn't sure how to explain something that had lived inside me for so long. Another drawback to hiding your most vulnerable parts.

"I think Danny and I grew apart a long time ago," I admitted. "Or maybe I forced myself to grow around him. You know those trees you see with twisted roots and limbs, searching for any bit of sunlight they can get. I was like that. Turning myself inside out to be who I needed to be. But I deserve my own space. I deserve to live out from underneath someone else's shadow."

Mac's blue eyes welled with tears, but she nodded.

"I don't want the life I had before," I insisted. "And, yes, I was devastated, but not anymore. Danny didn't break my heart." I fought to find the right words. "He . . . made me question everything I knew to be true. Not just about my marriage or love, but about the way I thought I could hold it all together. I was unhappy, lonely, and neglected, probably, too. But I thought I was managing. Through the illusion of control, I thought I could will everything to be okay. That I was stronger than something as flimsy and changeable as emotion."

"But Jack," I acknowledged, "he did the reverse. He denied himself—and me—in favor of control. I know he loves me. And he pushed me away despite that. Probably because he thinks I'm better off without him. Some misguided attempt to save me. Mac, it was like he couldn't believe that I would pick him, and *that* broke my heart."

My sister's gaze moved past my shoulder to the beautiful cabinet near the front door. I knew what she was seeing. All the time and effort. The details. The love that went into building it, whether Jack wanted to admit that or not.

"Well, that's what he's used to," she finally said, meeting my eyes once again. "People leaving. Feeling like he's not enough for them to stay. Maybe he didn't want to give you the chance to prove him right, too."

I nodded. Jack kept himself contained for a reason. He'd rebelled and acted out at a young age. It was easy to trace those mistakes back to his childhood and his abandonment issues. He'd grown up and taken charge of his life, but he still carried the scars. I hurt for that little boy who'd needed help falling asleep. For the teenager who hadn't been able to find a place he belonged, so he'd created his own.

And for the man in a bar across town who'd denied himself my love before I could take it away.

He might have been lying to himself about our relationship, claiming it was casual right up until the bitter end, but Jack had been right about some things.

I hadn't wanted to hear it at the time, but I did try to be perfect for everyone. I hid my emotions and faked being fine.

Mac wasn't the only person who'd seen the bright, optimistic version of myself instead of the messy real one.

Initially, I'd told myself that I was putting people at ease, keeping the peace with my lies. What did I have to complain about? I had a good job, a home, and a family who supported me. I'd been married to my high school sweetheart.

Sure, I'd been lonely, but it hadn't felt right to speak up. It seemed selfish and ungrateful to want more when I already had so much. Comparison was tricky like that. It provided the excuse to take what you got and claim it was what you deserved.

And when my life fell apart, wanting it back—even the solitary bits and the cheating husband—was easy and comfortable. That was the awful, painful truth. For once, in a moment of weakness, I'd been honest, and Jack had borne witness to it.

For whatever reason, he'd clung to that drunken confession with both hands and held me to it—held it against me. It had given him the excuse he needed to break things apart.

But I couldn't spend my life being afraid to be honest, and I told Mac as much.

"It's okay to let your guard down," she said sincerely, passing me a carton of ice cream. "People love you—and not just the perfect version everyone expects. They love *you*, the heart of you. And they want you to be happy, whatever that looks like. I can understand you not wanting to talk to Mom and Dad or Will about relationship stuff. But you can always talk to me or Larry. You should tell Candace what's going on, too. She's been so worried about you."

I winced, knowing that I hadn't been fair to my best friend. "She has the wedding so soon. I don't want to add more to her plate."

"Nu-uh," Mac mumbled around a bite of chocolate chip cookie dough. "None of those excuses. That's not how love works. It's not there only when it's convenient. The best sort of love isn't shiny or pretty. It's showing up when things are hard and messy and weighing you down. It's knowing you're hurting and hurting because of it. Let Candace be your friend. Let me be your family. Let yourself be vulnerable with us, and trust us to be able to be there for you. You're not something that needs to be handled, Bonnie."

Emotion stung my nose. "When did you get so smart, baby sister?"

She shrugged and licked her spoon.

"Is this Brady's influence?" I teased.

"First of all, rude. Second of all . . . yes, probably."

We shared a smile. Mine was a little watery, but Mac didn't call me on it.

Instead, she used her spoon to dig a bite out of my pint of ice cream before asking seriously, "Okay, can you explain the rabbit-stealing thing now? Because that has been driving me crazy."

My laugh burst out of me, but I hopped up and retrieved Oreo from the bedroom.

Then I made my sister an accomplice to petnapping.

Jack

Lia opened the door and then frowned.

I'd only rung the doorbell because my hands were full.

"Where's Bonnie?" she asked, looking behind me like I might be hiding her somewhere.

"With the Clarks, I imagine."

Then I passed my grandmother the bottle of wine I was holding so I could use two hands to support the bowl of mashed potatoes I'd made.

It was Christmas Eve, and as our two-person tradition dictated, we shared dinner together to celebrate the holiday. Lia made the ham, green beans, and rolls. And I brought the potatoes, deviled eggs, and pie. I'd whipped up the potatoes this afternoon, but the deviled eggs were courtesy of

Magnolia's kitchen, and the pumpkin pie was from Pied Piper over in Miller Creek.

"I thought you'd bring her," Lia called. She was still standing there with the door wide open.

Maybe she thought this was all an elaborate prank, and Bonnie was going to pop out at any moment and yell, "Surprise."

"Nope," I hollered back, unloading my burdens onto the countertop.

It wasn't like I needed Lia to remind me about Bonnie. Of course, I'd thought of her. That was all I'd done for the last week.

I could easily imagine her here, joining us in my grandmother's cramped kitchen, even though it had only ever been the two of us spending Christmas together.

Bonnie fit wherever she went. And that was part of the problem.

She sure as hell had carved out a space in my heart, making it hard to breathe when I thought about what I'd done.

I pulled the aluminum foil off the bowl of potatoes and added a serving spoon from the drawer. I placed it on the kitchen table along with the deviled eggs, but paused when I took in Lia's offerings, ready and waiting.

"You didn't make green beans," I accused. "You always make green beans."

Lia stood in the doorway wearing a frown that looked nearly identical to the one on my own face. "I made okra. Things don't always have to stay the same. Bonnie mentioned liking okra the last time she was here. So I made okra."

I stared at the offending deep-fried vegetable.

"So why isn't she here to eat my okra, Jack?"

Wincing, I straightened and cleared my throat. "It wasn't like that with Bonnie, okay? We weren't serious. She has her life, and I have mine."

"That's bullshit and you know it."

My grandmother stomped over and roughly gathered up the extra place setting that I'd missed earlier in my distraction over the green beans.

Lia had expected Bonnie for Christmas Eve dinner. She'd made space for her at the table and made okra for her, too. She'd obviously gotten her hopes up where Bonnie was concerned.

Well, hers weren't the only expectations I'd blown up recently.

"It just didn't work out," I replied, and it sounded lame to my own ears.

Lia turned her steely gaze on me. "Why? Because she was divorced? You think she has too much baggage?"

I frowned. "No, of course—"

"Or did she impede on your precious freedom and independence?"

"Jesus, Lia. No. None of that. Is that what you really think of me?"

She eyed me. "Well, how am I supposed to know? You show up out of the blue with a nice girl. Look at her like she hung the moon and the stars, too. And then you claim it's not serious. Sounds to me like you have commitment issues."

I stared.

"What?" she huffed. "I read things. I listen to podcasts. I know about the male loneliness epidemic."

I scrubbed a hand down my face.

"Which is complete bullshit, if you ask me," she added grandly. "Women have just finally gotten their priorities straight."

Exasperated and desperate to end this conversation, I snapped, "I'm just not right for Bonnie. She's meant for marriage and babies and someone worthy of her."

Her weathered face creased in confusion. "Why can't that be you?"

"Because of how I am."

A pause. "So, it *is* a commitment issue?"

Frustration warred with shame. Why was she making me spell this out? She knew my whole sordid history. Lia was the one person I'd expected to just get it. "It's not in my genes."

A beat passed while she stared, eyes wide.

"Oh, Jack." More than understanding or realization, her expression held so much damn disappointment.

"It's the truth," I countered defensively. "My father—whoever he is—never even tried to be in the picture. And Mom—Mom left. She'd rather be homeless or struggling or wherever she ended up than be saddled with me. I'm not a good bet for someone like Bonnie. She deserves so much more—so much *better*. Someone reliable. Someone worthy of the life she wants."

Not someone with a shitty reputation who'd only drag her down. Bonnie had goals and plans. I'd derail all of that. Changing things up just so she could be with me—starting over from scratch—would only make her resent me more. And once she figured out that I'd inevitably disappoint her, then it really would be over. Or worse, she'd stick it out and be miserable because that was the loyal kind of person she was.

Lia sighed heavily and dropped into the seat across from me, resignation practically radiating from her.

I sat too. Nothing about this conversation felt like having the upper hand, and standing over her made me feel worse somehow.

"Jack, you are my grandson, and I love you. But you are an idiot if you think you're anything like your parents. You are your own person. Always have been."

I opened my mouth to argue, to remind her I'd been a hellion, just like my mother.

But Lia raised a hand and kept talking. "Sure, you did some troublemaking in your youth, but luckily, people mature beyond their teenage years, thank God. It's silly to think that's the only version of you folks remember. People aren't assigned value at sixteen, for crying out loud. You grew up to be dependable and trustworthy. You're a hard worker and a good listener.

You're a good man, Jack. I'm damn proud of you. You take care of me and that bar and your employees. Those girls on your soccer team that you can't stop talking about. I don't think you see yourself very clearly at all."

Something squeezed my chest as a memory assaulted me. I remembered saying that same thing to Bonnie when she'd called herself broken, sitting on the stairs outside my apartment. I swallowed roughly. Basic factory settings and her hand clasped in mine.

"Do you think people really have a limit on their love?" Lia asked, voice as soft as I'd ever heard it. "That your mother's well ran dry and she didn't have enough for you or me? Do you truly believe she passed that on to you through blood? Because I don't think that's true. You have enough love for me and for the bar and your friends and staff and teammates. Are you worried you won't have enough left over for Bonnie, too? Is that it?"

"Of course not," I replied reflexively, throat tight. "I love her. I—" I broke off helplessly before finishing, "I love her."

"Good." Lia's smile was shrewd. "That's a start. Now what are you going to do about it?"

BONNIE

Christmas music was playing in my aunt Maggie's kitchen as folks filtered in and out.

We'd always celebrated Christmas Eve a little loosely.

When I was a kid, there'd been a movie on repeat in the den—usually *A Christmas Story*—while we'd taken turns decorating gingerbread houses at the kitchen table with my mom.

As Will, Mac, Larry, and I had grown older, the movie had changed— usually *Elf* or *The Nightmare Before Christmas*.

Now it was *Die Hard,* and we still decorated gingerbread houses. There was even a contest, and we voted on whose was the best. The winner got to smash the others, and we all took pieces home with us in giant Ziploc bags at the end of the night.

Extended family in ugly Christmas sweaters mingled in the kitchen, den, living room, and dining room, where everything was decorated to within an inch of its life with pine boughs and holly berries. There were various snacks and punch and a ridiculous amount of sweets scattered throughout.

I'd always loved spending this time with my loved ones. My favorite holiday, like I'd told Jack.

Last Christmas Eve had been difficult, though. Danny and I had been fighting, the news of his cheating fairly recent. But I'd been pretending everything was fine, putting on a show, while he'd hidden on the back porch in the cold, avoiding everyone.

This year, I was missing Jack, wishing he could be here with me. But I wasn't letting it ruin one of the most special times of the year.

Currently, I was decorating Maggie's kitchen tree. She had a total of six trees in the house. Earlier in the day, she, Becca, and I had made cinnamon ornaments. They were finally dry and cooled and smelled amazing. Becca and Mac were tying on the ribbon to make hanging loops, and I was placing them on the tree. I admired each festive shape—the bells and angels, reindeer and snowmen.

"I can't believe I never knew you could mix cinnamon, applesauce, and glue together to make ornaments," Becca said in wonder, and she cut another length of ribbon. She was wearing a headband with light-up antlers and a maroon *Star Wars* holiday sweater with Rey and Kylo Ren. Carl, the dog, had his head resting on Becca's thigh while she worked.

"We'll teach you all our ways," Mac said with a grin and a jangle. Her own ugly Christmas sweater had bells sewn on it, and she rang a little each time she moved.

"Except for Maggie's recipe for peppermint bark," I amended with a grin. "No one gets that."

"Oh." Becca frowned. "I helped her make some yesterday. Was that supposed to be a secret?"

"What?" Mac's mouth dropped open. "I have been asking Aunt Maggie for that recipe for *years*. She said she was taking it with her to heaven with her cast iron and her Aqua Net."

Becca and I laughed.

"She's fucking with you, Mac," Will said as he strolled over to where we were working. My big, grumpy cousin dropped a homemade butter mint into Becca's waiting mouth before pressing a kiss to her forehead, deftly avoiding the light-up antlers.

She grinned mischievously.

"Becca," Mac scolded. Then she grinned back. "That was devious. I'm impressed."

"Thank you," she said happily.

Mac stood after affixing the final length of ribbon to the ornament in her hand. She passed it to me with a questioning look in her gaze. I could tell my sister wanted to check on me, find out if I was okay. But after our talk a few days ago, I think she finally understood.

Maybe she'd spread the word to everyone to leave me alone about Jack, because I hadn't heard a word from my family, wondering how things were going or if the quiet bartender would be joining us. Maybe they knew things had ended, or they were just being polite. Either way, I was glad I didn't have to talk about it and could just focus on relaxing this evening.

Instead of the question I could practically see waiting on the tip of Mac's tongue, she asked instead, "Want me to grab you a peanut butter ball?"

Grateful, I smiled. "Yes, before Larry eats them all."

Our cousin was around here somewhere with Corie. The two were still dating and seemed happier than ever. In fact, Corie was planning on relocating to Kirby Falls in the new year.

It was Brady who delivered several peanut butter balls on a small party plate a moment later.

"Thanks," I told him.

Mac joined us eventually with a platter full of snacks.

As Becca and I put the finishing touches on the kitchen tree, we heard a knock from the back door. Most of the family in attendance knew to just come on in, so I was a little surprised.

"I'll grab it," Becca said before dashing off down the hallway toward the mudroom.

Just when I'd polished off the last bite-sized dessert on my plate, I heard Becca call out happily, "Brady, Lia's here!"

The peanut butter stuck in my throat, and I nearly choked.

Brady trotted off down the hall as Mac slapped me on the back. "You okay over there?"

But I couldn't get the words out. Surely that was not the same—

"Well, hi, Lia. Merry Christmas," Brady said in a booming voice that carried from the back porch. "Hey, Jack!"

My sister's eyes went wide, and I had to swallow several times in order to breathe.

"Holy shit," Mac murmured as footsteps sounded down the hallway to our right. "This better be some top-tier groveling. He was a huge idiot. Also, crashing Christmas. I give him bonus points for that."

"Do you think he's here for me?"

She gave me a look like I just might be a bigger idiot than the one crashing our family Christmas party. Then she sobered. "If you don't want to talk to him, I'll tell him to leave."

I considered holding on to my anger and righteous indignation. I could very easily hide behind my sister and keep my distance from Jack. But the truth was, I didn't want to. I didn't want to waste any more time.

"No. It's fine," I assured her. "If he wants to talk, I'll listen."

Just then, I saw Brady, Becca, and Lia trooping toward us.

"Lia's in my and Becca's knitting group down at Weaverly Place," Brady explained.

I knew Brady knit, and I knew Becca had learned from the ladies down at the yarn shop, but I didn't realize they were acquainted with Jack's grandmother.

On tentative feet, I moved forward to welcome our guest. Brady passed me with a little wink. And Becca mouthed, *Oh my God*, and squeezed my arm.

Then Lia came right up to me and kissed my cheek. "I brought you some okra. Merry Christmas."

Confused, I returned her hug. And sure enough, when I pulled back, the older woman had a covered dish in her hand that smelled like deep-fried heaven. "Thank you. I look forward to having some. Make yourself at home. I'm so glad to see you."

"I left your other present outside," she said. "But it's up to you if you want to return it or not. I wouldn't blame you."

My stomach gave a nervous clench at the implication. Jack was here for me. I could only imagine what sort of courage that took. He was a pretty self-contained, isolated guy. Not terribly social, especially not with people he didn't know. This was Christmas Eve with my family, and there were probably twenty cars parked outside in the field. Whatever he needed to say, it must be important.

My hopes started a slow and steady rise to the surface. But like I'd told Mac, I couldn't make this decision for him. I wouldn't fight this fight alone. Not anymore. Relationships went both ways. Not one person stitching things together, mending holes and seams just to keep everything from falling apart.

I loved Jack. I wanted to tell him that. I wanted a future with him, too. But if he still thought I was better off with Danny, then there wasn't much I could do about that.

After a few seconds, I realized Jack wasn't planning on trailing the others. So I made my way toward the back door and pulled my jacket off the coatrack as I went.

He had his hand raised to knock when I opened the door. Surprise flashed on his face, light from the hallway behind me illuminating wide hazel eyes and jaw scruff that was just shy of being a beard. He wore his favorite black leather jacket that I knew felt butter-soft beneath my fingertips.

"Hi," I breathed.

"Hey," he replied softly. "I was hoping we could talk."

So I nodded and stepped out into the cold air and shut the door behind me.

I led Jack over to a pair of rocking chairs on the edge of the porch. The night was clear and the moon was bright. Out here, away from the city lights, the stars sparkled, shimmering within a velvet black backdrop. You could see across the barren cornfields all the way to the tree line in the distance. Beyond that, mountains rose from the earth, cocooning our small valley like dark sentinels.

"I'm sorry for just showing up here like this. I know how important this time is with your family. But I just—" He paused and reached for my hand. "I just couldn't wait. I remembered what you said about Christmas Eve. The magic. The possibility. And I realized I wanted that . . . with you. If there was a chance I could fix what I'd broken, I thought tonight might be my best bet."

I smiled down at our clasped hands, barely noticing the chill in the air. My heart was beating wildly, and I could feel it too—the magic, the possibility, the hope of it all.

Jack squeezed my fingers, drawing my attention back to him. He watched me carefully, like I might leave at any moment, like I might not be willing to hear him out.

"I'm sorry for the things I said the last time we spoke, Bonnie. I tried to push you away. Did my best to hurt you so that I wouldn't disappoint you in the long run. And I fucking hate that I keep having to apologize. That I even need to say I'm sorry in the first place."

"I wouldn't say two times is a lot, Jack."

His brows pulled low. "No. I—I don't want me fucking up and then having to apologize for it to turn out to be a regular thing with us."

A regular thing with us.

Like we were a foregone conclusion. Inevitable.

"Well, I do," I argued.

Jack blinked.

"People make mistakes all the time," I explained. "I'd rather have your apology than your apathy. If you're so determined to compare yourself to my ex-husband, how about this? Danny never apologized after we fought or disagreed. He'd give me the silent treatment or make passive-aggressive remarks, sigh or roll his eyes. And then, just like that, he'd act like nothing ever happened. Like it was all fine. Completely normal to ignore your wife for days on end and eat dinner at your parents' house instead of at home. To come in late so I'd already be in bed and then wake up early to avoid me in the morning too."

I took a slow breath to steady myself, and Jack squeezed my hand between both of his. "I'd rather you acknowledge that you made a mistake than pretend it never happened. It shows you care and accept responsibility, and mean to do better. That's all any of us can hope for."

He nodded thoughtfully. "I'm sorry I hurt you. I was so scared of losing you—of you realizing that I'm not enough—that it seemed simpler to push you away first. I didn't want to be the person standing in your way, keeping you from what you really wanted. Even if that was your old life. I hated the idea of you fitting yourself back inside your past, making yourself small and twisting yourself up. But I didn't want to hold you back either. All the things I love about you—your goodness and loyalty and devotion—were things I respected. More than that, they left me in awe. I've hardly known dedication like yours in my own life. But to you, it's as natural as breathing. That's just who you are, deep down. You love and you love hard. I wanted that so badly. I just wasn't sure how to trust it."

For a long time, I'd been trying to figure out a way to let Jack know he was safe with me. That I'd protect his heart, if only he'd let me.

"So what happened? What made you come here?" I prompted.

"I had a conversation with Lia about my parents and all the baggage I've been carrying around with me. How I've let those things impact my decisions, my fears, and my relationship with you. I realized it's okay to be a little scared."

I smiled at the advice he'd given me and that I'd given him right back.

"Being scared doesn't mean I don't love you," Jack explained. "Because I do. And it doesn't mean I'm not ready to be in a relationship with you. Because I am. We already were. It was real, Clyde. All of it. For months. It was never *just* about sex."

"I know."

Jack might have been closed off and cautious, but he'd never been shy about making me a priority. And I'd known in my heart that he loved me. He'd just been too afraid to admit it. However, hearing him say it now was enough for warmth to fill me up. It was one thing to have that knowledge and another thing entirely to have it confirmed.

"I want to be with you," he went on, voice rough. "I want a life with you, if you'll have me. I want to take you to Lia's and spend holidays with your family, get to know them. I want to build something together. A home, a family, all of it. I'm hiring a manager for the bar. I want us to have a normal schedule, where we're not rushing all over, trying to steal moments together. And I want to help you remodel your house, to make it what you've always dreamed of. Because you deserve that, Bonnie. You deserve so much more than the leftover crumbs.

"I'd never thought much about marriage," Jack admitted. "But that day at the Rhododendron Inn, I liked the way you talked about it. How it should be. Being married to your best friend. You're that for me. I want to take care of you, to show you every day that you don't have to do it all alone. That you have a partner in me, a teammate. If you want it."

Emotion threatened to overwhelm me. All those things I'd wanted from marriage and had been denied, being made to feel like my expectations were too high, too lofty, were staring back at me now with dark eyes and genuine resolve.

Maybe Jack didn't realize it, but he was already doing those things.

"I want to take care of you, too," I agreed. "You've never once been shy about making me a priority. The cabinet and the teacups. Jack, you can't possibly know how much that meant to me. And I can't explain it in a way that doesn't make every version of me before this moment sound weak and cowardly. But you've been there for me and supported me exactly how I needed."

I explained, "Plenty of folks try to help. Or they ask what you want or what they can do, but I think you might be the first person who ever looked at me and said, 'What do you *need*?' Over and over again. And you didn't even realize you were doing it or the significance of it, but it meant the world to me."

Jack's thumb rose to my cheek and gently wiped away the tear that rolled down. His voice went impossibly soft, and he asked, "So what do you need, Bonnie? Right now. What do you need?"

The answer was right there, like an apple, ripe and ready for picking. I didn't even have to think.

"You," I confessed. "Just you."

Jack rose and pulled me into his arms. I laced my fingers behind his neck and pressed my body flush to his. I absorbed his warmth and his love and every single ounce of possibility. I let myself see the future playing out. And I let myself believe it.

I shifted away so I could see him, allowing my fingers to sift through the soft hair at his nape. "And I just wanted you to know, I don't need to fix you, Jack. You're not the boy you were in high school. You're smart. You're motivated. You work hard, and you've built so much more than just Magnolia Bar. It's not the only redeeming aspect of your life. You're a good man. You're caring and kind. You give your time and energy to people who need it. You support me and let my rabbit eat holes in every one of your socks. I don't want to change anything about you."

His eyes, bright and eager, searched my face. I hoped Jack was letting himself believe in the possibility, too.

"Maybe I had a crush on the bad boy with the motorcycle," I said. "But I want to spend the rest of my life with the man who owns my heart. I love you just the way you are."

"I love you too, Clyde."

I pressed up onto my toes, and Jack met me halfway. My hands cupped his scruffy jaw as our lips touched. There was heat and want, but it was a kiss of promise. An oath that gave us back to each other. A vow for a new beginning. One that allowed us the freedom to shape it any way we wanted.

When Jack's forehead rested against mine and the cold couldn't touch any part of me, I said, "Let's play a game. Three favorites. Ask me my three favorite places."

"Okay," Jack agreed. And the edge of his smile grazed my lips as he repeated, "What are your three favorite places?"

"Right here," I whispered and let my mouth touch his. "You and me." Another soft press of skin. "Forever."

JACK

Several months later

I'd just pulled the lasagna out of the oven when all my carefully laid plans for the evening went to hell.

The knock at the front door was my first clue. Bonnie shouldn't be knocking on her own front door. It wasn't even locked.

Then came the muffled voices from the other side. Two distinct voices. Ones that I recognized.

My hand went briefly to my pocket before I turned the oven off. Then I made my way to the entryway—the newly remodeled entryway.

Over the last six months, the house had undergone extensive renovation. Now we had a beautiful outdoor space, a screened porch, and a large deck for entertaining. There were even raised beds for a vegetable garden and lattice work beneath the decking for the blackberry plantings Candace and Mercer had given us.

We'd made upgrades here and there throughout the existing interior, but we'd also added a large bedroom, a walk-in closet, and an en suite bathroom. The new addition on the back of the house would be ours—mine and Bonnie's. All the rooms were now bright with natural light and neutral wall paint. No more dark paneling anywhere. The old carpet had been torn out, and the wooden floors beneath refinished.

And today was the day the crew had completed the kitchen, the last remaining piece in the remodel puzzle. The bay window and new cabinets made the space feel sunny and open. The pale granite countertops complemented the walls and flooring. My eyes snagged briefly on the light fixture over the kitchen table. Everything was the way Bonnie had envisioned it.

She'd seen the potential, and we'd made it happen. We were celebrating tonight.

At least, we were supposed to be.

I swung the front door open.

Standing on the porch was Brady Judd, supporting a giggling Bonnie. An unfamiliar minivan sat in the driveway, and MacKenzie Clark hung halfway out the passenger-side window, waving madly and shouting at her sister. I couldn't make out the rest of the figures inside the vehicle, but at least two more people were moving around.

I looked between Brady and Bonnie. "What is going on?" I asked.

"Just help me get her inside," Brady said.

"I am *fine*," Bonnie insisted, but the toe of her white sneaker caught on absolutely nothing as she passed through her brand-new front door.

To save time, I scooped her into my arms. She squealed in my ear, and instead of her honeysuckle-sweet scent, I caught something bubbly and dry with a whole lot of orange.

"They got hammered," Brady said from behind me as I settled Bonnie on the sofa.

I glanced his way, and he tossed his hands up in exasperation. "I don't know, man. Mac called me and said they needed a ride. I had to borrow my mom's minivan to get all their drunk asses home. Larry and Becca and Joan are in the car too. It was like herding cats, I swear. By the time I got one of them in the van, another left to go to the bathroom. They made me go through the McDonald's drive-thru and pick up French fries."

"And fountain Coke," Bonnie added helpfully as she leaned back on the couch and closed her eyes.

"That was probably a good thing," Brady said thoughtfully. "Something to soak up all the alcohol."

"I thought they were going to happy hour and drinking mimosas at Lonely Mountain?" I asked, baffled by the turn of events.

Bonnie had left my apartment, where we'd been living during the renovation of the house. I'd wanted to surprise her tonight with dinner in the completed kitchen, so I'd told her to have fun with her friends and then meet me here afterward.

Brady winced. "*Bottomless* mimosas, apparently. They were all trashed by the time I got there. Something about cheering Joanie up. I don't know. I didn't ask. My sister's sleeping it off in the back of the van. When I left them, Becca was singing her a lullaby and Larry was taking pictures of her with her phone."

I watched Bonnie reach out blindly and grab the blanket off the back of the sofa, eyes still closed.

"Smells good in here," Brady offered before taking in the scene. Tall taper candles glowed softly on either end of the kitchen table. A flower arrangement with roses and sunflowers and carnations sat dead center. The two place settings were arranged and just waiting for the next phase of tonight's plan.

"Thanks," I sighed.

"Sorry, she's . . ." He gestured to where Bonnie was slumped over on the couch. "Like this."

Just then, a series of aggressive honks came from outside.

Brady released a breath and pinched the bridge of his nose. "At least Bonnie gets sleepy when she's drunk. Mac just gets more Mac-like." Three more rapid horn honks sounded, followed by yelling. "Shit, I'd better go. See you at soccer practice on Tuesday."

"Yeah, see you," I said. "Thanks for bringing her home."

"No problem, Jack."

With that, Brady hustled back outside to the rest of the women.

I stared down at Bonnie, my hand finding the box inside the pocket of my jeans once more. Just to be safe.

Right then, her mouth dropped open, and a loud snore came from the back of her throat.

Smiling, I shook my head. At least she wasn't sick this time.

I let Bonnie rest on the couch while I blew out the candles and packed away the lasagna in the fridge. I wiped down the new counters and washed the few dishes I'd dirtied. Then I checked on Oreo and made sure she had enough food and water for the night.

The rabbit was ours now, officially. After winter break, Bonnie had talked to the second-grade teacher, who hadn't even realized her rabbit went missing every weekend. She'd been thrilled that Bonnie wanted to take Oreo off her hands. Bonnie had offered to bring her in once a month to visit the classroom.

I was proud of her for asking for what she wanted. And now the furry little sock destroyer had the best of both worlds, social time and a stable home where she was loved and wanted.

After I finished tidying up for the night, I went back to the sofa and sat down next to Bonnie. My hand, once again, worried the box's edge through the denim of my pants. As I watched the steady rise and fall of her breathing, I tried not to be too disappointed about my big plans. There would be more opportunities for romantic dinners and nights in. With the new full-time manager at Magnolia working five nights a week, my schedule had opened up. Bonnie and I had all the time in the world.

And now we were home, and nothing was going to change that.

I brushed a strand of blond hair back from her face and said softly, "Clyde, it's time for bed."

She groaned, and I laughed.

"Come down here with me," she urged, tugging on my arm, trying to get me to lie down with her on the couch.

"No, let me help you up. You'll be more comfortable in our bedroom. I can carry you, if you want."

Sleepy eyes blinked up at me. "Yes, please. You're so big and strong. And handsome. And sweet. And my favorite person."

I chuckled as I stood and slid my arm beneath her knees. "And you're drunk."

But I knew she wasn't lying. Bonnie showed me she loved me every single day. It wasn't so much proving it as it was simply living the truth she held in her heart. She was free and open with her affection. She showed she cared in a hundred ways, big and small, quiet and loud.

Once I lifted her and she was comfortably in my arms, Bonnie slid her fingers through my hair and started kissing my neck.

"Mayyyybe, I am a little drunk," she singsonged, her breath warm against me.

I cleared my throat and focused on getting her down the hallway and into bed. To sleep. That was all.

Our first time in our new bedroom was not going to be like this.

"Let's get you into some pajamas," I said, and placed her gently on the mattress.

I'd been bringing boxes of things over from the apartment to the house all week. Bonnie's clothes were hanging in the huge walk-in closet and folded neatly in the chest of drawers.

The bed had been delivered two days ago. She hadn't seen it yet.

Her hand petted the fabric of the bedspread as she gazed down. "This is pretty," she murmured dreamily.

She should think it was pretty. It was the bedding she'd saved on her Pinterest board under "Wish List for Later."

I bit down on my smile as I retrieved her favorite pajama pants and my tee shirt that she'd never given back.

With quick, efficient movements, I lifted her blouse over her head. It wouldn't do to get distracted right now, not even by the black bra she wore. *Christ.*

She apparently didn't need my help to undo the clasp and slingshot the lacy scrap of fabric across the room.

Grinning and topless, she leaned back on her elbows. "Okay, now it's your turn. Take it off."

I shook my head slowly from side to side, but I couldn't do anything about the smile on my face. Bonnie pouted adorably.

Well, I supposed I *was* getting ready for bed too.

With one arm raised, I reached back over my shoulders and grabbed a fistful of fabric. Bonnie clapped in delight, and the movement did very distracting things for her breasts, still fully on display.

But then I recovered and tugged my shirt up and over my head.

"Come here," she encouraged.

So I braced my hands on either side of her hips and leaned in close. I heard her breath catch and watched her eyes go dark as she reached for me. But I was quicker.

I pressed a kiss to the tip of her nose and said, "No," then straightened up to standing.

"Booo!" she called while flopping dramatically back on the mattress, one arm thrown over her eyes.

I took the opportunity to slide her jeans down, but before she could get too excited, I pulled her pajama pants on. After I'd urged her to sit up, I slid the tee shirt over her head and passed her a water bottle.

"Drink that so you're not miserable in the morning," I told her, handing over a couple of painkillers.

She gave me a thoughtful look. "This is like déjà vu."

"A little," I replied.

"I'm not puking this time."

"Luckily."

"I am in an unfamiliar bed, though."

"Yes," I agreed. "But you didn't steal my samosas this time."

Bonnie gasped and placed the water on the bedside table. "I did not."

"Oh, you definitely did. And you ate all my pakora. I had my takeout sitting on the bar, and I only turned my back on you for a minute, but it was long enough."

She covered her face with her hands and mumbled between her fingers, "I couldn't figure out why I was craving Indian food the next day. I always wondered what happened that night. You never really told me."

I folded back the covers and encouraged her to wiggle underneath. Then I lay down beside her.

"That was the beginning of the rest of our lives," I said simply.

She rolled over to face me, a soft, sleepy smile on her pretty face.

Something warm moved through my chest.

"I'll always be grateful you came to Magnolia that night instead of going to Mattie B's," I confessed.

"Even though I'm a troublemaking local?" she asked with a grin.

"Yep." I laced my fingers with hers in the narrow space between us. "You're the best trouble of my whole life. And I'm kind of an expert on the subject."

Her hand tightened around mine. "Not anymore. Now you're a respected business owner. A beloved neighbor and friend. An award-winning soccer coach. A dedicated grandson. A sexy woodworker. A rabbit dad. And"—she paused dramatically—"the love of my life."

The ring was still in my pocket. I could feel it digging into my thigh beneath the blankets. Her sweet words had my fingers eager to pull it free.

Tonight hadn't gone as planned, but I could still ask. Suddenly, I didn't want to wait for the perfect moment. Who needed perfection when there were moments like this? When my heart felt too big for my chest, and everything I never knew I wanted was close enough to touch.

But in the time it took me to wiggle the box out of the pocket containing it, Bonnie's eyes drooped. Two slow blinks later, and she was out.

I sighed, but I could feel the smile on my face.

There would be more opportunities. Our lives were filled with them.

In fact, my life was much bigger these days—fuller than it had ever been. There were more people in it, and strangely enough, I liked it that way.

I pressed a kiss to Bonnie's forehead. Then I turned out the light.

Sleep would find me soon enough, but I knew my dreams couldn't possibly compare to the life I had with the woman by my side.

Bonnie

I blinked awake in an unfamiliar bedroom. In the dim gray morning light, I found Jack by my side and breathed a little sigh of relief.

He was shirtless, his dark hair pulled back while he slept, a few strands loose around his neck and temple. I liked the way he looked in our bed.

Our bed.

The room had turned out beautifully. I couldn't believe Jack had sneaky-moved all the furniture in and had the bed delivered. Over the windows were the curtains I'd picked out, and I knew if I walked into the new bathroom, I'd find the fuzzy navy-blue bathmat I'd ordered.

Jack had been supportive throughout the whole design process for the remodel. We'd talked through options, and nine times out of ten, he'd agreed with whatever I wanted. I'd felt a little guilty until we'd had a long talk about what made us happy. Jack had promised that seeing me get the house of my dreams was what he wanted more than anything. I still had moments where I feared disappointing him, but they were few and far between these days.

I tiptoed out of bed to use the bathroom down the hall. I didn't want to wake Jack.

Curious about how the kitchen had turned out, I peeked into the room. My attention snagged on the kitchen table—the one Jack had designed and built this spring. I stepped closer and noted the flowers and the candles and the surface laid so beautifully with the good dishes and linen napkins.

Jack had planned dinner for us, and I'd ruined it.

My fingers trailed across the smooth surface of the dark wood as regret and remorse claimed me. On bare feet, I opened the door to the refrigerator. It wasn't stocked because we hadn't been living here. But on the middle shelf was a lasagna ready and waiting. There was also garlic bread and a bowl of salad wrapped up in cling film.

I bit my lip, miserable over what I'd messed up last night.

We'd been trying to cheer Joan up, and things had gotten a little out of hand, but that was no excuse. Jack had clearly planned a lovely meal for our first night back in the house.

And I'd gotten day drunk on mimosas with my friends. Then fell asleep.

I scanned the room, wondering how I could fix this, and my attention caught on something I'd missed initially.

The chandelier over the kitchen island was not the one I'd picked out—not the one we'd agreed on with the contractor.

I took in the clusters of delicate crystals and the way they layered and wove between each other in such a lovely, organic configuration. I'd recognize the fixture anywhere. It was the really expensive and extravagant chandelier I'd saved on my Pinterest wish list, not the more modest and reasonable one I'd shown Jack and settled on with the contractor.

Jack had done this for me. He was always doing things for me. In the last six months, he'd made me a priority in a million different ways. And he never stopped asking what I needed.

I swallowed down the emotion tightening my throat and padded quietly down the hall.

When I slid back into bed, Jack's hazel eyes slowly blinked open.

"What's wrong?" he asked immediately, dark brows drawing together.

"I'm sorry," I practically wailed and wrapped myself around him. "I feel awful that I ruined your plans last night."

He stiffened in my hold, muscles going briefly taut before he asked roughly, "My plans?"

"The dinner you made and the beautiful table you set. Our first night together in the house." I squeezed him even tighter. "I messed it all up, and I'm so sorry."

Jack relaxed and released a slow breath. His hands rubbed soothing circles on my back. "Hey, it's okay. You didn't know that I was trying to surprise you."

"I know, but—"

"You didn't ruin anything," he insisted as he cupped my nape and squeezed gently. "We can have a do-over tonight if you want."

I pulled back to look at him. "No, right now. I want lasagna for breakfast."

His lips twitched. "You do?"

"Yes," I replied eagerly. Then I tossed back the covers and hopped out of bed, renewed by the prospect of fixing what I'd broken.

I hurried into the kitchen and washed my hands. Then I tied on an apron I found hanging in the pantry and started pulling all the leftovers from last night out of the fridge.

The floorboards in the hallway creaked, and I knew Jack had followed me.

"You know, some foods are just good anytime," I babbled as I reached over to preheat the fancy new oven. "They shouldn't be designated as time- or meal-specific. You should be able to eat pasta for any meal. And pizza obviously. A classic for breakfast, lunch, or dinner. Also pancakes. I'm a big fan of breakfast for dinner."

When I turned around to find Jack, I gasped and slapped a hand over my mouth.

Because he was there, directly behind me, shirtless and in black boxer briefs. He was also waiting on bended knee with a ring box in his hand.

"Oh my God," I mumbled behind my palm.

"Sorry. I was impatient." He watched me with that same calm, solemn expression that I'd associated with him from the beginning. "Maybe it's too soon for you. Maybe you need more time. Maybe you don't ever want to be someone's wife again. But I want to be your husband—your teammate. Listening to you talk about marriage, I realized you were already all of those things to me. My secret keeper. My best friend. My roommate. My high-five giver. My partner. I want your loyalty and your heart. And I want to give you mine right back. I want to fight for you and fight for us. I want to be on your team for the rest of my life, Bonnie."

There were a number of appropriate reactions. Crying. Kissing. Shouting yes and throwing myself at him.

Instead, I blurted clumsily through the rising tide of my emotions, "It's not too soon! I'd marry you tomorrow if you wanted. At the courthouse or on a cruise ship by a ship captain. Or in Vegas with Elvis officiating."

Jack's lips lifted in amusement. "Or at a big wedding on the farm with everyone we know?"

Tears threatened, making my nose sting. How did he always know exactly what I needed?

I managed a shaky nod and took a step closer. "That too. You name the time and place, and I'm your girl."

He grinned. "You are."

I cupped his cheeks and pressed a soft kiss to his lips as visions of the future unspooled before me. Possibility. Hope. Love and devotion. Big moments. And small moments too. Partners in practice, not just theory. My coffee mug waiting on the counter in the mornings. And moonlit rides on the back of a motorcycle, butter-soft leather surrounding me. Someone who knew all my tender spots and protected them fiercely. A life lived together, side by side, heart to heart.

Jack reached up and loosened my hold. He placed the white ring box in one of my hands and held the other, lacing our fingers together. He cleared his throat deliberately and said low and rough, "Bonnie, will you marry me?"

"Yes," I breathed.

I let myself get swept up in the moment as Jack pulled me into his arms.

It was wild to think we'd ended up here. The bad boy and the good girl.

But that was only a part of the story and just fragments of who we really were. It had taken time and space, circumstance and heartache to bring us together. Not a perfect moment, but a handful of ordinary ones in every shape and size.

As our love grew and changed, so did we. And now we were exactly where we belonged . . . right here. Jack and me. Forever.

Want more of Bonnie and Jack?
I have a bonus epilogue for you! Get the heartwarming scene HERE when
you sign up for my newsletter.
If you have trouble with the link above, scan the QR code:

The fun in Kirby Falls continues with Joan's story in Leaf Well Enough
Alone, *coming May 26, 2026. Preorder your copy today!*

author's note

Just a quick note about the accuracy surrounding Bonnie and Danny's divorce. In the state of North Carolina, where *Leaf You Hanging* takes place, a separation period of one year is required before a divorce can be finalized and a marriage dissolved. Timeline-wise, I needed to speed things up, and so that part of the novel is inaccurate. Just wanted to put that out there. Also this is fiction, baby. I'm in the driver's seat. :)

also by laney hatcher

Kirby Falls Series

Take It or Leaf It: A Grumpy Sunshine Slow Burn Romance

Leaf It To Me: A Small-Town Slow Burn Romance

Leaf and Let Die: An Enemies to Lovers Small-Town Romance

Leaf You Hanging: A Reformed Bad Boy Small-Town Romance

Leaf Well Enough Alone: A Single Guardian Small-Town Romance

Cozy Creek Collection

Fall Me Maybe

Bartholomew Series

First to Fall: A Friends to Lovers Historical Romance

Second Chance Dance: An Enemies to Lovers Historical Romance

Third Degree Yearn: A Second Chance Historical Romance

Last on the List: A Surprise Pregnancy Historical Romance

Smartypants Romance

London Ladies Embroidery Series

Neanderthal Seeks Duchess

Well Acquainted

Love Matched

Find bonus content, reading order, and other news at my website:

https://laneyhatcher.com/

about the author

Laney Hatcher is a firm believer that there is a spreadsheet for every occasion and pie is always the answer. She is an author of stories both old and new where the HEAs are always guaranteed. Often too practical for her own good, Laney enjoys her life in the southern United States with her husband, children, and incredibly entitled cat.

Find Laney Hatcher online:
Facebook: https://bit.ly/3s6KnuY
Newsletter: https://bit.ly/3SbXg2v
Amazon: https://amzn.to/3IaOwU7
Instagram: https://bit.ly/3s4IRcS
Website: https://laneyhatcher.com/
Goodreads: https://bit.ly/3BD0Gme
TikTok: https://www.tiktok.com/@laneyhatcherauthor
Threads: https://www.threads.net/@laney.hatcher

Newsletter sign up

www.ingramcontent.com/pod-product-compliance
Lightning Source LLC
Chambersburg PA
CBHW032340310726
48973CB00007B/1788